As if he read her deepest longing his head, moving closer until their breath mingled and Emma could feel the beat of his heart against her own.

Perhaps her yearning had been there from the first moment when he had touched her in the coach. Mayhap it had grown from each look they had exchanged. She did not know. But the craving for him had grown until it writhed to unholy life within her, until she trembled with the force of it.

She had been warned about this from the time she was a small child, told time and again that she must not fall prey to the same mistake as her mother. Dragging in a shuddering breath, she tried to fight the demon of her desire, tried to recall all the reasons that she must beware of Anthony Craven, beware of the terrifying, captivating lure of him.

The full length of his hard body pressed against hers, trapping her between hot man and the cold wall at her back. The smell of his skin undid her, and she moaned softly as she brushed her face against his neck, his jaw. Wrong, so wrong, but the temptation of him made her blood sing.

He laughed, low and dark, the sound fully lacking in humor. And she thought he would kiss her now. Oh, please let him press his lips to hers, those lush, sensual lips. She moved her thighs together beneath her skirt, longing to push against his disturbing weight, while also longing to fist her hands in the fine cloth of his coat and drag him nearer still, to breathe the scent of him until he filled her lungs, her heart, her every sense. . . .

Books by Eve Silver

DARK DESIRES

HIS DARK KISS

Published by Kensington Publishing Corporation

HIS DARK KISS

EVE SILVER

ZEBRA BOOKS
Kensington Publishing Corp.
www.kensingtonbooks.com

ACKNOWLEDGMENTS

Thank you so much to my incredible editor, John Scognamiglio, and to my extraordinary agent, Sha-Shana Crichton.

With love to my family and friends, for all their unflagging support.

Eternal gratitude to Brenda Hammond and Nancy Frost, my dedicated, selfless critique partners.

And with all the emotion welling from my heart, to Dylan, my light; Sheridan, my joy; and Henning, my forever love.

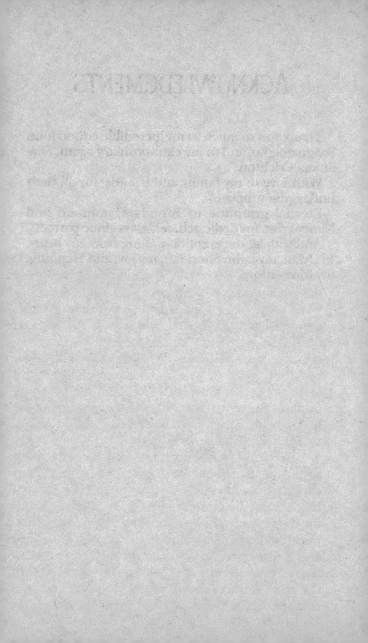

CHAPTER ONE

To travel on a day such as this was a task only for the addled or the desperate.

Allowing herself one small sigh, Emma Parrish pressed her back against the seat of the ancient coach, the hope and courage that had fueled her decision to leave Shrewsbury flagging under the onslaught of exhaustion and too many hours spent with naught for company but her own jumbled thoughts. A brutal rain battered the carriage as the high wheels dipped and lurched on the rutted road, threatening disaster.

A particularly violent pitch sent her careening across the bench, the harsh contact of her shoulder cracking the far wall, forcing a gasp. The stink of mildew and decay hung heavy in the stale air, sullying her very breath, and the storm eroded her composure. Rubbing her shoulder, she scooted forward and then rested one hand against the window frame. 'Twas better sitting thus. The contact with the solid frame kept her from sliding across the cracked seat onto the dark, wet stain that had grown with each passing hour as the rain leaked through the thin fissures that patterned the roof.

After a time, the rain eased, slowing to a drizzle, and Emma peered out the side window, hoping to catch a glimpse of the passing countryside. Bleak sky stretched as far as the eye could see, a dreary canopy of endless gray. Then the clouds parted. A single ray of brilliant light descended from the evening sun, breaking through the gloom to touch the earth.

A chill of foreboding raced along her spine. There, in the distance, silhouetted in sharp relief against the backdrop of that solitary ray of sunshine, stood a jagged shape, a stark Mephistophelean castle set high atop a lonely hill. Darkness in the light.

Manorbrier.

Her choice. Her future.

A whisper of unease teased her senses, making her skin prickle and her heart race.

The end of her journey was close at hand, though any comfort to be found in that thought was tinged with a heavy measure of apprehension. She had fled from the certainty of a fate she refused to bear to the possibility of one that was even worse.

And so she traveled on a day such as this. To a place such as this. To the home of the man who was—

Emma jerked back, startled, her musings scattering like raindrops in the wind as the churning wheels of the carriage flung up clumps of mud that splattered against the window with a solid thunk. And then the downpour resumed, drumming steadily on the carriage roof as the creak and sway of the coach marked the passing time and the deepening gloom heralded the dusk.

The minutes dragged into hours, and the shadows lengthened into the full blackness of night. Finally the vehicle rolled forward and back as it lurched to a stop, and after a moment the door was jerked open, letting a blast of damp and chilly air into the carriage. The coachman leaned in, lifting his lantern high, the sudden burst of light leaving Emma blinking against the glare.

"We're here, miss," he said, his gaunt face a study in shadows, the collar of his greatcoat pulled up about his chin. Water spilled from the edge of his low-crowned hat, and with a frown, he swiped at the damp brim. "Though I do question if here is where you truly want to be. Are you certain, then, that you don't wish to return to Shrewsbury? I'm thinking this is no place for an innocent young miss."

Emma pressed her lips together. *Shrewsbury* was no place for a young miss, at least not for this young miss. And innocent? Well, she had escaped her aunts' home with her virtue intact, but she had left the ashes of her innocence behind. She suppressed a shudder and leaned forward to look out the open door, peering into the darkness beyond. Night was upon them.

"Are we arrived at Manorbrier Castle?" she asked.

"No, miss. This be the meetin' place yer aunts told me to bring you to. There be another carriage to take you to Manorbrier. I've already given the gent yer bag." The coachman's face tightened with unease. "I heard it when I stopped to water the horses. There's tales that mark that place, miss. Stories that turn honest folk away."

Yes. She knew those tales. From the day she had

arrived on her aunts' doorstep, orphaned and alone, with naught save a single portmanteau housing her every possession, Emma had been besieged with stories of Manorbrier Castle and its dark lord. Sinister tales of murder. Tales of evil that could disquiet the most stable constitution. Her pregnant cousin Delia had died there, and Delia's unborn child with her. She was thrown to the bottom of a staircase by the man who had sworn to love, honor, and cherish . . . Lord Anthony Craven. Delia's husband. Delia's murderer.

Emma's new employer.

The coachman cleared his throat and said, "I can still take you back the way you came."

Back the way she came. Back to the home of her aunts, who viewed her as a terrible burden, an unwanted and unasked for responsibility tainted by the stain of her illegitimate birth. Back to the fate they had ruthlessly decreed was hers. She shivered, thinking of Mr. Moulton, with his broken teeth and groping hands. Her aunts had cared only for his fat wallet.

"Thank you, no. I will go on to Manorbrier Castle," she said firmly. "I am expected." *And I have nothing to go back to.* Her aunts had been only too eager to put her in this coach and send her to an uncertain fate. And if truth be told, she had been only too eager to let them.

She would never go back. She had made her decision and had no intention of reneging.

The wind swirled through the open door, and she shivered as the cold penetrated her worn cloak. His expression resigned, the coachman waited off to one side, his lantern casting out a paltry circle of light. Emma forced a weak smile, then turned her attention to the distance, to a second light that flickered and bobbed against the night sky. The lantern of the coach that had come to greet her.

Taking a fortifying breath, she dragged her cloak close about her person and stepped into the night. The heavens seemed to frown on her arrival, pouring forth a deluge that left her soaked to the skin before she had taken three steps.

She closed the distance between the two conveyances, shivering as she hastened toward the light of the unfamiliar carriage, barely visible now through the heavy sheeting of rain. Her heart pounded a wild and disturbing tattoo. A harsh gust of wind caught her hair from beneath her bonnet, tearing it loose from its secure roll at the nape of her neck. Wet strands twined about her throat, snarling in the fastening of her cloak.

Tugging at the tangled curls, she turned slowly back, eyes straining against the wall of darkness and storm as she anxiously sought a glimpse of the coachman who had brought her. One last look at a familiar and friendly face. But the light of his lantern was not there.

No kindly coachman. No hired carriage. Only black, black night behind her, and before her an open door and a single yellow light that bobbed and twisted in the frenzied wind, tethered by a precarious clasp to the side of the coach that had come to carry her to Manorbrier Castle. She was well and truly alone here in this bleak and distant spot.

Alone. No novelty that. She had been alone for a very long time, and this was her chance to end that loneliness, to build a life, a place for herself. To make a difference in the life of one small, solitary boy. *He* was the reason she had made this journey.

Bending into the storm, she took a step, and another.

"Stuff and nonsense. Stuff and nonsense." She chanted the words out loud to herself, a mantra against the tug of unease in the pit of her belly, but the raging storm snatched them from her lips and carried them away, to be drowned out by the drumming of the rain against the earth.

As she drew near, the looming bulk of the unfamiliar carriage blocked the worst of the wind. Resolutely, she grasped the edges of the door frame and pulled herself into the relative warmth of the vehicle. She settled herself on the seat and looked up to find that the hired coachman had not vanished after all. He had followed her, and now his broad frame filled the doorway, his face barely recognizable in the sickly light shed by the bobbing lantern outside. She forced herself to give him a reassuring smile before she realized that he likely could not see it, so wrapped was she in the shadows of the carriage.

He waited, squinting into the darkness, giving her one final chance to change her mind.

"Thank you," she whispered.

His shoulders slumped. Stepping back, he tipped his hat and shut the door, closing out the paltry lantern light, leaving her in inky darkness.

With a muffled thump the coach lurched into motion. Emma made an effort to right her ragged appearance and calm her anxious thoughts. Struggling to still the quaking of her chilled body, she forced her fingers to obey her mental command. After untying her bonnet and placing it on the seat, she began the arduous task of blindly unsnarling her wet hair.

Of her portmanteau there was no sign. She murmured a fervent prayer that the hired coachman had indeed passed it to the driver of the carriage in which she now rode. All her worldly possessions were in that bag. Small mementoes of her mother, of value only to a daughter's lonely heart. And her books, treasures whose well-thumbed pages whispered of hopes and dreams.

As Emma continued to work her fingers through her hair, the unkempt snarl was reduced to a slightly untidy mess, and even that soon gave way under her patient onslaught. Within a short time, she had rolled the wet strands into a tidy bun at the base of her skull and secured the lot with the pins she had dug out of the tumbled mass at the outset.

She could only hope that she would make an adequate impression upon her arrival at Manorbrier, and that her appearance would prove acceptable. That she was no raving beauty was in her favor, given that few wished to hire a governess who was considered a diamond of the first water. Her complexion was smooth and unmarked, and she did allow herself a small measure of pride in her thick, long tresses. She had inherited her dark hair from her mother, along with her brown eyes and her temperament, a cheery, practical nature that boded well for her success in the face of adversity, for she preferred to see life as an exciting challenge with trials and tribulations viewed as part of a pattern, like a detailed design on her aunts' best woven rug.

Lulled by the sound of the rain, which had abated to a dull patter on the carriage roof, she relaxed her posture and rested against the seat back to await her arrival at the castle. The inside of the coach remained a dark cocoon, enfolding her in its interior, blocking out the night.

A sound, so faint as to be almost imperceptible, caught her attention. Emma shivered. Surely she was imagining the steady rhythm of soft breathing. She sucked a slow, steady breath in through her nostrils. There was a slight whooshing sound as she pursed her lips and blew the air out through the tiny round hole she had shaped with her mouth.

The *other* sound continued, a soft, steady huff of inhalation and exhalation that was not her own. What had been suspicion coalesced into certainty. She was not alone in the coach. *Something* occupied the shadowed interior with her. Oh, what she would not do for a lamp. Even the tiny glow of a single candle would shed adequate illumination.

"Hello?" she whispered. "Is anyone there?"

Her imagination conjured a beast with glowing red eyes and a tongue that lolled from an open mouth replete with razor-sharp teeth set in massive jaws. Emma squinted into the darkness. There were no glowing red eyes looking back at her. No sharp teeth. No fetid animal breath. In fact, there was no longer even a hint of sound.

There was also no reply to her softly voiced query.

Perhaps she had imagined it. Imagined the faint breathing sounds. Just as she had imagined the beast in the corner, poised and ready to pounce. She almost laughed aloud at her own foolishness.

Then a quiet, scratching noise brought the worst of her fears swirling up from their subdued place, to surface again and take control of her every thought. Before she had opportunity to take those roiling emotions in hand once more, there was a flare of light that illuminated a being curled in the shadow in the far opposite corner of the coach. The glow came from a point close to the creature's face, but below it, thus allowing a play of light and shadow that cast eyes, nose, and mouth in fearsome relief.

Emma reacted without thought or logic and from the back of her throat came a tiny squeak of terror, which grew and gave way to a resounding noise that ricocheted off the interior of the carriage before escaping into the night. She paused to draw breath, and the brief silence was filled by clipped masculine tones.

"Good Lord, woman! Have you not the sense that God gave a mouse? My ears are ringing from the sound of you!"

She resented the comparison. Mice were meek creatures, and Emma was not meek. But she was cautious. Her fear subsided with near laughable speed, replaced by a niggling suspicion that the man across from her might be her new employer or, at the very least, was acquainted with him.

And she had shrieked in the man's ear. Oh, dear. Pressing one hand to her breast, she willed her racing heart to slow to a more reasonable pace.

The small flame glowed in the interior of the coach, continuing to reveal the planes and hollows of what she now realized was a man's face, and just below that, his hand holding the remains of a friction match. The fire raced down the length of the match, burning the fingers that held it. Emma knew that fingers had been singed because she heard a hiss of pain just before the match was abruptly blown out, leaving her alone with the man, and the dark.

"You startled me, sir," she ventured into the silence. "Had I known of your presence from the outset, I would not have reacted with such . . . such volume."

He did not reply immediately, but when he did, his voice reached across the carriage, deep and smooth. "See that you do not raise your voice to my son."

His reply gave confirmation of his identity. She was in the company of Lord Anthony Craven, and she had behaved ridiculously. Not an auspicious beginning.

Uncertain how to reply, she sat in tense silence, her back ramrod straight, a part of her thinking that he ought to apologize for giving her a fright.

"There is no need to perch on the edge of your seat like a little brown wren." He sounded more amused than angry.

Emma's eyes widened. The man must have the vision of a cat to be able to see *her* when the inky blackness veiled *him* from her sight. The eyes of a cat, and the manners of a baboon.

He made a sound low in his throat. "Do you think I purposely lurked here in the darkness, waiting for the opportunity to frighten you out of your skin?"

She had thought exactly that, but hearing the question put so bluntly made the idea sound preposterous. "No, of course not," she lied.

The silence lengthened, and then he grudgingly said, "I fell asleep. When I awoke, I had no idea you were unaware of my presence. And then you screamed."

"I see." Well, she now knew that her employer did not habitually lurk about purposely terrifying young women in his employ. At least, it seemed he had not done so on this occasion.

"Where is the chaperone I requested?" he asked.

Chaperone? For a moment she was strangely touched that he had thought to send funds for such. Yet the very idea was laughable. Aunt Cecilia would never spend money on a hired chaperone. She would consider it an arbitrary and foolish waste of coin, given that Emma was already tarnished beyond repair by the circumstances of her birth. In fact, given the choice, Cecilia would gladly have sold Emma into—

"Ah, let me guess . . . your Aunt Cecilia felt my monies could be better spent on herself, and your Aunt Hortense, having imbibed at least half a bottle of good brandy, hidden in her tea of course, was too insensate to argue on your behalf. Not that she would have bothered had she been conscious. She would have simply helped herself to more tea and muttered 'quite so, quite so.'" His tone was biting, but a subtle hint of humor softened the sound.

Emma swallowed a startled giggle at his irreverent monologue, a small amount of her fear allayed by his sarcastic, and accurate, description of Aunt Cecilia and Aunt Hortense. She frowned, wondering at this odd conversation.

Neither spoke for a time, and then Lord Craven said, "The rain has stopped."

She listened. There was no longer the sound of water beating on the carriage roof. "Yes, it has."

"Damned rain."

There was something in his tone that touched a place inside her, made her wonder why he disliked the rain so. And then she wondered why she cared.

She was saved from having to conjure a reply by the rapid jerk of the coach heralding the termination of her journey. The beginning of her new life.

A soft rustling signaled Lord Craven's movement on the opposite seat, and Emma sensed his nearness as he leaned close. She gasped, a sizzle of awareness jerking her upright at the feel of his warm fingers cupping her chin, the pad of his thumb brushing her cheek, her lower lip.

"So you came despite the storm, despite the rumors, alone, to a place far from home."

She heard something in his tone, admiration, or perhaps surprise. "I have no home," she whispered, and then wished she could call back those naked, far-too-revealing words.

He was close enough that she could feel the fleeting touch of his breath against her cheek, smell the subtle scent of sandalwood and man. She sniffed lightly, then deeper, enticed by the lovely aroma.

"And I gave my word to come," she blurted into the silence. Her word was her greatest treasure, her most valuable asset.

She felt a subtle tension lace his frame.

"Brave girl to come alone," he said softly. His voice held no humor now, and the words, along with the inflection, seemed to carry both praise and warning.

Brave? In the face of what danger? She opened her mouth, wanting to question him, uncertain of what query to pose. Before she could formulate her thoughts, Lord Craven moved from his seat and flung open the door.

A swirl of black greatcoat and a tall, powerful frame filled her vision as he left their conveyance and strode toward the house. Feeling oddly deflated by his abrupt leave-taking, she scuttled forward to the open door of the carriage and watched his progress. The wind had carried the storm away, leaving behind the clear night sky and the smell of clean, wet earth.

Lord Craven vaulted up the wide stone stairs, then paused and turned slightly, leaving his profile silhouetted against the light that poured from the lamps flanking the open front door. She thought his hair was dark, so it seemed from this distance, his chin strong and his nose straight and fine. More she could not see, but the overall impression was of a tall, forbidding man. Handsome in both face and form.

Tension coiled inside her as she stared at him, and her skin tingled in the place his fingers had contacted. She caught her lower lip between her teeth, wishing that he had not walked away so quickly, wishing that he had tarried. Sucking in a breath, she was left wondering why such thoughts should plague her, and why the lovely scent of him yet swirled about her, tantalizing her.

Unwilling to forfeit the sight of him just yet, she leaned out a little farther. Lord Craven inclined his head, appearing to speak to someone inside the doorway. Then with a swift glance in her direction, so brief she almost missed it, he turned and disappeared into the house.

A sound drew Emma's attention, and she glanced to her left to find a stranger standing near the coach. The light that shone so brightly closer to the house filtered to a timid glow this far from the source and left the man's face in shadow. Dark hollows and subtle highlights accentuated the terrible scars and puckers along his cheeks and chin, permanent marks that labeled him as one of the lucky.

Lucky because he had survived. Smallpox killed so many of those it touched, and scarred those whose lives were spared. Emma met the man's gaze, silently wondering what loved ones he had buried while he lived on to mourn them. Tears burned the back of her eyes as she thought of her own mother, a victim of the same terrible plague, dead these many years but never forgotten.

"Is this Manorbrier, then?" she asked, with forced brightness. She had no doubt as to her location, but she wished to open a conversation and dispel her melancholic mood.

"Yes, miss," the driver replied, his expression blank as a child's fresh slate.

"And your name is?"

The man stared at her for a long moment. "Griggs," he replied.

Emma heaved a sigh of relief. For a second she had feared he would not answer at all, but would turn and disappear like his enigmatic master, leaving her alone on the front stairs.

"I am pleased to make your acquaintance, Mr. Griggs."

"No mister. Just Griggs. And you be Emma Parrish. Now we's got the introductions all done, let's get you in to Mrs. Bolifer."

As Griggs helped her down from the carriage, Emma spun slowly about, taking in her surroundings. The manor house appeared sizeable, a great, dark shadow against the vast backdrop of night sky. Two large lanterns flanked the open door and spilled light onto the stairs and the closest part of the cobbled drive. Emma stared at the front of the house for a moment, perplexed. There was something odd about the windows. Then understanding dawned. Every window was dark. Not a single light shone from the face of the manor, save that which radiated from the lanterns.

Struck by the strangeness of the place, Emma turned and examined the drive. It was cobbled and long, passing through a huge gate set in the crumbling remains of a wall that surrounded the bailey. Like a diamond hidden in a lump of rock, the newer house nestled within the crumbling shell of the original Manorbrier Castle.

To the south of the gate rose the silhouette of a round tower that looked to be as old as the wall. It leaned slightly to the right, giving the impression that it might tumble to the ground in a tumult of stone and mortar. This she saw by the light of the moon, giving the whole an eerie, shadowy cast that Emma assured herself would be gone when she saw the place on the morrow in the brightness of day.

Suddenly, near the top of the tower she saw a brief flash, a rapid burst of brilliance that was extinguished almost before she registered its existence.

"Oh!" she cried. "Did you see that, Griggs? There, at the top of the tower?"

"No, miss. I saw nothing at all."

"A flash of light in that tower. It was there but a second."

Griggs hefted Emma's luggage with a grunt. Ignoring her comment, he started toward the front door of the manor house. Emma lifted the hem of her still-damp skirt and followed, casting a glance over her shoulder toward the tower.

"What you got in here? Rocks?" Griggs asked, looking back at her.

"No, books." Again she glanced at the tower. "But, Griggs, I did see a light. A very bright flash. A flare. Almost like . . . I don't know . . . a match.

No, brighter than a match . . . the light was bigger somehow, and then it vanished. . . ."

Griggs stopped so suddenly that Emma trod on his heel before she could stop herself. He turned slowly to face her, his eyes narrowed. "If I was a new governess come to Manorbrier," he said, drawing out each word, "I would pay no mind to the Round Tower. No mind at all."

Taking a step back Emma met his gaze, a strong flash of annoyance rushing through her. She had been uprooted from her home of the past five years. Despite her aunts' malevolent attitude, Emma had taken pleasure in parts of her life as a sojourner in their house. She had loved Cook, and Annie, the downstairs maid, the flowers in the garden, and her stolen moments of freedom in the afternoons when her aunts slept. Whatever small sense of security she had enjoyed had been wiped out on her journey to this rain-washed castle so far from anything known and familiar. Griggs's warning was the last straw.

Pulling herself up to her full height, which barely reached the hulking man's shoulder, she tilted her head to glare at him. Intent on politely but firmly setting some rules for their future association, rules that included an absence of veiled threats and warnings, Emma was startled into silence by his next words.

"There's death in the Round Tower, miss. Death in the very air. You stay away from that tower." Griggs looked at her with focused intensity, as if willing her to heed his warning.

She shivered as she realized he meant it. Every word. Griggs was afraid of the tower, and he meant for her to be afraid as well. "What . . . ?"

Ignoring her startled query, the man adjusted his grip on her bag and turned away.

A shadow fell across the lighted doorway, and Emma looked up to find a woman blocking the entryway. Her gray hair was coarse and wiry, with long strands poking out from the coil she had rolled in an attempt to tame her appearance. Her gray eyes were flat and seemed coldly unwelcoming, an impression bolstered by the fact that her thick brows were drawn together and the corners of her mouth pulled down in an expression of distaste.

"The servants' entrance, if you please." The woman held firm as Griggs approached.

"Bag's heavy." He shifted his stance. "This way'll do for tonight, Mrs. Bolifer."

Emma swallowed and took a step forward, more than willing to enter by whatever door would create the least controversy, but, to her surprise, the woman moved to the side to let him pass.

"Griggs," Mrs. Bolifer said, "you may take her bag to the blue room on the upper floor."

He paused, looking down at Mrs. Bolifer, his mouth open as if he wished to say something. Her expression grew even more forbidding.

"The blue room," she repeated firmly. "Until we know what sort she is."

With a nod, Griggs moved on and thudded up the wide staircase at the end of the entrance hall, leaving Emma standing just outside the house on the top step, prevented from following by the barrier presented by Mrs. Bolifer's stout body. Bewildered by the odd exchange, she peered past the woman to the interior of the hall, gleaning the quick impression of geometric black and white floor tiles and a polished rosewood center table, complete with an arrangement of dark red roses.

Returning her attention to the woman who barred her entry, Emma hesitated. She was tempted to bob a curtsy to the housekeeper, but as the new governess, she thought the action inappropriate. Instead, she smiled and extended her hand.

"I am Emma Parrish. So pleased to make your acquaintance, ma'am."

"We are not at a tea party, Miss Parrish," Mrs. Bolifer snapped back, ignoring Emma's proffered hand. Her cold gaze scanned the girl from head to foot, and then she turned and made her way toward the stairs, the skirt of her stark black dress floating outward with her movement. Mrs. Bolifer pushed it down with her hands.

Or rather, *hand*. It was then that Emma noticed that Mrs. Bolifer's left sleeve ended in a gathered band, empty from just a bit below the shoulder. The woman used subtle movements to keep her empty sleeve out of sight, rolling her shoulder to hold what remained of her arm behind her when she faced forward, and ahead of her when she turned.

"Come along," she said, without looking back, and Emma followed.

Mrs. Bolifer carried a single candle to light their way as they climbed the stairs and walked the length of a dark corridor. Each room they passed was dim and quiet. The housekeeper climbed a second flight of stairs and a third. They reached the landing and proceeded to a room at the end of a hallway, in the farthest corner of the uppermost floor. The air smelled stale, laden with dust and disuse.

Eyes trained on the candle that had been left

burning in the room, Mrs. Bolifer jerked to an abrupt halt just outside the open door. Emma could not be certain, but she thought the housekeeper's expression held something akin to fear.

"The blue room," Mrs. Bolifer intoned, standing stiffly to one side.

Emma peeked past her and saw that Griggs had left her portmanteau on the floor beside the narrow iron bed. On the far side of the bed was a small table and on it a single flickering candle, which cast dancing shadows across the walls and floor. An armoire was angled in the corner, and the only other furniture was a spindly chair beside the fireplace, softened by a pretty blue-and-white cushion.

A cheerful blaze danced in the hearth, bringing warmth to Emma's damp and chilled form. She smiled. Griggs must have built the fire for her. Perhaps she had made one friend here in her new home.

Turning toward Mrs. Bolifer, who waited in silence, her posture angry and unyielding, Emma spoke quickly to hide her embarrassment as her stomach growled loudly. "Thank you for showing me to my room, Mrs. Bolifer."

The woman stared at her and after a moment said, "You'll use tallow candles here in your own chamber, but there're wax ones for when you move about. His Lordship has no liking for the stench of tallow."

"Yes, of course," Emma murmured, masking her surprise at the use of wax candles, for they were so frightfully dear. She pressed her lips together as her stomach rumbled yet again.

"I'll not bring you a tray," the housekeeper said brusquely.

Emma opened her mouth to protest that she held no such expectation, but Mrs. Bolifer shook her head and glared her into silence.

"But I will ask Cookie to make you a little something in the kitchen. Down the stairway to the left, and then down a second flight, along the hall, down the back stairway to the right, take the first turn on the left. And from now on you are to use the back stairway and the servants' entrance unless you are accompanied by the young master." With a final glower, the housekeeper turned away. "Get yourself dry now."

Dear heaven, it would be a miracle if she found the kitchen at all, but Emma sensed that her companion had no intention of repeating those directions.

Standing in the doorway of her room, she watched the light of Mrs. Bolifer's candle recede into the darkness. Partway down the hall the bobbing flame stopped, and Emma could barely discern the housekeeper's black-clad form.

"Do not leave a flame burning unattended," the woman admonished in an eerie singsong voice. Her words drifted back to Emma, the empty hallway causing the sound to echo in an unnerving way. "Never, never leave a flame unattended."

The shadows swallowed Mrs. Bolifer as she continued on her way until it seemed that the small and distant candle floated through the air, weightless. Then the light disappeared, leaving Emma alone to ponder what little she had seen of this unfamiliar household, her thoughts awhirl with confusion and unease. What a peculiar and somewhat eerie place.

The scarred coachman, Griggs, who regarded

her with fear-darkened eyes as he whispered vague warnings.

Mrs. Bolifer, the one-armed housekeeper who watched the flames with a wary eye.

And Lord Craven, with his flowing black cape and dangerous beauty, which she had seen outlined against the light. The touch of his warm fingers against her chilled skin. The low, rich sound of his voice.

Emma sucked in a breath, wondering why the thought of her enigmatic employer made her feel restless and beset by uneasy emotion.

Brave girl to come alone.

CHAPTER TWO

After changing in to dry clothes, Emma left her tiny chamber, carrying the lighted candle to guide her way. As she walked, she noticed that the doors to the other rooms on her floor were closed, and no sliver of light shone from beneath. Curious, she paused and gently turned a handle. Locked. As was the next and the next that she tried. Frowning, she pondered this peculiar circumstance, wondering what secrets were hidden behind these locked doors. Again, her stomach rumbled, and she quit her impromptu exploration in favor of a speedy trip to the kitchen.

With only three wrong turns and a single moment of panic, she managed to follow the housekeeper's directions down the flights of stairs to the first turn on the left. There, a narrow hallway opened into the comfort of a warm and well-lit kitchen.

Mrs. Bolifer sat at a long, scarred wooden table with a pot of tea and three cups in front of her. A second long table, this one higher than the first, spanned the far wall of the kitchen. Behind it stood a woman in a faded brown dress. She was tall, and thin as reed grass, her brown hair streaked with gray and scraped into a tight bun at the back of her head. The harsh hairstyle accentuated the sharp angles of her cheekbones. Her brown eyes were time worn, and deep lines bracketed her mouth. Emma suspected she had seen much in her lifetime, and not all she had seen was good.

"Hello, I am Emma Parrish."

To Emma's surprise the woman's austere face lit in welcome and she rounded the table to take Emma's hand and pump it with enthusiasm.

"Call me Cookie," she said, her voice high and girlish. Such a contrast to her appearance. Her smile deepened the creases in her cheeks and made a network of lines fan out from the sides of her eyes. Nonetheless, the woman's smile took years from her appearance and did much to soften her angular looks.

Emma surreptitiously assessed the cook. No visible scars. And she seemed to be in possession of all her limbs. After meeting both Griggs and Mrs. Bolifer, she had half expected a missing leg or, at the very least, a pronounced limp. But Cookie seemed hale and hearty, save for the look in her eyes that hinted at scars somewhere deep within her soul.

Smiling in return, Emma let the cook guide her to a seat opposite Mrs. Bolifer. The housekeeper poured three cups of steaming tea, and Cookie put a plate of bread, cheese, and cold meat in front of Emma.

"And how was the trip, dear?" Cookie asked just as Emma filled her mouth with a bite of bread and cheese. "Quite long, I should think. And all alone in a hired coach." Fortunately, Cookie seemed quite capable of carrying on a conversation all on her own, saving Emma from being unmannerly by answering with her mouth full, or appearing rude by continuing to chew and giving no answer at all. "Poor thing! The wind is quite dreadful tonight, and I vow that the water coming from the sky put me in mind of Noah and his ark. Last year it rained for three weeks without pause. The road was a river of mud. A river, I tell you."

Cookie talked. Emma chewed. And Mrs. Bolifer glared into her steaming cup of tea.

"Such a dreadful night, such wind, such rain. And His Lordship. Poor man. A full day and a night in the village without any rest."

At the mention of Lord Craven, Emma's heart sped up, and she waited for Cookie to continue. Curiosity, she reassured herself silently. The unsteady state of her pulse had nothing to do with the odd heat that had suffused her at his brief touch in the carriage or the way that his voice had echoed through her thoughts long after he had left her.

Heaving a deep sigh, Cookie shook her head. "At least this time he didn't come back drenched in blood. His coat was good for nothing but the rag bin after that."

Emma nearly choked as a mouthful of food was sucked in along with her startled intake of air. As she coughed into her napkin, Cookie reached over and pounded her on the back. "Tea's cool now, love. Take a sip. There's a good girl."

Blood? She must have heard wrong. But, no, she was certain she had heard Cookie say the word "blood." Her gaze slid from Cookie to Mrs. Bolifer, who continued to examine the tea in her cup as if it held the answers to the mysteries of the world.

"And I suspect they gave him naught to eat," the cook pointed out mournfully. "I took him a tray. Left it by the door. Never would I go in the tower. Just left it by the door."

"That tray will be by the door come morning." Mrs. Bolifer nodded. "He takes not a bite when he gets like this. You know that as well as I."

Gets like what? Emma swallowed her food, looking back and forth between the two women. She was inordinately curious about her new employer, parched for any tidbit of information her companions might share, and she found her fascination both odd and unsettling.

"I thought I saw a flash of light in the tower," she said.

Two pairs of eyes swiveled to stare at her.

"You stay away from there," Cookie said somberly.

Why? The question hovered, unasked, and both Cookie and Mrs. Bolifer turned their attention to their teacups. Emma frowned, puzzled and a bit unnerved by the clear message that the Round Tower was not to be visited, not even to be discussed.

She looked up to find Mrs. Bolifer staring at her. The two women had grown silent during Emma's musings and they now regarded her as if expecting an answer to a question she had not heard them ask. She finished the last morsel of bread and smiled her apology.

"I am terribly sorry, but I seem to have been wool-gathering."

Mrs. Bolifer's lips tightened in a frown, her face creasing into what appeared to be her customary expression.

"That's all right, love." Cookie patted her hand. "I was just asking . . . how old were the last set of children you cared for? You seem a mite young for a governess with much experience."

"Oh!" Emma felt her cheeks heat with embarrassment. "I haven't actually been a governess to anyone's children. Though, before my mother died I did go to the farm down the way and teach the children their numbers and letters. And the children taught me to milk a cow. They were a good bit better with their letters than I was with the cow." She smiled at the memory of farmer Hicks's children. "The worst of it was, I caught the cowpox, just like any milkmaid."

Both women stared at her, unblinking.

"My mother was a governess," Emma said quickly, feeling as though her qualifications for the position had been found distinctly lacking. "She often told me that the best way to manage a child is with a hug, a smile, and a steady set of rules."

Neither of her companions said a word, and then Mrs. Bolifer stood abruptly and nodded once to Cookie. "Good night, then," she said, stalking from the kitchen with a rustle of her stiff black skirt.

Unnerved by this rapid departure, Emma glanced uncertainly at the cook.

"Don't mind her, love." Cookie rose and cleared the tea things from the table. "Mrs. Bolifer is soft under all those prickles. Especially when it comes to the boy."

"Tell me about him," Emma urged. What little she knew about the child was colored by the bilious tinge of the venomous barbs Aunt Cecilia had aimed at the father.

Cookie arched a brow. "He's a six-year-old boy. That should tell you enough."

"I so want to make a difference in his life," Emma whispered.

Narrowing her eyes, Cookie asked warily, "What sort of difference?"

"Is it terribly selfish of me to imagine that I can offer Nicholas, a child I have never met, love and comfort and, at the same time, perhaps glean some of the same emotions for myself?" Emma sank her teeth into her lower lip and immediately wished she hadn't blurted her thoughts aloud.

"Is that why you came here? Looking for love and comfort?" Cookie's questions pitched high in surprise.

Rising, Emma gathered her plate and cup, using the action as an opportunity to choose her words with care. She had no illusions about her prospects. Penniless and illegitimate, working in her aunts' home as scullery maid and step-girl and laundry maid all rolled into one, or if Cecilia had had her way, being sold to the first man who offered a fat purse—

No, she would not think of that now. Not ever. The arrival of Lord Craven's letter could not have been better timed. Her aunts seized the opportunity to rid themselves of her presence, given that she had defied their best-laid plans. The fact that there had been a monetary settlement to help compensate their loss had definitely swayed them. And despite the rumors that painted him a monster, Lord Craven's employ, the chance to care for his son, had appealed to Emma far more than Mr. Moulton's rancid embrace.

"I came *looking* for nothing," she said at length. "But *hoping* for a way to love a child the way I was loved."

Cookie met her gaze, shadows and worry beating back the warmth of her smile. "The poor mite has had a hard go of it. But you might well do, Emma Parrish. You might last longer than the others."

There was something in Cookie's tone that made Emma flinch. "The others?"

"Twelve governesses in four years. With His Lordship so exacting, they hardly survive a few weeks before they're gone."

"Hardly *survive* a few weeks?" Emma echoed, her thoughts spiraling back to Cookie's earlier reference to Lord Craven returning home drenched in blood. Surely she couldn't mean—

"Then they're gone." Cookie snapped her fingers. "Just like that."

Gone? "Where do they go?" Emma whispered.

"Don't know where they go, dear. But His Lordship makes sure they never come back."

Early the next morning, Emma watched pale fingers of light creep past the lace curtains of her window, to trace patterns on the wooden floor. The fire had long since died, the gray ashes lending no warmth to the chilly room. But a cold hearth was no novelty. Her aunts had seen no need to waste coal on Emma, and her tiny room in the attic of their home had been frightfully cold in winter and dreadfully hot in summer. By comparison, her current chamber was a luxury.

Raising her hand, she stifled a wide yawn. Tormented by Cookie's words late into the night, her thoughts before she had fallen asleep had been filled with hazy visions, terrible imaginings of Lord Craven, his hands covered in blood, a faceless governess lying murdered at his feet, and then the woman had become Delia, broken at the bottom of the stairs.

Slumber had been long in coming.

She tossed back the counterpane and climbed from the bed. Shivering, she crossed to the pitcher of clean water that Cookie had sent up with her the night before. Carefully doling out tooth powder onto her brush, she acknowledged that she felt a little foolish for having let her imagination and the exhaustion of her long journey influence her thoughts and observations the previous night.

Don't know where they go, dear. But His Lordship makes sure they never come back. She shook her head as she thought of all the possible sinister scenarios she had attributed to that statement. Ridiculous. She was a sensible girl, not prone to wild exaggeration or fanciful musing. Surely the exhaustion of her long journey was to blame for her morbid thoughts. Obviously the previous governesses had not suited, and they had moved on.

After donning her dress and pinning her hair in a neat coil, Emma followed the same path she had taken to the kitchen once before, making only a single wrong turn along the way. As she paused, uncertain of her way, a chill of unease slithered along her spine. She spun, her gaze darting about, searching the dusty shadows.

A dark premonition gripped her, making her blood pound thick and heavy through her veins. Someone was watching her. She could feel his eyes upon her, sense a threatening and malicious intent. Tamping down the urge to flee this deserted corner of the house, to run pell-mell through these unfamiliar halls, she turned a slow circle, every sense attuned. A mad flight would only serve to lose her way even more than it was already.

She squinted into the darkness, turning slowly about. There. She heard it. The rough sound of a breath drawn and released, again and again, mingling with the wild and wretched pounding of her own heart.

Mrs. Bolifer's instructions sounded in her mind: *down a second flight, along the hall, down the back stairway to the right*. . . . Resolutely Emma turned, away from whatever lurked in the dust-laden shadows, away from the whisper of evil that crawled, unseen, through this house. She carefully picked her way along the path she had trod the previous night, her pulse slowing to a more regular pace as she heard no footfall in her wake, no hint of someone giving chase.

She might have convinced herself she had imagined the whole of it, but for the deep certainty that for at least a short while she had not been alone. A sinister distress plagued her as she wondered who had been watching her, and why.

As she neared the kitchen, Emma hesitated, unsure if she should voice her concerns to the others. She had no proof, only a story of losing her way, imagined sounds, and a dark feeling of unease. There really was nothing to tell.

"Nicky! You are to breakfast with your father and new governess. Put that scone back this instant." The housekeeper's voice was gentle, but firm.

Emma felt a jolt of surprise as she stepped into the kitchen. Mrs. Bolifer was smiling, as was Cookie. They were both looking at a small boy who kicked at the floor with his toe before putting the scone he held back on the platter. The child looked as if he had dressed himself from the ragpicker's bag. His breeches sported a large hole at the knee. His stockings were mismatched. And his dark hair stood up in unkempt tufts from his head.

"And perhaps we should do something with your hair. You are to meet your new governess at breakfast."

"I hope Papa makes her go away, just like the others."

Cookie exchanged a worried look with the housekeeper before crossing the room to kneel in front of the little boy.

"Oh, no, Nicky," she said as she wrapped her arms around him in a warm hug. "Miss Parrish is quite nice, lovey dove."

"I don't know," the boy replied, his voice muffled by Cookie's shoulder. "I haven't met her yet. But if she is like Miss Strubb or Miss Rust or . . ." The child shivered and hesitated briefly before saying the woman's name in a hushed whisper. ". . . Mrs. Winter, then I think I should not like to meet her at all. And certainly if she is like Mrs. Winter, then she should go away and never come back. Papa could send her off in a pine box. Just like he sent Mrs. Winter."

A pine box? Emma stood frozen, digesting the implications of all she had overheard. Clearly the child was frightened and had quite possibly been ill-treated by his previous governesses. That he had suffered was a sad thing, to be sure, but his trust could be gained with patience and love. So she worried not overmuch as to Nicky's opinion of her, but the mention of a pine box for the unknown Mrs. Winter gave her pause. There was only one type of pine box he could mean.

A chill crept across Emma's skin. It seemed that

Mrs. Winter had left Manorbrier in a coffin, and by the child's account, it was Lord Craven who had put her there.

Even as she struggled with that thought, the boy looked up and caught her in her unintentional eavesdropping. His blue eyes widened and all color left his cheeks as he huddled deeper in Cookie's embrace.

"Good morning," Emma said brightly as she crossed to him and quickly knelt so that her face was on level with his. "I am ever so pleased to meet you, Master Nicholas."

If possible his eyes rounded even more.

With a quick look at the housekeeper, Emma continued, "I heard Mrs. Bolifer address you as Nicky, and I trust you will allow me the same familiarity. And you shall call me Miss Emma. I rather think that 'Miss Parrish' is too stuffy sounding."

The child sucked in his cheeks. He was all pursed lips, hollow cheeks, and great round eyes as he studied her suspiciously. But he did take Emma's proffered hand and shake it in a gentlemanly fashion, thus confirming for Emma that he had a modicum of tutelage in fine manners.

Emma rose and quickly brushed the front of her skirt before turning back to her young charge. "Well, Nicky," she said with a smile, "I will have to ask you to escort me to the breakfast room. I have no idea where it is, and I am sure we do not wish to keep your father waiting."

She sucked in a fortifying breath. The thought of seeing Lord Craven this morning gave her an odd feeling, half apprehension, half nervous anticipation.

"A gentleman escorts a lady so." Emma positioned Nicky's arm and laid her hand gently in place. He looked up at her uncertainly, and Emma's heart gave a little kick. Clearly he was wary of her, perhaps even fearful. She turned the full magnitude of her smile on him and gave a brief nod. "Lead on, sir."

Nicky hesitated, his gaze sliding from hers, focusing on her hand where it rested on his arm. Then he cast a desperate look at Cookie, who smiled and nodded her encouragement.

"That's just fine, love," the cook said gently. "You take Miss Parrish on in to breakfast."

Cookie's encouragement proved to be all that Nicky needed. With a nod he hiked his arm up in recognition of Emma's greater height and led her from the kitchen. Rather, Nicky galloped and Emma took long strides in order to keep up. She found it promising that the child maintained the position of his arm and escorted her to the best of his ability, rather than shaking off her touch. A most approvable beginning.

Although, it seemed that Mrs. Bolifer did not agree, for as they walked past, Emma noticed that the housekeeper sent her a look of unconcealed distrust.

Entering the breakfast room, Emma paused. There were three settings at the table, and the aroma ascending from the foods held in silver chafing dishes on the sideboard permeated the air.

Nicky skirted the dining table and threw himself into the seat closest to the window. His movements were so exuberant that Emma feared he might dislodge the pristine white tablecloth, and all of the china and crystal with it. She gave a tiny sigh of relief when he was safely seated with the tableware still intact.

"Good morning, Nicholas," a deep voice rumbled from the doorway behind her.

Startled, Emma spun so quickly she nearly lost her balance. Lord Craven was directly behind her, his broad shoulders filling the door frame. He reached forward and grasped her elbow, steadying her.

"And good morning to you, Miss Parrish. I trust you are recovered from the fatigue of your journey." That voice. Warm and lush, it stroked her senses, made her want to lean closer and revel in the sensuous baritone.

"Good morning, my lord." Her heart skittered within her breast as she looked up and took in her first clear view of Lord Anthony Craven. *Why, he is young,* she thought in surprise, *no aging tyrant but a man of perhaps three decades, vital and strong.* He was tall, well formed, the tailored cut of his coat caressing his frame. Dark hair, overly long and sinfully thick, hung straight to his collar, framing the hard planes of his face. She had the oddest urge to reach out, to run her fingers through the shining strands of his hair, to test the softness.

Dear heaven. He was more than attractive. He was masculine perfection. Emma wet her lips, stunned by his stark, male beauty, and by her own inexplicably strange reaction to it. The full, sensual curve of his lips pulled taut, and she held her breath waiting for his smile.

"And thank you, yes, I am quite recovered from the fatigue of the journey." She felt breathless, akin to the sensation elicited by a vigorous walk.

The smile she anticipated never came, and she found herself oddly disappointed. He stared at her intently, as if he could read her every thought, his gaze locking with hers, and then dropping lower to peruse her person in a most indecent manner.

Emma's pulse raced as he returned his attention to her face. She felt undone by the look he settled on her. Somehow, the way he looked at her, with pupils dilated and dark, rimmed in an eerie topaz green, made Emma think that Lord Craven was hungry. For her.

Her breath left her in a rush.

"Then you slept well?" he inquired. "Undisturbed by things that go bump in the night?"

Emma's shoulders tensed at this oblique reference to the terror she had exhibited in the coach the previous night. "I am rarely disturbed by things that go bump in the night, my lord. My constitution is normally quite steady."

"Indeed. Not prone to overwrought imaginings, Miss Parrish?"

She had no answer for that because he had already seen her at her worst, with ridiculous flights of fancy spurring her to uncharacteristic behavior. Worse, she had spent the night exactly as he described, struggling to fall asleep as she waged an out-of-character battle with her overwrought imaginings, and then again, on her way to breakfast, when she had been so certain she was being followed. . . . Had that been nothing more than foolish fancy?

No. She thought not.

Chewing lightly on her bottom lip, Emma looked up to find her employer staring with marked intent at her lower lip in the place she held it caught between her teeth. She sucked in a quick, ragged breath.

Lord Craven was not looking at her in a way that a gentleman might look at a lady.

And she liked it. She *liked* the way he stared at her, his gaze warming her, touching her, making her body tingle in a foreign and wicked way. The realization shocked her, leaving her feeling disoriented and uncertain.

As if from a distance she heard the sound of Nicky's voice, and she latched onto his words as though they were a signal light in a wild storm.

". . . and I escorted her to breakfast, and here we are," he said.

"You were very helpful, Nicky." She turned to him, smiling encouragingly, grateful for the distraction.

Recovering herself, she glanced down at Lord Craven's lean fingers where they yet curled along her forearm. The length of time that he had maintained the contact was quite improper, and Emma frowned in confusion, half relieved, half disappointed when he finally let his hand drop away.

Nicky bounced up and down in his seat as his father rounded the table and leaned forward to place a kiss on the child's brow. Emma masked her surprise at this outward display of fatherly affection. Somehow she had assumed that Lord Craven would be a disinterested parent, at best. Then she recalled the man's admonition that she not raise her voice to his son, and she had the bewildering sensation that she had somehow misjudged the situation. Whatever information she had about this father-son relationship was based on gossip, supposition, and the opinion of Aunt Cecilia, who was herself a bitter and cruel guardian. Clearly these were not solid groundings on which to form an impression.

Lord Craven moved around the table and held Emma's chair, the one across from Nicky. She felt awkward as she made her way to her seat, her skirt brushing against her employer's muscled legs as she took her place, the sandalwood scent of him teasing her, making her long to draw nearer still and inhale until she had enjoyed him to the fullest.

She was acutely aware of a fluttering sensation low in her belly, and she felt certain it was caused by neither hunger nor fear. The experience was new to her. It made her feel hot and restless, and she fought the urge to press her thighs tightly together beneath her skirt. This, then, was attraction, she thought. Dangerous, foolish attraction. The kind that had drawn her mother into a web of heartbreak.

Emma sought to steady her galloping pulse. She, who was the product of her mother's unfortunate liaison with a nobleman, who had spent her life burned by the brand of illegitimacy, knew better than to fall prey to the physical allure of her employer. On that path lay only danger and disaster.

Doubly so, given that Lord Craven was a widower rumored to have murdered his wife, Emma's own cousin. The thought felt wrong, and that wrongness made Emma wary. She did not know this enigmatic man, and she would be most wise to avoid swift judgment of him, whether to good or evil.

She glanced up once more. He was watching her, his changeable eyes glinting like finest gems, his expression revealing little.

And still her blood pounded, thick and strong in her veins. Oh, why was it Anthony Craven made her pulse race as it had never done before, made her every nerve tingle? She was foolish in the extreme to allow her thoughts to travel this path.

What was it about him that . . . stimulated her so? The way his clothes caressed his lithe frame, or the hint of dark stubble along the sculpted line of his jaw? She busied herself with smoothing her skirt, praying he would step away and leave her with some semblance of sanity. She had seen the man exactly twice. This . . . attraction was surely a temporary madness.

After a moment, Lord Craven withdrew to his own chair and sat watching her in narrow-eyed contemplation. His intent regard held a degree of puzzlement, and Emma wondered if he, too, felt the inexplicable current that pulsed between them.

He looked away as Griggs arrived with another warming dish. Emma wondered at the peculiarity of this household to have the coachman serve as footman, and heaven knew what else.

Rising, they each served themselves from the array of foods offered, with Lord Craven helping his son to fill his plate. Emma noted absently that there was a boiled rice pudding dotted with currants and flavored with cinnamon and vanilla, an unusual breakfast choice unless one was a six-year-old child. Nicky was especially excited about it, demanding a huge scoop alongside his eggs and bacon.

Once seated, Nicky chattered to his father and sent Emma several uncertain glances, as if expecting some reprimand. She smiled reassuringly when she caught his eye but refrained from entering the discussion. Still grappling with her inexplicable physical response to Lord Craven, she felt unequal to the challenge of polite conversation. Moreover, she wanted to take this opportunity simply to observe Nicky and learn a bit about him. She had a strong suspicion that the child would come around to her fairly quickly, if this morning's experience was any indication. Had she been alone she would have laughed out loud at her recollection of Nicky galloping down the hallway dragging her behind.

Nicky stuffed a piece of scone smothered in strawberry preserves into his mouth, then gathered up a fistful of shirt from over his chest and rubbed it forcefully across his jam-stained lips. He stopped mid-action and turned a frozen stare in Emma's direction, his mouth a little round "O" of terror. Stomach clenching at the sight of his fear, Emma raised her serviette from her lap and blotted it delicately on her own lips. She held Nicky's gaze the entire time, then purposefully looked down at the serviette that lay on the table beside his plate. The child's eyebrows shot upward as he grabbed the linen square and enthusiastically scrubbed his mouth.

Glancing up, Emma found Lord Craven watching her, studying her with a slow perusal that left her feeling as though her skin tingled in the wake of his regard. Then he nodded once, an action she read as silent approval of her handling of his son.

Again Emma felt that odd sensation of having her expectations turned upside down. She had assumed that all the previous governesses had fled from Lord Craven's evil influence. Yet, given the conversation she had overheard in the kitchen, and Lord Craven's evident concern for his child, she was faced with confusing and conflicting information. It was feasible that Lord Craven had merely dismissed those women from his employ. She had barely formulated that thought when the words Nicky had spoken in the kitchen slammed through her mind. *Send her off in a pine box. Just like he sent Mrs. Winter.*

Before Emma had a chance to ponder further that chilling possibility, Griggs returned to the breakfast room and leaned over to whisper something in Lord Craven's ear. Whatever news Griggs imparted seemed to cast an immediate pall over His Lordship's mood. No explanation was forthcoming. He simply placed his serviette beside his near-empty plate and stood.

"You will excuse me, Miss Parrish." His gaze lingered on her for an unsettling moment before he strode from the room, pausing only long enough to ruffle his son's dark hair.

Lord Craven's exit brought the return of Emma's appetite and she proceeded to empty her plate with ladylike precision while discussing Nicky's favorite topic—horses. Several times she glanced up to find Nicky watching her handling the utensils and copying her movements.

"Well, Nicky"—Emma placed her knife and fork together on her plate and smiled when Nicky did the same—"we shall begin your lessons this morning."

The child's expression took on a wary cast. Emma rose and crossed to the window. The sun peeked from behind a cloud, shining down on an expanse of manicured lawn.

"Could you tell me the normal schedule of your day?"

"Normal schedule?" Nicky echoed.

"Yes"—Emma glanced over her shoulder at him—"the things you do and the order in which you do them. I should like to practice our letters and numbers before luncheon. But the day is so lovely that perhaps we could spread a blanket and take our lessons outdoors. Do you have a slate?"

"Outdoors, Miss Emma?" He shook his head vehemently from side to side. "Miss Rust only let me outside for a walk in the afternoon. After lessons were done. And Mrs. Winter never let me out at all."

"Not at all, Nicky?" Emma asked, with a hint of laughing suspicion in her tone. "Not even to play?"

Nicky huddled against the back of his chair. "Mrs. Winter said play was evil. Sometimes, she left me alone in the nursery. She told me to kneel and recite my prayers. Then she would go away for a very long time." He cast a quick glance at Emma, and his voice dropped near to a whisper. "If I thought she'd be gone long, I would sneak out to the stables to see the horses. But one time she caught me and switched my legs until they bled. Then Papa sent her away. In a coffin that was nailed up tight."

Emma winced at this horrifying tale, even as a dull thud of anger pulsed through her. She thought that if Mrs. Winter were here, she, too, might be tempted to send her away in a pine box.

"Oh, Nicky," she whispered, turning fully and kneeling by his chair, touched beyond measure that he had trusted her with this ugly tale. Slowly, she reached out and laid her hand on his head. "I do not have a switch. My mother was a governess. She was very kind, and she taught me that if you work very hard, then you must play very hard. That way you keep a balance in your life. Play is not evil, Nicky. It is a child's way of practicing for the future."

"Your mother was a governess?" Nicky asked. "What was your father?"

The unexpected question caught her off guard,

digging at an old wound. A nobleman, she thought. A cad. A man who promised a young girl the world, then left her ruined, pregnant, without so much as a good-bye.

"My father died a long time ago." That much was true. He had been crushed to death when the carriage he was racing overturned.

"Oh. So did my mother." He glanced at the window and heaved a mighty sigh. "There is Papa now. I wish he had stayed a little longer."

Rising, Emma turned, her heart doing a strange little dance when she watched Lord Craven crossing the long drive. The sun glinted off his dark hair as he strode briskly toward Griggs, who stood waiting in the shadow of the tower.

There's death in the Round Tower, miss. Death in the very air. You stay away from that tower. It seemed that Griggs did not heed his own advice, for there he stood not an arm's length from the very thing he so feared.

"Nicky," Emma said, an inexplicable chill creeping along her spine. "Do you know what is in the tower at the end of the drive?"

"Yes, Miss Emma."

Something in his tone made her turn.

"Can you tell me?"

He stared up at her in a way that made her pause, his eyes grown wide and wary. Clearly Griggs was not the only one afraid of the Round Tower.

"No, Miss Emma," Nicky said tremulously, then finished in a whisper, "and you cannot make me."

Her heart wrenched at the fear that shadowed his eyes.

"Come show me the nursery," Emma said brightly, moving toward the door. She held out her hand, waiting as Nicky cautiously clasped his small fingers around her larger ones. "We will find the things we need, and we will take our lessons outside in the sunshine today."

Her mood lightened as he gave her a shy smile, then pulled ahead to lead the way. Still, she felt disconcerted by the child's revelations, wary of things unspoken.

Moments later, Emma and Nicky settled on the grass, having gathered all they needed from the nursery, and a blanket from a sullen-eyed upstairs maid who bobbed a curtsy but hurried off before Emma could ask her name.

One hour spun into the second and the third, and the morning fled past. Nicky was bright and sweet, soaking up everything she offered, and then asking for more. She had hoped he could count to twenty, but she quickly found he could go even further, treating the lesson like a game. Emma was pleased that he seemed to so enjoy learning, and again she wondered at his experiences with his previous governesses. With the resiliency of childhood, he had quickly left behind his initial reticence and now embraced her company with obvious affection.

Emma found that she, too, could forget some of her initial apprehension of the previous night, and for this morning at least, Manorbrier seemed fine indeed. In the bright light of day, she could see tiny flowers poking through the chinks in the ancient wall. The stone of the manor house glowed a soft, warm gray and the many windows glinted in the sun. A gentle breeze drifted past, carrying the subtle scent of roses from the garden. Even the grass beneath her was soft and inviting.

Lessons complete, Emma and Nicky flopped on their backs to study the great blue expanse of sky.

"A sheep. That one is a sheep, Miss Emma." Nicky poked his finger at a fluffy cloud directly overhead. Emma thought it looked more like a rabbit with floppy ears, but she allowed Nicky to take the lead.

"That one looks like a fancy carriage, with four horses in front," she said.

"And that one looks like a fox." Lord Craven's deep voice joined their banter.

"I did not hear you approach, my lord," she said, pressing one hand to her chest as her gaze met his. His eyes were a deep, rich green, bright against the frame of black lashes. The most stunning eyes she had ever seen.

Unnerved by such personal and inappropriate thoughts, Emma recalled herself and scrambled awkwardly to her knees. She made to rise, acutely aware of her disheveled state and unladylike pose, aware, too, of the lure of her beautiful, dangerous employer. Lord Craven motioned her to remain where she was.

"Papa!" Nicky cried. His eager gaze scanned the heavens. "That cloud there with the bushy tail? You think it looks like a fox?"

"I do." Lord Craven smiled at his son. He wore no coat and the white cloth of his shirt outlined the breadth of his shoulders. His sleeves were rolled back, revealing strong forearms defined by ridged muscle. Emma wet her lips, wondering that he walked about like this, so uncaring of convention and formality. Wondering if his skin would be warm to her touch, his muscle solid and hard.

He turned his head and caught her staring at

him. Emma's heart gave a hard thud, and she dropped her gaze, a flush of embarrassment heating her cheeks. Dear heaven, what was wrong with her that she thought such unsuitable things and stammered and blushed each time this man drew near? Her life had been neither sheltered nor protected. She knew much of the truths between man and woman, though she had never experienced such for herself. She was no schoolgirl caught in the throes of childish infatuation. Yet never before had she felt this restless unease, this fascination. There was something unsettling about Anthony Craven, something dangerous. Even the briefest encounter left her breathless, with her thoughts in turmoil.

"A fox, Papa?" Nicky squirmed on the blanket, twisting his head this way and that as he searched out the shape in the clouds. "Are you certain? That one there? Looks like a big, fat toad to me."

Emma laughed, and when she glanced up, Lord Craven was still watching her, his eyes hooded.

The hard line of his lips curved in a small smile as he reached down to ruffle his son's hair, and Emma found herself wishing she could see him smile in truth, unfettered, hear him laugh without restraint. "A toad it is, Nicholas mine."

"Stay with us, Papa," Nicky pleaded, his eyes sparkling.

Emma watched the easy affection between father and son and felt her perceptions tilt off kilter once more. This was a child who loved his father. Felt safe with him. Secure.

How, then, to explain Mrs. Winter and her dreadful switch? Had Lord Craven condoned such treatment, as so many of the quality were wont to do? Yet he had forbidden Emma to so much as raise her voice to his son. She could not imagine he had condoned a whipping as just punishment.

Shaking his head, Lord Craven said, "Not today, Nicky. I have business that will not wait. But tomorrow I shall take you to the paddock." He turned his gaze on Emma, his perusal intent, and she had the sudden insight that he had not stumbled upon them by accident. He had been watching her at her duties, assessing her.

"Please," he said softly, gesturing to the blanket, "I did not wish to intrude on such lofty study."

She could have read his words as condemnation, but something in his eyes made her think he approved of her methods.

"Miss Parrish." He inclined his head in farewell.

"Lord Craven," she replied, feeling awkward as she continued to kneel before him on the grass. He turned and strode away, his lithe muscled form moving with perfect grace.

Heart thudding in her breast, she faced the disturbing and disconcerting truth.

A large part of her was relieved to see him go.

A tiny part of her wished he had chosen to stay.

Chapter Three

"I think, Master Nicholas, that we deserve ice cream as a treat," Emma whispered conspiratorially to Nicky as they sat in the nursery some days later. Her heart swelled as Nicky's eyes widened with glee. His smiles brought her untold joy, and his laughter was like the finest piano concerto playing across her soul. *I will make a difference in this child's life,* she had vowed, and she had begun to fulfill that solemn promise to herself.

"Oh, Miss Emma! Ice cream? Truly?" Nicky ran his sentences together, bouncing up and down in his seat. Each bounce jarred the cadence of his speech, making him sound as though he were sitting in a wagon on a very bumpy road, rather than at the small desk in the nursery.

"It is not every day that a boy can print each word on his spelling list without a single mistake," she pointed out.

"So I suppose I do deserve ice cream," Nicky agreed. "But Cookie will be cross when we tell her. She says that it is too much fuss and bother, and she will only prepare it for very special occasions."

"Then we shall do everything ourselves." She smiled as she recalled the times she and her mother had prepared ice cream. It would be a pleasure to share the experience with Nicky, the anticipation, the first sigh of pleasure as the frozen cream melted on their tongues. "Turning the icing pot will be fun. We shall even fetch the ice from the icehouse."

Nicky stopped bouncing and stared at her for a long moment. "Papa says I am not to go near the icehouse."

"Why ever not?"

"Miss Rust fell off the ladder to the bottom. No one found her for hours and hours."

"How very unfortunate for Miss Rust!" Emma exclaimed, frowning.

"Yes. It was unfortunate for her." Nicky tapped his fingers on the desk and then spoke without looking up. "But not for me. I was happy when she went away."

Snatches of overheard conversations skittered through Emma's thoughts, and a chill of foreboding chased along her spine. She wondered just how one asked a child if there was evil afoot in his home, if some nefarious scheme had led to Miss Rust's departure. She ventured a gentle question as she laid her hand across his.

"Nicky, is there something you wish to tell me about Miss Rust?"

"She said someone made her fall."

"Oh-h-h." Shocked, Emma stumbled over a reply and then recovered. "Who made her fall?"

Nicky's expression turned mulish, and he shook his head quickly from side to side. "I told Papa I wasn't near the icehouse that day. I wasn't. I promise. And she wasn't hurt much. Not *that* day."

The child's distress tore at her, gouging her emotions. Clearly, the subject of Miss Rust was most upsetting, and one that Nicky preferred to avoid. And, dear heaven, why was his denial so vehement, so desperate? A chilly whisper of distress raised the hairs at the back of her neck.

"Nicky," Emma began only to stop when he pulled his hand from hers. As she looked at him, with his tousled black hair and enormous blue eyes, he looked inordinately small and frightened. Barely out of swaddling. Far too young to be faced with the visions he had hinted at. He was a child who should be free of the ghosts and fears that haunted his expression. She cleared her throat. "Nicky, if Miss Rust wasn't hurt when she fell in the icehouse, then when was she hurt?"

"She wasn't ever hurt. Not really," he said.

Emma had less than a second to enjoy the feeling of relief that swept over her, before his next words dashed her complacency.

"She wasn't hurt. She was just dead."

The sound of distant drums beat a heavy rhythm, pounding at Emma's temples. Then she realized the sound was not distant at all, but the forceful pumping of her own heart, the rushing of her own blood.

"Dead, Nicky? Are you certain?" she whispered.

"Oh, yes. Just like Mrs. Winter. Papa sent Mrs. Winter away in a pine box." Nicky frowned. "But I don't know what he did with Miss Rust." His expression brightened. "Perhaps she is still in the tower."

"Nicky!" Emma exclaimed. "You cannot mean . . . that is . . . you must be mistaken, darling. Miss Rust left." She spoke the last sentence firmly, as if saying it with certainty would make it so, though her thoughts were a jumble of confusion and concern. "I am convinced she went home after her dismissal."

"I saw Griggs haul her to the tower. But if you are convinced she went home . . ." Shrugging, Nicky smiled, appearing well pleased by her solution. "May we go now?"

Emma glanced at the nursery window, her shoulders tensing. Miss Rust could not possibly be ensconced in the tower, moldering for months on end. Surely the smell would attest to her presence. . . . *Oh, dear heaven.* There was no smell. There was no cadaverous Miss Rust. It was all the fancy of a six-year-old boy and his overly imaginative governess. What in heaven's name was she thinking? That Anthony Craven had murdered not only his wife and infant daughter, but a stream of governesses as well? Or perhaps, that Griggs, the great bulky footman, had done the deeds? Mrs. Bolifer? Cookie?

"Let us proceed," Emma said brightly, deliberately putting tight rein on her own outlandish imaginings. "I shall fetch the ice from the icehouse and you shall turn the icing pot. We each have our duty to perform, and then we will have our chilly sweet."

Emma held her hand out and the boy took it without hesitation. Together, they made it as far as the kitchen, where they retrieved the largest pot they could find.

"And what are you two up to?" Cookie regarded them with mock severity, hands firmly planted on her hips.

"We are going to make ice cream!" Nicky's excitement was extreme. He struggled to control himself, but he fairly quivered, like a hound after a scent. All sign of his earlier distress seemed to have evaporated.

"Are you now?" Cookie's brows shot up. "Don't forget to pound the ice very fine, and add a peck of coarse salt before you pack it round the ice cream freezer. There's a tub you can stand it in stored in the pantry there." She nodded her head in the general direction.

Her words were all the encouragement that Nicky needed. He was off like a shot, and Emma exchanged a smile with Cookie as the child struggled out of the pantry, tub in tow.

"What a fine job," Emma said, clasping her fingers around the edge of the tub and helping him to drag it to a corner of the room, as far from the fire as possible.

"Here, Nicky. You take this side"—Emma gestured to the handle of the pot she had retrieved earlier—"and I shall take this one. Off to the icehouse with us."

He froze, his small fingers curled over the edge of the pot as he stared up at her with wide, uncertain eyes. "You know I cannot go in, Miss Emma. Papa said."

"Of course." She smiled at him reassuringly, all her earlier unease flooding back. "You may wait by the door and then help me carry the ice back here and put it in the tub."

He seemed content with her suggestion, and together they left the kitchen.

Set far to the back of the manor, the icehouse was at the end of a meandering path surrounded by several shade trees. In the winter, ice was hacked from the nearby frozen pond and stored in the deep hole in the floor of the icehouse for use during the warmer months.

They had strolled a good way along the path

when Nicky pulled up short and dropped his side of the pot.

"Papa!" he cried as he tore across the lawn toward his father's tall figure.

Emma's heart fluttered. She watched Lord Craven approach with his long-limbed easy stride, his muscles moving beneath the cloth of his trousers, the sun glinting on his dark hair. He seemed to exude power, energy, confidence. Her pulse began to pound a fast, unsteady rhythm, and she struggled to slow the tempo of her breathing.

"Good afternoon, my lord." She spoke with a calm equanimity that she was far from feeling.

"Miss Parrish."

His voice—that beautiful, luscious voice—was low and rough, the cadence sending an odd jolt to the pit of her belly. And, oh, she recognized that jagged heat for what it was. The sweet pull of desire, the delicious heat of carnal attraction.

The promise of ruin. The certain end to the life she had hoped to build here.

Emma looked into his eyes and stumbled back as she read the intensity of his thoughts, the need that matched her own.

Sucking in a sharp breath, she tore her gaze away and focused on the child, who ran now along the hedge, chasing a butterfly. "Nicky and I were heading to the icehouse. We are going to make ice cream."

Lord Craven's gaze flicked in the direction of the small building, and when he looked back toward her, Emma noted that the hint of a frown marred his brow.

"The icehouse," he repeated softly.

Recalling Nicky's earlier statement that he had been forbidden to venture there, Emma hastened to reassure. "Nicky will wait for me while I go inside to fetch the ice. He did tell me that he is not allowed to venture inside."

Lord Craven nodded slowly. "I thought I would take him to the stables."

Hearing the last of his father's comments, Nicky scooted over and looked uncertainly between the adults. He adored spending time with his father, but the promise of ice cream held strong sway over his child's mind.

Emma smiled. "Might Nicky not do both, my lord? He could visit the stables while I fetch the ice and gather all we need. When he returns, he can assist me with the preparation of his sweet."

"May I, Papa?"

Bending, Lord Craven scooped his son into his arms and spun him about until the child squealed with glee. Emma watched, her heart catching in her breast. The scene was too sweet, too warm, and the smile that curved Lord Craven's hard mouth too enticing. She had waited so long to see that smile, and it did not disappoint. White teeth against dark skin.

She wanted him to turn the bright gift of that smile on her.

She wanted him to press those beautiful, sculpted lips to hers. The thought was both frightening and alluring.

Dear heaven, was this the temptation that had led her mother astray? She could not help but wonder if she had inherited this terrible wanton streak, if she was doomed by the circumstance of her birth to suffer the same enticement.

No. There was more to it than that, for never before had she felt this fascination, this wild excitement that heated her blood and pounded in her heart. 'Twas Lord Craven who lured her. The physical strength of him, banked in gentle kindness to his son. The mystery of him. The sadness and pain that lurked behind his infrequent smile.

She had a sharp and bittersweet longing to hear him laugh, full and loud, unfettered by the shadows of his past.

Foolish wishes. Foolish girl.

Resolutely she turned her attention back to Nicky. "If I am to work so hard at the fetching and carrying, then you must do the most difficult job of all."

"What is it?" Nicky asked, his eyes wide and serious as his father set him back on his feet.

"You must turn the freezer by increments, halfway round and back. Then scrape the cream from the sides every ten minutes," she said.

"I can do that!"

"I know you *can* do it, Nicky, but *will* you do it?"

"I will! I will! I will!" he pronounced, punctuating each exclamation with a nod of his head.

"Very well. I shall see you anon."

With a smile that lit his face, Nicky spun and ran toward the stables. Suddenly, he skidded to a stop. Turning, he rolled his eyes at his father, who remained standing by Emma's side.

"Come along, Papa!"

The corner of Lord Craven's mouth twitched in the hint of a smile. "A moment to speak with Miss Parrish, if you please."

Nicky glanced at Emma, his expression puzzled, and then he shrugged and ran off toward the stables.

"It would seem that my son prefers the company of horses to people."

"And you, my lord? Do you prefer the company of people?"

He tilted his head to one side, the action making him seem almost boyish. "In comparison to horses?"

In comparison to dead governesses whose bodies you hoard in your shadowy tower. With a shiver, she thrust the thought aside. Dear heaven, she was well and truly losing her mind.

"I don't know." She drew a shaky breath. "I am for the icehouse, my lord. I promised Nicky ice cream, and I intend to honor my word."

"As you wish," he said, then added in a hard voice, "be careful on the ladder. A fall could be disastrous, Miss Parrish."

She had just begun to move away, but at his words her head jerked up and she paused. "Was the fall disastrous for Miss Rust?"

An almost imperceptible tension crept into Lord Craven's hard-muscled frame.

"She was bruised," he replied obliquely.

"And after she healed from her bruises?" Emma pressed. She knew the folly of her questions, recognized the danger that she might be horrified by the answers. And the danger that her prodding might unearth far more than she wished to know. Still, she could not seem to stop herself.

"After she healed from her bruises?" Lord Craven's brows rose and his tone held a sardonic edge. "Well, after she healed, Miss Parrish, she was no longer bruised."

"You make sport of me," she whispered, hugging the empty pot she carried, sensing the dark undercurrent to the words he left unspoken.

"No," he replied, moving closer. Slowly, he reached out and lifted a stray curl from her shoulder. The breath left her in a rush and her heart thudded at a turbulent rate. "I merely try to deflect your curiosity," he continued. "But it is apparent that you will not rest until you dig up the sordid remains, so here they are. Before Miss Rust could heal from her fall, she died."

His blunt statement struck her like a blow, for she had held out hope that Nicky was mistaken.

"Died?" Emma repeated numbly, struggling with the shock evoked by his words and the tumultuous emotion stirred by his nearness, his touch. She had known the truth of it, and still she had hoped for a different reply. Dead wife. Dead governess. Perhaps more than one. How to call such mere coincidence? Driven now to have her answers, she blurted, "And Mrs. Winter?"

"Dead as well." His tone was flat. "And I must admit, I liked her much better after her demise."

Emma stared at him in dismay, horrified by his callous words. "You cannot mean that," she whispered.

"Oh, but I do." His green-gold eyes were flat and cold, leaving her no hope that he might mean other than what he said. Where was his kindness now?

Suddenly, she recalled Nicky's assertion that Mrs. Winter had taken a switch to him. Did Lord Craven know of the incident? Could that be the reason behind his pitiless assertion?

He stepped closer still, and his voice was low and rough as he spoke, stroking her as surely as any caress, horrifying her with its seductive appeal. She should not feel this way. "Please do heed my suggestion that you exhibit caution on the icehouse ladder, Miss Parrish. It would not please me should tragedy befall you."

"I cannot pretend that it would please me any better, my lord." He was so close, separated from her only by the width of the pot, which she yet held clutched against her chest. The luscious scent of him surrounded her, the heat of his body shimmering around her and through her as a delicious awareness flooded her, leaving her feeling light-headed.

Her gaze dropped to his mouth, the sensual fullness, the hard masculine line. And then one side curved in the hint of a smile, and a strange longing whispered insidiously through her every vein, strumming her senses to heightened alert, thrumming hot and strong in her blood.

And she had the terrible, enticing, wonderful thought that she would like to kiss him, to lean forward and press her mouth to his and taste his forbidden warmth.

Raising her eyes, she found him watching her. Heat. Intensity. Studied concentration. His hand strayed from her wayward curl to the column of her throat, and her breath froze at the sensation of his blunt fingers running lightly along her skin, hovering over her fluttering pulse and then gliding lower to the curve of her collarbone.

With a gasp, she stepped back, her movement breaking the extraordinary connection. Surely she was on a wild descent into madness, for what other explanation could there be for her uncharacteristic and dangerous longings?

Lord Craven studied her for an instant, his pupils dark and wide. Dear heaven, did he *know*—could he read her every wanton thought etched in her face? Mortified, she held her breath, lost in a tempest of confusion and chagrin.

"Have a care on the ladder, Miss Parrish," he said, by way of farewell, and then he turned away and strode along the path.

Her emotions in turmoil, she stood, frozen,

relieved to have a goodly amount of space between them, yet perversely disappointed as she watched him go. Then Lord Craven stopped and turned to face her once more.

"Griggs mentioned that you brought a portmanteau stuffed with books. Do you, by chance, enjoy the works of Mrs. Radcliffe, Miss Parrish?" he asked.

"Yes, I do, my lord."

"Ah, so you appreciate a Gothic novel. Pray tell me your favorite. *The Mysteries of Udolpho* perhaps? Or *The Romance of the Forest?* I cannot recall, but I am certain there was a corpse in one of them." He rubbed the sculpted line of his jaw. "And a haunted castle . . . and, yes, I recall a villainous lord."

"Ooooh!" The breath left her in a rush. He was implying that she was *imagining* the whole of Miss Rust's terrible fate, though he had affirmed the truth of her every suspicion. She could hear the light censure in his tone, see it in his eyes. "Miss Rust is dead. By your own admission she is dead. And Mrs. Winter, as well. Do you deny the veracity of those statements?" Her voice was sharp. She could not help it.

"I deny nothing."

"You speak in riddles. I do love a horrid novel, but I have no wish to *live* a horrid novel." She sank her teeth into her lower lip.

"Do you sense evil here, Miss Parrish?" Lord Craven regarded her calmly, posing the question with the casual interest of a man inquiring after the weather. He might have asked if she sensed rain. "Do you suspect a monster lurking within these stone walls?"

"I do not know," she said miserably, haunted by the untimely passing of those who had lived within these walls. Delia and her infant daughter. Mrs. Winter. Miss Rust. Far too many deaths to be mere chance.

"Then why do you not leave? Flee this place for the safety of another?"

Emma sighed, forcing her roiling thoughts under control. "I believe I am a person of intelligence and sense, my lord. I have no proof of any wrongdoing. It seems ridiculous to flee in a frenzy of supposition." Then she spoke aloud the most convincing reason of all, the one that was irrefutable in its simplicity. "Besides, I have come to care for Nicky. I cannot imagine leaving him, nor can I betray my word. I made a commitment to serve as his governess, and I do not take my commitments lightly."

Lord Craven stared at her, a piercing look that she thought must surely strip her bare, revealing her innermost thoughts and convictions. "So you value your word," he said softly.

"I value honor."

The silence lengthened like a winter shadow, dark and all consuming. Somehow, she thought her reply both pleased and disconcerted him.

When she could bear it no longer, she said, "Do you think I ought to leave, my lord? Flee because of an indistinct feeling of unease? Leave Nicky, whom I hold dear?" She shook her head and then continued in a fierce tone. "I am made of sterner stuff. I will *not* leave him."

He regarded her steadily. "And I am extremely glad to hear it."

Emma swallowed. Dear heaven, the way he looked at her, his eyes hot and hungry. He left her feeling dizzy. Flushed. Wishing for something that could never be. Something dangerous.

She raised her chin a notch and met his gaze with

what she prayed was calm equanimity. "I believe that your son awaits you at the stable, my lord."

His brows shot up in surprise. "Do you dismiss me, Miss Parrish?"

Awkwardly clutching the large pot against her, Emma met his astonished gaze. Such eyes. Green and gold and thickly lashed. Stunning.

"I believe that I do, my lord." The words came out in a breathless rush. She was acutely aware of her own audacity, but the insidious longing that thrummed through her body was too perilous to ignore. She wanted to be away from him before he surmised her wicked thoughts. Dangerous thoughts of touching him, feeling the play of sculpted muscle and solid bone beneath her hands. Her gaze flew to his, and in that moment she had little doubt that he knew exactly where her treacherous mind had wandered.

"As you wish," he replied, and she thought she heard laughter in his tone. With a brief tilt of his head, he turned and continued on the path until the trees veiled him from sight.

Moments later, breathless, more from her own dreadful, wonderful thoughts than from any exertion caused by her walk, Emma pushed open the outer door of the icehouse. The first door led to a small dirt-floored vestibule and then a second, inner door. The better to keep the cold air inside and the large chunks of ice frozen. Her hands filled by the empty pot, she took three steps forward before coaxing the inner door open with her shoulder. The interior of the icehouse was not overly large, the air dank and cold, and in the gloom she could just barely discern a thick snake of rope hanging above a dark, open pit.

The cold was welcome. Perhaps it would chill

her heated thoughts of Lord Craven, cool her fervent imaginings.

With a tilt of her head, Emma squinted into the dim chamber and examined the pulley system that was attached to an overhead beam. It resembled the simple mechanics of a bucket and rope used to dip water from a well. She set the pot on the ground and then contemplated the problem of her skirt, for it would hamper her descent into the abyss that loomed before her. Pulling the folds of material between her legs, she tucked the tail of her skirt into the waistband and began her climb down the long ladder that led to the ice stored at the bottom of the pit.

Retrieving the ice was a simple task, one she had performed as a child. The crater was quite dark, with only a paltry light filtering from above, and she was left with a nervous feeling that gnawed at her. She quickly filled the bucket with hunks she chiseled from one of the large blocks and used the pulley system to send the bucket upward. Hiking her skirt once more, she climbed the ladder and dumped the fruits of her labor into the pot, repeating the entire process twice more until ice chunks overflowed the rim and she was certain that she would stagger beneath the weight of her unwieldy burden.

She hefted the pot and made her way awkwardly toward the inner door. The chill of the icehouse had cooled her body considerably. In fact, gooseflesh was raised along her arms. She would welcome the heat of the afternoon sun.

As Emma neared the inner door, she heard an odd scraping sound that set her teeth on edge, as if she had bitten into the ice she carried in her pot. Squatting clumsily, she placed her load of ice on the ground, then rose and pulled on the door handle.

The heavy wooden door would not budge.

Heaving an exasperated sigh, Emma wrapped both hands around the handle and tugged with greater force. Nothing.

And then the laughter began.

Cold and harsh, it was an eerie sound that seemed to float from all around her, bouncing off the walls and into the deep, damp crater, the echo swirling about her like a dank mist. Emma pulled harder on the handle of the door. Then harder still.

The laughter ebbed and flowed, vibrating in the confines of the small building. The door held firm even as she pulled and shook it with increasing frustration and dismay.

"*Ehhhmmmaaaaa . . .*" A voice drifted over her, touching her with icy talons that held a tangible threat, wrapping frozen tendrils about her heart. "*Ehhhhmmmaaaaa . . .*"

She spun about, peering into the shadows, her blood racing through her veins and her breath coming in harsh gasps. A smell, vaguely familiar, swirled around her. Lemon, she thought. Only laced with something dark, something wretched. Peering into the gloom, Emma tried to see who shared the small space with her, for there was someone here, someone with foul intent. The laughter reached a horrible crescendo and then broke, leaving an abrupt silence that was perhaps even more terrifying in its absolute lack of sound.

"*Run, Ehhhmmmaaaaa . . . Let me see you run.*"

Run? Where? Straight into the pit? She thought of Miss Rust, dead, dead Miss Rust. With renewed vigor she tried the door, rattling it frantically on its hinges. The sound of a sharp crack rent the silence, and so suddenly did the portal open that Emma reeled back and stumbled to the ground, the great yawning crater opening like a dark maw at her back. Scrambling to her feet, heart pounding so wildly that she was left feeling faintly ill, she bent and curled her fingers round the rim of the pot, dragging it to the outer door. There, she leaned her back against the solid bulk, panting from exertion and distress, every sense attuned lest the laughter begin anew.

"Stuff and nonsense," she whispered, and then louder, "stuff and nonsense."

Someone had been here, someone who meant to frighten her. Or worse.

Well, she was not such easy prey.

"Show yourself!" she cried, squinting at shadows. "Who's there? Show yourself!"

The frantic thud of her own pulse was her only reply.

Fear merged with anger, a heady mix, but Emma tamped both down with rigid control. Knowledge was her most favored ally, and with that certainty in place she waited as her pulse slowed and her breathing became less labored, then she turned and carefully examined the door frame of the inner entry. There was no lock. No latch. What, then, had held the door shut firm against her? And why?

The latter question was beyond her ken, but perhaps she could answer the former.

Running her fingers around the edges, she gasped as a sharp splinter pierced her flesh. A large, red drop of blood welled from the wound as she managed to get hold of the shard of wood with the edge of her nail and pull it free. Undaunted by the injury, Emma continued her exploration. There was no hidden lock that she could find.

She crouched and searched the ground until finally her fingers closed around a thick length of wood. A long, slow breath escaped her. Yes, someone had been here, had fitted this stick in the handle to make her a prisoner. But who? And, for heaven's sake, why?

Shivering, as much from agitated emotion as from the damp chill, Emma rose, determined to unravel the mystery. She closed the inner portal slowly from the outside and fitted the rough staff through the handle. Pushing on the door with all her might, she found it held firm, just as it had when she had been trapped on the opposite side.

"To what purpose?" she mused aloud as she pulled the makeshift lock free.

The episode had unsettled her, but she felt certain that the perpetrator had intended it to do more. The realization was horrifying and brought to mind the fate of the previous governess. Had Miss Rust been subject to the same sinister sounds of mirth? Had fear precipitated her fall?

Emma pulled open the outer door and shoved the wooden stick into the ground at its base to hold it ajar. Her quaking limbs refused to lift the ice-filled pot, but she was determined not to leave it behind, so she bent and dragged it out, kicking the stick aside and allowing the door to swing shut behind her. Some prescience made her look to the hedgerow, or perhaps it was simply chance that her glance slid in that direction. Through the thick foliage she glimpsed a pair of buff breeches and polished boots. The copse was too dense to see more.

Blood rushing in her ears, Emma froze in an

agony of mixed anger and dread. Leaving go her hold on the pot, she straightened, took a step forward, and another, great gasps of air filling her chest, and a dark terror surging through her veins. Someone lurked in the shadows, watching.

The leaves rustled wildly and the sound of twigs snapping carried to her on the breeze. The breeches and boots disappeared just as Emma sprinted to the edge of the thicket. She pushed through, branches catching at her, scraping tender flesh, but there was no one there. Catching her lower lip between her teeth, Emma stared into the shrubbery, feeling numb and suddenly drained. Whoever had been here was gone now, her chance lost. But she had a terrible certainty that the perpetrator would return. For *her*. There was a thought that brought no comfort.

Shivering, she began the arduous trek toward the warmth of Manorbrier's kitchen, dragging behind her the cold pot that overflowed with chunks of ice, determined to finish the task she had set for herself.

She froze as a hazy memory sprang forth, shimmering until it coalesced and she saw it in her mind's eye with distinct clarity.

When she had encountered him earlier, Lord Craven had sported buff breeches and shiny Hessian boots.

CHAPTER FOUR

Cookie was not in the kitchen, or the garden, so Emma was alone without companion or confidante, a large porcelain bowl balanced against the front of her hip, her right hand moving in a rapid circular pattern, beating the whites of eight eggs. She had already boiled the milk and thickened it with arrowroot before setting the mixture on the table to cool. The sweet smell of warm milk scented the air.

Increasing the force she was using to beat the egg whites, Emma poured her passions into the action, releasing her anger, her fear, her confusion, all the tumultuous emotions that had been birthed by her terrifying experience in the icehouse.

Someone had purposely set out to frighten her, perhaps even to agitate her enough to cause her to fall. No, not perhaps. Of a certainty.

Her hand froze over the stiff whites that stood out in crisp peaks with slightly curled tops. *Someone at Manorbrier wished her harm.* Or perhaps he wished her to flee. Whatever the case, the person in question would quickly learn that she was made of sterner stuff. She had finally found a place where she was needed, wanted, and she would let no one frighten her away.

For too long she had let the vagaries of her life and the will of others buffet her to and fro. But no more. In making the decision to come to Manorbrier she had found her determination, and she had no intention of forfeiting it now.

Suddenly, the kitchen door was hurled back against the stone wall, the force sending a loud report through the kitchen. Emma's already strained sensibility was pushed to its limit, and with her heart slamming against her ribs, she whirled about with such haste that she nearly overturned the egg bowl.

Nicky tore across the room and sniffed the air beside the pot of warm milk and arrowroot. "Is it ready? May I taste it?"

Setting the bowl on the tabletop, Emma swallowed. From the corner of her eye, she caught a glimpse of Lord Craven, one arm resting negligently on the door frame, the breadth of him filling the open space. Heart still pounding, she turned toward Nicky, hoping that her expression betrayed none of her inner turmoil.

"Not quite ready, Nicky," she said. "We have a bit of work to do still."

Raising her gaze, she found Lord Craven regarding her speculatively. Black lashes. Green eyes beneath straight, dark brows. Those eyes, dear heaven, those amazing, disquieting eyes. And hard masculine lips formed in perfect sensuality. Carnal. Beckoning.

Emma felt hot color rise in her cheeks. She looked away, busying herself with measuring out a pound of powdered sugar and setting it on the table next to the cooling milk. She needed just one brief moment to calm her racing pulse, and she was honest enough to admit that her reaction was only partly caused by the fright of Nicky's precipitous entry, and mostly caused by Lord Craven's presence. The hard, steady cadence of her heart pounded her excitement, her pleasure at being in his company.

Despite his odd behavior. Despite what had just happened to her in the icehouse. Despite every fear and justified suspicion. Foolish girl that she was, his mere presence brought her joy, made her spirits soar with shameless delight.

"Pour the sugar in a little at a time, Nicky." She handed him a wooden spoon. "Stir it in, and then add a bit more."

"You sound funny," Nicky said, taking the spoon from her. Then he laughed. "Sort of stiff and full of air, like the egg whites."

Emma said nothing, merely passed him the sugar she had measured. She watched as Nicky followed her instructions until, satisfied that he could handle the task on his own, she stepped away.

"Miss Parrish, are you quite all right?" Lord Craven spoke softly from directly behind her.

She froze, tension seeping into her shoulders and neck. She could feel the brush of his arm, his side, as he moved to face her and laid the back of his hand across her brow, trailing it down the curve of her cheek. Touching her. He was *touching* her. Warm, strong hands against her skin, and his body so close she could feel the heat of him.

Drawing a ragged breath, she struggled against the urge to rub her cheek against his fingers.

"You are flushed," he observed.

"I am fine, my lord. Just warm from beating the

eggs." Ducking her head, Emma pulled away from his touch.

Mortified by the madness that ran molten through her veins, she could not look at him. He was too close, and her mood was too uncertain.

As she moved her head, her eyes were drawn to Lord Craven's breeches and boots. *Fawn-colored breeches. Mud-caked Hessians.* Like those she had glimpsed in the shrubbery outside the icehouse. At a frantic pace, her thoughts capered this way and that, sending a dark edginess through her, an ugly distress.

Had it been Lord Craven at the icehouse, his eerie laughter taunting her while the chill air pricked her skin and the black pit loomed before her?

Emma shook her head to clear it, forcing her thoughts back to the present, inviting her practical nature to ease her fears. The same mud was on the drive, or the field, or any garden to be found on the estate, not to mention the stables, where she knew with certainty Lord Craven had been. No sinister secret lay in that mantle of drying dirt. Someone else had skulked in the bushes. Someone evil.

"Miss Parrish, you are no longer flushed." There was a touch of irony in Lord Craven's tone. "You are now white as a shroud."

"I have something on my mind, my lord," she mumbled.

"Some*thing* or some*one*?"

Sucking in a quick breath, Emma met his sardonic gaze. Did he know, then, that he haunted her every thought, her every secret wish? The corners of his mouth curved slightly, deepening the dimple in his cheek. She wanted to touch that mouth, to run her fingers over the full lips, to test their softness. She felt her cheeks heat once more.

"Allow me to correct myself. You are, indeed, flushed." Again he laid the back of his hand on her skin, this time in a gentle caress along her cheek, her chin. Her skin tingled each place he touched, and she bit back a moan.

His smile broadened. She was stunned by the warm glow that cascaded through her. Perfection. Yes. She had wanted the beauty of his smile turned on her, and here he had done just that. A flash of white, straight teeth. Drat the man! Even his teeth were beautiful.

"Miss Emma!" Nicky's call broke the intoxicating spell. "I put in all the sugar! What shall I do next?"

"Oh! You must . . . that is . . ."

Lord Craven dropped his hand to his side, his gaze shuttered, his smile fading. "My son has impeccable timing, and I have pressing business." He inclined his head. "I bid you good afternoon."

Disappointment warred with relief. Emma dragged in a breath, turning her attention to Nicky, helping him add the egg whites to the mixture. But she could not resist a single sidelong glance at Lord Craven as he departed. Broad, square shoulders. Narrow hips. Tight buttocks that bunched with each step.

Dear heaven, she was chasing madness.

She let out a long, slow sigh, wondering what it was about this unfathomable, inscrutable man that drew her like a flower to the sun, and why, despite rumor, innuendo, and indeed her own firsthand knowledge of his oft intimidating nature, she could not find it in herself to believe anything but good about him.

Perhaps she was a woman of rare insight.

She shook her head. Perhaps she was a deluded, infatuated fool.

In the weeks that followed, though she wished it otherwise, Lord Craven haunted Emma's thoughts, invaded her dreams. Each time their eyes met across the drive or through a doorway, she was painfully aware of the thrill that spiraled through her at the mere sight of him. Her mind whispered of the danger, but she could not seem to stop this elemental reaction, this fascination with the man.

Yet, there was more to his appeal than mere physical beauty. He was unfailingly polite to her, nay, more than that, he was genuinely interested in her thoughts and opinions, listening with careful attention during their morning discussions over breakfast with Nicky.

There was the loving kindness he bestowed on his son. The way he swung the child up onto his shoulders and strode along the drive, or joined their lessons for a brief time, encouraging, supporting. Ever the fine parent.

Emma was so glad for Nicky that he had what she had never known. A father's pure and genuine love.

Still, there were times when she was left with a wrenching unease, times when Lord Craven disappeared into the Round Tower and a pall of anxiety and distress settled over the whole of Manorbrier. Those days were the hardest, for none would share the truth of what went on in that crumbling pile of stone and mortar, leaving Emma to imagine what she would, and to remember Nicky's childish assertion that Miss Rust yet remained in the tower, a dead, decomposing governess, or perhaps only a child's macabre fancy.

Yet even such chilling thoughts could not dampen her forbidden interest in her employer. Sitting in Lord Craven's study late on a Friday afternoon, Emma delivered her weekly update of Nicky's progress, her senses attuned to the man who stood across the room, legs braced shoulder's width apart, arms resting on the window sash.

"All in all, my lord, that sums it up. Your son is a lovely, bright child and I am thoroughly enjoying our time together—" She broke off, feeling slightly disconcerted that she had delivered the entirety of her lengthy report to Lord Craven's back.

An unwanted spark of attraction prickled through her as she studied his broad-shouldered form, his lean hips and muscled thighs, the length of his thick, dark hair where it kissed his collar. Hitching in a breath, she forced her attention away from the enticing image he presented and looked around the room. His Lordship's study. It was a man's room. Dark paneled walls were lined with shelves that boasted a wonderful selection of books in several languages. A large mahogany desk was positioned in front of a window draped in dark velvet. Emma sat rigidly on the edge of one of the two heavy brocade chairs that faced the desk.

She shifted uncomfortably in her seat as her employer continued to peruse the garden, seemingly content to let the silence lengthen and grow. But a tiny seed of suspicion whispered that he was no more oblivious to her presence than she was to his, and something in the set of his shoulders, the subtle tension lacing his frame, implied a weighty matter resting heavy on his thoughts.

"You will dine with me tomorrow evening, Miss Parrish?" Lord Craven turned to her as he spoke. The words were phrased as a question, though his tone held a steely note of command, and Emma knew that this, then, was the issue he pondered.

"I . . . I shall be delighted, my lord. And Nicky . . . ?"

"We shall dine after he is abed." Lord Craven lifted a sardonic brow, obviously reading her hesitation in her expression. "Come now, *Cousin Emma.* Surely it is not inappropriate for me to wish a charming companion to entertain me at table. You are family, are you not? Not merely a governess, but my own cousin."

Emma looked down at her hands, attempting to hide her confusion. Lord Craven was asking, nay, ordering, her to dine with him. She was disinclined to seek his company, disturbed by the maelstrom of unfamiliar emotions he roused in her, and for the past weeks it had appeared that he was of like mind. He had not been rude, merely distant. Other than their daily breakfast with Nicky and the few occasions he had stopped by to watch their lessons, he had made a point of spending time with his son in her absence, specifically suggesting that she might like a moment of freedom to take her tea with the staff. She had been glad of it in a way, for his proximity was both enticing and unsettling in the extreme.

Glancing at him through her lashes, she noticed the coiled tension in him, the power in the breadth of his shoulders and muscled thighs. He was like a beautiful wild beast meant to be admired from afar, but far too dangerous at close confines. She blew out a breath, thinking ruefully that these were things no proper governess would notice.

As to his reference to their familial bond, it

would likely be imprudent of her to tell him so, but Emma could not imagine regarding Lord Craven as her cousin.

She was the cousin of his dead wife. His *murdered* wife. Or was that his intent? To remind her of exactly that? Strange, contradictory man.

"I scarcely think of you as family, my lord. We are only recently acquainted." So much for prudence.

He gave a short bark of laughter. "You are outspoken, *Cousin Emma*. Ah, look at the mutinous expression that clouds your fair brow. Have I insulted your sensibilities by calling you outspoken? Or is my use of your given name the cause of that frown?"

"As a gentleman, my lord, you should not make free with my given name until such time as I give you leave." Emma swallowed hard, her heart thumping a harsh rhythm. She dared much to speak to him so. But she feared that if she set no limits for him, like a small child, he would set none for himself.

His voice was deceptively soft. "As a governess, Cousin Emma, it hardly behooves you to question my behavior."

He moved toward her, each step a study in masculine grace, his eyes—those beautiful, startling eyes—locked on hers as he rounded the desk to settle his lean hips against the gleaming wood. Her heart kicked up a notch. He was far too close, one booted foot resting against the right front leg of her chair, the other against the left, his long limbs stretched out, splayed to each side.

"And, pray, what made you think I am a gentleman?" His tone was rich and dark as warm chocolate.

Emma shivered as the sound caressed her skin.

No. He was no gentleman, and in his presence, she was painfully tempted to act less than a lady.

She could lift one hand, such an easy thing, and lay her palm on his muscled thigh, feel the solid flex of muscle and sinew. Her breath caught in her chest. She tipped her head back and found him regarding her with a quizzical expression, such powerful contemplation. Puzzled. But something else, as well. Something that tugged at the core of her and lit her insides with a slow, lazy burn.

"I . . . that is . . ." With a shiver she straightened her spine, pushing herself against the brocade back of the chair.

The room was too warm. She wondered that it suddenly seemed so. Again she opened her mouth. What to say? Nothing. There was nothing. She stroked her tongue against her too-dry lips, realizing at once that it was the wrong thing to do, for his interest sparked, flared. She read it in the subtle shift of his expression. His green-gold eyes settled on her and snared her, forcing her into immobility.

They stared at each other, she into the handsome face of a man who both frightened and beguiled, a man of mystery and shadow. She wanted to touch him, to explore the chiseled edge of his jaw, the lovely curve of his lip, the straight line of his nose. Her breath came in shallow gasps, and her body tingled in most unladylike places.

She had never felt anything quite like this. Attraction. The feeling was so complex, so simple.

He blew out a short huff of air. Rolled his shoulders. And even that stimulated her senses. Enticement, over nothing more than simple movement. He looked away, and she thought he wrestled with some secret demon, struggled with some inner tumult, and then, finally, mastered whatever private fiend gnawed at him.

"Thank you for your report. I am well pleased with Nicky's progress." He paused and then finished softly, "My son is everything to me."

At that stark admission, Emma's heart twisted within her breast, making her painfully aware that she *liked* this inscrutable man, and that liking was more dangerous than anything else, for it enhanced his seductive appeal. Attraction was one matter, something she could wrest into submission. But *liking* him was another beast entirely.

She wet her lips, looked up to find him watching her once more. So close. He was so close, perched there on the edge of his desk, she had only to rise and lean forward and brush her lips across his. Kiss him as she so longed to do.

A fantasy. Only a fantasy, for to do so in truth would be sheer folly.

With a small moan she bolted to her feet, intent on escape. Lord Craven rose in the same instant, and they stood chest to chest in the small space between the desk and Emma's newly abandoned brocade chair. The shallow pull of air, in, out, made the tips of her breasts nearly brush his shirtfront. He wore no coat, perverse man, and disdained to button his white lawn shirt. She could see the hollow of his throat, the hint of muscled chest and golden skin.

A day's growth of beard shadowed his jaw. He looked unkempt, tousled, untamed. Wickedly, darkly handsome.

She made a sound, half moan, half gasp, as she stood poised to flee, darkest desire pooling inside her like a living, writhing thing. And this from a mere look. Dear heaven, one touch and she would surely be lost.

Raising his left hand, he moved as if to stroke the

backs of his fingers along her cheek. Emma stared at his hand, and he froze midmovement, his gaze following hers.

The tip of his index finger was missing, cut off at the farthest joint.

She was drawn back to the stormy night of her arrival when she had first seen Griggs's scarred face, first discerned Mrs. Bolifer's empty sleeve, and she had wondered if all the inhabitants of Manorbrier were marked in some terrible way.

"Does it offend you?" He hesitated at the word "offend," and Emma suspected that he had intended to use some other, harsher word.

"I never noticed it before. Your hand, I mean, your finger." Frowning, she looked straight ahead, at the crisp white shirt that covered his chest, her heart fluttering wildly, confusion coursing through her. She wanted to tell him that her heart wept for his suffering, that she would heal him if she could, not only the scar she could see, but those hidden from view, deep inside, the ones she sensed marked his soul. Instead, she said, "I just never noticed it before."

"Delia hated it. She thought me mutilated. Repugnant." The words sounded curt, as though pulled from him against his will. Lord Craven lifted his maimed hand, turning it palm up, then palm down, before resting it again on the smooth surface of the desk. "She never wanted me to touch her with my left hand. As if the loss of a tiny bit of finger made me less than whole."

As he spoke, Emma heard something in his tone. Bitterness? Regret? Or something darker still, some live, twisting thing that ate away at his soul? Did he love her still, his Delia?

Or was it hatred that tinged his words? Hatred enough to lure him to do murder?

"Did you . . . suffer an accident after you met her?" she asked softly, thrusting her wild conjectures aside. He had given her no cause to spin such suppositions, only spoken a handful of words in a tone bleak and raw. It was her overly sensitized emotions that made her think such things.

Her confusion swelled and she wondered how her sparking attraction had descended to this suspicion. He had given her no cause, no grounds for such. Perhaps, then, it was her own defense against the sensual lure of him, the forbidden fascination.

If she feared him she would not want him. There was both safety and a touch of the absurd in that thought.

A moment of silence drew out long and taut. Emma finally lifted her gaze, searching his face. His expression was shuttered, his jaw tense.

"I suffered much after I met her." His voice was harsh. "And there was nothing accidental about it. Delia knew well what torture she was about."

The words seared her, for they painted a cheerless picture. She wanted to touch him, to calm the pain of his memories. If she dared to lean forward, just the barest inch, she would be pressed against the width of his chest, her mouth a breath from his. The thought was wildly appealing. And equally frightening.

There was her answer. It seemed she wanted him no matter what. Or perhaps it was that she could not find it in herself to truly fear him. Only herself, and her terrible wanton need.

Emma felt a stirring of panic. He could consume her, this intense and enigmatic man. There would be nothing left of her, of her principles, of her good and pure intentions. Her secret imaginings would come to fruition, her mouth pressed wetly to his, her body hard against him, and while she treasured the fantasy, she was horribly afraid of the reality and where it must lead. No good end could come of such folly. Only heartbreak and loss.

With a soft cry, she whirled and fled to the door. She thought only of escape. Not so much from Lord Craven, but from her own unspeakable, and quite irrational, longing for him.

"Miss Parrish," his tone was crisp, controlled, stopping her short. Her fingers clasped about the cold metal door handle. "I shall see you at supper tomorrow. Promptly at eight, if you please."

She knew well the danger he posed, and so she definitely did not please. But she hardly thought it mattered.

CHAPTER FIVE

". . . and King Arthur called that magical place Camelot," Emma whispered, smoothing Nicky's hair gently. The boy stirred but did not open his eyes. How sweet he looked, his dark hair rumpled, his cupid's-bow lips soft with sleep.

With a smile, she left the nursery and set off for her room on the third floor to prepare for her meal with Lord Craven. She would tidy herself and pin her mother's cameo brooch to her bodice. The brooch was the only piece of jewelry that her mother had owned, a treasure of little monetary value, but immeasurable sentimental worth to Emma. The simple decoration would have to suffice, for she had nothing finer than her ragged and faded day dress to wear to supper.

Unbidden, a childhood memory of sitting on the landing hidden from view watching the fine lords and ladies dance at a midnight ball sprang to mind. Her mother had come to find her, warned her not to set her sights for one of those well-dressed young men. Just look where such girlish dreams had led *her*. Then she had taken her daughter's hand and escorted her away, but Emma had been unable to resist the temptation to look over her shoulder one last time and watch as a gilded couple swirled about the floor. To her innocent eyes, they had seemed touched by the fairy magic she read about in her books.

The memory shifted and blurred, and suddenly it was Lord Craven—dressed in elegant evening attire—who spun the woman in a heady dance. And the beautifully gowned woman was . . . herself. She was held in Lord Craven's embrace, her lips a mere hair's breadth from his.

Clapping her palms against her flushed cheeks, Emma hurried down the corridor. Though she acknowledged her fantasy as stuff and nonsense, she could not push aside the wish that she had such a gown to wear this evening, some delightful confection to make her feel beautiful.

When had her feeling of resentment at Lord Craven's invitation turned to anticipation?

"Emma Parrish," she muttered. "You are a woman grown. Far too old for a silly schoolgirl fantasy." She didn't dare voice aloud the thought that Lord Anthony Craven was less the stuff of schoolgirl dreams, and more the sort of man who made chaperones a necessity. Too masculine, too bold. Too hauntingly appealing.

Anthony Craven was no sweet prince.

She pushed open the door to her chamber and nearly stumbled at the sight that greeted her. For a moment, Emma thought that the gown she had woven in her fantasy had taken flight and landed with stunning accuracy right in the center of her bed. There, laid carefully across the coverlet, was a magnificent dinner dress of shimmering blue silk.

Perfect for her meal with Lord Craven. Had he brought the dress and laid it here for her to find? How strange.

Taking a step forward, Emma hesitantly reached out and stroked the rich silk. The fabric was smooth to her touch. She thought the gown lovely, though the idea that Lord Craven had secretly entered her chamber and laid the dress across her bed was somewhat unsettling. It did not behoove a gentleman to enter a lady's chamber, especially when that lady was in his employ.

And, pray, what made you think I am a gentleman? He had been quite clear on that point.

Emma frowned as she considered her options. She could simply tidy her hair and attend dinner as she was, garbed in her well-worn day dress. Pin on her cameo brooch as she had planned. But Lord Craven had troubled himself to provide her attire. Surely it would be churlish to refuse the dress.

Conversely, she could argue that it would be inappropriate to accept such an obviously costly gift from her employer. Pressing the backs of her fingers to her lips, she narrowed her eyes, contemplating her decision.

"The aunts would have apoplexy!" The words popped out, and Emma smiled. The idea of her aunts falling to the ground, insensate, simply because she donned a blue silk dress gifted to her by the man they named monster was enough to make her decide in favor of the gown. Though they would never see it, she would know, and that would have to be enough. Not terribly grown-up of her, but reasonably satisfying nonetheless.

She quickly divested herself of her much-mended day dress. Lifting the shimmering gown from the bed, she slipped it on. The skirt billowed around her ankles, the yards of material draping as only truly expensive cloth could. With gentle hands, Emma pressed at the creases that marred the bodice and one side of the skirt. She wondered if the gown had been folded away somewhere. The wrinkles suggested it might be so.

Twisting, Emma tried to see herself in the tiny looking glass above the washstand but could catch only fractured glimpses of her appearance. The sleeves came off her shoulders, bowing gently about her upper arms before ending in a gentle pouf just above her elbow. Brussels lace trimmed the neckline then looped cleverly about itself in a pretty rosette before falling in a rich cascade down the front.

The gown could have been measured for her frame, save that the hem was a trifle long. But Emma was glad for the length, which hid her plain serviceable shoes from view.

Frowning at her naked hands, Emma wished that she could solve the problem of her lack of evening gloves as easily as the hem had solved the problem of her footwear. Suddenly, she recalled her mother's gloves, a remnant of her genteel youth, a memento she had kept until her death, and Emma had kept since. She leaned over, pulled her portmanteau out from under the bed and withdrew the gloves from the side pocket. The soft kid leather was only slightly yellowed with age, the seams a little frayed, and there was a smudge of black on the tip of the right index finger.

She thought that even their faded glory would be better than no gloves at all, and so she slipped them on. The fingers were a trifle overlong, but the gloves reached to her elbow. Emma felt they completed her ensemble quite nicely. At least, she hoped they did. Just as she hoped the gown looked as fine as it felt.

Freeing her long hair from the pins that confined it, Emma picked up her mother's ivory inlaid brush and ran the bristles slowly through her unbound tresses. Then she twisted the whole into a simple knot at the base of her neck in a looser, softer style than the one she customarily wore.

She had no diamond pins to sparkle in her hair, no necklace to grace her throat. Nonetheless, she felt the fairy princess of her fantasy, for this was the finest gown she had ever worn. Taking a deep breath to steady her nerves she stepped from the room, raised her hands, and pinched her cheeks for color. She had seen the eldest daughter of her mother's employer do that once. It had made the girl look vibrant, fresh. Emma hoped it would do the same for her.

Although, she supposed it might simply make her look like she had eaten something that gave her a rash.

The servant's staircase brought her close to the kitchen. Emma paused, considering a quick visit to show Cookie her finery, but she could well imagine Mrs. Bolifer's face screwing up in that pinched frown, the one that screamed of disapproval. No, she would not let the housekeeper ruin one moment of her evening. Even sensible girls had a right to their dreams, no matter how frivolous or unlikely they might be.

Hurrying along the hallway, Emma paused outside the doorway of the dining room. She smoothed her gloved hands over her skirt as her stomach somersaulted with nerves. Never in her life had she attended a dinner party. Or walked through the park with a handsome man. But tonight, she had been given the opportunity to pretend, and she intended to enjoy it to the fullest.

Tomorrow, she could go back to being Miss Emma Parrish, poor relation, spinster, governess, daughter of pitiable Elizabeth Parrish, who had made a terrible, unforgivable blunder and paid for it the rest of her life. Tonight, she was Miss Emma Parrish, the loveliest lady in the room. She bit her lip to keep from laughing out loud. She would be the only lady in the room, but that did not signify.

Emma stepped into the dining room. The wainscoting and dark color of the walls seemed to pull the room inward, making its large proportions seem less than they truly were. The rich mahogany dining table was laid for two, one setting at the head, and the second to the immediate right, rather than at the foot. Dinner and side plates, gleaming silverware, and three crystal glasses for each diner. How very formal they looked. And ever so intimate, pushed to one end of the large expanse of tabletop.

A candelabra glittered with the flames of several candles. Sniffing delicately, Emma could ascertain none of the foul odor that normally accompanied a tallow candle. Wax candles were frightfully costly, yet it seemed that this dinner warranted them. And then she recalled Mrs. Bolifer's blunt observation that Lord Craven hated the smell of tallow.

"Miss Parrish, your punctuality is commendable."

Drat the man. He had done it again. Come upon her and caught her unawares.

Emma turned, her breath catching in her throat as she saw Lord Craven, his broad shoulders delineated by the dark cloth of his evening coat. A white neck cloth graced his throat. Oh, handsome, handsome man. The corner of his mouth was curved slightly, hinting at a smile. She ventured a smile in return. "Good evening, my lord."

He stepped closer. She tilted her head back, holding his stare. Parting her lips, she tried to draw enough air to fill her suddenly starved lungs. Her lips felt swollen, hot. How odd; they had felt just fine only a moment ago. Lord Craven's nostrils flared as he stared down at her, and the dark centers of his eyes dilated until Emma thought she would be pulled inside of him to drown in the infinity of his soul.

Whirling away from him, she struggled to get her unruly emotions under control. Was she to be condemned to the onslaught of insanity each time Lord Craven entered a room?

"How lovely the table looks," she mumbled inanely, resting one hand on the ornately carved back of a mahogany chair as she looked at him over her shoulder.

His gaze flicked briefly to the table before settling back on her. He scanned her, his eyes resting for a heated second on the bared skin just above her décolletage, before moving on to take in the remainder of her person. Emma's heart lurched as his eyes narrowed and his mouth tightened in disapproval.

"Where did you get that dress?" The tone was not rude. He spoke softly, deliberately enunciating each word. "Where did you find it? Some dusty old trunk?"

Perhaps it was the lack of inflection that frightened her.

Emma swallowed, confusion and unease squelching the sizzling attraction she had been subject to only a moment past. Her bewilderment robbed her of eloquent speech.

"You gave it to me. At least, I thought . . . what I mean to say is that when I found it, I thought you had—"

A rapid slash of Lord Craven's hand through the air was enough to still Emma's attempted explanation, freezing the words on her tongue.

"Come with me." Again that toneless voice. The overly controlled cadence of his elocution implied a fury so great as to be barely contained.

Emma stepped away, her head moving slowly back and forth. "Perhaps I should return to my chamber."

"Perhaps you should. But not just yet."

This, then, was Lord Craven's temper. This frozen fury that permeated the air like a bitter winter wind. And the cause of it . . . she had no idea.

She sidled around the chair, deliberately placing its bulk between them, as if that paltry barrier could offer protection.

"Come with me," he said again, reaching across the chair and closing his fingers around her wrist. "I do not know your intent in donning that gown, Miss Parrish, but you were misguided." The anger was there, leashed like a wild beast, writhing and undulating, desperate to burst free.

Emma tugged tentatively on her trapped limb. Though he did not apply enough pressure to hurt her in any way, Lord Craven's firm grasp ensured that she could not escape.

"My lord, my sole intent in donning this gown was to dress for the evening meal. Obviously, you do not approve. Now, if you will unhand me, I think it best for me to return to my chamber." Again she pulled on her wrist, adding a little twist as she attempted to free herself.

"Unhand you?" His brows rose in surprise and he glanced at his fingers where they curled about her wrist, as though they belonged to someone other than himself. "Forgive me."

Without further preamble, he dropped her hand. The suddenness of the release caused Emma to stumble back a pace.

"You may return to your chamber if you wish. But first, there is something I will show you." He gestured gallantly, indicating that she should precede him from the dining room, and when he spoke, his voice was low and rough. "After you, Cousin Emma."

Pressing her lips together, Emma stepped around his formidable frame. Despite his apparent return to congenial behavior, she knew he made no request but, rather, demanded her compliance.

"I really—" she began, only to stop midthought as Lord Craven stepped to her side and placed her hand on his arm. The muscles beneath the smooth black cloth of his evening coat were firm and taut. Emma glanced at him from the corner of her eye. He was a large man. A strong man. A frightening man.

A man who bound his emotions with a fence forged of strongest steel.

He will not hurt me. The words represented a certainty, not a spurious hope. She could not say from whence the thought came, but she was comforted by its presence, confident of its veracity. She thought of his expression when he realized he held her wrist, his grasp in no way painful. Still, he had looked surprised. A little appalled. *Forgive me.* She cast him a sidelong glance. No, he would not hurt her.

He made no further effort to restrain her. Emma accompanied him, spurred now by her own curiosity and free will, and they walked in silence, their way lighted by a candelabra that Lord Craven took up in his free hand.

Stopping before an ornate gilt frame, his expression cold and forbidding, he set the candelabra on a small table that stood to one side. "Delia," he said softly, his fingers resting briefly on the edge of the painting.

Emma looked at the picture of her dead cousin. A chill stole over her, and the gown she had worn as her fairy-tale dream suddenly felt like a shroud. Her skin shrank from the cool silk, and a faint nausea turned in her stomach.

"She is wearing *this* gown," Emma whispered as she stared at her cousin's perfect porcelain beauty. "Why would you give me Delia's dress?"

"Indeed, why would I? That dress is particularly repugnant to me. She was wearing it the night—" He shot her a sidelong look and then continued, "I thought it was burned years ago."

She glanced at the portrait, at Delia arrayed in this very gown, looking confident and lovely, just as Emma remembered her. "If you did not give it to me, then how did it come to be lying across my counterpane?"

Lord Craven scowled but made no reply. She met his gaze unflinchingly. There was no warmth in him now. He stared down at her with a remoteness that acted as a solid barrier between them.

"I had no idea. About the gown, I mean." Emma looked away from his grim expression, back toward

Delia's portrait. His reaction clearly indicated that he could not bear to see another attired in the belongings of his beloved.

Such a bitter tonic, that realization. She had wondered if he loved her still, his Delia, and now she had her most unwelcome answer.

"You must have loved her very much," she whispered. Impulsively, she reached forward, twining her fingers through his and squeezing gently. Offering small comfort in the face of his loss.

Silence was the only reply, but she could feel restless emotion shifting the currents of the air, cold eddies that licked the edge of her skirt, up and under, raising gooseflesh.

"No wonder you were so angry when you saw me garbed in this dress." She cleared her throat nervously when he yet held his silence. "Are you angry still?"

He turned to her then, and Emma realized her mistake. His predator eyes glittering with all the dark fury he had earlier held in check. "I am *angry*, though that single word can hardly aspire to describe adequately the black pit of utter rage that burns my entrails like an evil humor."

His fingers closed firmly around hers where she had so foolishly linked their hands, and she felt the surge of his temper hovering just under the surface, a writhing thing that once unleashed might be impossible to control.

Leaning close, he held her gaze, mesmerizing her. "So you see, Miss Parrish, you are wrong on two counts, and right on only one. I did love Delia, once, if love can be named as the obsession of youth. And then I hated her, with the powerful hatred of a man. Hatred strong enough to wish her gone from my life.

Gone from this earth. Gone to Hades, where she could meet her just match."

"No," Emma whispered, pulling her hand from his with a desperate twist, backing away from him in disbelief, stunned by the intensity of his emotion.

"I wished Delia dead," he said flatly. "I hated her with enough passion that I dreamed of wrapping my hands around the delicate white column of her throat, snapping her neck like a dried twig. And for that I cannot grant forgiveness to myself. What think you now, Miss Parrish? Do you still cast your maiden's glance at me? At my lips? My chest? My thighs?"

Dear heaven, he knew her every thought, had seen each languid, longing glance. . . .

He stalked her, both with his words and with his body. For each step Emma retreated, he pressed forward, until the wall pushed against her back and she could retreat no more.

"No," Emma whispered again, leaning against the cold, unyielding wall as if she could seek protection there. What he was saying was too terrible to consider. And she had thought him lost in his lamentation at the early death of his beloved. Foolish girl. He spoke of darkest thoughts and deeds. Tears welled in her eyes, and a single drop escaped, to roll down her cheek. She could not believe it of him. Did not want to believe it of him.

"There are demons in my soul that you can have no wish to see." Words wrenched from him, rough as gravel.

"Do you name yourself murderer? Do you?" She choked on a sob, every rumor, every ugly insinuation she had ever heard churning together with this horrific confession into a repulsive and frightening brew.

One last step and he was before her. Slowly, deliberately, he raised his maimed hand and wrapped a dark tendril of Emma's hair around the scarred remnant of his finger, then rested his open palm on the column of her throat where her pulse beat a frantic rhythm. And she could not will herself to pull away.

"Tears, Emma? For Delia?" His voice rolled over her, rich and deep and tantalizing. She could smell the faint intermingled scents of sandalwood soap, and brandy, and man, so tempting and lush, even now in the moment of her utter distress.

Emma shook her head, dashing at her tears.

"For me, then, Emma. Do you cry for me?" Now his tone was faintly mocking.

"For myself," she answered with pained honesty, the words insufficient to express the cause of her sorrow. Yes, she cried for Delia, dead these many years. And for Lord Craven, this beautiful man with his tormented soul. But, most of all she cried for herself. For as she listened to the words he spoke, the stark utterance that painted him a monster, she still could not chase away the near overwhelming urge to press her lips to his, to breathe hope and succor into his bleak world. To ease his pain.

To be the one who could save him.

Emma cried because she was well and truly lost. She might sooner try to save Lucifer himself.

As if he read her deepest thoughts, he angled his head, moving closer until their breath mingled and Emma could feel the beat of his heart against her own. She stood, frozen, a bewildered yearning spilling through her, drawn to him despite the tortured confessions of his soul. Drawn to him because of them. And certain that he knew of her longing, of the hot need that poured through her veins, the ache that cried out for his touch.

Perhaps her yearning had been there from the first moment when he had touched her in the coach. Or the moment when she had watched him hold Nicky in his arms, smiling down at his son. Mayhap it had grown from each look they had exchanged, or each time she had watched from a distance as he bestowed a kindness upon a servant. She did not know. But the craving for him had grown until it writhed to unholy life within her, until she trembled with the force of it.

She had been warned about this from the time she was a small child, told time and again that she must not fall prey to the same mistake as her mother. Dragging in a shuddering breath, she tried to fight the demon of her desire, tried to recall all the reasons that she must beware of Anthony Craven, beware of the terrifying, captivating lure of him.

The full length of his hard body pressed against hers, trapping her between hot man and the cold wall at her back. The smell of his skin undid her, and she moaned softly as she brushed her face against his neck, his jaw. Wrong, so wrong, but the temptation of him made her blood sing. She wriggled against him, aware of the press of his pelvis to hers.

He laughed, low and dark, the sound fully lacking in humor. And she thought he would kiss her now. Oh, please let him press his lips to hers, those lush, sensual lips. She moved her thighs together beneath her skirt, longing to push against his disturbing weight, while also longing to fist her hands in the fine cloth of his coat and drag him nearer still, to breathe the scent of him until he filled her lungs, her heart, her every sense.

Breath hissed from between his teeth. She wondered if he was as overcome as she. And then, shifting slightly, he brought his mouth against her ear, and she was stunned at the hard twist of disappointment that clutched at her.

"Run away, Emma," he whispered, even as his hand wrapped around the nape of her neck, his thumb caressing her collarbone. His breath caressed her as surely as if he had touched her, skin to skin. "Does my admission, nay, my confession, not strike the fear of God in you? Fly away from me."

He made a harsh sound in his throat, and Emma felt the cold rush of air that replaced the warmth of his body as he slapped his open palms against the wall and pushed himself away from her. The chill brought the return of sanity. And the rush of mortification. Something about this man caused her to reject all that she knew, to forget her mother's life-long admonitions, to yearn for him in a way that consumed her.

With a small cry, she sagged against the wall, her emotions churning like the darkest clouds of a winter storm.

"I do not fear you." She was horrified to realize that she spoke the truth. Fear him? No. Instead, she wanted him with an intensity that burned like a hot coal in the pit of her belly. This was madness. Fear was the wiser course.

Lord Craven chuckled, a hard sound that might have been aimed at her, or himself.

"Fear what I may do to you, Emma. For if given the chance, do it I shall." He turned from her, walking slowly away, his withdrawal marking his words for the lie they were, for he had done nothing to her. Nothing at all.

And to her true and utter horror, she wished that he *had*. She melted to the floor in a heap of rumpled silk and damaged dreams.

His self-accusatory words rippled through her thoughts, and she realized that despite all he had said, there were truths yet unspoken. Perhaps those truths lay in what he had *not* said.

"You said you dreamed of killing her," she called out.

The dwindling sound of his footsteps stopped abruptly, and the silence was heavy with secrets and implications.

"You said you *dreamed* of killing her," Emma whispered, her voice choked with her tears. "You never said you killed her."

He did not answer, and for a long while Emma huddled on the floor, the harsh rasp of her breathing gradually calming as she gathered her shattered nerves into some semblance of order. The steady sound of his footsteps resumed, ricocheting hollowly in the cold, empty gallery, imitating the echo of his silence in Emma's heart.

CHAPTER SIX

"It would seem we are of like mind, Miss Parrish. Bothered by unpleasant dreams?"

With a wary sense of resignation, Emma looked up from her plate of cold beef, cheese, and bread, her heart pounding at the sound of Lord Craven's mellow voice. He had haunted her thoughts these many hours, chasing the possibility of sleep from her mind. And now he was here in the kitchen, standing before her in glorious disarray, breeches slung low on his hips, white shirt tossed casually across his shoulders, apparently driven by the same wakefulness and hunger that had brought her to the kitchen in the wee hours of the night. Strange, strange man that he did not simply ring for a servant to bring him food.

"Bothered by the practical need of an empty belly, my lord," she replied. "And you? Haunted by nightmares?"

"By the past," he said and then looked as though he wished he had not.

He studied her for a moment before striding forward, heedless of his half-naked state. Emma stared in fascination at the hard planes of his chest, the supple ridges of his abdomen. Her mouth felt dry. She had the appalling, alluring thought that she'd like to touch him, to run her hands over his smooth skin, to press her palm to his chest and feel the steady thud of his heart, the rhythm of his blood pounding in his veins.

A fine dusting of dark hair shadowed his chest, narrowing to a thin line that ran down his belly to his breeches. If she reached out, laid her finger on that line of hair, traced it, a mysterious path, to the final outcome . . .

With a sharp intake of breath, she lowered her eyes, but the image of his linen shirt hanging open, revealing the ridges of his belly and the hard planes of his chest, was branded in her mind. Had the man no modesty, no decency?

"What—" she exclaimed, startled, as he pinched his thumb and forefinger on the flame of her candle, then set his own in the center of the table.

"I detest the stench of tallow," he said.

"Tallow is frugal," she pointed out.

He stared at her for a moment, his eyes, the endless verdant green of them, dark and glittering, hard and bright. She thought he must surely discern her thoughts, her wanton, wicked thoughts.

"I have no need for frugality, only a desire to breathe untainted air."

"Why do you dislike the smell of tallow?" she ventured boldly.

"It smells like death."

She swallowed, having no response to that statement, completely unnerved at having to face Lord Craven again so soon after the debacle in the portrait gallery.

"I see you had thoughts similar to my own." He gestured at the half-full plate before her, smiling ruefully as his stomach growled, the sound loud in the silence of the darkened kitchen. "I shall join you."

Emma opened her mouth to suggest that he join the devil but thought better of her reply. Her years of guarding her tongue—and her thoughts—against her intrusive aunts had taught her to measure words with great care. She was angry at his earlier treatment of her, dismayed that despite his horrid behavior she could not help but feel a sizzle of awareness whenever he was about.

And despite his attempts to brand himself the villain in her eyes, she had her doubts. The question was, why did he wish her to view him through a haze of suspicion and fear, and if such was his intent, why was he behaving now as though naught had occurred? Perhaps he was unsettled. Addled. Completely mad.

With silent grace he strode past her, moving out of her line of sight.

Emma sat rigidly on her wooden seat, determined to resist the urge to turn her head and follow his progress. She heard the clatter of a plate being set on the high wooden table behind her, the sound of liquid pouring, then nothing. The inclination to check on Lord Craven's exact location within the kitchen was tempting in the extreme.

Concentrating on her meal, she broke off a chunk of bread and laid a slice of cheese across it. She could only wish that if she ignored him, he would go away, for she was as yet unprepared to cross rapier-sharp words with him once more.

"Here," he said, leaning close beside her, the open edge of his linen shirt brushing her shoulder.

The contact was negligible, but Emma's senses hummed to life. She could feel the slightest graze of cloth against cloth, and it strummed her nerves like the touch of a musician to a harpsichord. Closing her eyes, she inhaled the scent of his nearness.

With a thud Lord Craven placed a full mug of ale in front of her. Her eyes snapped open.

"Thank you," she murmured, a little flustered to realize that the master of the house was serving her. From the corner of her eye she watched the play of muscle across his taut belly as he straightened. Drat the man! His very presence rankled. Why could he not simply leave her alone?

Summoning her courage, Emma met his gaze as he sat down opposite her, his plate filled with the same makeshift meal she had foraged for herself. Perhaps she should unnerve him as he did her.

"What shall I do with the gown?" she questioned bluntly.

Lord Craven paused, his mug poised halfway between his lips and the table. Regarding her through narrowed eyes he took a slow pull on the ale, then set the drink down and casually drew the back of his hand across his mouth. Emma found the coarse action entrancing, and her eyes followed the movement of his knuckle across his full lower lip.

"Burn it."

His answer was not at all reassuring.

They ate in silence, though Emma wondered that she could stomach a single morsel. Only hours ago she had huddled on the floor, convinced that she was in the realm of a madman. Now she sat with that same man, sharing a companionable meal.

As if reading her thoughts, Lord Craven waved

his hand negligently and asked, "Do you think me mad, Miss Parrish? A snarling beast fit for Bedlam?"

"Does it matter what I think?"

He blinked, clearly surprised, and then he smiled, a slow curving of his lips. She loved that smile, the open warmth of it, a rare gift. "Yes, for some unfathomable reason, what you think *does* matter."

"I think you are . . ." she paused, searching for the right word. He watched her intently, waiting for her answer. "Unusual," she finished at length.

His brows rose.

"Yes, unusual," Emma temporized. She could hardly tell him that despite his unpredictable behavior, she found him intriguing. Enticing. Compelling. But there was one truth she could share. "You frightened me, you know. Was that your intent?"

His smile faded. "The shock of seeing you gowned in that—" He shook his head. "Originally, I had no intent, Miss Parrish. My actions were governed by a sad lack of control over my temper. And then I thought that perhaps a little fear might not be a terrible thing."

Emma chewed thoughtfully, digesting his words, thinking it strange that he claimed a lack of control when she had borne witness to his icy restraint, and wondering why he wanted her to be afraid of him. She met his gaze, read the sensual knowledge there, and found her answer. He had surmised her infatuation and had set about removing it, her inappropriate and obviously unwelcome fascination.

He was far wiser than she. Mortification sloshed over her in a hot wave.

"Will you flee with the morning light, Miss Parrish? Run from this place?" He paused. "From me?"

Her breath caught. Something in his tone made

her think that it mattered greatly to him what her answer might be, that he had no wish for her to leave, despite his earlier instruction when they had stood in the gallery and he had urged her to flee. Strange, contradictory man.

"I do not wish to be frightened again." Her heart pounded as she said the words. Forcing herself to meet his gaze, she regarded him frankly.

"Then you must make every endeavor to ensure that you are not," he observed dryly.

"As must you," she replied briskly.

"Yes. As must I."

"Was that an apology, my lord?"

His eyes were the color of burnished brass, reflecting the flickering light as he stared at her. One moment green, the next gold. Changeable. Unpredictable. Beautiful. As was the man himself.

He gave a short bark of laughter. "An apology, Miss Parrish? No, I think not. Merely a statement."

Again silence reigned. They ate the remainder of their meal with studied concentration, the only sound the hiss and sputter of the candle as the melted wax puddled around the wick. At length, Emma rose.

"Good night, my lord. And, no, I will not flee with the coming of the light. As I have already told you, I would not leave Nicky. I have come to care for him." *I have come to care for you.*

Something flickered in his gaze, and for one terrible moment she wondered if she had somehow blurted that last thought aloud. Then he inclined his head and said, "Constancy is an amazing gift. I thank you for offering yours to my son."

Emma could think of no reply to the warm admiration that shimmered in his words, and the pain that hovered just beneath it. Who had betrayed him

in the past that he valued fidelity and constancy so?
'Twas not the first mention of such he had made.

"Good night, Miss Parrish," he said.

She picked up her tallow candle, the one he had
snuffed with his fingers. Carefully, she relit it from
the wax candle on the table as he watched her from
beneath hooded lids, his expression unreadable.
Crossing the kitchen, she paused, her back to him,
her hand resting against the door jamb.

"I accept."

"Accept?" he echoed, his tone hinting at curiosity.

"I accept your thanks. And your apology," she
said softly. And then she fled the kitchen as if followed closely by a horde of demons, when in truth
she was followed only by the rich sound of Lord
Craven's laughter.

Several days later, Emma took advantage of the
free hour when Nicky was at the paddock to stroll
outside in the sunshine, novel in hand. She carried
one of her favorites, *The Romance of the Forest*, intent
on enjoying a few stolen moments of quiet freedom. The sound of a horse and cart coming up the
cobbled drive caught her attention. She paused
and watched as Griggs stopped the wagon near the
Round Tower, set the brake with meticulous care,
and nodded to her as he climbed down from the
seat and made his way around to the back.

Griggs hefted what appeared to be a large sack
out of the bed of the cart. The load was nearly as
long as the coachman, and he clearly strained
under the weight as he adjusted his burden over his
burly shoulder. He made a sight, his scarred face

twisted with the effort of carrying the heavy thing, his back hunched. He staggered toward the tower.

Wrapping her arms around herself, Emma shivered, a strange sense of foreboding crawling slowly up her spine. Unbidden, the memory of his warning the night of her arrival at Manorbrier sprang to mind. *There's death in that tower, miss. Death in the very air.* There had been no mistaking his fear that night. It had oozed from his pores and hovered about him like a swarm of flies. Yet, here he was, moving toward the tower, carrying a burlap-wrapped object that made Emma inexplicably uneasy.

She strode forward casually, studying the odd bundle.

Griggs paused, squinting at her as she approached. "Stay where y'are, miss. Don't want you coming near."

"And good afternoon to you, Griggs."

"I means what I says, miss. No place for you near here. You go on back to the kitchen, or the garden, or wherever you was before." He shifted the sack as it slid down his shoulder.

"What do you have there, Griggs?" Emma pressed her lips together as she wondered at her own perverse curiosity, but there was something so odd about the shape of the thing, rounded at one end, tapered at the other.

"Naught that concerns you, missy," he said with a scowl.

She was tempted to agree and move on, but something held her in place.

"Do you need my help?" she asked, eyeing his load apprehensively. Were those *toes?* There at the end, poking through a loose fold of sheeting? She shivered.

Griggs turned the full force of his disapproving glare on her. She stopped cold. The intensity of his gaze warned her that he was not simply talking to hear himself speak. There was an unspoken horror that lurked in his eyes. Whatever he carried, he wanted her as far away from it as possible.

His expression accomplished what his words had not. It sent a harsh tremor of fear slithering down Emma's spine, and a wild swirl of worry tripping through her belly. Suddenly wary, she took a stumbling step back.

They *were* toes. And *legs*, and *arms*, barely concealed by swaths of cloth. Dear heaven, it was a body, a dead body he carried.

True fear roiled in her belly. Griggs's eyes widened, and Emma realized that he knew she had recognized exactly what it was he transported.

"You be wise, missy."

He bid *her* be wise? Where was the wisdom in carrying a corpse up a tower?

Emma watched in frozen dismay as Griggs made his way laboriously toward the Round Tower. Pausing at the doorway and shifting the bundle across his shoulder, he reached for a leather thong that hung about his neck. With an impatient tug, he pulled the thong from inside his shirtfront and bent forward to push the key into the lock.

The weight of the load combined with his bent posture sent Griggs's long bundle sliding down his shoulder, and as he stumbled in an attempt to regain his equilibrium, the stained gray sheeting that wrapped the thing became disarrayed.

From the bottom of the bundle dangled a human hand, the fingers curled like talons, the skin wrinkled and pale save for a terrible blackened lesion that marred the flesh, the center glistening wetly in the sun. Emma gasped and lurched away. 'Twas not just any body, but a terrible, frightening thing riddled with disease.

Taking another involuntary step backward, she held up one hand palm forward. Such a futile gesture aimed at warding off the horror that confronted her. She swallowed against the bile that crawled from her stomach up toward her throat, as frozen talons of true horror gouged her heart.

Griggs looked down, taking in the horrible tableau reflected in Emma's eyes.

"His Lordship likes 'em fresh," he said. "Says it's best for the harvest." With a grunt, he hefted his morbid parcel, turned his back on her, and disappeared into the tower.

Swallowing convulsively, Emma closed her eyes, but her imagination conjured the exact vision she tried so desperately to block. A long-forgotten whisper popped into her head, one she was familiar with from a local outbreak when she was a child. *Malignant pustule.* She knew what that lesion was, knew the name they called the terrible disease that brewed wounds dark and shining like lumps of coal.

Anthrax.

A shudder shook her frame. In her mind she saw the oozing blackened pustule that marred the corpse's arm, the curled fingers, the shriveled skin.

Dear heaven. What manner of place had she come to? A flood of horrified thoughts cascaded through her brain, and none of them made a stitch of sense. Anthrax *killed*, turning the blood black as coal, congealing it like mutton drippings gone cold. And here Griggs claimed that Lord Craven wanted the body *fresh*, wanted to carry out some macabre *harvest*.

Heart pounding so hard she felt ill from the force of it, Emma began to back away, one step and the next, until her back bumped against the wooden slats of Griggs's wagon. With a cry, she whirled and fisting her hands in her skirt, she ran full tilt down the cobbled drive, her chest tight and desperate for air, her blood thick and sluggish. Away. She needed to be away from Manorbrier and that horrible tower, and the image that was branded in her mind's eye.

The image of death.

She ran until her lungs protested and each breath was forced past her lips with a painful gasp. Her feet ached and her thighs burned, and still she pressed on, unseeing, reckless in her flight. Manorbrier lay behind her. But she could not say what lay ahead.

The sound of a horse at full gallop chased after her, and her name, a cry on the wind. Emma spun about to find Lord Craven mounted upon a great sleek beast bearing down on her. His unbound hair was caught and cast about by the wind, and his countenance was dark and forbidding. The pounding in her breast mingled with the drumming of the animal's hooves.

She could not hope to outrun him, but she could not seem to slow the rhythm of her flight. Her feet tripping over each other, she tried to run while glancing back at her pursuer. A sharp pain knifed through her ankle as she stumbled on the uneven terrain, and losing her balance, she cried out. The ground came rushing toward her.

Arms outstretched, she landed in a graceless

heap among the wildflowers. Oddly, she noticed the smell released as the tender buds were crushed by her fall. The scent swirled around her, strong and sweet. And the smell of grass and damp earth, rich and primal, filled her nostrils. The wind, the trill of a bird, the buzz of a bee, all seemed exaggerated, slowed to an abnormal pace, while her entire focus was riveted on Lord Craven's approach.

His Lordship likes 'em fresh. Says it's best for the harvest. Oh, dear heaven ... Emma tried to summon a prayer, but her mind was numb with fear. Fear of him. And fear of herself, for despite the corpse and Griggs's horrible assertion, despite the implication that Lord Craven played dark games with a deadly plague—mounting evidence all of the evil that lurked in his soul—she desperately wanted to absolve him of wrongdoing.

Yet, she had witnessed with her own eyes the human remains that Griggs had carried to Lord Craven's tower lair. What possible explanation could he offer for that? What explanation would her foolish heart accept?

Pushing herself to her knees and then higher still, Emma tried to take her weight on her injured limb. To no avail. The ankle was already swelling and the pain was sharp and intense. Again, she stumbled and collapsed to the ground.

No escape now. Lord Craven was upon her.

With a snarl he flung himself from the saddle, landing with inhuman grace on the balls of his feet. "Are you hurt?"

Mutely, she shook her head. He stalked toward her, stopping when he reached her side, booted feet planted shoulder width apart, fisted hands resting on his narrow hips. His expression was thunderous as he glared down at her.

"Miss Parrish." The words were bitten off with military precision. "I had believed you to be a sensible girl. It seems my impression could not have been more incorrect."

Hunkering down beside her, he shoved her skirt up above her knees. Emma felt a hot flush stain her cheeks as his hands slid impersonally along her legs.

"Please, my lord." She tried to return her hemline to a more modest level.

He moved her hands aside and again pushed at her skirt. With a firm but careful touch he probed her ankle.

"I suspect you are done with running for today." His tone had gentled somewhat. "Does this pain you over much?"

"No, my lord." *Not as much as my heart,* she thought as she stared at his square jaw, his firm lips, the chiseled curve of his cheekbone. She was caught between the urge to reach out and lay her hand against his skin, and the urge to shrink from him in horror.

Something in her tone caught his attention. He tilted his head and looked into her eyes, probing more than her ankle.

"It appears that our discussion the other night was for naught. You have again allowed yourself to succumb to irrational fright."

She blinked. *Irrational?*

"Mrs. Bolifer came rushing to the stables, frantic with worry." Emma had difficulty trusting the veracity of that statement. Frantic with worry? Mrs. Bolifer? "It seems she caught the tail end of your rather frantic escape," he continued. His tone and the chastising look on his face implied that he expected more of her.

Emma felt a cold anger start in the pit of her belly, pushing aside her fear and taking its place. He was *chastising* her. A man who hoarded dead bodies in some secret room in a moldering tower was taking her to task for worrying his housekeeper. Dead bodies! And he called her fear *irrational.*

"Griggs was carrying a corpse, my lord." Her tone could have frozen hot coals in the pits of damnation.

He raised his brow inquiringly, and his expression revealed polite puzzlement. "And?"

Emma stared at him, aghast. "He carried a dead man into the tower." She swallowed. "The wrapping came loose. I saw the man's hand."

Polite puzzlement gave way to outright confusion. "You fled because of a hand?"

"I fled because of the *corpse.*" She could not fathom his perplexity.

"Why?" He was looking at her intently, as if her reaction was outside the realm of comprehension.

A soft sound of frustration escaped her, and her irritation grew as her fear diminished. Somehow, she felt less afraid sitting here in the green field far from the tower, though, in truth, the cause of her trepidation had changed in nothing but proximity.

"Would not any being of rational mind flee from a dead body that dripped pestilence on the ground?" She wondered again if perhaps Lord Craven was mad. And Cookie. And Mrs. Bolifer. And Griggs. And even herself. An entire castle full of Bedlamites, for surely that was the only explanation for this bizarre conversation.

"The body was dripping pestilence?" His tone was sharp, indicating his concern. Here, at last, was something he did seem to understand. "Did you see a drop fall?"

Emma shook her head. "No. But I saw an arm. With a terrible carbuncle. But like no carbuncle I have ever seen. It was black and shiny, with a raised red rim. The sight was one I shall not likely forget."

"Ah."

Emma waited for him to say more, but he seemed lost in thought. The cold anger inside her began to bubble anew, heating to a slow simmer. He still crouched beside her, but his mind was obviously somewhere else entirely.

"Ah?" she repeated, stunned at his lack of response. Completely at a loss as to how she could be sitting in a slightly damp field of wildflowers discussing a dead man with a madman, her voice rose with more than a touch of anxiety. "That is the only word of explanation you offer? Ah?"

For one minuscule portion of a second she allowed her fury free reign. Her terror and confusion and, yes, her anger boiled from her heart down her arm to her clenched fist, whereupon she delivered a blow that would have stirred envy in a professional pugilist.

Her fist connected with Lord Craven's shoulder and the force rolled him from the soles of his feet onto his lordly backside. He landed in an ignominious heap with an expression of stunned amazement on his perfectly hewn features.

Then he raised his gorgeous green-gold eyes and stared at her in confusion. She could not say which of the two of them was more shocked by her actions.

Shoving her skirt down around her ankles, Emma drew herself to her most ladylike pose, searching deep within herself for hidden reserves of genteel calm.

"Lord Craven," she began, her elocution clear and distinct, "I have just seen your coachman carrying a dead man into the Round Tower. In and of itself, that tableau is most distressing, but there is greater depth to my unease. From the coal black sore I saw on the dead man's arm, I believe he died of a most heinous plague."

She had finally won his undivided attention, and given the spark that ignited in his eyes, she thought that perhaps he understood at last.

Sucking in a deep breath, she voiced her suspicion. "I believe he died of anthrax."

"Miss Parrish, we shall return to your monumental skill as a pugilist in due time. I would sincerely like to know where you learned that right hook." Rubbing his shoulder, he looked pointedly at her reddened knuckles. "But for the moment I should like to explore your knowledge of disease. Anthrax, Miss Parrish? Why would you say that?"

"I was teaching the children of our neighbor, Mr. Hicks. One day I overheard him telling a story about the cattle of a farm near Cheltenham. He said that they died of anthrax and that the soil harbored the evil humor for decades."

"To my knowledge, the disease may lodge in the soil for thirty years or more," Lord Craven mused, continuing to rub his shoulder absently. "What other bits of lore did the good farmer impart?"

As Emma struggled to remember that long-ago story told by Mr. Hicks, she could not help but note that Lord Craven was looking at her with a degree of admiration. "He said the disease could be seen in more than one manifestation. An attack of the lungs. Or a bloody flux. Or a malignant pustule. Black as coal, he said, shiny and the edges red and raw. He described the pustule quite literally, having no idea that I was intrigued by the conversation."

"I do not suppose that oozing pustules are a subject of great interest to many young girls," Lord Craven observed wryly.

"No, I do not suppose they are," Emma agreed. "But I have ever been unlike other girls of my acquaintance."

"Yes. I can easily believe that." He stared at her for a long moment and then continued, "So you caught sight of Griggs carrying a body with a black lesion evident on the . . ." His voice rose questioningly.

"On the forearm and palm," she supplied.

"And upon seeing the carbuncle—to use your earlier description—you diagnosed anthrax and immediately fled the vicinity. A most reasonable response, I suppose."

Except his tone suggested that he found her actions most *unreasonable*. Emma heaved an enormous sigh. Flight in the face of a horrifying tableau *was* a reasonable response. Yet, somehow, when he described the episode in such dispassionate simplicity, her reaction seemed rather overblown.

"But how did you come to be so certain, Miss Parrish? Have you ever seen such a pustule before?"

"No. Well, yes . . . I have seen a depiction of such." She huffed out a breath. "My mother took me to an exhibit of paintings once. The artist was quite fascinated with disease, and all his works depicted—" She shivered in recollection. "Suffice it to say that I recall that exhibit in vivid detail."

"Enough detail to recognize what you saw today

as the same disease." He studied her for a moment, true admiration in his gaze. "Amazing, really."

That single word of praise shimmered through her, warming her. He thought her amazing.

"Why did you come here, Miss Parrish?"

His question took her by surprise. "Oh, well, I did not plan to arrive at this particular field. I simply ran."

His smile was small. "I meant to question your arrival at Manorbrier. We have already ascertained how you came to arrive in this field."

"You sent for me, my lord," she said very slowly. "Do you not remember? You wrote to my aunts, Cecilia and Hortense."

Lord Craven made a slicing motion with his hand, and a hiss of exasperation escaped his lips. "Of course I remember that I sent for you. I know well enough what was in *my* mind. I am asking what was in *yours*. Why did you choose to come to Manorbrier?"

"Oh." Emma was not certain that she wished to divulge the details of her thought processes to Lord Craven. Somehow, her unhappiness and desperation to escape her aunts' home, her hope of finding a place of her own, seemed too personal to share. But he clearly expected some response, and her emotional stores were too depleted to muster the energy to lie. The truth would have to do. But dare she tell him the whole of it? Dare she trust him even a little, this enigmatic, secretive man?

"My aunts are somewhat—mmmm—unpleasant," she began, hedging.

Lord Craven gave a hoot of laughter, leaving Emma to wonder how a man of such brooding disposition could be so free with his laughter. And why the sound of it should please her so.

"Miss Parrish, you are the mistress of understatement. Cecilia is a harpy, and Hortense is as dull as tarnished silver."

"Yes, well, as I said, my aunts are unpleasant. Their home was not mine. I was merely a sojourner in their townhouse, an unwelcome burden on their frugality." She raised her eyes to his and spoke bluntly, for he seemed to wish it. "And my aunts decided it was time for me to take up what they considered my true position in life. They arranged for me to meet several . . . men."

"You declined an offer of marriage?" he asked, his tone gentle. "Why?"

Her humiliation was complete. " 'Twas not marriage they had in mind," Emma whispered, looking away, unable to meet his gaze a moment longer. All the fear and desperation of that night rushed back upon her, bitter as horseradish. "My lord, it may surprise you to learn that my aunts had decided to sell me to the highest bidder."

There was the root of it laid bare. So ugly in the bright light of day, but not half as ugly as the truths she left unsaid. The words brought all the terror and horror swirling back to her, a clammy fog of recollection and despair. Mr. Moulton, with his grasping hands and fetid breath. The drugged wine that he had bid her drink. The terrible sound of rending cloth as the dreadful man tore at her bodice. And worse, the awful sense of betrayal. She had known her aunts viewed her as a burden, but she had never discerned the depth of their contempt for her.

Dragging in a breath, she raised her chin a notch. A lethal tension coiled through Lord Craven's frame, as though he read her very thoughts.

"I trust their intent did not see fruition," he said darkly.

She blinked at his tone, for it seemed as though he was angry on her behalf.

"No. My ingenuity and your kind offer of employment saved me from that." She had punched Mr. Moulton, hard, right in the center of his face. Her desperation and his rather drink-laden state had won her escape, leaving her virtue intact if not her naiveté. Lord Craven's letter had arrived the very next day, had included a most generous bank draft for her aunts, and had offered Emma a last desperate hope. One she had grasped like a drowning woman at a jagged shard of barely floating wood.

For a moment Lord Craven said nothing. "The failure of their plan ensures Cecilia and Hortense's continued comfort."

Startled, she glanced at him, unsure of his implication, though his words seemed quite clear. His gaze had chilled like a frozen pond, cold fury, tightly leashed. Did he mean to say that he would have harmed them if her story had had a different conclusion? Was he capable of such? Surely not.

"They believed that the fact that I am the product of an illicit affair between my mother and a young lordling who went and got himself killed in a carriage accident gave them leave to do with me what they would."

Oh, reckless tongue. Her illegitimacy was cause for dismissal from her post. And then she recalled the fact that he had likely known of her circumstance before he had ever sent for her. He had been married to her cousin Delia, after all.

Though he said nothing, the muscles of his jaw tightened.

"My prospects are few," she finished softly. Did he judge her? She could not say, but somehow she thought not.

"So you came to the home of a man rumored to be a killer? That was the choice left to you?"

She looked at him sharply. He definitely sounded angry on her behalf, which made no sense at all, for she could not imagine why he should have a care for her. "I came to the home of a man in need of a governess for his son."

"Only moments ago you fled with the hounds of hell nipping at your heels. Or perhaps the hounds of the tower. Yet now you sound so certain of my innocence."

"Certain of your innocence? Nay." *I am certain you left innocence behind you long ago,* she thought, aware of how close he was, the heat of him, the strength. "But neither am I certain of your guilt."

"So you prove yourself to be a sensible girl, after all," he mused, reaching out to run his finger softly along her jawline.

The contact sang through her body. If she turned her head ever so slightly his fingers would caress her cheek, her lips. What was wrong with her that she was so very tempted to do just that? She jerked back and slapped at his hand.

"I readily admit that I am a woman of no fortune, no beauty, and too sharp a tongue. I suppose that sensible is a no more offensive label than those." She could not contain the hint of waspishness that seeped into her words, though it seemed that Lord Craven did not find her words off-putting.

"I find I have a liking for sensible." Like a wild-fire, his expression changed. No longer musing, but hot and sensuous. Dear heaven, his presence was irresistible. Enticing. He had only to murmur such words of approval, and a glow of pleasure suffused her.

Emma struggled against a rush of confusion. Was she such a desperate miss that she ached for admiration, and from a man who was so dangerous to her on every level? There could be no good end to this fascination. She was governess to his son. He was her employer, a man far beyond her rank. A man who hoarded bodies in a tower . . . a man rumored to be a killer. . . .

He drew the pad of his thumb across his lower lip as he studied her. And then he spoke in that beautiful, compelling voice: "You name yourself no beauty, Miss Parrish. Have you not heard that beauty is in the eye of the beholder? Some men value a quick mind." He reached out and stroked her hair, a light touch, there then gone. "Intelligence. Loyalty." The words were softly seductive, his tone both smooth and rough, and so enticing that she almost leaned into his caress. "Dark flashing eyes. And skin soft as finest silk."

She held herself still, though her pulse ran wild at his touch.

Run away, so her common sense whispered. Lord Anthony Craven was more dangerous to her than any evil humor. Men of his position would offer nothing to a governess. That knowledge had been drummed into her until it was as much a part of her as her skin or her heart.

Worse still, he had secrets, terrifying secrets. A wife dead under circumstances most strange, governesses killed while in his employ. And corpses carried to the top of his tower lair. What manner of man was he in truth?

And what manner of woman was she to want him so?

Run away, Emma thought once more. 'Twould be the prudent course. But she could not run. Her ankle still throbbed, and she could feel the swelling that made her stocking seem to fit one size too small. And if truth be told, she would not run even if she could.

Lord Craven rose, towering above her, framed by a backdrop of blue sky. Tilting her head back, Emma took in the picture he presented. No portrait could have done him justice. Then he bent and drew her up until her weight rested on her one good foot, her body supported by his.

Heat sluiced through her. She pressed against him, aware of her guile, for she pretended 'twas her injury that made her do it, when in truth it was the hard kick of wanting. He had never kissed her, and wanton, foolish girl, she wanted him to. So very much. Let her have this, her secret pleasure. What harm one kiss?

Sucking in a breath, he closed his eyes, then slowly, slowly, lifted his dark lashes. Whatever battle he waged, he was lost. As lost as she.

Her heart knocked wildly against her ribs as he reached out slowly to weave his fingers through her hair, leaving the long curling strands tumbling over her shoulders, her habitual knot in disarray.

A wicked tingle chased across her flesh, sensitizing her skin to his touch. She wanted to arch her neck, to feel his lips against her throat, where her pulse beat with ever increasing fervor.

Her gaze slipped to his mouth, his wonderful, generous mouth. His lips curved in a dangerous smile. Knowing. Hungry. She tipped her head, up, toward him, luscious anticipation and the slow burn of desire cycling through her.

Tightening his arm about her waist, he set his lips to hers in a brief caress, paused, came back to taste her, harder, stronger, his mouth opening on hers and his tongue tracing the outline of her lips, her teeth. No tentative touch, but a masculine claiming. Openmouthed, wet and deep, the kiss spilled through her, hot, so hot, rushing to her breasts, her belly, the juncture of her thighs.

On some level she thought it was indelicate, unrefined, crude, the way he licked her tongue, thrust then withdrew, increasing the pressure of his lips on hers. But she did not care. The feel of him, the taste of him were beyond wonderful. And so she licked him back, dragging a groan from deep inside him, the sound stroking her spiraling desire.

There was ecstasy in his kiss, his touch, so much better than ever she had dreamed, and the feel of his long, hard body pressed against her and the drum of his heart.

"No." She could not stop the soft cry of denial that escaped her as he pulled away.

He stared at her for a long moment, his expression a study in confusion. "You are beautiful," he rasped, sounding both bewildered and dismayed.

Chest heaving as she struggled for breath, she stared at him, passion thrumming in her veins. Delicious. Enthralling.

Running her tongue over her lower lip, she tasted him, his passion, his need. Here then was her answer. Here was the harm of one kiss.

She would spend an eternity yearning for more.

CHAPTER SEVEN

Some hours later, the pain of her ankle throbbing beneath the coverlet woke Emma from a restless slumber. Hugging herself, she moved her palms up and down against her upper arms in a reflex action of comfort as she struggled free of the hazy images that haunted her. She had been dreaming of pestilence. And endless fields of wildflowers.

Burrowing deep beneath the blankets, she shivered, though a fire burned in the grate. The flame of a candle stub flickered on the bedside table, sending dark shadows writhing and dancing against the wall. She wondered if it was yet day.

"I see you are awake." Lord Craven's deep voice drew her from her musings.

Startled, she glanced up to find him standing framed in the doorway holding a candle in his left hand. The hall behind him was dark. His face was shadowed, cast in sharp relief by the glimmering light. Her heart clutched at the sight of him, so handsome, so fine. So mysterious.

Emma opened her mouth to ask all the questions that jumbled her thoughts, but wariness held her silent. Questions would garner answers, and for the moment she was uncertain if she wanted to hear them. Dropping her gaze, she stared at his hands. Strong hands with long fingers. She remembered the feel of them as he ran them over her legs, evaluating her injury, and the solid strength of him as he had carried her to her bed, for she had been unable to bear weight on her injured limb.

Heat rushed through her veins. His strong arms, his solid chest, and the smell of him, fresh, clean, and far too delicious—so much so that she had barely suppressed the urge to bury her face in his neck and inhale the scent of his skin, to dart her tongue from between her lips and taste him, to press her mouth to his . . . A sharp hiss of air escaped her.

"It seems, Miss Parrish, that you will be alone for much of the next few days. I doubt your ankle will support your weight on those stairs." He stepped into the chamber, placed the candle he carried on the table by her bed, and snuffed the remains of the tallow stub with his fingers. "Why have you not moved to the room next to the nursery? This ridiculous trek to the third floor must be bothersome. Especially when you have a desire to launch a midnight assault on the kitchen."

Traitorous heart that it swelled so at the reminder of a shared moment.

"I suppose this ankle will preclude any such assault for some time, my lord," she replied, forbearing to mention that she inhabited the room she had been assigned by his housekeeper.

Lord Craven held out his hand. "You will likely need this in the coming days."

Emma realized that he grasped her novel, the

one she had been carrying when she began her wild flight into the field.

"Thank you, my lord." She reached out and closed her fingers around the worn leather, her skin contacting his. A crackle of energy passed between them, hot and raw. Carnal.

Her gaze shot upward. Despite all that had passed, she wished he would lean close, press those firm lips to hers, let her taste him, touch him once more. He did nothing to entice her, nothing overt, but there was a dark undercurrent of sensuality that was as much part of him as his skin or bone.

"Miss Emma!" Nicky scrambled round his father's long legs and threw himself onto Emma's bed.

The moment dissolved and Emma jerked away, the book falling to the bed with a muffled thud. Wrapping his arms around her, Nicky buried his face in Emma's shoulder. "How is your ankle?"

"My ankle is feeling much better now that you are here to hug me."

"Truly?" Tipping his head back, Nicky scrutinized her face, looking for the truth of her words.

"Truly." Emma confirmed, giving him a gentle squeeze. Her eyes met Lord Craven's over the child's head. She quickly looked away from the heat of his gaze.

"Papa says you must rest for at least three days. But I am to leave tomorrow, and who will take care of you?" Nicky's brow wrinkled in concern, and his blue eyes watched her with serious intensity.

"Leave?" she echoed, sending a glance at Lord Craven.

"Nicky and I journey on the morrow to visit my father and stepmother. We shall be gone for a fortnight."

What a terrible maelstrom her emotions were in. She was torn between relief and regret.

"I shall just have to take care of myself, Nicky," Emma said, giving him another gentle squeeze.

"And I suppose you will have Cookie and Mrs. Bolifer, too. Especially Mrs. Bolifer. She always takes care of me when I get hurt. I'm sure she will take the very best care of you."

Emma pressed her lips together to keep from laughing. The vision of a stern-faced Mrs. Bolifer, gray hair standing out in springy coils, chest heaving with the exertion of climbing the stairs as she carried a tray to Emma's chamber, was as unlikely as a bull giving birth to a calf.

Lord Craven made a noise that sounded suspiciously like a snort of disbelief. Obviously, he shared her thoughts on the matter. "Time for bed, Nicky. We have an early morning, my lad."

With a last hug, Nicky hopped off the bed and raced into the hall. Then he popped his head back into the room. "Will you move to the room next to mine, Miss Emma?"

Emma glanced at Lord Craven. Prior to this evening, he had made no mention of a desire to reassign her chamber, but she supposed his earlier comment, however cryptic, was mention enough.

"I shall, Nicky. By the time you return from your adventure, I will have moved to the room next to the nursery."

"Good." He gave a swift nod of satisfaction. "May I carry the candle, Papa?"

"Be very careful. Hold it straight." Lord Craven handed the candle to his son. With a grin lighting his face, Nicky left the room, and Emma could hear him singing to himself as he made his way down the hall.

"Lord Craven," Emma stopped him as he turned to follow the boy, "I was unaware of a planned trip. Do you wish me to accompany Nicholas?"

"I suspect your injured ankle would hamper your ability to chase after a six-year-old, Miss Parrish. Something you may wish to consider the next time a sudden urge to run pell-mell to the winds strikes your fancy." His tone was mildly sardonic. Emma felt a flush heat her cheeks.

"The urge will likely lie dormant until the next time I am confronted with a dead body bearing a terrifying malady."

"Touché." He shot her a quick glance, his expression unreadable, his eyes glittering in the dim light.

He had offered no explanation, no excuse. A dead body lay in the Round Tower, and Lord Craven offered nothing to calm her mind. She had wondered earlier what possible explanation she could accept. And now she had her answer. He had offered nothing, and foolish girl that she was, she had accepted even that. But did he intend to leave the dead man to rot in the tower while he vacationed elsewhere? The thought was . . . unthinkable.

"In any event, the trip is a yearly adventure in which my son and I indulge. Other than the dubious pleasure of my stepmother's company, it is a trip both Nicky and I enjoy."

She nodded, sensing that this interview was near its end, yet loath to see him leave.

"Perhaps you would be so good as to mention the issue of the rooms to Mrs. Bolifer. I would not wish to have her think I was overstepping myself by making demands in your absence."

He smiled, that perfect curving of his lips that made Emma feel as though he were a work of art that she could admire for eternity. "As you wish, Miss Parrish. Is there anything else?"

She sank her teeth into her lower lip, her thoughts whirling this way and that. *Why do you have a dead man in your tower, and what in heaven's name do you wish to harvest? What happened to the last governess? And the one before that, and the one before that?*

A choked sound of dismay escaped her, and she shook her head, unable to find the words, or the courage, to ask. "It was kind of you to bring Nicky up to say farewell. I shall miss him."

"I am not kind, Miss Parrish. Never mistake me for a man who is kind." Lord Craven's voice was a whisper, the tone caressing her, though the words made her shiver.

The need to touch him was a wicked torment that gnawed at her, a fierce hunger. One kiss was not enough. It could never be enough. She longed for more, ached for more.

For one arrested moment, she thought the intensity of his gaze would devour her. And then he crossed to the fire, breaking the sizzling connection that arced between them. Picking up the poker, he jabbed at the log, creating a flurry of sparks accompanied by a series of hissing and popping noises.

Then the meaning of his words surfaced in her jumbled thoughts. *Never mistake me for a man who is kind.*

"Why do you say that? I have seen you treat Nicky only with benevolence." She wondered why he refused to acknowledge any goodness in himself. A part of her was afraid of him, truly afraid. Of the secrets he hid, of the mystery that enshrouded him.

Yet, that fear was tempered by the conviction that he would do her no harm. More than that, he would let no evil touch her. That certainty was clear and strong, and she did not wonder at its source.

"I love my son," he said at length. "And he has formed an attachment to you. If there is any kindness left in me, that kindness is for him."

Emma's heart skittered to a stop, then resumed the regularity of its pace. Was he trying to convince her, or himself?

"Yes, of course," she murmured, fighting the swell of disappointment that his words produced. Had she hoped for some declaration of affection?

"You will be here when we return?" He turned his attention from the fire and now regarded her with that peculiar intensity that so disquieted her.

"Yes," she whispered, looking down at the coverlet. "I will not leave Nicholas." *I will not leave you.*

She could feel him watching her but dared not look up to meet his gaze.

"You are a most unusual woman, Miss Parrish." Warm, lazy words, spinning through her senses with a slow sensuality.

A rush of air escaped her. "Unusual? Why? Because I ran like a madwoman across the field?"

"Nay." She heard the scrape of his boots on the floor as he covered the short distance between them and caught her chin in his hand, tilting her face to his. The contact sent a lush heat coursing through her. "You are unusual because you have a rare and precious constancy, a steadiness of nature I value above all else."

A thrill of pleasure thrummed in her veins, and then she exerted her practicality, tamping down the feeling until it simmered lightly, held in tight confine.

Constancy. He valued her constancy. She would be wise not to read any greater meaning into his statement. Surely he valued her as a master values a servant. 'Twas not the first time he had mentioned such. There was some current in his words, some truth she sensed but could not define. Who had betrayed him that he found honesty and loyalty to be so rare, so special?

She swallowed against the constriction that clogged her throat, and she found the courage to ask, "About the corpse, my lord . . ."

"The corpse, Miss Parrish?" His dark brows drew together in a frown. "A local man with no family. I shall see that he receives a proper burial."

"So you brought him here to bury him?" How odd to drag the man's body up to the tower only to bring him down once more.

"No." He glanced at her, his eyes glittering in the firelight. "I had him brought round so I could harvest his organs. His blood."

Dear heaven. The ghastly calm of his voice. A choked sound escaped her.

"There is beauty in death. And lessons to be learned," he whispered, warm breath brushing her cheek as he twined his fingers through her hair. "I could show you, Emma. I could show you wonders that would make you understand. You have a quick mind. It would only take time to teach you, but you could have untold knowledge." He paused. "Anthrax is only the beginning. There are smallpox and the other pox—syphilis."

"Syphilis!" she squeaked, horrified. "What are you saying? I cannot . . . you cannot mean that you . . ." Stunned, she pulled away, a sudden jerking movement that tore her hair from his grasp.

Her eyes filled with tears at the sharp sting, but she welcomed the pain, for it brought her back to reality. "Do you mean that you suffer from such?"

"No." A harsh laugh escaped him. "And I am utterly astounded that you asked."

She astounded herself but had no intention of telling him so. "How can you say these things to me?"

"You asked," he said as he watched her intently. "You asked and I answered."

Was he mocking her? She could not be sure, but somehow it seemed that his derisive laughter was aimed not at her, as she had originally thought, but at himself. There was a coldness to him now, a distance that he had erected. Emma thought perhaps he had whispered those words on purpose to alarm her. To push her away more surely than if he had used his body to thrust her from him. To protect her from himself.

Lord Craven had set out to establish the boundaries, and he had succeeded. Suddenly, Emma wished to be as far from him, from his inexplicable behavior and cryptic actions, as possible.

She twisted the coverlet about her fingers and stared at the stub of the candle by her bedside. In the silence she imagined she could hear a spider spinning its web, or the dust gathering on the furniture, so great was the absence of sound. Then the log crackled, the noise dispelling her imaginings, making her jump at its suddenness.

Lord Craven rose and crossed the room. "Good night, Miss Parrish. Sleep well." He paused for a moment in the doorway, his back to her, his palms resting on the door frame, and then he moved on, his footsteps fading as he left her to her solitary thoughts.

"Good night, my lord," she whispered, though only the shadows remained to hear her.

Walking in the afternoon sunshine ten days later, Emma could not contain a grimace. The uneven terrain of the field caused her gait to be slightly unsteady as she made her way carefully to avoid reinjuring her ankle, which throbbed a bit as she walked. She welcomed the discomfort. It meant she was healed enough to put weight on her injured limb. Good thing, that. Because Nicky had been gone just over a week and a half and her days were a study in boredom. Ten days had passed with the rapidity of a snail making its way across a hay field.

At first she could not leave her bed, forcing Cookie to brave the stairs in order to care for her. And twice she had sent the downstairs maid, Glynnis. Of Mrs. Bolifer there had been no sign. Once the swelling decreased enough to let her move around, Emma found that she had nothing to do. No Nicky, no responsibility, and too much free time with nothing to fill it.

Nothing, except thoughts of Lord Anthony Craven, and Emma preferred not to allow herself to spend two long weeks mooning over her employer.

With a sigh, she resolutely pulled her mind away from Lord Craven, from his demons and secrets. From the dark, sweet taste of him and the tug of her own drugging desire. She had spent days lying abed thinking about nothing but him. Foolish, foolish girl. She regretted the wasted energy of spinning her thoughts and dreams about him, just as her mother had spun a web of false hopes in regard to her father only to have those hopes so cruelly dashed. Though she was a poor hand at it, and detested it to boot, Emma should have better poured her efforts into embroidery. Something constructive. Anything to occupy her hands and mind.

Unfortunately, she was in possession of neither colored threads nor cloth. So instead of patterning a sampler, she was left spinning fantasies in thin air.

Increasing her pace, Emma walked briskly along the field, enjoying the sun, the birds, the breeze. Days ago she had fled the castle in a full panic, running through this field as if the demons of the underworld nipped at her heels. Today she walked through the exact same field, but at a more sedate pace, taking the time to enjoy the clumps of wildflowers, the buzz of a bee.

The weather was warm, with just a hint of cooling breeze. She paused, closing her eyes and turning her face to the sun.

"Hello."

Emma jumped at the sound of a voice behind her. Spinning round, she found herself facing a man. He was neither overly tall nor overly large. Maintaining his distance several feet away from her, he stood regarding her with a perfectly amiable expression on his face. He was handsome, with sandy hair and light eyes, but there was something . . .

"Hello," she returned the man's greeting somewhat warily, resting her palm against the base of her throat. She was in a deserted field with a man she did not know. Though the situation ought not to be threatening, neither did it feel completely safe.

"Lovely day for a walk."

"Yes, it is."

"I am Leonard Smythe. Dr. Smythe. From Bosherton." He inclined his head.

"Emma Parrish. Recently arrived at Manorbrier."
She inclined her head in return, letting her hand
drop back to her side. He was a doctor. A healer.
No one to fear. "How far to Bosherton?"

"Hmmm. 'Bout half hour to the west at a good
pace."

She nodded. "I have yet to visit the village."

"You must be the new governess," he said, taking
a single step toward her.

"Yes. How did you know?" Emma fought the urge
to take a single step back. What on earth was the
matter with her? The man was not the least bit ob-
trusive; in fact, he was gentlemanly in both manner
and appearance. His sandy hair was neatly trimmed,
his features regular and even.

"Talk is that Lord Craven has brought in a cousin
to help with the boy." He arched a brow inquiringly
at Emma. "You are his cousin?"

Emma frowned.

"I am." Despite the warmth of the sun, she felt
gooseflesh rise on her arms and a chill seep
through her body. Wrapping her arms about herself, she wished she had her sweater. A breeze had
taken on a chilly nip. "Lovely to have met you, Dr.
Smythe, but I should be getting back now," she said,
knowing that her dismissal bordered on rudeness,
but suddenly desperate to be away. There was something in the way he looked at her, something in his
eyes that unnerved her.

Turning toward Manorbrier, Emma took several
steps. Her ankle was taxed from her long walk, and
she could not help the slight limp that crept into
her gait.

"Miss Parrish, you have hurt yourself. Shall I have

a look, then." He was beside her before she had time to protest.

She shook her head, anxious to be away from him but uncertain why. "Thank you, no."

"Did he hurt you?" His voice was a hoarse rasp.

Emma could not think whom he meant. She stared at him, trying to decipher his meaning.

"Forgive me," he muttered, stepping away from her, clasping his right hand with his left. "I should go. I am sorry to have troubled you. It is just— Be careful, Miss Parrish. He is a dangerous man."

It struck her then.

"Sir, do you refer to Lord Craven?" she ventured uncertainly, completely baffled by this odd man and his even odder comments.

"*Lord* Craven," Dr. Smythe mused. "He is lord of nothing, Miss Parrish. Merely the sixth son of a marquis. A courtesy title, nothing more."

His statement came as no surprise. Cookie had told her as much several days past, though her tone had been ever so much more polite as she had said it. "What is your purpose in telling me this?"

He seemed taken aback by her question. Perhaps he had expected some stronger reaction, though, truly, Emma could not imagine what his intention was, and he did not seem inclined to elucidate. The silence lengthened, and Dr. Smythe's eyes narrowed as he looked at her. "You have been beguiled, Miss Parrish. I offer this unsolicited opinion because of my grave concern for the well-bred young lady you most certainly are. Beware."

Oh, dear. Yet another cryptic warning. She sighed.

"Beware of what, Dr. Smythe? I have yet to encounter any threat to my person." Save for the anthrax-riddled corpse in the Round Tower, and the person who had spied on her that first day at Manorbrier, and the frightening episode in the icehouse. She caught her lower lip between her teeth, wondering if he detected her deception.

"Not all threats are obvious, Miss Parrish." Dr. Smthye paused, then continued in a softer tone, as though he was hesitant to impart gossip. "The last governess at Manorbrier died a terrible death."

He must mean Mrs. Winter. "What sort of death, Dr. Smythe?"

"She died of anthrax, Miss Parrish. I found her body on the side of the road to Bosherton, haphazardly clothed, a small portmanteau by her side. From all appearances, she was fleeing Manorbrier with utmost haste."

Emma stared at him in dismay. *Anthrax.* She had died of anthrax.

"How terrible," she whispered, her mind conjuring the image of the horrific lesion on the corpse that Griggs had carried to the tower.

"Miss Parrish, you look rather pale. I shall stay until you recover." Dr. Smythe gestured toward a large boulder near the edge of the field. "Come. Sit a moment."

"No, thank you. I must return." She backed away, suddenly overwhelmed by the desire to return to Manorbrier, to its familiar crumbling enclosure. Pressing her palms together, she brought her fingers to her lips, acknowledging the ridiculous dichotomy in the fact that she wanted to scuttle back and seek comfort in the very place that housed the pestilence to which Dr. Smythe referred.

"As you wish." Dr. Smythe gave a curt bow.

Emma took several steps before the sound of his voice

stopped her. "You may rely on my assistance should the need arise. Until we meet again, Miss Parrish."

Bewildered, Emma paused for a moment, sending a glance over her shoulder. Dr. Smythe watched her in narrow-eyed contemplation. Anxiety and a wary distress crawled through her as she turned and began the long trek back to Manorbrier castle.

Emma awoke before dawn the next morning. After so many days of inactivity, she was near mindless with boredom. With minimal effort she had convinced Mrs. Bolifer to give her the key to the locked third-floor rooms, and to allow her to clean them. She was glad for the task to busy her hands.

Meg, the quiet maid who performed her upstairs chores without ever being seen, was in the scullery when Emma arrived, bending over a bucket, her back toward the door.

"Good morning, Meg," Emma said, surprised to have actually encountered the girl. She was like a wraith, seen only in glimpses, and this was the first time Emma had spoken to her since her arrival at Manorbrier.

The maid straightened so quickly that she nearly overbalanced herself. Pressing her hand against the wall for support, Meg hesitated, then turned slowly.

Emma noticed the girl's eyes first. Huge and blue, they were clear as a winter morning. She was very young, perhaps fifteen or sixteen. Resting one hand against the wall, Meg clasped the other protectively over her abdomen. The gesture called Emma's attention to the girl's belly, which strained against her apron, molding the cloth to the shape of a large, round ball. Clearly, Meg was far advanced in her pregnancy.

"Good morning, miss."

"Please call me Emma." Frowning, Emma stared at Meg's face. "You are not the maid I met the day after my arrival. She was older than you, and none too happy to be here."

"My sister," Meg replied. "Alice. She helps out on days I feel peaked, but she has no liking for work."

Silence followed that statement, and the two women stood in the fledgling light of dawn looking at each other uncertainly.

Finally Emma spoke again, terminating the protracted silence. "Meg, I know it is none of my concern, but should you be carrying out the heavy chores in your condition?"

Meg stared at her for a moment, then answered with surprising candor.

"Miss . . . I mean, Emma," she said, her voice as high and clear as a child's, "I'll tell you true 'cause I think you're asking out of genuine concern. I've been watching you with Master Nicky, and you seem like a fine governess, not yelling at him or switching him like the others."

Turning, Meg began to gather her cleaning supplies as she spoke. "I ain't got a bun warming in the oven by choice. Weren't one of the village lads that done it. The babe's father ain't going to claim it, or me. Quality never do."

Sadness welled in Emma's breast. So that was the way of it.

Meg heaved a sigh, then continued. "My da's dead. My ma has consumption. She coughs up blood and can't drag herself from her bed. And I got six brothers and sisters at home, all with hungry bellies. Lord Craven kept me on, even when he knew I was in the family way. Aren't too many places that wouldn't have tossed me out right quick." Her supplies gathered, Meg tugged at her apron and looked Emma straight in the eye. "And he pays me thirty pounds a year."

Emma could not suppress a startled gasp. The amount was outrageous. Even the finest London lady's maid would likely earn only fifteen pounds per year. Suspicion nagged at the edge of her mind. Was Lord Craven the father of Meg's babe? The thought was like a blade in her belly. She did not wish it to be true, could not deny the pain that such a possibility brought to her soul.

Yet, it would explain his generosity. Thirty pounds a year.

She stared at Meg's freckled face. The girl was so very young to bear such a harsh burden, the task of finding a way to raise an illegitimate child.

"Lord Craven doesn't want us to starve," Meg continued, her tone indicating that she thought his actions noble. "And Dr. Smythe'll come to physic Ma only if I give him the coins ahead of time. When I first came looking for work I told that to His Lordship. He tossed me two shillings. Told me to think of it as an advance on my wages. Only when it came time to pay me, he never deducted the two shillings off." Meg winked at Emma, a knowledge far greater than her age ought allow evident in her expression.

"And if Lord Craven's a mite odd, always wanting to look at a dead body before it's buried, carrying soap and a jar of water in his carriage so he can wash his hands all the time, well, ain't no never mind to me. His coins feed my family, and that's all I care about."

Emma wondered at the odd behavior Meg described. "Why does he want to look at the bodies, Meg?"

She shrugged, unconcerned. "I dunno. Maybe all doctors do."

Her words startled Emma. "What do you mean all doctors do? What has that to do with Lord Craven?"

"Dunno . . . just that doctors and bodies are oft found together."

"Do you mean to say that Lord Craven is a *doctor*?" Emma asked, utterly perplexed by the possibility. He was wealthy. A lord. Physician was an unlikely title for one of his class.

Meg looked at her strangely and nodded. "Everyone knows it."

The idea seemed outlandish to Emma. She hardly imagined that Lords of the Realm made a common practice of seeing to those in need.

"Does Lord Craven ever," Emma hesitated, then used Meg's word, "physic the people of the village?"

"No, he don't do that anymore. Not since the mistress died."

Emma almost asked why and then thought better of it. The maid would not be privy to the inner workings of Lord Craven's mind.

Her thoughts were awhirl with all she had learned. Lord Craven was a doctor, though he no longer practiced his profession. What a strange and unlikely disclosure. Still, it explained the fascination with death, with disease. Such a riddle was Anthony Craven, but each piece she fitted to the puzzle seemed to deepen the mystery even more.

Well, she would have ample time to ponder the conundrum while she scrubbed floors and windows. She gave a small sigh of resignation. Here she had planned the day's chores in an effort to clear him from her thoughts, yet it appeared she was destined to dwell on him in the end.

"Meg, I'll need some rags and a broom. Oh, and a mop and bucket," Emma said. "I am going to clean the rooms on the third floor."

"Rooms on the third floor are locked. I'm not required to clean 'em."

Emma fished through her pocket and pulled out the key that Mrs. Bolifer had given her the day before, holding it up like a trophy. "They will not stay locked for long."

"Oh, well then, miss . . . I mean, Emma. There's an extra bucket in the corner. And rags on the shelf. Take what you need."

Meg turned to leave, hefting her bucket of soapy water.

"Meg," Emma's voice stopped her.

Meg looked up, holding the bucket handle with both hands, her face pink with exertion.

"Why did you avoid me? Before today, I mean. I should have liked to have met you sooner."

"Didn't know if my"—Meg looked down at her enormous belly—"my *bun* would offend. I watched you sometimes, just to see what sort you were."

"Watched me?" Could that explain the odd sensation she had felt in the corridor the morning after her arrival?

The maid pressed her lips together and nodded. "I thought it best to stay out of your way till I knew if you were like the others."

"The other governesses, you mean? The ones before me?"

Sliding her gaze away from Emma's, Meg studied the contents of her pail as if something of great interest was contained therein.

"Meg, who is the father of your child? Perhaps he could somehow contribute, at least financially. . . ."

The girl shrugged and stared down into the depths of her bucket, her face flushed red now, though Emma was not sure if the color was caused by the exertion of holding the heavy pail, or by the emotions that Emma's questions elicited. "He pays me some. He can be right generous at times." She paused awkwardly. "I have to get busy with my chores now, miss. Excuse me."

Left alone in the scullery, Emma began to gather her supplies, and her thoughts.

He pays me some. Lord Craven was paying her thirty pounds a year. Was he the father of Meg's babe? The thought was heartbreaking to her. As the product of such a union, Emma knew only too well that it was common for a man of the upper class to enjoy himself well, and leave the woman to face the consequences. What had Meg said? *The babe's father ain't going to claim it, or me. Quality never do.*

Emma sighed as she lifted her own bucket and slowly made her way to the servant's stairs. Meg's circumstance was only one more reminder that she must not succumb to the dark lure of her attraction to Anthony Craven.

Not unless she wished to find herself round with an unclaimed *bun.*

CHAPTER EIGHT

Wipe the walls. Wash the windows. Scrub the floor. Emma found that just as Mrs. Bolifer had warned, cleaning the upstairs rooms was proving a monotonous task. The locked chambers held no secrets, only dust. But at least her hands were occupied and she was carrying out a useful task. The rooms had been neglected. The thick layer of dust on the floor and the stale smell of the air suggested they had not been opened in some time.

In one room Emma discovered a delicately fashioned rosewood writing desk with painted panels on the two lowest drawers. The paint was most unusual, with a metallic sheen glinting in the vivid hues.

She knelt on the floor, running her finger over the front of the desk. It was clearly a piece of furniture designed for feminine use, small and intricately detailed, with painted flowers, and a parrot off to one side.

With a fresh rag, she carefully wiped the dust from the desk. Then her imagination took hold. She thought of the novels she loved so well, in which a desk might hide a secret compartment, or a painting obscure the entry to a dark tunnel. A laugh escaped her. Though she had given in to the childish urge and examined each room she had cleaned thus far, she had discovered no secret passages, no dark tunnels wreathed in cobwebs. Only walls and windows and dust. Still, imagining that she might discover some secret or treasure had made her tedious chore quite a bit more bearable than it otherwise might have been.

Turning her attention to the desk, she drew forth the center drawer, her breath catching in her throat as she waited for the contents to be revealed to her. It was empty.

Undaunted, Emma slowly opened each drawer in turn, only to swallow her disappointment as she found nothing. Rolling her eyes at her own ridiculous notions, she continued with her cleaning, working methodically to set the room to rights. Once done, she closed the window and fastened the latch, then turned to exit the chamber. The desk caught her attention once more, and she recollected a novel she had read. A false bottom in a drawer had secreted an important document, shielding it from prying eyes. Of course, she knew that life was not a work of fiction, but there was no harm in looking one last time.

Again Emma examined each drawer, this time searching for a hidden catch or unusual hollow sound when she tapped her fingers against the wood. Nothing was forthcoming. Disappointed at the absence of any significant discovery, she attempted to return the last drawer to its closed position, but it would not push in all the way. Frowning, she withdrew the drawer completely, setting it on the floor beside her. Then she tipped her head to the side and peered into the dark opening.

There, at the very back, was a small rectangular object. Emma stared at it, excitement stirring in her breast. She wiped her hand on her apron, then reached in. Her fingers closed around the thing and she drew forth a finely tooled leather-bound book. She riffled the pages and a jumble of words sped past, the decidedly feminine script indicating that her discovery was a woman's diary. Tucking the small volume away in her pocket, she rose and moved on to the next room, intending to examine her prize when she had a free moment.

After opening the window of the final chamber, Emma set her thoughts and her hands to finishing the task she had begun. She dipped her rag in the bucket, and then wrung the excess moisture from the cloth. Pushing a stray hair from her forehead with the back of her wrist, she swiped the cloth along the window ledge, wiping it clean. Fresh air swirled through the open window, the cool breeze welcome on her flushed cheeks.

She had worked for some time, with only the floor left to wash, when she paused, every sense alert. Perhaps a sound caught her attention, or a movement from the corner of her eye. Or perhaps it was only the secret wish of her heart that made her think she was no longer alone. She froze, her heart accelerating with a mixture of trepidation and hope.

Slowly, she turned away from the window, every nerve alight with a shimmer of awareness. Her breath left her in a rush.

In the doorway stood Lord Craven. He leaned against the threshold with arms folded, one booted foot crossed over the other. His dark hair was wind-blown, a single strand caressing the hard angle of his jaw.

For a moment, she thought she had imagined him, conjured him from the cauldron of her secret desire.

"You are returned earlier than expected, my lord." Those words she spoke aloud, though the remainder of her thoughts were hers alone. *I missed you, dreamed of you. Your touch. Your kiss. I am undone with wanting you.*

His intent gaze roamed over her face, her body, leaving her feeling hot and flushed each place it touched. And she could not help but wonder if he knew the secret thoughts and fantasies that left her hot and restless in the night.

Moving with languid grace, he entered, his polished Hessians tapping on the bare floor, the sound echoing hollowly in the empty room. The corded muscles of his thighs rippled beneath the cloth of his buff breeches. He had not bothered to divest himself of his square-cut coat but came to her smelling of sunshine and fresh air.

And Emma did not doubt that he came to *her*. She felt it in every fiber of her being. Her blood pounded in her veins, leaving her breathless, aching.

You will be here when we return? He had asked her that before, and she had registered somewhere in her consciousness that her answer was important to him.

He stood so close she could feel the heat emanating from his body, see the hunger in his eyes.

"My lord," she said, backing up a step, her foot brushing against the bucket. Abruptly, she recalled her disheveled state, her stained garments and work-roughened hands. Her foot nudged the broom.

"Anthony," he said huskily. "Say my name, Emma."

"Anthony," she whispered, struggling to draw breath.

"I could not stay away," he said, his tone bewildered, as though he could not fathom the reason. Reaching out, he brushed a stray tendril from her cheek, tucking it behind her ear. Though his touch was gentle, Emma read a savagery in his eyes that kindled wicked sparks and sent a bolt of longing racing through her body, bringing her to aching, throbbing life.

She tried to slow her breathing, to stop the flood of heat and damp that pooled between her thighs. Dear heaven, he came upon her like a storm, wreaking havoc with her composure. And all he did was stand there, looking at her with those green-gold eyes, the promise of untold pleasure in his gaze.

She retreated, sliding her feet backward step by step, thinking that distance might sever the bond that surged between them. Each movement of her limbs stroked her, accentuating the exquisite anguish that she barely comprehended.

As he watched her, Anthony's mouth curved in a hard, sensual line, empathy clear in his expression. He knew. Dear heaven. He knew what his mere presence was doing to her.

"Come here," he said softly, his voice thick.

"I—" She tried to speak. The sound she uttered was a hoarse croak, so unfamiliar that she was stunned into silence.

Anthony held his hand toward her, a simple gesture that drew her more strongly than any pretty phrases. She wanted to go to him. To step into his arms and feel their hard strength surround her. To live for a single second the dream of being loved by him. He wanted her. Of that she was certain. Just as she was certain that he offered her nothing.

"What do you want of me?" She forced the words out. They might have sounded plaintive had she used a different tone. Instead, the question sounded like a challenge. Better to have him say it than to let her mind conjure his thoughts. After all, she might be wrong.

"What do I want of you?" His brow furrowed as he contemplated her question; then he gave a self-deprecating bark of laughter. "I want what I have no right to. I want to see you naked in my bed, your hair unpinned and spread on my pillow. Or to see you clad only in your black stockings, nothing more. So I can peel them off slowly. Run my tongue along the back of your calf, your thigh, to your pretty round bottom."

His words were scandalous, terrible. Wonderful. He should not speak to her so. *Oh, but he should,* a tiny voice whispered. He should say those things and do those things, because if the mere sound of his voice could send such unbearable pleasure ripping through her, what then would she feel if he matched action to thought?

She sank her teeth into her lower lip and shook her head in confusion.

When she did not speak, he continued, "That night in the portrait gallery, I could have taken you."

He paused, perhaps waiting for her to contradict him. Closing her eyes, Emma longed to cover her ears, to block out the truth of his words. But she offered no denial. He *could* have taken her that night,

there against the stone wall, with the portrait of
his dead wife looking on. Even then she had been
enthralled despite her fear, half in love with the
Lord of Manorbrier.

Anthony took a single step closer. "But I have no
desire to *take*. What do I want of you, Emma? Only
that which you wish to give."

"I do not wish to give you anything." The words
came out in a breathy rush, jumbling together in
their haste to leave her tongue. They were a pitiful
attempt to deny her feelings, her overwhelming
desire for him. If she did not force the lie out
quickly, she would not be able to say it at all.

Emma's retreat brought her to the wall. Her back
pressed against the solid surface. Burying her fingers
in the coarse weave of her skirt, she thought of her
mother's warnings, ringing in her ears from the time
she was a child, and she thought of Meg. *The babe's
father ain't going to claim it, or me. Quality never do.*

Was that what she wanted? To be like Meg? Like
her mother? Pregnant and alone? She would jeop-
ardize her place here, her chance to make a difference in Nicky's life, her opportunity to love and
raise him.

A low moan of distress escaped her. She felt
unbalanced, besotted.

Looking at him, the perfection of Anthony
Craven, Emma tried to sort through her thoughts.
He offered her nothing. But was that true? He did not
offer marriage. Respectability. Home and children. But she had no chance of those, regardless.
He offered her a taste of life. For a moment, a
week, a month, she could have *him*. And when it
was done, she would have the memories of him

for a lifetime. The idea was a temptation of the most compelling kind.

"Why me?" she asked breathlessly. "You could dally with a village girl, or go to London. I am certain you would have little trouble satisfying your—" She stopped abruptly, unable to form the words to reflect accurately the shadowy picture in her mind.

"I could," he agreed, apparently taking pity on her. Allowing her the dignity of leaving her thoughts unspoken.

Why me? Why me? Her question hung between them, unanswered. Emma had the sudden insight that perhaps he could not explain their attraction. He simply felt it, as did she.

"I could not endure it if you send me away. From Nicky, I mean. I do love him, my lord." Her breath came in short, shallow gasps that accentuated each sentence she spoke.

He did not reply, merely held her pinned by his hot gaze, plundering her soul with the desire she read there.

She ought to make a sensible decision, though that hardly seemed possible while her heart pounded in her chest and her mind invented unfulfilled images of Anthony touching her. And she touching him.

"Anthony," he reminded her in a rough whisper, taking another step closer. "The way your breath catches as you whisper my name pleases me."

With a quick dart of her tongue Emma wet her lips. They felt swollen. She felt swollen. Her breasts and, there, between her legs.

He took his time crossing the remainder of the space that separated them. His gaze remained locked on hers and she thought he must know the secrets of her deepest thoughts, her private yearning, her unutterable confusion.

"Do you understand what goes on between a man and a woman?" His voice was soft, pouring over her like warm honey.

Unable to speak, Emma nodded. One could hardly grow up in a rural setting and not acquire some basic knowledge of procreation. Though she doubted that human activities were an exact replica of barnyard animals, she had a basic idea that two bodies merged as one. And when she had lived with her aunts, Annie, the downstairs maid, had been fairly forthcoming in her tales of the nocturnal activities in which she had participated, along with suggestions of how a girl could avoid getting caught.

Anthony leaned closer, the luscious scent of him and the heat of his body such potent lures. She had ample time to flee, to deny the craving that gnawed at her feminine core with an intensity that was almost painful. Though her mind warned her that her chosen course was folly, she stood unmoving, her back pressed against the solid wall.

Her body wanted this, ached for it. She wanted this, wanted him.

She gasped as Anthony's palm came flat against the wall, just above her left shoulder. Turning her head, she looked at his splayed fingers and then returned her gaze to his.

"I do not wish to be a sensible girl," Emma whispered. Her heart pounded in delicious expectation, and she was darkly, fiercely glad that he had come to her.

He made a sound low in his throat, half groan, half laugh; she couldn't describe it. But it triggered a crashing wave of desire that tore through her body with the violence of a storm. Emma was thankful for the support of the wall at her back, else she might have melted into a boneless puddle at his feet. The sound of her breathing—or was it his?—registered in her mind, harsh and rough.

Again she licked her lips. He took it as an invitation, leaning forward enough to run his tongue along the corner of her mouth. She cried out softly, stunned by the contact. As her lips parted, he pressed his mouth to hers. His tongue slid inside, just a bit, just enough to let her taste him. And then deeper, lips and tongue and teeth. Wet, dark pleasure.

He braced himself on outstretched arms, holding his body from her, touching her only with his mouth. It was not enough. The tips of her breasts strained against the cloth of her bodice. Emma arched her spine, wanting more, wanting to feel the whole of his hard length pressed against her. Such heat. Such need.

"Ah-h-h-h." A lingering, slow exhalation resonated with her pleasure as Anthony deliberately lowered his weight, pinning her to the wall, his long body molding to hers, his muscled thigh between her own. Lush sensation, foreign and far too enticing.

She inhaled through his mouth, through hers, light-headed with longing, the taste and feel of him spilling through her with that luscious endless kiss. With a low groan he slid his body on hers, rubbing against her as he pushed his tongue into her mouth, making her ache and want and gasp, on fire for him. Tilting her head, she sucked him deeper, then caught his lower lips between her teeth, biting, sucking, sliding her hands around his waist, and lower, until her palms pressed against the hard

globes of his buttocks, the cloth of his breeches soft
and smooth to her touch.

She curled her fingers, felt the fine flex of muscle
as she pulled him closer, rubbing slowly back and
forth, moving with blind instinct, her hips tight to
his, and the wet throbbing heat of her desire
pounding at her core. Poised on the edge of a
precipice, if she simply took a step she would fall
into . . . into . . . *something*. But she had no idea
which way to step, how to relieve this pressure that
built inside her like steam inside a covered cooking
pot. She was boiling and churning—

"Oh, please. Oh, I . . . I need . . ."

Pulling back, he looked down at her and pressed
his fingers to her lips, cutting off what she might
have said. Emma slid her tongue into the crack between his fingers, licking, tasting. A sharp hiss of air
escaped him, and she felt a profound feminine
thrill, for whatever wild yearning writhed at her core,
its mate lived within him. She felt it calling to her.

"You want me," she whispered, half seductress,
half pleased innocent.

"I do." His voice was deep and raspy. So masculine.

A last vestige of common sense made her speak.
"You will honor your word . . . you will not send me
away from Nicky? When we are done? When it is
over?" Oh, that she was so beguiled by him, that the
words escaped her on a breathy gasp, that she truly
intended to deny all she had been, all she was, the
illegitimate daughter of a woman who had made
exactly this mistake.

At her question, something shifted in his eyes,
heat and need fading to cool bottle-green glass. She
frowned, oddly distressed, sensing a change in him
as he slowly blew out a breath and pulled away.

"No." All her disappointment centered in that one word, crushing, terrible disappointment as he pulled back even farther. She loved the feel of his kiss, the way his lips and tongue stroked, caressed, and his teeth, gentle nips and slow bites. More. She wanted more.

"Shh . . . shh . . ." Anthony stroked her hair, leaning forward to press his lips to her temple. She wriggled against him, wanting the press of his hips flush with hers. She had been so close, so close to . . . to some unknown thing that would happen if he would only push his hips back where they had been, if he would only kiss her as he had a moment past.

"Greedy girl," he murmured, as though reading her thoughts. Or perhaps she had whispered her need. ·

Lost. The moment was lost. She could sense it in him, and she wished she could grab hold and pull back whatever it was she had said that changed his mood so.

"Am I the first to kiss you?" he asked, one brow lifted questioningly. There was something in his tone. Though he was not smiling, she thought he might be laughing at her, enjoying some dark, private humor.

Knowing she could not possibly speak, Emma nodded her head. The kiss they had shared in the field the day before he left, and now this . . . this kiss that made a lovely pulsing ache throb hot and wet in her loins.

"*This* from an innocent." Now he did laugh, the sound grating, rife with self-mockery. "You would kill me in my bed, Emma Parrish. I should die from exhaustion, I suspect. And likely I would love every moment of it."

She frowned at his words, not grasping his meaning. At length, her heart slowed its breakneck pace, and her breathing could almost be described as normal. She licked her lips slowly, enjoying the feel of her tongue against the soft skin, the taste of him that lingered still.

"I don't understand."

"I know." He ran the pad of his thumb across her lower lip. "I am thinking that I am a lucky man to have discovered you. And that I am a fool not to take advantage of my good fortune."

What is it? What have I done wrong? Emma fought the urge to reach out and drag him back against her. One minute he was kissing her, touching her, rubbing his body against her until she thought she might go mad with the teasing tantalizing pleasure of it, and the next he was gone. Walled off from her behind that icy reserve. "Why?" she whispered.

His expression altered as he stared at her, a subtle shift that changed him from lover to remote lord. "I can offer you nothing but a mindless dalliance. You deserve far more, and I am incapable of giving it. When you asked if I would honor my word . . . you reminded me that you deserve to be treated honorably." He frowned, glanced away then back. "You are a woman of rare integrity, Emma mine. You merit far better treatment and consideration."

So she had stopped him with her words. Unwittingly. A part of her was so very proud that she had saved herself from disgrace, from ruination, from the path of the same terrible mistake that had been her mother's. But, oh, her body ached with the disappointment of the broken spell.

Stepping away, he bent and retrieved her discarded broom, then crossed the room to lift the bucket of dirty water. Emma watched his strange actions, feeling bereft and confused. He was correct. She did deserve more, and she was horrified that for even the briefest moment she had considered accepting less.

Anthony turned to face her with a clear look of regret. "Do you remember, Emma, when I told you that I am not a kind man?"

"Yes." Her every feeling—relief, disappointment, dismay—poured into that single word.

"I am about to do something kind, though I am sure that a certain part of my anatomy will ill appreciate my generosity." He made a crude gesture toward the rigid prominence that strained the buttons of his breeches.

Emma glanced away, at once offended and equally fascinated. She suspected he had known exactly what he was about, had acted on purpose to distance himself from her.

"And what is this kindness you speak of?" she asked, though she already knew.

"I want you, Emma Parrish." Words spoken low and rough, sending a fresh wave of longing pulsing through her. She stared at the floor, unable to look in his eyes. "I want to take the clothes from your body, touch you, your legs, your waist, your breasts while I pin you beneath me, warm and willing. I want to thrust myself inside you, my tongue in your mouth, my body pushed deep inside yours."

"I . . ." What? What could she say to that? She had thought to kiss him, to press herself against him and run her hands over his corded muscle. Through the safety of shirt and breeches. She had thought no further, though she had claimed she had. When he asked her if she knew the way of a man and a woman, she had said she did. There was no lie to the words, but she had not thought what they meant. To her. To him. Dear heaven. *My body pushed deep inside yours.* The words made her feel flushed, confused, strangely enticed and repelled at once.

He blew out a slow breath. "I shall refrain from accepting the precious treasure that you offer." Her gaze slammed back to his, and she found him watching her through eyes hard and bright, edged with barely banked lust. Then his expression softened, and his next words were spoken in a tone of wonder. "Because I find that I *like* you, Emma Parrish. Truly, and in the finest sense of the word. And more than that, I admire you. Strange, to say those words." He shook his head. "I admire your courage, your honest and true heart."

His words made her heart swell in a terrible mixture of elation and despondency. Such idle commentary to him, but to her, the finest compliment she had ever heard. He admired her, and she could hear in the cadence of his speech, the soft incredulity of it, that his thoughts surprised him. And how did she feel about that?

"I have no wish to see you ruined. You are saved by my fond regard." A rueful smile curved his lips. "And I am damned by it." He exhaled slowly, a harsh huff of air. "I shall return these things to the scullery for you."

Turning from her, Anthony lifted the cleaning implements that he had gathered and quit the room, leaving Emma alone and baffled. Lord Anthony Craven had cleared the room, no better than any scullery maid, sloshing dirty water on his fine boots, and all to escape her simple wiles.

You are saved by my fond regard.

"Saved?" She drew a shaky breath, struggling to let go of the tight yearning that wound her in knots, the longing for him, the insistent throb between her legs that demanded surcease. "Saved from you for the moment, perhaps," she whispered. "But what will save me from myself?"

Emma paused to gather her composure outside Lord Craven's library the following afternoon. She was wary of him, of being alone with him, tied in knots by the heated recollections of his touch, his kiss, the press of his muscled body on hers. When Mrs. Bolifer had requested that she carry a message to the library, it had been all Emma could do not to turn and bid the housekeeper deliver it herself, but Nicky was well occupied helping Cookie bake a cake, leaving Emma without a viable reason to decline the housekeeper's request.

She did not want to face him yet.

Through the partially open door she watched as Lord Craven paced his library like a caged beast. Twelve paces across. Twelve back.

He had bid her call him Anthony, but to do so was so intimate, so tempting. Even in her thoughts she would be wise to maintain her distance.

The thought of facing him now, with this new and intimate knowledge between them, was unsettling in the extreme. Yet reason decreed that 'twould be better to face him sooner rather than later.

Lord Craven stood beside his desk, contemplating a half full glass of brandy that sat on one corner near the edge. After a moment, he picked up the drink and tossed it back in a single swallow before moving to stand by the window. She thought he looked pensive, a touch forlorn. For her? Did he carry such melancholic burden because of what had passed between them? Her heart lurched at the thought.

Drawing upon her reserves of composure, Emma bolstered her courage and knocked on the door.

"Come in." Lord Craven turned away from the window and circled the desk.

"I am sorry to intrude, my lord. Mrs. Bolifer sent me with a message." Emma stood hesitantly in the doorway, feeling uncertain. Her nerves remained in shambles, her emotions yet to recover from the wild passion that had overtaken her the previous afternoon. She forced herself to meet his gaze.

His expression betrayed nothing, a cool expanse of absent emotion. How very adept he was at masking his thoughts.

"Nicky is baking a cake," she said, then hesitated, wishing she could simply turn and run, knowing that she must face him, face her own yearning and wrest it into submission if she wished to remain at Manorbrier. "Mrs. Bolifer sent me."

"So you said." Lord Craven glanced at the empty brandy glass in his hand, as if only now recollecting it, or perhaps hoping it would provide a means of escape. With deliberate care he set it on the desk, then returned his gaze to Emma.

Why, he is as ill at ease as I am, she thought in surprise.

"Did Mrs. Bolifer mention anything about Bosherton?" he asked.

"None dead. None sick. That is the message she sent." Pursing her lips, Emma frowned, confused as to the meaning of such cryptic communication as much as by the inaccuracy of it.

Lord Craven nodded.

"But the message makes no sense. Meg told me that her mother has consumption. Surely she must count among the sick." Emma glanced away, unable to meet his eyes, her thoughts centered on the memory of Meg's pregnant belly, and the unanswered question of who was the father. She thought of Anthony's kisses, those lovely, heady kisses, and her heart twisted at the possibility that he had kissed Meg the very same way.

"Meg's mother is coughing her life away," he muttered.

She glanced back to find him staring at the floor, his hands shoved deep in his pockets, as though he could not bring himself to look at her.

Or as though he would succumb to wild and desperate passion at the mere sight of her. Her cheeks heated, every thought drawn back to the very subject she so wished to avoid. Lord Craven's kisses, the scent of him swirling around her, and the lovely stroke of his tongue, inside her, inside her mouth, the glide of his lips across hers.

Look at me, she thought. Turn your gaze upon me and warm me to the depths of my soul.

"Cookie says spirit of saffron will help," she blurted into the growing silence, her gaze fixed on his full lower lip, the dark shadow of his jaw, the strong column of his throat. She shook her head, desperate now to clear it of these tempting and wholly inappropriate thoughts.

"The woman needs something more than spirit of saffron if she's to last out the year, Emma." His tone was laced with genuine regret.

"Can you not help her?"

At her softly voiced question, Lord Craven lifted

his gaze to meet hers, and there she saw a bleak and sad despair. "No, I cannot. I attempted to ascertain the causal agent of her condition. But Meg's mother would have no part in it." He shook his head. "Like as not, she thought me a lunatic."

"No!" Emma exclaimed. "Surely she knew you would help. . . ."

He shot her a sardonic glance. "The villagers think me cracked. The Mad Lord of Manorbrier, who locks himself in the tower with corpses, who rides to the village in the dark of night to take blood that flows no more from a body that will never move again. I pay them well, the mourners who circle like anxious hens, clucking and moaning while I do my strange work. Blood money ensures that none remain in the room while I practice my macabre arts."

She had surmised some small bit of this from the words Meg had spoken during their conversation in the scullery. Still, he painted a ghoulish scene, one that left her feeling horribly uncomfortable, as she was certain he had intended. He presented himself in a manner that could only be described as off-putting, as a fiend, a terrible beast with dark and mad intent.

"But why do you let them think that? Why do you encourage it?" She was appalled that he nurtured and fed such ludicrous suspicions, could not understand why he did not defend himself. Suddenly, she recalled her own suspicions and fears, and his lack of explanation even to her. The realization hurt, even though she understood the source. He wanted to hold her far away, to cultivate and maintain a distance between them, his border of safety where she might not pass.

Was that her answer, then? Did he dare let no one near, using his odd behavior as a shield, the frightening stories as a buffer to hold any and all at bay?

To hold *her* at bay.

Lord Craven took a step toward her. "They think me unbalanced, yet my coin buys their cooperation. More often than not, that coin is all that stands between an entire family and starvation. Desperation always proves to be an excellent motivator, and I am left to do as I will. Better that they are wary of me. I want no one to see me as a savior, no one to think that I might play the hero and snatch them from death's cold embrace."

"But . . ." Emma stumbled over her question, confusion tangling her tongue. Dropping her gaze, she studied the pattern in the carpet that covered the polished wood floor. She did not understand this man or his motivations.

He was unutterably attractive, titled, wealthy.

Damaged. Wounded.

She longed to take away his pain, but how to heal a wound she could not see or name?

A current stirred the air and she felt his presence beside her. Raising her head, she met his gaze, and suddenly, she understood him very well, for in his eyes she read desire. Blatant. Hot. Barely suppressed. Mirroring her own sharp and vivid longings.

"Emma," he rasped, running the pad of his thumb along her cheek, "so tempting, so innocently sensual in your response. You rubbed yourself against me like a kitten looking to be petted."

Mortified, she could not answer. There was no denial, no defense against the naked truth of his statement. His words embarrassed her, even as they made her burn with agonized heat. She stood, frozen, reveling in the feel of his hand cupping her cheek, knowing she should pull away. No good could come of this mad infatuation.

"You are my son's governess, a woman in my employ, under my protection. What manner of man would take advantage of such a situation?"

The question made her think again of Meg, of her overlarge belly and practical disposition. She stared at him, trying to see into his soul. "Have you ever?"

He blinked, his brow furrowing in puzzlement. Then her meaning dawned, and he dropped his hand to his side.

"Have I ever taken advantage of my position?" He gave a strangled laugh. "Yesterday, I carried the broom and bucket of dirty water to the scullery like a common servant in order to avoid the temptation of remaining in the same room with you. The temptation to finish what I had started." His lips curved in a bemused smile. "I do not think I have been to the scullery in my entire life."

Was that an answer? Emma wondered. Did the man never say a simple yes or no?

Still, the knot in her heart eased just a little.

Striding to the window, Lord Craven flicked open the curtain and stared out at the garden awash in the glow of the late afternoon sun.

"I can offer you nothing." His tone was flat. "That will not change."

He could offer her nothing. At least he offered her the truth, refraining from giving voice to lies and pretty promises he had no intention of keeping.

"In order to offer you anything save a tawdry liaison, I must offer my heart on a platter, offer it to be shredded, betrayed." He looked back at her, watching her, eyes narrowed and unblinking. "That I will not do a second time."

A second time.

"Delia," Emma whispered, more to herself than to him, stunned that he had shared so much of himself. She had never expected that. In vivid detail, she recalled his anger that night in the portrait gallery, his pain. Again, her doubts surfaced, and she wondered what hold his dead wife had upon him, for she was no mere ghost. She was a solid wall, as real and true as mortar and stone, cold, hard, unyielding, circling Anthony Craven's heart.

Dragging in a breath, Emma turned toward the door, desperate to be away from this room, from him, from dreams and wants that could never be. She drew up short when she saw Mrs. Bolifer's stout form filling the doorway. How long had the housekeeper been standing there and what she had overheard? Her expression was shuttered, providing no clue.

Wariness flooded Emma as she wondered why the housekeeper had sent her with a message, then come to the library herself.

"Mrs. Bolifer." The air stirred, and there was the shush of booted feet on carpet as Lord Craven moved from the window. Emma felt him draw close behind her. "There is smallpox in Derrymore. Sally Gibbons's mother hails from there. You are certain there are none sick in Bosherton?"

"Yes, my lord. I asked Meg this morning. She said all is well. Even her mother seems to be feeling a touch better. Sat out in the sun for a bit yesterday. Though the day before that was bad. She coughed up enough blood to change her handkerchief red. Consumption's a terrible thing." Mrs. Bolifer skewed her lips to the side and then let out a quick huff of air.

Emma sidled toward the door, hoping to slip away undetected, desperate to be alone with her confused thoughts. At the last moment, she cast a wary glance over her shoulder and found Lord Craven watching her, his expression unreadable. She slipped into the hallway and pushed her hand into the pocket of her dress.

Oh, dear. The key to the upstairs rooms. She had meant to return it to Mrs. Bolifer, but the task had slipped her mind. Turning back, she paused just outside the open door, waiting for a break in the conversation before announcing her presence.

"Was there anything more?" Lord Craven asked.

"My lord, there is one thing." The housekeeper lowered her voice. "She *met* him. They spoke."

"Did they?" His tone was cold and clipped. "Here? He came to Manorbrier in my absence?"

"No, he did not come here. Miss Parrish was out walking one day and came across him quite by accident."

The sound of her name gave Emma a start. How odd. They were speaking of *her,* and after a moment she realized they discussed her brief interview with Dr. Smythe.

Lord Craven swore softly. "There was nothing accidental about it, you may be sure. Not on his part. How did he know she would be out that day?"

"She was out every day."

"You let her roam about? Why was no one with her?"

"I could hardly lock her in her room, my lord," came Mrs. Bolifer's aggrieved tone. "She is a woman grown. There was little enough to occupy her in your absence. I suspect she was bored."

"Mrs. Bolifer," Lord Craven's voice was silky, interwoven with a thread of steel, "do you take me to task for the governess' boredom?"

"No, my lord. I simply point out that she took up the habit of walking, and you made no mention of setting a watchdog at her heels."

"I assumed her injured ankle would keep her close to home," he replied. "I should have guessed that our Miss Parrish would not settle for a life of leisure." A brief silence followed, and Emma pressed her back to the wall as she agonized over the inappropriateness of eavesdropping on this conversation. She had not meant to, had intended merely to return the key, but she was curious as to how they had known that she met Dr. Smythe. She had not hidden the fact, but neither had she had a reason to mention such an innocuous meeting to anyone.

"You have been in my employ too long, Mrs. Bolifer. Your tongue has grown free, and your manner disrespectful." The subtle humor in his tone softened his words. She recalled such wit from the night he had so irreverently, so accurately, mimicked Cecilia and Hortense.

"Someone must remind you that you are only human, my lord."

Emma stifled a gasp at the housekeeper's temerity.

"I know exactly what I am, Mrs. Bolifer," Lord Craven said quietly. "There is no need to remind me."

"My lord—" Mrs. Bolifer began.

"Tell Griggs to send word that if there are signs of smallpox I am to be notified immediately," Lord Craven interjected. "I'll take the blood of the dead. The blood of the ill and dying, even better."

CHAPTER NINE

Less than an hour had passed since Emma had overheard the exceedingly odd conversation between the housekeeper and Lord Craven, and her understanding of their dialogue was no clearer now than it had been then. Thrusting her hand into the pocket of her skirt, she curled her fingers around the key to the upstairs rooms, the cold metal ridges pressing into her skin. A convenient reason to seek out Mrs. Bolifer. An opening for a long-overdue discussion.

Closing her eyes briefly, she stiffened her resolve before rapping lightly on the closed door of Mrs. Bolifer's private apartment.

"Yes?" The housekeeper's voice sounded impatient.

Emma smiled. It was nice to know that some things would always be as expected.

"Mrs. Bolifer? May I speak with you?"

A rustling sound, the scrape of a chair along the wooden floor, then the door was pulled open a crack. Mrs. Bolifer glared at her through the thin opening, gray eyes narrowed in undisguised irritability.

"I am working on the household accounts, Miss Parrish. What do you want?" She opened the door a fraction of an inch wider, and a soft scent drifted into the hallway. *Like freshly squeezed lemons*, Emma thought, frowning. There was something familiar about the smell, something odd. A medicinal quality that made it less than pleasant.

"I should like to speak with you for a moment, if I may." Emma angled herself into the opening, hoping that the housekeeper would not slam the door in her face.

"Only for a moment." Grudgingly, Mrs. Bolifer stepped back, indicating that Emma might enter.

Emma stepped through, surreptitiously studying her surroundings and finding them rather unexpected. She would have predicted the housekeeper's apartment to be drab and gray, not unlike the woman herself. Somehow, she had imagined that Mrs. Bolifer would live in a stark and dark environment, with heavy furniture and cheerless decoration. Instead she found a bright room painted buttercream yellow, with curtains of a slightly darker hue adorning the windows. They were pulled back with tasseled ties, letting the daylight stream through the glass panes.

A lovely embroidered settee was against the far wall, and a matching chair angled toward the hearth. On the mantelpiece sat a cut-glass vase with pale pink roses that had yet to reach their full bloom. Two small gilt-framed miniature portraits flanked the vase. Emma caught a glimpse of a stern-faced man portrayed in one, and a young girl, her lips turned up in the hint of a smile, depicted in the second.

The housekeeper crossed to a small round table

with two delicately carved high-back chairs. She sat down in the chair facing Emma. With unblinking gaze and taciturn mien she flipped the cover of her journal closed and rested her open palm against the dark leather jacket, her fingers splayed outward, as if holding in the secrets of the tome they rested upon.

Though the second chair stood empty, Mrs. Bolifer did not offer it.

"Well? What do you want?" The housekeeper drummed her fingers on the book as she waited for Emma's response.

"I came to return the key to the rooms on the upper floor."

The drumming stopped abruptly. Mrs. Bolifer's fingers hung frozen above the leather journal, curled like unsheathed claws. "Give it here, then."

Pulling the key from her pocket, Emma drew closer. The odd smell she had noted earlier grew stronger. Lemons. Only laced with something disagreeable and foul.

Her breath caught in her throat. She *knew* that medicinal scent, recalled it too well, for it had swirled around her when she had stood in the icehouse. 'Twas the scent of locked doors, of malice and cruel intent.

"You did not find any secrets there, did you?" Mrs. Bolifer rubbed her maimed shoulder through the cloth of her dress, and the pungent aroma grew stronger, surrounding Emma in a rank eddy, leaving her belly roiling with a faint nausea.

For a moment she thought Mrs. Bolifer spoke of the icehouse, openly acknowledging what she had done. But, no, she referred to the rooms on the third floor, Emma realized. She swallowed. "No. I found nothing save a thick film of dust and heavy, stale air."

Her gaze fastened on Mrs. Bolifer's hand, working her shoulder round and round, and the smell growing ever stronger. *Had* the housekeeper locked her in the icehouse, intending for her to fall? Did Lord Craven know, and was that the reason for the odd conversation she had overheard?

The thought seemed ludicrous, as did the possibility that Lord Craven would countenance his housekeeper stalking governesses like prey.

Anxious now to be away, Emma dropped the key on the table and quickly crossed to the door. She heard the rustle of Mrs. Bolifer's stiff black skirt as she adjusted her position, and the faint creak of the chair. With her hand resting on the brass knob, Emma spoke over her shoulder, spurred by some inexplicable need to know for certain just who her enemy was.

"Do you smell lemons?" she asked.

When no reply was forthcoming, Emma turned toward the glacial silence of the room. The housekeeper sat with quill poised midair over the journal. Her cheeks were flushed and her brows drawn down in a scowl.

"My liniment. Cookie swears by it. She obtained the recipe from the village doctor, and she mixes a batch for me every few weeks. Goose grease melted with horseradish juice, mustard, and turpentine. And a grated rind of lemon with the juice added just to cut the smell." Mrs. Bolifer grunted. "I use it for my arm. The one that is gone."

From the village doctor? Did she mean Dr. Smythe? "Does it pain you still?" Emma asked, a flutter of sympathy tugging at her heart.

The housekeeper laughed mirthlessly. "Not as much as the deed itself. Less than two minutes it took. But the longest two minutes of my life. Sometimes, I wake at night and think it's still there. I reach for the glass beside my bed. I can feel my fingers close around it. But, of course, they don't. The fingers are gone, and the glass is left standing on the table."

Emma made a soft sound of sympathy. "How terrible."

"Terrible? Maybe. But it was either this or a shroud and a cold grave. So he cut it off. I begged and screamed, but there were none to save me. My man was dead. My arm was worse than dead. Rotten to the core, stinking worse than a rancid meat pie . . ." Mrs. Bolifer's voice trailed away, and she stared at a spot on the ceiling, her eyes glazed and distant.

"Dear heaven." The images wrought by the housekeeper's words were appalling, and the ghastly sensibility made Emma light-headed. She moved to the table and sank into the empty chair, uninvited.

"You would think a person would forget after seven long years. But there are nights when the pain is as fresh as yesterday. And today, well, today I'm glad for Cookie's liniment."

"Have you mentioned this to Lord Craven? Perhaps he has some cure . . . ."

"Oh, aye. He has a cure." Mrs. Bolifer gave a sharp squawk of laughter, the harsh sound grating on Emma's nerves. "He's the one who cured it in the first place, and faster than any he was."

Emma pressed her fingers to her lips, her eyes stinging with tears of empathy, and then the horrifying understanding of Mrs. Bolifer's implication set in, leaving her thoughts spinning and her heart racing. "Lord Craven cut off your arm," she whispered.

"And paid a price for it himself. He wanted to spare my suffering, and worked faster than the wings of a hummingbird, so I've been told. But his own hand got caught in the blade and he carved himself at the same time as he did me. Didn't stop him. He finished the deed, and only when it was done did he tend to his own wound."

The words slammed into Emma and a dark haze narrowed her vision as bitter bile clawed its way up her throat. The room spun and swayed and a shadowy tunnel narrowed her sight.

"Don't you go and faint on me, girl. I don't keep smelling salts." Mrs. Bolifer slapped her lightly on the cheek.

"No, of course not," Emma murmured, then continued in a stronger voice. "I have never fainted in my life."

"Well, if you didn't just fall into a faint, my girl, then what would you call it? A nice nap?" Mrs. Bolifer laughed, a short, sharp sound. "What set you off? My story of how His Lordship lopped off my arm?"

Emma cringed. "The notion is rather unsettling," she conceded, though in truth the concept so horrified her that she felt ill. Yet, Lord Craven had saved Mrs. Bolifer's life and been hurt himself in the process. She thought back to their conversation in his study, when he had told her that Delia had hated his maimed hand. He had saved Mrs. Bolifer's life but paid for his good deed both with his own blood and with his heart.

Mrs. Bolifer stared at her for a protracted moment.

"The notion is rather unsettling," she mimicked. Then to Emma's overwhelming astonishment, the woman threw back her head and laughed, loud and full, no restraint to her mirth. And then as she settled back, the housekeeper pulled a small tin from the pocket of her voluminous black dress. She held the tin in her palm and used the tip of her thumb to flip the lid off, with amazing dexterity. "Lemon drop?"

"No, thank you." Emma eyed the sweet with revulsion. Never again would she regard anything with a lemony scent or taste in quite the same way as she had in the past.

Placing the open tin on the table, Mrs. Bolifer helped herself, tucked the candy in her cheek, and spoke around it.

"I was burned in a fire," she said matter-of-factly, answering a question Emma had not dared to ask. "My man was dead from the smoke. I only thank God he didn't live long enough to burn. My arm was charred blacker than coal, and the pain was worse than any I ever thought could be. No wonder there are fires in hell. Don't think there is a worse pain a body could suffer." Mrs. Bolifer fell silent for a moment, her eyes focused on some distant vision of the past. "Except, maybe, the pain of loneliness."

"How terrible for you," Emma whispered, reaching over to place her hand over Mrs. Bolifer's, intent on offering comfort. Her own unsettled stomach seemed a paltry discomfort in the face of the other woman's suffering. To be burned in a fire, and lose her husband that selfsame night. . . .

"No wonder then," she murmured. At the housekeeper's blank look, Emma explained, "The night I first arrived at Manorbrier, you warned me never to leave a candle unattended. And most of the house was dark. The whole thing was a bit unsettling, but now it makes perfect sense."

"Hmm. Does it now?" Pulling her hand away from Emma's gentle grasp, Mrs. Bolifer stood and crossed to the hearth. She took one of the miniatures from the mantelpiece. Gazing at the picture for a long moment, she moved to Emma's side and held it out for the younger woman's inspection.

"My husband," she said, a wealth of emotion buried in those two simple words. Pain, loss, and heartbreak, softened only slightly by the intervening years. Mrs. Bolifer's marriage had been a love match, Emma realized with surprise.

"He buried it under the rosebushes."

"I beg your pardon?" Emma breathed, disoriented by the housekeeper's disjointed statement.

"I could not bear the thought of my arm being tossed out like refuse. And I do love roses."

"Your arm is buried under the rosebushes?" Emma glanced at the window, appalled. She walked beside those bushes almost every day. Never would she look at them in the same way.

"Not here," Mrs. Bolifer snapped. "Under *my* rosebushes. I had a small cottage on the outskirts of London. My daughter's husband rebuilt it after the fire. She lives there now, with him."

Emma had always imagined Mrs. Bolifer to be a lost soul, alone in the world, trapped in Lord Craven's employ.

"Were you in Lord Craven's employ before the fire?" she asked.

"No. No. I never knew Lord Craven before that day. But his offer of a position is what kept me sane. Gave me a purpose where I had none." She paused.

"My daughter was married by then, with a little one on the way. And her husband is a decent sort but not fond of my company." Mrs. Bolifer jerked her chin toward the miniature that remained on the mantle. "So there you have it."

Gave me a purpose where I had none. As he had done for Emma, offering her a home, a place, a child to love. She saw it now, the glittering thread of good that wove through his actions. He took those scarred by life and loss, and he offered them hope. "And Griggs? And Cookie?" she asked. "Did he give them a purpose where they had none?"

"Aye."

"Where are Cookie's scars?" Emma asked softly, barely daring to ask, but certain she wished to know. They were there. Hidden where none could see.

"In her heart. Her son died."

"Ohhh . . . Oh, how terrible." Emma felt the salt sting of tears prick her eyes. Poor Cookie.

"He died and she wanted to be with him, tried to be with him. Thought no child should be separated from his parent."

Emma stared at her, and then growing certainty made her flinch. Had Cookie tried to take her own life, to follow her child to the hereafter? She could not make her lips form the question, and so she sat in unhappy silence.

The housekeeper glanced up, then down. "Enough of idle chat, now," she muttered and then briskly flipped open the journal she had been working on earlier, her actions signaling the end of the interview. Emma eased to her feet, feeling more confused than when she had first arrived. The conversation with the housekeeper had answered little and given rise to a slew of fresh questions and concerns.

* * *

Nicky was asleep. Emma sat at his bedside, her own eyelids drooping. The child had chattered endlessly about ice cream and ponies before exhaustion overtook him at last. Placing a kiss on his forehead, she rose and went into her own adjoining chamber, the one she had moved into at Lord Craven's behest.

Leaving the door between the two rooms slightly ajar, she walked softly across the carpeted floor, her fingers trailing along the heavy curtains of the large canopied bed. She glanced at the nearby table and paused to retrieve the diary that sat, forgotten, on the polished surface. She had tossed it there the day she discovered it and had yet to find the time to read it. No. That was untrue. She had not wished to look at the diary, for it brought to mind unsettling emotions and thoughts of the other things she had discovered that afternoon—the sweet ache of desire to be found in Anthony's arms, the yearning fueled by his kiss.

Her mouth felt dry, and she licked her lips. She could hear his voice, his sensual baritone, stroking her, promising untold delights. *I want to thrust myself inside you, my tongue in your mouth, my body pushed deep inside yours.* She could think of naught else. Her wayward imaginings burgeoned and grew until she closed her eyes and gave in to her longing. She could almost taste him, feel the wet thrust of his tongue, twining with hers, teasing her until she was molten and burning with dark passion. A gnawing hunger tugged at her breasts, and low in her belly, and there, between her thighs.

The temptation to hurry from her chamber and seek him out was nearly overwhelming.

A soft cry escaped her and she paced forward, back, until, resolutely, she yanked her thoughts from places they should not wander and focused on the small leather journal in her hand. Mild curiosity teased her, and she welcomed it, anything to relieve the mad yearning that chewed at her insides. She carried the diary to the low window seat and sank down onto the cushioned surface. After removing her boots, she tucked her stockinged feet underneath her.

Carefully opening the diary to the first entry, Emma ran her finger over the delicate, feminine script. She recognized her cousin Delia's flowery hand from the letters that she had posted with regularity to the aunts.

I am ever so happy, Emma read. *I have met the man I shall marry. And like a princess in a fairy story, I shall live happily ever after.* Pity tugged at Emma's heart. There had been no happy ending for her cousin, only an early death.

I met L.S. and am quite enamored of him. But, alas, he is a simple country doctor, without title or vast means. A shame that our association can have no future, for I sense in him my kindred spirit, my true mate. Instead, I have decided to marry Lord P. Emma's brow furrowed in confusion. Lord P.? Who was Lord P.? She read on, her curiosity piqued. The pages spread before her an endless catalogue of balls and soirees, and tidbits of nasty gossip that illustrated how sad and shallow Delia's life must have been for her to find her only joy in the misfortunes of others.

Miss C. was caught kissing Lord Q. in the garden, Delia wrote. *Lord L. wore a stained cravat and the ladies laughed behind their fans. The Dowager Countess of S. passed wind at the opera.* And at the end of each description of each ball, Delia listed the initial of a lord she had decided to marry. It seemed the same lord was never listed twice.

Emma was stunned by this insight into Delia's character. The aunts had always led her to believe that Lord Craven had swept into Delia's life, convincing her to be his bride before she could lend thought to her decision. The implication was that Delia, a sheltered and naive girl, had been given no opportunity to consider any other suit. The aunts had presented Lord Craven as a jaded monster who plied Delia with false promises to gain her hand. But clearly, by Delia's own written admission, this was not the case.

The musicale was enchanting. I met Lord C. He is terribly handsome, terribly enamored of me already, and rumored to be rich as Croeseus. I think I shall marry Lord C. I mean it this time, dearest diary, my only confidante. Lord C. is the man I shall marry, for he is the wealthiest of the lot.

There was a shift in tone and content after that statement. The fervor of Delia's writing and thoughts no longer reflected her earlier frivolity but, instead, depicted a single-minded purposefulness. She had become the hunter, and Anthony the hunted, though Emma guessed he had not known it at the time. According to Delia's recitation, she had been extremely careful to allow her prey the impression that in truth he pursued her. It was difficult for Emma to imagine that Anthony had ever been the young man that Delia described, a man who would easily fall under the spell of fluttering lashes and pouting lips.

She paused, index finger resting lightly on the last word of the page. Not only was the written description of Anthony so one-dimensional as to make it almost laughable, but there was something else missing from the story. Emma tapped her nail slowly on the paper, then stopped abruptly as the answer came to her.

Strangely, Delia forbore to mention the proposal, the first kiss, what it felt like to be held in Anthony's arms. Emma knew from her own experience in Anthony's embrace—her own taste of his lips—that were she given to keeping a journal, she would have devoted boundless prose to those thoughts and the feelings engendered by his touch.

Frowning, she skimmed the pages that itemized the contents of Anthony's London house, Delia's shopping trips and the agonies of being forced to choose between the pink gown or the blue. And then the tone of the diary changed once more.

I have no wish to go to Wales. I have no desire to see Manorbrier. Anthony has ever doted on me, acquiescing to my every demand, save for the one where I asked him to give up that horrible surgery in the East End, where he ministers to the poor. That one small request he denied me. And now he has turned against me altogether. I have begged him to let me finish the season, but he is adamant, tyrannical, even cruel. And all because I made one small choice that he disapproved of.

All right. Perhaps he has his point. Perhaps the choice was partly his to make, but he never would have agreed with me, never would have let me finish the deed. Sometimes I think I hate him.

Emma was as much startled at the emotion evinced by the written words as she was by the content of the statements. So lacking had the diary been in all but the most superficial information regarding Delia's thoughts and feelings toward Lord Craven that her sudden vehemence was made more extraordinary in contrast. And to what deed did Delia refer? What choice had she made that angered Anthony so?

I hate Manorbrier. Anthony locks himself away for hours, even days, in that horrible crumbling tower, and I am left to my own devices. There is no pleasure to be taken in good society. The village, Bosherton, with its peasants and farmers, has no fine shops. I am bored, bored, bored. I cannot say why we are even here. The village has no need of Anthony, as they already have a doctor. Though I must say that I have begun to become reacquainted with Dr. Smythe, and a kinder and more solicitous man could not be imagined. It seems that he knew Anthony from London, but when I suggested to my husband that we might invite his friend to supper, he became irate. He stormed and scolded, his voice thunderous before he stalked away from our dinner of larded pheasant. I am afraid of his moods. They have become more frequent since we came to this horrible place.

Afraid of Anthony? Emma could not fathom it. Even in the face of his icy rage the night she had inadvertently worn Delia's gown, she had never felt truly afraid. Nay, she had been certain that he would never harm her.

Leafing ahead, Emma scanned the dates at the tops of the pages. Weeks and, toward the end, even months, passed without an entry.

I have not seen Anthony in days. He locked himself in the tower, and when I ordered Griggs to unlock the door, he refused me. Imagine the gall. A servant refusing the mistress entry. But that is the sad truth of it. I am not mistress of Manorbrier. Instead, I think I am prisoner here.

Though no iron bars span the windows, and no jailer locks me in at night, I am not free to go. The other day I went walking and upon pausing to study a hyacinth I caught sight of the housekeeper, that horrible one-armed creature, following me at a distance. She saw me look at her and all she did was smile. I must find a way to leave the manor without her notice.

My only friend here is Dr. Smythe, who remains steadfast in his support. He is my confidant and I bare my soul to him when we meet.

But I must be careful of Griggs. Like the housekeeper, he, too, is my husband's minion. Only the cook, simple being that she is, is kind to me.

And now that I have come to a most terrible realization, the danger to me increases. I cannot write the words, for to see them on paper would make them too real, and that I cannot bear to face. Not yet. Not until I must. I shall tell Dr. Smythe—Leonard—first. He will advise me, as he always does now.

What terrible realization could Delia mean? Emma flipped the page, anxious to read on, and was disappointed to find that the next entry held no answers, instead embarking on a minutely detailed description of Delia's visit to her aunts, Hortense and Cecilia. There was a lengthy diatribe against the weather, and an even more verbose attack on the quality of Anthony's coach and four.

With a sigh Emma closed the diary, her heart heavy.

She had not loved him. Delia had not loved Anthony Craven, had, in fact, detested him. Emma blinked back tears, wondering for a moment at such melancholy. And then, with a sad little laugh, she acknowledged the source. It was *because* Delia had not loved him, while he had treasured her with all his youthful ardor. All Emma could think was that if Anthony Craven had given his heart into *her* keeping, she would have treated it like the greatest treasure.

What had he said to her that night as he stood before Delia's portrait? *I did love Delia, once, if love can be named as the obsession of youth. And then I hated her, with the powerful hatred of a man.* Dear heaven. He had loved her, and she had broken his heart, never returning his love, never offering her own heart for his safekeeping. Emma sighed, Anthony's loss twisting her insides in a hard, sharp knot, her mind focused on the wish that she could take away his heartbreak.

She wondered if he mourned her still. No. From what he had said, Emma surmised that he had finished mourning his lost love long before Delia died. But what of the terrible hatred he described? Was it merely because of unrequited affection, or was there some deeper tragedy to this tale? Did it have something to do with the choice Delia had made, the one she had described in her diary?

Rubbing her hand slowly across the leather binding of Delia's diary, Emma stood and went to replace the journal on the table. She had no wish to read more right now, for it seemed the small volume contained no answers, and in fact served to increase her unease rather than assuage it.

She returned to the window seat, allowing her thoughts to wander where they would, and in doing so brought the focus of her attention to the very place she least wished it to be. Lord Anthony Craven.

Closing her eyes, she struggled against her inner turmoil, her tangled thoughts revisiting Lord

Craven's kiss, the touch of his hand on her skin, the feel of his hard-muscled frame pressed close to hers. Dear heaven, she wanted him with a longing that bordered on pain. She wanted to run her tongue along the hard line of his mouth, to taste him, to touch him, to lie with him. She dreamed of it with a hot hungry yearning that left her aching and weak. And what did that make her?

She, who was the product of an illicit union, branded with the ugly mark of illegitimacy, knew only too well where such an alliance would likely lead. She must steel herself, unless she wished to end up like her mother or Meg, pregnant and alone.

Yet, it was not only his touch, his kiss she craved. She longed for his presence, his discourse, the way he looked at her with startled admiration and interest and even humor.

With a soft exclamation of bitter frustration, Emma turned her head toward the window. Through the panes of glass she could barely discern the silhouette of the Round Tower against the star-tossed sky.

The tower that was ever kept locked.

The tower that hosted the dead.

Suddenly, a flare of light burst against the night sky and then abruptly disappeared. Dousing her own light, Emma returned to the window and pressed her nose to the glass, peering into the darkness. A shadow shifted, a bare hint of movement, there but a second, then swallowed by the night.

Snatching her boots from the floor, she laced them with all haste. She had had quite enough of shifting shadows, whispered warnings, and veiled allusions. Enough of snippets of conversation that led only to confusion, and hazy threats that boded ill.

Tonight she would have her answers.

Carrying a tallow candle, Emma made her way through the silent house, out the kitchen door. She marked her good fortune at failing to encounter a single soul on her nocturnal journey across the well-manicured lawn.

Pausing in the shadows of the tower, she recalled with vivid clarity the image of Griggs, the cloth-wrapped corpse hoisted across one hulking shoulder as he fitted the key that hung round his neck into the lock on the tower door, and she wondered how she might gain entry. Her concerns proved to be for naught. The door was already unlocked, a gift of luck that sent a shiver of unease skittering across her skin. Breaching the fortress was proving to be all too easy.

Dampness oozed from the lichen-covered walls. The stone stairs were ancient, slick, the centers worn away. No balustrade marked their winding course; no handrail guided the unwary person along this treacherous climb that wended its way up the interior of the tower. The meager illumination fanning from the paltry flame of her candle could not adequately light her way, and she felt as though the chill from the stones crawled deep inside to the marrow of her bones.

Lord, what strangeness lurked in this place that it so inspired the fear of those who dwelled at Manorbrier?

The air was rank with the smell of mold and decay. A faint scratching sound leached down from above, the noise dampened by the thick stone construction. Emma shuddered. Rats, she suspected. But even the threat of repulsive vermin could not sway her from her course. Firmly planting the sole of her boot on the next stair and the next, she ascended toward she knew not what.

The stench grew stronger. Her stomach roiled as her senses recognized a vileness to the aroma that permeated the crumbling walls. Not the simple decay of an old castle. The tower reeked of death, and with each step she took toward her destination, the smell advanced until she fancied she could taste its bitterness on her tongue.

Splaying the fingers of one hand against the stones, she continued her climb. Nearly there now. The steady beat of her heart accelerated until it roared in her ears like a river after a storm, turbulent and frantic.

At the top of the staircase she paused, extending her arm, holding the candle at the end of her reach in order to amplify the scope of its illuminative power. The glow flickered against the far wall. With a subtle shift of her hand she moved the flame so its light fell across a closer structure, a table, on which she saw papers piled with meticulous care. Gliding closer, Emma examined the worn wood surface, stained dark in places by age and use.

She ran her fingertips lightly over the wooden ribs that defined the back of a simple chair pushed neatly against the table. Lifting the candle high, she watched as the light spilled across the plain furnishing, and she squinted into the gloom of the far edge.

Something looked back at her with sightless eyes.

A squeak of dismay escaped her. Empty sockets set in the yellowed bone of a human skull looked back at her, holding her shocked attention. Her stomach rolled, and she swallowed against the bile that clawed upward, demanding release. She would not throw up. She would not allow fear to overcome reason.

She had known from the outset that her expedition was not for the faint of heart.

"Stuff and nonsense, Emma Parrish," she said firmly, peering into the gloomy corners of the room. Her eyes slid back to the skull and her voice trembled slightly when she spoke again. "Be sensible. Be strong. There are no monsters here. Just dry bones, and silly imaginings."

As if in response to her words, the wind picked up, rattling the shutters and whispering through chinks and cracks, the sound of its eerie wail snaking along her spine and sending her stomach plummeting to her toes.

The candle flame flickered, its beam bouncing off a series of glass jars on a second table that stood against the far wall. She moved forward cautiously, the rank aroma of rotting matter growing stronger as she approached.

Setting her candle on the table, Emma looked at the collection of glass.

Something moved.

Jumping back, she pressed her open palm against her heaving chest. With a nervous laugh, she again leaned forward to examine the contents of the jars.

Her horrified gaze remained locked on the writhing contents, even as her thoughts rebelled. Maggots. Dozens—no, hundreds!—of thick, fat maggots oozing through what appeared to be a collection of rotting flesh.

Human flesh? Dear heaven.

Instinctively, Emma turned her face away, sucking in a desperate gasp of air. Slamming her eyes shut, she pressed the flat of her fingers against her lips and swallowed convulsively. What manner of man was Anthony Craven? This place, his realm . . . it was disgusting.

With determination she picked up her candle and moved on to yet a third table, which abutted the second. In the dark, she could make out the outline of even a fourth table, set back in the farthest corner.

Frowning, she stared down at a collection, plate after plate of what appeared to be dantzic jelly, or blood pudding, gone bad. There was a film across the top of each shallow plate, and a second glass saucer covered every one of them. Reaching out, Emma meant to touch the murky growth, to smell it, to determine exactly what it was.

Suddenly, Griggs's face flashed before her eyes, and his harshly whispered warning ricocheted around in her mind: *There's death in that tower, miss. Death in the very air.*

Emma snatched her hand back to her side. *Death.* She stared at the innocuous saucers and shivered. Again the wind howled, and the scratching sound she had heard earlier returned. Glancing at the stones beneath her feet, she half expected to see a rat gnawing at her booted toes. With a shiver, she stepped away, into the shadows of the darkest corner.

The last table held an assortment of larger jars crowded against each other, their macabre contents floating in clear fluid. A small dead pig. What appeared to be a cow's heart.

With slow, even tread, she walked the length of the table, pausing to bring the candle close and examine the contents of each jar in turn. The damp chill penetrated cloth and skin and even bone, and the fine hairs at her nape prickled and rose.

Emma whirled to face the gaping, dark entry to the stairs. "Who is there?" she called out apprehensively, straining to see in the dimness. The mounting wind howled a mournful reply.

Girding herself against what she might find, she faced the specimen jars once more, silently reassuring herself that they contained nothing to fear. Merely pickled pieces of meat. Yes, she would think of them as such. Like a pickled tongue or brisket that could be sliced and served cold. She grimaced.

The image revolted her.

Emma thrust the candle before her and turned her full attention to the last jar at the end of the row. The jar was neither larger nor smaller than the others. It contained the same clear fluid with a specimen floating therein, preserved against decay ad infinitum. Emma stared and the specimen took shape, the nature of what it was becoming clear. As her mind assimilated that which her eyes saw, her hand that held the candle began to shake. A slight tremor slid insidiously from fingers to palm to elbow, and all the while a horror took hold and grew inside her, a poisonous flower. She was past nausea, past fear. She was past even rational thought.

The thing floated, white and dead, shriveled despite its wet milieu, and Emma gaped at it in abject revulsion. She could not reason, could not think at all.

Staring back at her from a glassy prison were human eyes, devoid of consciousness. A human mouth gaped wide, forever frozen in a parody of a soundless scream. A head, *a human head,* severed cleanly at the base of the neck, hung suspended, buoyed by the liquid that bathed it.

Emma cried out, but her horror dulled the sound to a dry croak. She was caught in a tableau of obscene unreality.

The wind howled once more. The shutters rattled, and then stopped, the sudden silence somehow more ominous than the din. Her candle flickered, sputtered, failed, leaving her in the darkness. She clutched at the candle holder, but her trembling was so great that it slid from her nerveless grasp. She heard it clatter against the stones, the sound hollow and ghostly.

Frozen by dread and disgust, she stood for a moment in the blackness, assaulted by keen, sharp terror. Then she ran in the direction of the stairs. Something snagged the edge of her skirt. She fell, her knees slamming against the hard stone floor. Scrambling to her feet, she pressed on, tears streaming unheeded down her cheeks.

She reached the stairs at last. Some wispy remnant of common sense warned her to slow her pace. Too late. Her foot slid and she went careening forward. With a cry, she flung out one hand to steady herself, her fingers closing around emptiness.

CHAPTER TEN

"Emma!"

Strong arms closed around her as she teetered on the edge of the precipice, a breath away from crashing like a rag doll in a mad tumble down the stairs.

Too numb to struggle, she allowed Anthony to scoop her against his hard chest. He carried her back to that terrible room, that chamber of abominations. A murmur of protest escaped her lips but did not halt his progress. He set her on her feet, leaned her against his solid frame, offering the support of his body as he took something from his pocket. There was a faint scratching sound and a Lucifer match flared to life. Sliding one arm about her waist to balance her, he leaned to one side and touched the match to the stub of candle that sat near the edge of the table—the one that held nothing more threatening than yellowed papers and a brittle skull.

"Th-th-th . . ." Still trembling, she could not speak, could not form an articulate sound, let alone string together a series of words to form a sentence.

"Are you hurt?" His voice held a harsh urgency as he ran his hands firmly along her arms, her ribs, then down to her thigh and the curve of her calf as he bent low.

"N-n-n-n—" She shook her head.

He straightened abruptly and turned toward the table that held the rows of saucers. Stepping closer, he dragged her with him, one arm securely wrapped about her waist. She was glad for the firm support of him, for if he let go she would surely pool at his feet with all the solidity of melted wax.

"Did you touch any of these? Did you remove the covers?" He spoke brusquely, his diction painfully precise. Facing her, he clasped her shoulders, his grasp firm. "Tell me, Emma. Tell me."

"I touched nothing." She shook her head to emphasize her words, sensing that her answer was infinitely important to him.

The tense lines that furrowed his brow relaxed, and the rigid carriage of his frame eased.

"Ah. You have regained your voice," he said.

She nodded, uncertain of his mood.

He glanced at the glass saucers once more.

"Do you know what grows there, Miss Parrish?" He nodded toward the table.

"No," she whispered.

Holding her shoulders, he looked into her eyes. "Death. All manner of death. Anthrax. Gangrene. And I am attempting to breed consumption, though I have been less than successful thus far."

His words made no sense to her, but she could read an intensity, a frantic resolve in his gaze and feel the tension in the pressure of his fingers on her shoulders. Then she realized it was fear. He was afraid for her.

"I touched nothing," she said, feeling the need to reassure him of her safety. For some reason, he was troubled, nay, more than that—terrified—by the possibility that she had handled those dishes. And she almost had. The thought made her shudder.

"More than a century ago the Royal Society of London published the English translation of the findings of one Antoni van Leeuwenhoek. He was a Dutchman whose hobby it was to grind magnifying lenses, then peer through them and see what they revealed. His hobby led to his discovery of what he called 'wee animalcules,' tiny living beings that could be seen only with the help of those lenses."

"You believe tiny animals that no one can see are the cause of disease?" Emma frowned in puzzlement. The thought was fantastical, ridiculous. And perhaps just outlandish enough to be true. She squinted at her palms. "What does this have to do with those dishes?"

"You wondered about Miss Rust, and likely about Mrs. Winter, as well." His tone was brisk.

Emma stared at him mutely as her pulse leapt once more. He was quite correct. It was the former governesses or, at least, their fate that had brought her here in the dark of night. And now it seemed that at last she would have the answers she sought.

"They were curious. Like you." His tone held a hint of censure. "Their curiosity cost them their lives. Mrs. Winter slunk in here under cover of darkness. She was careless, knocking one of my glass plates to the floor. In addition, she was foolish, because she lifted the broken pieces and hid them away in her skirt pocket. As if I would not know that one dish was missing." He made a soft sound of frustration. "We were lucky she did not spread the pestilence through the entire household."

So Anthony believed these dishes harbored disease. How strange. Emma sank her teeth into her lower lip, working up her courage. Finally, she asked, "What happened to her, to Mrs. Winter?"

"She must have cut herself on the glass shards. Weeks ago, Miss Parrish, you recognized anthrax. But have you ever watched it eat a person from the inside outward? Fever, headache, vomiting—all mild symptoms in comparison to what followed. She developed malignant pustules, and her blood was poisoned by the disease. It ate away at her, and she hemorrhaged inside, where none could see." He raked the fingers of one hand through his hair, pushing the thick, dark strands from his face. Emma stared at him in appalled fascination, the image of Mrs. Winter's dreadful demise too horrific to contemplate.

"She did not come to me for help. Instead, in her fevered and weakened state, she tried to flee to the village, to Bosherton, and seek the care of a physician there. She was found dead by the side of the road the next morning. She never arrived at the village." He shrugged. "It would have made no difference if she had. Mrs. Winter's fate was determined the moment the glass pierced her flesh and the disease took root inside of her. Few survive once the malaise taints the blood."

"No more," Emma whispered, turning her face away from his intense gaze. "I do not wish to hear more."

Gently, he pressed the side of her jaw with his index finger, moving her head so she looked at him once more. His eyes glittered in the dim light.

"Now, tell me again." His words were softly spoken, but his tone demanded her compliance. She could feel the kiss of his warm breath against her skin. "What did you touch, Emma?"

Emma. Not "Miss Parrish." His use of her given name was an indication of his concern. "Nothing, my lord. I touched nothing."

Breathing deeply, she tried to still the dizzying tumult of emotion that assailed her. Fear. Confusion. Horror. And yes, terrible irrational attraction that made her long to fling herself into Anthony Craven's warm embrace and seek safe harbor there even as reason whispered that she guard herself against such dangerous longings.

Slowly, as if in answer to her secret yearning, he pulled her against him, wrapping his arms about her. Emma turned her nose into his chest, inhaling the smell of him, the fresh clean scent of sunshine that seemed to cling to him even here in this loathsome place. He rested his chin against her crown. They stood thus, wrapped in each other's embrace, isolated from reality. His explanation filled her mind, cutting through the misty suspicions she had built and then argued against during her weeks at Manorbrier.

Inexplicably, she felt tears gather on her lashes, threatening to fall. Did she cry for herself, or for an unknown dead woman? She couldn't say.

Emma closed her eyes, but she could not block out the images of Anthony's laboratory. This place was his wretched domain, his ghastly realm, as much a part of him as his eyes, his nose, his heart. She found it rank. Putrid. Repulsive. It was difficult to equate the place with the man.

"And Miss Rust?" she whispered against his shirt.

For a long while she thought he had not heard her.

"She came searching for secrets and found her death instead. Nothing appeared to be disturbed. I suspect she never made it to the top of the staircase, but fell on her way up. She lay broken at the bottom of the stairs when I came the next morning." His tone held no apology. No regret. He merely stated a fact.

Broken at the bottom of the stairs. Those words painted a picture too abhorrent to contemplate. Emma wondered if she could ever learn to regard death and suffering with such equanimity. Aunt Cecilia's accusations rang in her thoughts, for Miss Rust's fate was chillingly similar to that of Anthony's dead wife, Delia. A fall down a treacherous staircase with death's chilly embrace waiting at the bottom. Had Miss Rust been thrown down the stone steps, or had she slipped on the slick surface, as Emma herself had nearly done?

Pulling back, she tipped her head and met his gaze. "This is a terrible place," she whispered.

"Is it?" Something dark flickered in his eyes. "I find it to be a place of enlightenment."

"Enlightenment?" she cried in anguish. "Here, where you are surrounded by darkness and death? What manner of man are you? What manner of doctor? *There is a head in that jar!*" Emma made a frantic motion in the direction of the far table as a bubble of hysteria welled up from her core. "*A head.* A human head that once held thoughts and dreams and fears. You keep it in a jar next to a dead pig!" The sound of her voice escalated until she yelled in earnest, and tears coursed down her cheeks.

Taking great gasping breaths, Emma struggled for calm. And through her tirade, Anthony said nothing.

"You grow death like others grow flowers," she said at length. "You are a harsh man, unyielding as rock, who spends his leisure hours here, in a place that I could never have imagined. From the depths of my darkest fears, I could not have dredged thoughts of such a place." She felt raw, flayed by the night's events and all she had seen. "Yet there is a gentleness in you that I cannot deny. The love you shower on Nicky is pure. And your heart is good."

He made a rough sound of denial. "Do not paint me with rose-tinted hues, Emma. If you see me at all, see me as I am in truth. I have made the mistake of looking only at the surface. Believe me, the shock of discovery—and, yes, it does come—the shock of peeling away layers to reveal a rotten core is unpleasant in the extreme."

Delia. He spoke of Delia. "I do not paint you with rose-tinted hues. Nor do I paint you the villain. I know what you did for Mrs. Bolifer, offering her the position as housekeeper to ensure that she chose life—a *useful* life—over one of despair. And Griggs. And Cookie. And Meg, whose family would starve if you did not pay her a ridiculous sum." She hesitated and then whispered, "And for me."

"Do you list my virtues in order to convince me, or yourself?" he asked dryly.

As she looked at him now, he was splendid. The candlelight played across his sculpted features, highlighting planes and hollows. Emma reached up and laid her palm against his lightly stubbled jaw. He made a low sound but did not pull away.

What terrible malady had overtaken her that despite everything she had seen here she yearned for him so? He was the demon who haunted her night-mares, the angel who graced her dreams.

"I am so confused," she whispered, dropping her hand to her side.

He caught her wrist. Drawing her palm to his lips he kissed the fleshy part at the base of her thumb, then gently pressed his teeth against the sensitive skin.

A flame seared her, running from her arm to the pit of her belly with lightning speed.

"Oh!" she cried, trying to snatch her hand away. Such feelings were not appropriate, least of all here, amidst the death and decay.

With a low laugh, he licked the place he had grazed with his teeth. As his tongue played across her flesh, she closed her eyes in confusion. She had challenged him, demanding to know what manner of man he was, when, in truth, she should be posing that question to herself. What manner of woman was she to fall under his wicked spell without struggling in the slightest?

"You ask what manner of man I am." His voice was thick and rough as he revisited her earlier question, deciphering her thoughts with unerring accuracy. "I am a man who grows death—" At her startled look he affirmed her words with a nod. "Your description was most precise, sweet Emma. I grow death as others grow flowers. I research the nature of contagion. My interest is no longer in the living. I do not physic them or tend to their ills. My dominion is the realm of the dead. And I revel in it."

He pulled her against him, so close she thought they would meld into one. His fingers tangled in her hair, and his thumb caressed the angle of her jaw. Her heart thudded, pumping blood that felt thick and hot, warmed honey in her veins.

"I am a man who keeps a head in a jar." Anthony's expression grew hard. He leaned close, his lips touching her ear, and when he spoke, the movement caressed her skin, sending a cascade of tingling pleasure to every nerve. "Make no mistake, Emma. I am a man who is part monster. Cold. Hardened to human suffering. That I freely admit," he whispered harshly. "Do you want such a man?"

He had pared away all pretence, all nicety, and bared the heart of the matter. Did she want such a man?

Dear heaven, she did. With all that she was, she wanted this man. But at what cost to herself? She closed her eyes tightly, weighing the merit of any answer she might give. In the end, she responded to his question with one of her own.

"Why do you keep that abomination?" She gestured toward the macabre contents of the specimen jar, leaning back enough to see his face.

One side of his mouth curved, a parody of a smile. "To remind me of my humanity."

Emma drew a deep, shuddering breath. "So you do acknowledge that you are human," she mused.

He made no reply, merely held her trapped in his embrace. His fingers gently massaged the back of her neck. She closed her eyes, letting the sensation of his touch warm her, tease her, bring her to life.

Before her loomed a choice, a forked road with one well-trod path, the path of genteel poverty, living life within the dictates of society, but only on the fringes of true fulfillment. She would never have a home, would instead live as a governess, raising someone else's child, cast aside at the whim of whatever employer she served. She would be as her mother had been. Oh, but when her mother had been alive, Emma had felt that she *did* have a home, for home was her mother's love. Could she live the rest of her life without love, adrift and truly alone?

She could feel the warmth of Lord Craven's body, a mere breath from her own. *He* was the second path, less defined, ill understood. The path that would carry her to the role of lover, mistress, fallen woman. And to make such a decision here, in this ugly place, fraught with mystery and fear . . . it was nearly more than she could bear. Yet, this was the perfect place, for here, Anthony was laid bare, presented as nothing other than the man he truly was.

Sucking in a sharp breath, she stepped away, needing space and distance and clarity of thought. Her gaze skimmed the table, strewn with papers, the glass dishes harboring the promise of a slow, agonizing death. Emma hesitated. She glanced at the maggots, writhing in the fetid rot that served as their home. Then, she confronted the bottles that held the macabre specimens, her mind spinning through conjectures and endless possibilities. Finally, she turned to Anthony once more.

"You research the nature of contagion," she reflected. "For what purpose?"

"Purpose?" he repeated, then shook his head.

"What purpose, my lord?" Her tone was insistent. "To breed death and disease? To kill unwary governesses?"

"Don't be ridiculous," he muttered.

She thought him uncomfortable with his own nobility, determined to present himself in the worst possible light. Perhaps he genuinely saw himself as some sort of fiend.

"Then why?" she pressed.

"To know the nature of contagion. To stop the onslaught of pestilence and plague. To stop the suffering and death." He made a harsh sound low in his throat. "There is no cure for anthrax. For smallpox. For diphtheria. For sepsis of the blood."

"So you wish to save lives," she said triumphantly. "To lessen human misery." Whatever macabre experiments were performed by Lord Craven, his motive was pure. His response, and her reasoning, had provided her with an answer she could accept.

He clicked his tongue impatiently. Emma watched him and waited. At length, he spoke.

"Do you imagine me to be a hero, Emma? A gilded prince who will fulfill your every fantasy? I am no mythical champion. Just a man. And if you build me up to some outlandish degree, I will disappoint you, my dear."

"As you were disappointed?" Something flickered in his gaze, a warning perhaps, and Emma sensed he was not ready to tread that particular path this night. She shook her head. "I neither build you up, my lord, nor cut you down. I simply seek to base my choices on truth." She moved her hand to encompass his laboratory. "Is this the castle of a prince? Hardly that. Yet I have doubt you are the monster you claim to be. My observations and deductions prove that is untrue. A moment ago, you admitted that you are a man, nothing more, nothing less. A flesh and blood man. One with noble goals. And that is what I perceive you to be. Not hero. Not monster. But man."

"Always the sensible girl," he murmured.

"Not always," she said softly, knowing her heart shone in her eyes. "Once before I told you that I have no wish to be a sensible girl. You rebuffed me."

"I did. As I ought refuse you now." He laughed, low and soft, the sound stroking Emma like a caress. "Again, proof that I am merely a man. I have not the strength to deny you."

He moved his hand to indicate the slitted window that overlooked the yard. "Do you know that the day after your arrival I watched you playing children's games with my son? Laughing and twirling, all innocence and purity. Your skirt moved up to reveal practical boots and sensible black stockings. And all I could think was that I wanted to peel them from your naked skin and run my hands over the limbs they covered."

A low sound escaped her, half denial, half pleasure. So he had wanted her all this time, longed for her as she had for him. The thought was heady, delightful.

"But it was more than that, Emma."

The stroke of his low tones across her senses was as tantalizing as any physical caress. She was melting inside, aching to simply throw herself against him and drag his mouth down to hers. "I wanted to hear you laugh for me. To see your pretty mouth curve in a smile for me. To see you hold your arms wide in welcome."

"I promise you nothing, Emma Parrish. My heart has no room for love, my life no place for a wife." He looked at her intently as he spoke, assessing the impact of his words. "But I do . . . care for you."

Oh, that precious admission, dragged from him in gruff, stark disclosure. He cared for her. It would have to be enough.

Emma swallowed, fearful of the leap she was about to take, yet strangely unable to choose another course. This was the path that felt right.

"I understand," she said. "At least you have been honest with me."

"*Do* you understand, Emma?" His voice was hoarse, with an urgency that she was beginning to recognize as desire.

She nodded slowly. "You will not marry me. You will not love me. And you offer me nothing. These things you have said quite clearly, my lord."

"Anthony," he corrected her.

"Anthony," she repeated, savoring each syllable. How many times had she whispered his name to herself in the darkness of the night, dreaming of his touch, his kiss? The slow, steady pounding of her heart accelerated, beating a rapid tattoo that seemed to cry out against the enormity of her decision. Or, perhaps, it beat with encouragement, hastening her fall.

Taking a deep breath, she continued, the words pouring from her in a rush. "When you are done with me, will you send me away? I do not wish to leave your son, for he has worked his way into my heart, and I believe I have made my way into his. It would be hurtful to him were I to leave. Damaging, even. I cannot make this choice at his expense. I must be absolutely certain. . . ."

Using their clasped hands to draw her even closer, Anthony stared into her eyes. Emma's head dropped back as she held his gaze. With infinite slowness he lowered his mouth to hers, brushing a fleeting kiss across her lips. The contact singed her, a dark flame searing her body, sending a heightened awareness zinging through her limbs.

"You asked me this before, the day I came upon you washing floors and windows." He raised a questioning brow as he pulled back, watching her. "And if I promise you this, you believe I will keep my word?"

"You would never do anything to harm Nicky in any way. Of that I am certain. And you are a man of honor. I do believe your word is your bond." Simple statements spoken with naked sincerity. She believed those words.

He gave a harsh bark of laughter. "A man of honor who would take my son's governess to my bed. A virgin maid under my protection, and under my control. Where is the honor in that?"

"Though your code of chivalry is your own, Anthony, I believe it is one you cleave to. Tell me, will you deny your own code?"

His nostrils flared as he drew a breath, his head tilting back slightly. Her arrow had struck home.

"No, I will not deny my code."

"Then I ask you again. Will you give me your promise not to send me away?"

"What? No demands for jewels? No attempt to secure the promise of a house, a coach, servants of your own?"

Emma sensed that his words were calculated to wound, to put distance between them and give her one last chance to escape.

"Do you think so little of me?" She could not help the tiny catch in her voice as she spoke.

He rested one finger beneath her chin and tipped her head back until he could look into her eyes, his gaze hot and fierce. "I think *everything* of you, my Emma."

The breath left her in a rush. *My Emma.*

"I will not send you away." He spoke the words in a low, hard voice, the way one would swear a vow. "But I make no promise that you will not wish to flee of your own free will and determination. The likelihood is that you will regret this foolish choice."

Emma smiled, a bittersweet curve of her lips. "There will undoubtedly be times when I will feel regret. But there will also be times in my life when I will take out the memories of our time together, revisit them with wistful pleasure, then carefully store them away." She remembered the times that her mother's eyes had held a pensive longing. She wondered now if that longing had been for the foolish young man who had been her one true love and only lover. "For one night, or one week, perhaps even a month . . . it matters not. I shall have a love affair. Do you understand?"

She filled her lungs on a slow inhalation, unwilling to explain that it was *his* desire that made her burn, the intensity of it, the heat that pulsed from him in waves, catching her up and consuming her. The promise of his touch, his passion, his tenderness tugged at her until she was weak with it.

He pulled her roughly against his chest and his lips came against hers with the urgency of a man starved.

"Remember, Emma." She could taste him as he spoke, feel his breath enter her open mouth. "Remember that I warned you and gave you one last chance to run."

"I have no wish to run."

"You bare my flaws until I stand in the worst possible light. And still you want me."

Decide. Now. She could still walk away, and she knew he would not follow, though he would want to with the same deep throbbing need that haunted her. But, oh, the cost of such a choice. She could have him. Anthony, her prince of dark and shadow, and all she needed to do was say.

"Yes." She tossed her head, defiant now. Certain. "Still I want you."

His eyes widened, narrowed, and then he tucked her hand securely in his, lifted the candle, and led the way down the winding stone staircase and out into the fragrant night. He pulled her into his arms and spun her round and round on the cobbled drive.

Emma sensed a freeing of Anthony's reserve, as if by breaching his stronghold, his tower lair, she had breached his personal defenses as well, and he had shared something of himself with her this night. He smiled in a carefree manner, and for a moment she glimpsed what he must have been like as a youth.

"I believe this is my dance," he whispered, his arm a solid strut at her waist.

She had not expected him to be lighthearted. His jaunty mood was contagious, and she responded with an ebullience that obliterated all concerns, all doubts.

The light of the moon poured over them, and the risen wind whipped Emma's skirts about, belling them out like a fancy crinoline beneath an evening dress. Caught in the moment, she could pretend that she was a maiden fair with jewels sparkling at her throat. Her hair, already in disarray from the questing caress of Anthony's fingers, tumbled loose, falling free down her back. She laughed as he twirled her, and kissed her, hard male lips and the delicious thrust of his tongue, leaving her breathless and dizzy.

Emma tipped her head back and watched the stars spin overhead, sparkling bright and clear against the night sky. The crickets were her orchestra, the cobbled drive her dance floor. She laughed, a pure and free sound of joy.

One-two-three. One-two-three. The rhythm of the waltz hummed in her veins, and Emma danced in the arms of her beau, caught in the gossamer web of a dream.

CHAPTER ELEVEN

Emma walked softly as some time later they picked their way through the darkened house. Her heart yet pounded from the exertion of their dance, and from the heady feeling of freedom that had spun through her as they twirled in the rhythm of their waltz.

His warm hand clasped in hers, Anthony led her to a closed door at the far end of the hall. Her own chamber, and Nicky's adjoining one, were at the opposite end of the house in a separate wing.

Anthony opened the door and stepped back to let her precede him. Entering his room, Emma was struck by its size. Her gaze was immediately drawn to the large bed that was the focal point of the chamber. No curtains surrounded it. Instead, the bed stood alone and unveiled, stark in the gleaming moonlight that streamed through the window-panes. Of its own accord, an image of Anthony lying in that bed sprang to the forefront of her thoughts. It was a disturbingly tantalizing image, but an incomplete one that tested the limits of her paltry experience.

Nervously, Emma stared at the bed. The dark wood headboard was large and simple, with several pillows resting against it. She could not discern the color of the coverlet in the moonlight, but it was puffed with down and she suspected it would be warm on a cold winter night. Anthony's presence just behind her generated a heat of its own, one that had nothing to do with the temperature of the room. Without looking, she sensed that he stood so close that the smallest movement on her part would bring her in contact with his body.

Her palms felt damp and her heart fluttered in her chest. Moving hesitantly into the room, Emma crossed to the window. There was a certain amount of security in standing with her back to the bed, and to him. At least she could control the nearly irrepressible craving to dissolve in a fit of hysterical laughter.

Oh! This would not do. Could a man make love to a woman who tittered like a schoolgirl?

She hugged herself, wrapping her fingers around her upper arms, and looked through the panes of glass to the darkness beyond.

"Emma." Her name was a whispered caress.

A creaking sound sliced the silence and she turned from the window to find that he sat on the edge of the bed. That terrible, frightening, enticing bed. The mattress dipped beneath his weight, the perfectly smooth coverlet wrinkling beneath his thighs.

She wanted to skirt past him, to alter her decision, so carefully made. At the same time she wanted to join him on the soft surface of the bed, to sink into the mattress and the warmth of his embrace. Opting for prudence, Emma stayed exactly where she was, frozen in an agony of indecision.

All her life she had been warned against choosing this path. Now, uncertainty waged a tormented battle inside her and her fingers curled and clenched, fisting at her sides. To stay. To flee. She had thought the decision made, but faced with the reality of Anthony's bed, the scent of him light in the air, she was afraid.

Leaning forward, Anthony lit a candle on the bedside table. Emma blinked against the sudden flare of light. Her gaze flicked abruptly to his face, then back to the flame. She had preferred the darkness, the anonymity of it, the ability to make her choice in the shadows. But he was a man who would accept nothing less than her heartfelt clear assent.

Emma watched the flame jump and dance, and she knew that, on some level, her choice had been made that very first night when he had startled a laugh from her with his witty mimicry of her aunts, then left her in the carriage, alone. She had had a choice, then, as now, to scurry back to the life she knew or to leap forward into the unknown.

Anthony rose and closed the space that separated them. Standing before her, he seemed inordinately tall and broad. The top of her head barely reached his chin. He stood close and she felt his breath stir the strands of hair at her crown. Taking her hand, he gently pried her curled fingers open and brought her palm to his mouth. She felt his soft kiss but could not bring herself to look up and meet his gaze. To do so would be to risk losing herself in the fathomless depths of his soul, risking her own in the process.

The neck band of his shirt was open. Emma

stared at the vee of bared skin, the hollow at the base of his throat that was cast in light and shade. Hesitantly she reached out and traced his collarbone with the tip of her index finger. She felt him tense beneath her touch.

"Do you know that when I am with you I cannot breathe?" she asked, surprised by the thick, husky quality of her voice.

He lifted her chin, tilting her head so she was forced to meet his gaze.

"Yes," he said, and though his expression remained impassive, she could hear the beginnings of a smile in his voice.

"And that my heart races like a runaway cart?"

Now the smile blossomed across his sensual lips, curving the corners upward. "Yes."

"And that I shake as one ill with the ague?"

The smile grew, a flash of white teeth.

"Yes."

She opened her mouth to ask how he knew, but he bent forward, joining the firmness of his lips with her own, touching his tongue to hers only long enough to tease her senses. The kiss was featherlight, like a butterfly come, then gone. Her finger was still on his collarbone, and his movement flattened her palm against the hard muscles of his chest. She could feel the pounding of his heart, the rhythm keeping time with the rushing of her blood, synchronized.

Beneath her palm his chest rose and fell with each breath. Faster now, and deeper, too. It would seem that she was not the only one to experience difficulty drawing air into her body.

"You are trembling," he whispered, gliding his hand along her forearm.

The room tilted crazily. Anthony slid his arm around her waist, drawing her against his muscled thighs.

He still smiled, but there was a subtle shift, a change. There was no humor in his expression now. The smile was wolfish, a fleeting baring of his teeth before he swooped down and claimed her mouth with his. Tilting her head, Emma welcomed him.

She whimpered, arching into him and opening her mouth to his exploration. Her qualms and maidenly unease evaporated, scorched away by the hunger that consumed her with a suddenness that was overwhelming.

The firm touch of his hand stroked her waist, her back, and lower, to cup the rounded curve of her bottom. Heat pooled between her thighs, an ache that gnawed at her. She wriggled against him, seeking surcease. Closer. Oh, to touch him and feel him, the heat of him, so much better than her cold, lonely dreams.

His kiss deepened, so hot and sweet that she licked him and bit at him, tasting him on her tongue. Honeyed wine could not compare. She lay half swooning in his arms, reveling in the feel of his hands as they roamed freely over her back and buttocks.

Each touch inflamed the hard edge of her desire, making it sharper, keener, feeding the hunger that consumed her. Her fingers tangled in his hair, then moved to touch his shoulders, his back. He was hard and warm, the heat of his body seeping through his shirt. She wanted to touch his bare skin, to feel the contours of his body beneath her hands.

Oh, God! She was on fire. A blue flame ate at her from the inside out and she knew that only he could

quench the heat, ease the near unbearable pain
that swelled and grew in the core of her femininity.

Emma rubbed against him in an agony of desperation. The rough moan that rumbled in his chest
answered her need. She could feel the hard ridge
of his flesh thrusting against her belly. Her bosom
felt swollen, the dress too tight to bear. The sensitive tips of her breasts pressed against the cloth of
her bodice, and she wanted the bodice gone, the
dress gone. It seemed the only way to get close
enough to him, to douse the blaze within.

Her nipples ached. Emma made a soft sound, a
gasp of surprise, a moan of delight, as he dragged
his knuckles across the fabric-covered peaks. Back
and forth, softly at first, then with increased pressure until she whimpered and strained toward his
touch, the pleasure so acute it was almost pain.
Frantically, she tangled her fingers in the fine lawn
of his shirt, pulling at him, searching for release.

His fingers closed around the aching tip of her
breast, pinching gently. Emma cried out, the sensation exquisite. Her legs buckled beneath her as
desire overwhelmed her. She could not feel the
floor beneath her feet. There was only Anthony,
solid and firm, and between them raged emotions
that stole her breath, her thoughts.

"Oh, please." Emma tugged ineffectually at her
buttons. So many buttons.

His warm fingers brushed hers aside. She felt
them dip in the hollow between her breasts as the
buttons came undone. Then the rough pads of his
fingertips slid down her shoulders, skin to bare skin.

She was unclothed. She could not think how, but
suddenly she was clad only in her stockings, bathed
in moonlight and the single candle flame, her dress

a dark blot on the carpet at her feet. Vaguely she recalled the impression of her chemise floating against her skin, pulled over her head and tossed aside. Had he done that? Emma could not form coherent thought. It did not matter. Her body was a cauldron of heat and yearning that negated all whispers of conscience.

Anthony stepped back, his head tilted slightly to one side as he stared at her, unblinking, intense desire casting his features in sharp edges. He caught her wrists as she tried to cross her arms, suddenly shy.

"Better than my imagination," he rasped, lifting one hand to run the pad of his thumb across her nipple. His touch sent a jolt of unendurable pleasure hammering through her.

She cried out in abject misery and absolute bliss. As her legs collapsed beneath her, he caught her, preventing her unceremonious descent to the thick carpet at her feet. Anthony lifted her into his arms, nuzzling the side of her neck as he shifted her to the bed. Glorying in the sensual slide of soft cloth against even softer skin, Emma moved her arms languidly against the smoothness of the spread.

He stood above her, his eyes roaming over her naked skin, and she felt beautiful, desirable. Her gaze locked with his and he smiled, a slow, lazy flash of white teeth that was rapacious and conspiratorial at once. She was his collaborator, his consort. His smile held the promise of shared ecstasy. Emma felt her mouth curve in answer and she held her arms open as he came to her, the weight of him settling over her.

"Emma, my queen of passion," he whispered beside her ear, then reared back, leaving her bereft.

"No!" she cried out against the loss. Once before he had left her so. But not tonight.

Fisting handfuls of his shirt, she tugged at him as he pulled back. His buttons tore away, leaving the shirt hanging loose, revealing the hard planes of his chest, the ridges of his abdomen. No marble sculpting this, Emma thought in awe, but a flesh and blood man. Then she realized what she had done—tore the very clothes from his body—and she rolled away to bury her face in the pillow, mortified at her wantonness.

A rustling sound accompanied his soft chuckle, and the edge of the bed sagged beneath his weight. She burrowed deeper, hiding from him, from herself. The moist lap of his tongue on her spine left her skin sensitized in the wake of his caress. Her yelp of surprise dwindled to a low purr of pleasure.

The bed shifted and creaked, and she felt him against her back, flesh to flesh, lying alongside her. The hard ridge of him jutted forward, impudent and proud, no longer confined by his breeches, urgent against her buttocks.

"Come out from under the pillow, Emma."

She merely shook her head and hid, breathing in the smell of the pillowcase. His bed, his sheets, holding the luscious scent of him. She moaned.

"Come now, I won't bite." There was a pause, and she felt his lips on her shoulder blade, gentle nips and kisses along the bend of her ribs. Then his teeth sank into the fleshy round globe of her buttock. "Or perhaps I will. You are too tempting a morsel to ignore."

With a squeak of surprise, she rolled quickly, tossing the pillow at his head. Deflecting it with his elbow, he came on top of her, the muscles of his shoulders and arms corded as he held himself above her.

"I am cold," she whispered, staring transfixed at the curve of his lips, overcome by a strange yearning to suck and nip his mouth, his chest, the skin of his belly. She curled her fingers in the bedclothes, undone by the force of her desire.

"Let me warm you." Anthony lowered the length of his body to hers, gliding the tip of himself against the wet, slick core of her. He felt smooth, like the finest silk.

Brazen, she reached down between them and ran her hand along the thick shaft, tracing the broad, round head, curious and entranced. She closed her fingers around him, feeling the dull thud of his pulse, or perhaps her own. Dear heaven, how would such a thing fit inside her?

"Hhh-hnn." The breath left him in a rush, the sound of it stoking the scorching flame inside her to even greater heights. Her touch gave him pleasure. Of that she was certain, and, oh, the pure delight of that knowledge, the deep, feminine pleasure of it.

Emma wet her lips, then lifted her head from the cushions and darted her tongue out to lick his perfectly sculpted mouth. As she fell back against the pillows, he followed her, his kiss roughly sensual. She felt it puddle and spread through the pit of her belly. Liquid heat. Beautiful, glorious madness. Her stomach leaped, dropped, and she was light-headed with desire.

Anthony moved, taking her nipple in his mouth, sucking on her until she let out a low sigh, the sinful luxury of his lips and tongue and teeth even more stirring than the touch of his hand. He licked and sucked and oh!—bit her—and she arched up wanting more, panting, throbbing, the rasp of his tongue driving her to lunacy.

His fingers nudged her waist, traced the line of her hip, the dark boundary of her stocking, coming to rest on her inner thigh.

Disconcerted, she moved her legs restlessly but made no protest. Excitement overshadowed mortification. With a soft laugh, Anthony squeezed her thigh gently and then shifted, replacing his hand with his mouth. Shocked, Emma stared at his dark hair, fanning against the pale skin of her limbs. She felt a tiny sting as he nipped her there, then the soft touch of his tongue when he laved away the hurt.

With a dazed squeak, Emma wiggled away from the wet kisses he trailed upward, but his grasp on her waist held her fast as he licked and probed, his attention focused on one sweet, sensitive part of her, the rough-smooth scrape of his tongue winding her tighter and tighter. The breath left her on a sigh, then a moan.

If he was debauched, then she was his true match, for she reveled in his wickedness.

With that thought in her mind, and his name on her kiss-swollen lips, she arched her hips in a frantic rhythm, wanting, aching, so close, quivering and panting until she thought she could bear no more. Too exquisite, this strange pleasure that built and built until she thought she must surely shatter.

And then the pleasure drove her, harder than she could ever have dreamed, until her limbs quaked and a high keening cry was torn from her lips, her body contracting and writhing, arching against his hot, wet mouth, pressing tight against him as she shuddered and sighed, her breath ragged, her senses shattered by absolute delight.

She lay, gasping, eyes shut as the room spun and her body became her own once more. He moved, coming to lie beside her and hold her and stroke her with long, slow, flat-palmed caresses.

Anthony probed between her legs, his fingers gliding into her, and she stiffened at the alien encroachment. There was a vague sense of embarrassment at the slide of his hand, slick and wet from her body, but then he pushed deeper, widening her, and the strangeness became a strange pleasure.

The feel of him, muscled male body pressed against her own, the soft hairs of his chest brushing her skin, and the scent of him, deliciously appealing, wrapping her in sensual haze. He moved above her, pressing her back into the soft coverlet, the weight of him glorious as he reached between their bodies and positioned himself at her opening, replacing fingers with the thick, hard length of him. Hot. He was so hot. She felt a pressure, an intrusion, solid and demanding, and somehow right.

On instinct, she reared up, ran her tongue along his flat male nipple, as he had done to her. He tasted of salt and man, inexplicably delicious, and the rough sound of his pleasure stroked her senses. Falling back to lie flat beneath him once more, she again followed instinct, wriggling against his shaft, that hard, proud rod that pressed into her, a little, then a little more, and she angled her hips, pumping up against him. The pressure increased and the sense of fullness, and she felt his corded muscles tremble against her. He pulled back, pushed forward, again, and then again. More. A brief flash of pain. A sharp burn.

She exhaled, fast and sharp, surprised.

He stretched her, filled her.

Emma made a soft noise, uncertain now. The muscles of his arms bulged as he held himself still above her. Reaching between their bodies, he rubbed his thumb across her, slow, gentle, stroking her sensitive flesh until the pain receded, replacing uncertainty with urgent need. With a gasp, she surged against his hand, loving the feel of each sensitized stroke, and yes, even the feel of him inside her. Then he moved, thrusting into her slowly at first, then deeper, harder, building to a rhythm that made her buck and whimper. She wanted him to push it in again, push it in—

"Mo-oo-o-re, Anthony!" Emma cried his name, clutching his muscled shoulders, thrusting against him recklessly, wantonly. And she could feel his pleasure, sense it matching her own with every pumping thrust of his body, and his enjoyment only enhanced her own.

She ran her hands over the smooth skin of his back, his buttocks, stroking and clutching the bunching muscle. Oh, this sweet, sweet joining. He was hers and she was his and together they made this journey of wonder and delight.

Her breath rasped, mingled with his, and the pounding of their hearts, their blood, together. She knew only that she wanted him deeper, tighter, there between her thighs, and she rocked her hips, bringing her legs up to wrap tight around him, pulling him closer still.

"Christ, Emma." Oh, the sound of her name, torn from him, and the hiss of pleasure that came from deep inside him.

The precipice was there. She climbed, climbed,

then tumbled over the edge again, falling through gauzy clouds and overly bright stars. Clinging to him, the only solid bulwark on this dazzling, whirling journey, Emma sobbed her release.

"Emma!" Anthony cried, the sound ripped from him with grating force, his hips pushing against her hard and fast. His body jerked and shuddered. "My— Emma!" Thrusting deep, he held himself, trembling, and she could feel the throb of him deep inside her. He let his weight come full upon her, and she held him, and he held her, and she smiled in secret celebration of newfound knowledge and joy.

"I am a fallen woman." Emma lay on her side in the curved embrace of Anthony's right arm, her head pillowed on his shoulder, contentment humming in her soul. She wondered that she was not bothered by her downfall. Twining her fingers through the dark hair that dusted his chest, she traced its path downward where it drew a thin line along his taut belly to the base of his now quiescent flesh.

"And it seems that you have fallen, as well," she murmured as her fingers reached their destination, and she stroked him lightly, curious about him in this new form. Suddenly, she drew back in alarm as the outer covering of his shaft seemed to come away in her hand. A soft sound of distress escaped her.

Anthony laughed as she jerked back. "Nothing to fear, Emma mine. It is only a French letter."

"A French letter?"

"A sheath designed to catch a man's pleasure, to

ensure that you do not become pregnant," he explained. "Nothing sinister."

Emma stared at him in amazement. She had not known such a thing existed. And then the magnitude of his statement struck her, warming her. "You have protected me."

"There is no foolproof method, Emma, but this is the safest measure I know. And the least vile. Pulling out at the moment of delight is the worst torture I can imagine."

She blinked, thought about that, thought about how it would feel if he stopped his stimulation of her at that critical instant, and she found she could sympathize with his aversion. "Yes," she said slowly, moving back across the sheets toward him as he held out a hand in invitation. "I think I understand."

He caught her hand and brought it to his mouth for a kiss.

"Should it fail, know that I would never abandon any child of mine." His softly voiced declaration poured through her heart.

In his eyes, she read the truth. He had protected her to the best of his ability, and should that fail, he would not abandon her, pregnant and alone. She had seen him with Nicky, knew how desperately he loved his son. He would never desert his own child. On some level, she had known that all along. Perhaps that knowledge had influenced her decision, lending her reassurance.

Anthony would not abandon her if she became pregnant, cast her into the same cruel world that had spurned her and belittled her all her life. He would never send his child to face the uncertainty of such a fate.

"Thank you," she whispered, unable to say more to explain how much his actions meant to her.

He looked startled, opened his mouth to speak, but she did not want to talk anymore. Not of this. Leaning forward, she pressed her lips to his, emptying the emotions of her heart into him. Yet, a tiny seedling of insecurity sprouted within her. He would never abandon the pregnant mother of his child, but once such a child was born, would he then send her away? *I would never abandon any child of mine.* But what of her? Would he abandon her?

His mouth was warm on hers, and she let his heat wash away the cold uncertainty that taunted her. With a soft moan, she kissed him harder, deeper, opening her mouth to welcome him.

"Do not tempt me, sweet Emma. You need time to recuperate."

She snuggled against his side and he drew the covers over them, cocooning them in his great bed. Listening to the sound of his breathing, inhaling the scent of his skin, Emma wanted to purr with contentment.

The silence stretched between them, comfortable and secure. At length he spoke.

"I should have told you earlier, Emma. I leave in the morning." His tone held a hint of regret.

"Leave?" She jerked upright and stared down at him in confusion. "But . . . that is . . . oh!" Words failed her. She had no claim on his time, no right to question his comings and goings. Nonetheless, she felt betrayed and hurt, confused by his surprising pronouncement.

He pulled her back into the shelter of his arms, kissing her brow tenderly.

"Three days, Emma. I must visit someone. My stepmother rarely asks anything of me, and this I cannot deny her. The arrangement was made months ago. Two days' travel, one there, one back, and a day to deal with the matter at hand."

His explanation softened the blow. He had not owed her one, and the fact that he offered it was comforting somehow.

"Is Nicky to go as well?"

"No," he replied. "Nicky stays with you."

He trailed the back of his hand along her jaw, her neck, the valley between her breasts. "Mmm. Perhaps I could take you with me."

Once more she bolted to a sitting position.

"That would hardly be proper. One does not take one's paramour on family business," she stated primly, looking at him the way she would look at Nicky if she caught him with his fingers in the cookie jar. "I think I can survive for three days without you."

"Absolutely. It would be improper to take you there," he said, his expression somber. Then with a grin, he dragged her down and rolled until he had her beneath him. "But not improper to take you here."

He kissed her. Something inside her unfurled, gently at first, then stronger. *Kiss him. Stroke him. Touch every lovely muscled plain and valley. Rub your body against his. Yesss. Like that.*

Her response drew a low groan from his throat.

"I thought you said I needed time. To recuperate." She laughed, but the sound dissolved into a moan as he caressed her.

"Now seems like a very good time," he murmured against her mouth, then turned her so she lay face down, her back to his front. As he pushed into her, slowly, hot and slick, she gasped and arched her back to take him deeper still, her hands fisting in the covers, her breath coming in short, sharp gasps, and she let herself fall into the dark rich pleasure of him.

CHAPTER TWELVE

Tick—tick—tick. Turning her head, Emma found the source of the sound. A small brass clock stood on Anthony's bedside table. The sight of it brought a tinge of sadness to the pleasurable haze that yet surrounded her, reminding her that time would plod on regardless, its passage steadfast and firm. Wistfully, she wished she could halt that passage and freeze it in this perfect moment.

She leaned forward and kissed Anthony's mouth, then turned her head and brushed her lips across his maimed finger.

He drew a startled breath.

"Does it pain you?" she asked.

"No."

"Mrs. Bolifer told me you injured yourself the day you . . . the day you . . ." She hesitated, unsure what wording to choose.

"Lopped off her arm?" he finished dryly. "'Tis the phraseology she herself chose. For the shock value, I suspect."

"Yes, I suppose you are right." She took his maimed hand and sandwiched it between her own.

"Why do you no longer practice medicine?"

He gave no answer and the silence stretched taut between them. Emma looked up to find his gaze shuttered.

"Tell me. Please," she whispered. "I so long to *know* you."

"I would say you now know me very well indeed."

His answer near broke her heart. He had shared his body with her in both rough passion and gentle caress, but he would share no part of his secret soul. The barrier of his reticence held her at bay, bringing a tinge of sadness to her mood.

He caressed the line of her jaw with his free hand, letting his fingers slide along the column of her neck, and lower to the swell of her breast.

At her stern "governess" look, he smiled.

"You could help many with your healing skills," she pressed, driven by her own dark memories, her recollection of her mother's horrific death, her body ravaged by smallpox. There had been no coin to pay the physician after that first wasteful visit, and even if she had been wealthy as a queen, 'twould not likely have changed the outcome. Emma swallowed. He could help many, but not all. Was that the reason, then? Because he could not save everyone? Delia's diary claimed he had once ministered to the needy, the poor. Why had he stopped?

"You choose to go to the village only for the blood of the dead," she continued. "Why, Anthony?"

He gave her a sharp look but made no answer. She rolled up onto his chest, hoping to glimpse his thoughts. Something dark and cold flickered in his gaze, a shadow that was discernible even in the dim light.

"Answer me. Please." She needed to know. Somehow, she needed to piece together the puzzle of Anthony Craven.

"Leave it, Emma. Perhaps someday I shall bare my soul to you, dark as it is. But not today."

Closing his arms around her, he settled her head against his shoulder, effectively terminating her searching look. They lay thus, wrapped in soft sheets and the afterglow of recent passion, but an undercurrent pulsed and writhed. Its presence, however subtle, was unmistakable.

"I cannot," she whispered, nuzzling into the place where his neck met his shoulder, her words muffled against his skin. "I cannot leave it at that. You are a part of me now. I think that your joy is my joy. Your pain, my pain."

Anthony sat up so abruptly that Emma tumbled back into the sheets and gave a small cry of alarm.

"No," he said fiercely, his fingers curling around her shoulders, his eyes glittering in the dim light as he loomed over her. "Emma, do not lose yourself in me. Do not bear my burdens as your own." His voice was raw. "You will be pulled in, destroyed. There is a darkness to my soul that I cannot, will not, explain to you. Remember what I offered you."

"Nothing. You offered me nothing." As she said the words, a flicker of concern sparked inside her, a twinge that made her wonder if she had chosen a path that could only lead to heartbreak, and then she pushed the thought aside. Though she was a woman of little experience, she intuitively recognized emotion in the touch of his hand, in his interest in her pleasure. She smiled and ran her fingertips across his lips. "But you care for me."

His eyes widened slightly, then narrowed. "Yes, I

care for you," he rasped, the words dragged from him by unseen forces, an undeniable truth that overcame his reserve.

"Anthony," she whispered. And then she laughed, climbing atop him, her heart soaring free as she straddled him. Impishly, she kissed his mouth, his neck, his muscled chest, her hand sliding along his ridged belly as she wriggled along the length of him, lower, and lower still, until the hot, smooth jut of his erection teased her.

With a low growl, he rolled her beneath him, reached out and dragged open the drawer of the night table, and pulled forth a sheath. His mouth was hot on her neck as he kissed her, licked her, nipped at the tender skin, then ran his tongue over the spot to ease the sting. He shifted, took her mouth in a hot, deep kiss that stole her thoughts, stole her soul. Nay, not stole. She gave it all, and willingly. His mouth opened over hers, and she moaned, wrapping her arms tight around him, pulling him close.

"I like to hear your pleasure," he whispered, running his fingers over her taut nipples, pinching them lightly until she gasped her delight. "I like to feel your body soft and yielding beneath mine, to hear your gasp as I push inside you."

Matching action to word, he thrust into her, and she did gasp, and then moan, arching to meet each luscious thrust, her body instinctively searching for release. She closed her hands around the hard globes of his buttocks, squeezing the taut muscles. He was so hard. So hot.

Faster. Deeper. Until each thrust made her cry out softly and she wriggled and moaned, bending her knees and pressing her heels against the soft mattress. Sensation spiraled ever tighter, and she slapped her palms against the sheets and fisted the soft cotton, dragging it into great mounds until the sheer pleasure pushed beyond bearing, and she screamed her release, the sound caught by Anthony's mouth as he kissed her, rough and hot, his body rigid as he found his own final pleasure.

She closed her eyes, wrapped in the warmth of his embrace, breathless from the weight of him but reluctant to push him away. She liked the feel of him, hard and solid, and she made a soft protest as he rolled away, gathering her in his embrace.

"Sleep, Emma mine," he whispered.

Emma mine. She smiled, and closing her eyes, she slept.

When Emma awoke, she realized that Anthony yet held her in his embrace, his chest against her back, one arm tossed across her shoulders. And she sensed he, too, was awake. Glancing at the window, she saw the first rays of dawn streaking the sky.

"I should return to my chamber before Nicky awakens to find me gone." Sinking her teeth into her lower lip, she closed her eyes, feeling suddenly shy and strange, now that the light of day was creeping through the window.

"I cannot argue your logic, though I have no wish to let you go just yet." Anthony stroked her hair, shook his head in bemusement. "Some part of you will always be reasonable and steady."

She had no wish to go, but, yes, reasonable and steady girl that she was, she knew that it was time. She frowned, thinking of the trek she faced to reach her own chamber. "Why do you sleep in a separate wing from your son?"

He laughed, his breath caressing the nape of her

neck. "And some part of you will always be a most curious puss. It is not unusual, Emma, for a man to set up a nursery in a different wing."

"No, not unusual," she agreed, "but somehow, it seems unusual for you."

So long was his reply in coming that she thought he would not answer, and then he said, "My dreams are haunted by the past. I have no wish to wake Nicky in the dead of night."

Dreams. Nightmares. Did he mean that he might cry out in the night? Frighten his son?

"Are your memories so very terrible?" she asked softly, rolling to face him.

He made no reply but kissed her then, hard and demanding. And there was her answer. Dreams so frightful he would not speak of them.

Pulling away, he looked toward the rising sun, the dawn growing brighter with each passing second. His lips curved in a rueful smile.

"I must be away, Emma."

"The sooner to return, my—" She broke off before she uttered the fateful word. She had been about to say my *beloved*. Was he? Dear heaven. Was she in love with Anthony Craven? There was no doubt that she was entranced by him, desired him, yearned for his company both in the bedchamber and out . . . but had she been so very foolish as to give him her heart? She thrust the thought aside, unwilling to examine the possibility. That road could lead only to disappointment and disaster.

"My lord," she finished hastily, improvising in the face of his questioning glance.

Rising gracefully from the bed, Emma gathered her discarded garments and dressed herself with an economy of movement. As Anthony made to don his breeches, she shook her head emphatically.

"No, Anthony. If Nicky is awake, he should not see us creeping through the house like criminals. If I am found wandering about at this early hour, I will simply plead a restless sleep and the need for a breath of air."

Finishing with the last of her buttons, Emma leaned forward and brushed her lips across his in a fleeting caress. She gazed at his face, intent on memorizing every detail. That he would visit her dreams while he was gone—and likely even her thoughts during waking hours—she did not doubt.

"Safe journey, safe return." With that softly spoken farewell, she forced herself to turn away and slipped from the room into the cool, silent hallway.

Emma stood at her window, hidden from view by the heavy velvet hangings. She watched as Anthony swung into the saddle atop the black horse she had seen him ride before. Though it was early still, the sun was bright, glinting off the steed's gleaming coat. Leaning forward, Anthony spoke to Nicky, and then to the stable master, Henry, who stood at the horse's head. Though she could not hear the words, Emma surmised that some small joke was exchanged between the two men, because Henry laughed jovially and nodded at his master as he patted the great beast's side.

A small gasp escaped her as Anthony tipped his head and looked toward her window. Heart pounding, she almost drew back into the shadows of the drapery, suddenly shy, yet uncertain why that should be so. Forcing a smile, she raised her hand in silent farewell, her fingers splayed across the glass. Then, unwilling to watch him ride away, her emotions too new, too strange, she turned her back to the window, her heart sinking as she heard the hollow clack of the horse's hooves on the cobbled drive, growing fainter, and fainter still. She stood motionless, aching to pull back the shutters and call her good-byes, knowing that such a thing could not be done.

What in heaven's name was the matter with her? She was not one for melancholy farewells and brooding regret. With Nicky off to the stable for a riding lesson with Henry, her time was her own, and for a moment she wished she had not agreed to this alteration in schedule. Nicky's disarming presence would be a very welcome diversion at the moment.

Pacing restlessly, her mind full of wild thoughts and recollections of her night spent in Anthony's arms, Emma deliberately crossed to the armoire and retrieved a novel. She would lose herself in the heroine's story, and for the moment, she would forget her own. Her emotions were too fresh, too confused, and she was not ready to examine too closely her feelings for Anthony. Smoothing her skirt, she was about to settle on the window seat when there was a soft knock at her door.

As Emma opened the door a crack, Meg bobbed an awkward curtsy, her enlarged belly precluding graceful movement.

"Meg!" Emma smiled in genuine pleasure. She pulled the door open wide. "Come in."

The maid darted a nervous glance along the empty hall and shook her head, keeping her eyes downcast.

"I've a message," she mumbled, fumbling through the pocket of her skirt.

"A message?" Emma frowned, startled by the pronouncement and perplexed by the girl's odd behavior.

The maid held a small folded sheet toward her. It was sealed in dark red wax. She thrust the missive in Emma's direction, her hand shaking slightly as she did so.

"Meg, are you ill?" A prickle of alarm crawled along Emma's nape. "Come in and sit for a moment. Is there aught amiss?"

"Take it," Meg whispered miserably, shoving the letter into Emma's hand. "I have to get to work now." She turned away.

Leaning into the hallway, Emma watched in bemused silence as the girl hurried to the end of the hall, her gait made awkward by her heavy burden.

After a moment Emma turned her attention to the note, and upon examination, she found her name scrawled across the front in a masculine hand. There was no indication as to whom the sender might be. She sank her teeth into her lower lip, a flare of hope bursting through her, to sparkle in her veins. Anthony. Could the note be from him?

Closing the door softly, she returned to the window seat and sank down on the soft cushion as she considered the blob of melted wax. It bore no seal, its smooth surface giving no hint as to who might wish to contact her.

Carefully, she pulled the wax apart and unfolded the sheet but frowned down at the message, her heart sinking as she realized the sender was not the one she had desired.

Miss Parrish,
  I must speak with you. Please. Great danger lurks.
Walk in our field at teatime tomorrow. Leave the boy
behind. I shall find you.

                                              Smythe

Our field? He must mean the place she had met
him before, when Anthony and Nicky had been
away. Odd that he should send such a missive. To
what danger did he refer? The tower? She had already faced that demon and emerged unscathed.

With a sigh, Emma glanced at the window. A
memory of the icehouse washed over her, sending
glacial talons to flay her composure. She recalled
the sensations of fright and dismay, the danger, and
the ugly laughter that had spun through her mind,
ricocheting off the frigid walls. Though there was a
possibility that Mrs. Bolifer was the culprit, Emma
had never actually identified the perpetrator of that
cruel jest, nor had she determined whether someone truly wished her ill. Rubbing her hands against
her arms she tried to warm herself, but the chill
persisted, clawing at her with icy tenacity.

Could Dr. Smythe be the one who had carried
out that spiteful joke, attempting to frighten her
from Manorbrier? Why then would he send this
curt warning? He may have tried to frighten her in
order to chase her away, thus protecting her from
the evil he claimed inhabited the castle. Or he may
have . . .

Pursing her lips, Emma narrowed her eyes at the
scribbled letters. Conjecture was pointless. Better
to meet with Dr. Smythe and simply query as to his
intent. Heavens, she barely knew the man, and

here she was spinning shadowy scenarios, when there was likely a simple answer to be had.

Nicky usually had his tea a bit early, taking his riding lesson with his father while Emma shared tea with Cookie and Mrs. Bolifer. Anthony had said that Henry would oversee the lesson in his stead while he was gone, and while today's lesson had been moved to the morning, there was no reason that tomorrow's could not be had in the afternoon. Hence, finding a way to occupy her young charge while she walked would prove no great hardship.

Letting out a small huff of air, Emma made her decision. Dr. Smythe would have a companion for his afternoon promenade, and with any luck, she would have some answers.

The next day flew quickly by, and Emma found that teatime arrived before she realized it. She walked with Nicky toward the stable, listening to him chatter about the visit he had had with his grandparents. What manner of people were they? she wondered. She did know that Anthony's mother was dead, and that the woman whom Nicky referred to as Grandmama was Anthony's father's second wife.

"The day we got there, Grandmama started asking me questions," Nicky said.

"Did she?" Emma murmured. "Questions about your pony?"

"No." Nicky skipped three steps forward, then turned to look at her. "She asked me if I'd like a new mother, if I wanted Papa to find a wife."

Emma gasped at the unexpected pain wrought by those simple words, the sensation twisting her heart in a viselike grip until she felt nauseous by the intensity of it. A wife. Dear heaven.

"And while we were there, Grandmama had so *many* women to tea." Nicky huffed and flopped his arms, indicating just how deplorable the situation had been. "She wanted Papa to go calling, but he would not leave me and she was very cross. Grandmama said I was too little to go along, and Papa said that if I was not to go, then he would not go, for he had no interest in finding a wife."

As Nicky tossed out that comment, Emma's mood brightened a small bit.

Snatching up a large stick, Nicky lunged as though engaged in a duel, continuing his story as he charged his imaginary enemy. "Papa seemed pleased not to have to go out, and on the last day he was definitely pleased when the Misses Felicity and Prudence took their leave. They kept rubbing his sleeves and picking bits of lint from his coat, but I never saw any lint, only they kept picking it, and finally Papa asked if they would like him to simply remove the garment, and they giggled and giggled until it hurt my ears."

Closing her eyes, Emma struggled to calm her racing pulse. This she had not considered, this terrible possibility that Anthony might marry, might bring his bride here, to Manorbrier.

Nicky gave a violent war cry, and Emma's eyes snapped open once more. He looked up at her and smiled.

"Then I told Grandmama that the only new mother I would have is *you*."

"Oh, dear," Emma breathed.

"Yes," Nicky said, his brow furrowing. "That is *exactly* what Grandmama said. 'Oh, dear.' And then she said that you are most unsuitable, Miss Emma. That you are illy . . . illy . . . illy . . ." He let out a great huff of air. "Does that word mean you're ill?"

Uncertain whether to laugh or cry, Emma shook her head. "No, Nicky darling. The word 'illegitimate' means something else entirely."

"Oh, good. Because I would not like it if you were ill, Miss Emma." And then he threw his arms about her, burying his face in her skirt and hugging her as tightly as he could. "And I think Grandmama is wrong. You are very suitable, *perfectly* suitable for me."

Resting her fingers on his silky hair, Emma allowed herself one single moment to dream, to wish that this amazing child were hers to love for a lifetime. She pressed her lips together. Foolish dream for a foolish girl.

"Here is Henry," she said, gently loosing the child's embrace. "Enjoy your ride, Nicky."

"I will, Miss Emma." And with a jaunty wave he was gone, leaving Emma to ponder his words as she hurried toward the appointed meeting place with Dr. Smythe.

A cloud drifted across the sun, the dark shadow a reflection of her thoughts. So Anthony's stepmother wished to see him wed. Why was she surprised? Despite the rumors that swirled about him like a fetid mist, he was a man whom many would consider an excellent match. A man of wealth and standing. Titled, with fine family connections.

Handsome. Strong. Brilliant. With hands that turned her blood to fire, and lips that—

She quickened her pace. He was a man who would marry a lady of his station.

And she was the bastard daughter of a long-dead lord.

Was that where he had gone? To some country retreat to meet a woman of his stepmother's choosing? Was it possible he had lain with her, made such wild and sweet love to her, and then followed his stepmother's behest that he find a suitable wife? Dear heaven, the thought was too terrible to be borne.

Emma shook her head, thrusting those unpleasant possibilities from her mind. He had made no promises, save one—that she could remain by Nicky's side. She had known from the outset that there was no future for them, only a present that she was determined to relish to the greatest possible degree.

"Miss Parrish, I had feared you would not come." Dr. Smythe's greeting interrupted her musings, and she jerked back in surprise, pressing one hand to her breast as she scanned the vicinity, searching for him.

He stood in the shade of the hedgerow, his face shadowed by a dark cap.

"I startled you," he observed. "I apologize."

Dropping her hand, Emma turned to face him. "You seemed most inclined to speak with me, Dr. Smythe."

Stepping from the shadows, he removed his hat and peered at her closely, concern etched in the fine lines that bracketed his mouth. "You are in good health?"

"I am, thank you." Mindful of the time, she said, "Please be brief, sir. Nicky's riding lesson will last only one hour. I must return posthaste."

"Has he followed you?" Glancing in the direction of Manorbrier, Dr. Smythe made no further move to approach her.

Emma shook her head, confused. "Nicky?" she

asked, and then she understood. "If you refer to Lord Craven, he is away from home."

"There are others in that household who could follow. His minions."

Emma blinked at his choice of words. His softly voiced observation brought to mind both the suspicion Delia had written of in her diary—that Mrs. Bolifer dogged her every step—and the troubling conversation she had overheard outside Anthony's study. *You let her roam about? Why was no one with her?* Emma wondered what Dr. Smythe knew that she did not, and she could not help the quick turn of her head, the questioning glance over her shoulder, just in case she had, in truth, been followed.

"Ah! So my words cause you no surprise," he observed sadly, as though distressed to find that he was correct. "I had hoped you would be spared."

"Dr. Smythe," Emma said in a firm tone, determined to remain unmoved by yet another whispered warning, "please state the reason you wished to meet in this clandestine manner. I am uncomfortable with the whole of it."

"You would be even less comfortable if I did not warn you that you are in grave danger, with none about to save you. Do you know that there have been deaths at Manorbrier?" His eyes were fixed unblinkingly upon her, his gaze open and earnest.

"Yes, I do know. My cousin, Delia, and her newborn daughter died there some years ago." Emma noticed that his features tightened at the mention of Delia, and she recalled from what Delia had written that the two had been acquainted. "And the governesses, as you have mentioned before."

"Your cousin knew what he was." He nodded as he spoke, a slow rocking of his head that hinted of some great insight, some secret knowledge. Smythe took a step closer, speaking in a low voice that implied confidentiality. "Not at first. But slowly, over time, she began to see what she had married. She paid for that knowledge with her life."

"You believe the rumors that my cousin was murdered?"

He studied her for a long, uncomfortable moment. "No rumor, but undiluted truth. She was most definitely murdered."

Emma gasped. "How can you be certain?"

"I am a physician. There were definite signs on the body. Bruising about her throat . . . And there are others who have died a painful and terrible death. An untimely death brought about by all too human malice."

Taking a step back, Emma swallowed, pressing her hand to her own throat. Though she knew of the other deaths already, something in his tone made her shiver, and a horrible feeling of dread crawled over her at his assertion that there was proof of Delia's murder.

"I am aware that two governesses died. Mrs. Winter and Miss Rust. Both dead by sad *accident*." A flicker of surprise tinged his expression at her statements.

"Do you dismiss them so easily?" he asked softly. "They died because of *him*."

Anthony. He marked Anthony as a murderer. Emma shook her head. "What is your implication, sir? That there has been foul murder perpetrated at Manorbrier castle? Go, then, to the authorities. And if there is proof of my cousin's murder, take that to them as well."

"The proof was buried with her. And what will the magistrate do without proof? He will be swayed by

Craven's title and wealth, and he will not be the first." He stepped closer still and in his eyes she read his concern. "But I fear for your safety, Miss Parrish. I offer you aid. The time may come when you find yourself in desperate straits, convinced of the danger to both body and spirit. Evil abounds, permeating the walls of Manorbrier. The Round Tower . . ." His voice trailed away.

"The rumors of murder are just that—rumors."

"I do admire your bravery," Dr. Smythe said solemnly. "But I yet fear for your safety. Craven is not what he seems. Beware, Miss Parrish. Beware. When your desperation eats at your heels, biting at you faster than you can flee, come to the village. I will help you escape. The child as well, if need be."

"Escape? From what?" Though the day was warm and the sun kissed her skin, Emma wrapped her arms about herself to ward off a chill that ate at her from the inside. "Do you think me a prisoner?"

"Remember, Miss Parrish. Come to me. I *will* help you. And Nicholas." His gaze strayed from hers, and he scanned the field behind her, his brow furrowing.

"Nicholas!" she exclaimed. "He is in no danger. Lord Craven loves his son, would protect him at all costs—"

"Love takes many forms and does not always offer protection." He made a soft sound of dismay. "Even now he plans—"

He stopped abruptly, his expression turning wary.

"Dr. Smythe," Emma began, intent on questioning him about the dangers he perceived, and the reason for his allusion to Nicky. What did he think Anthony planned? She found this conversation most distressing, especially so in light of Dr.

Smythe's obvious sincerity. Evidently, he truly perceived great danger, believed that she was at risk, and worse yet, that some harm might befall Nicky.

She sucked in a breath, and a familiar scent teased her senses. *Lemon* . . . Frowning, she leaned toward Dr. Smythe, struggling to isolate that smell.

A twig snapped behind her and Emma whirled around to find Mrs. Bolifer bearing down on her with the haste of an industrious ant. Her face bore an expression of extreme displeasure, with narrowed eyes and downturned lips, and cheeks flushed red with exertion.

Had the lemony medicinal aroma—the one that she recognized from the icehouse, and again from the housekeeper's apartment—come from Mrs. Bolifer now, carried on the breeze? Or from Dr. Smythe?

"Your jailer, Miss Parrish," Dr. Smythe said, shaking his head sadly.

The housekeeper's unexpected arrival seemed to substantiate his claims, and Emma felt a tingle of apprehension.

Mrs. Bolifer was at her side now, huffing and heaving as though the hounds of hell had chased her clear across the county. Her eyes narrowed as they rested on Dr. Smythe, who inclined his head and uttered a cordial greeting. Mrs. Bolifer grunted her reply.

"Time to return, Miss Parrish," the housekeeper instructed, then turned to Dr. Smythe and said in a low, hard voice, "Mind where you step, doctor. This girl is under His Lordship's protection." Suddenly Mrs. Bolifer seemed less like jailer and more like protective mother hen.

"Perhaps it is His Lordship's protection she should fear." He gestured toward the housekeeper's empty sleeve. "You are living proof of the man's handiwork."

"I am, and lucky for it. I'd not be alive today if he had not done what he must."

"One opinion, to be sure. Though some may not agree." Dr. Smythe closed his eyes for a moment, then opened them, his expression revealing both sympathy and dismay.

A dull red flush suffused Mrs. Bolifer's cheeks, and Emma felt caught between these two, as though some knowledge was shared by both yet secreted from her.

"We should return," Emma urged, uncomfortable with the interplay between them. "Nicky will be looking for me."

After a protracted pause, Mrs. Bolifer gave a short nod. Emma could feel Dr. Smythe watching her, sense the intensity of his regard upon her retreating back. Her thoughts were a tangled skein. Mrs. Bolifer's sudden appearance seemed to lend some credence to his claims that Emma did not possess the freedom she had assumed was her due.

She shook her head. Dr. Smythe's intimation that she was a prisoner was ridiculous. As was his insinuation that Lord Craven might do harm to his son.

Sending one last wary glance over her shoulder, Emma saw Dr. Smythe standing exactly as she had left him, shoulders tense, and at his back the dark clouds of a gathering storm.

CHAPTER THIRTEEN

The sweet embrace of Morpheus eluded Emma
that night. She tossed restlessly, her legs tangling in
the bedclothes, her thoughts a snarl of supposition
and turbulent emotion. Anthony's face haunted
her. His touch, his smell, the green-gold beauty of
his eyes—all were evasive wisps held just beyond the
realm of consciousness. Each time sleep began to
take hold, to carry her to the world of pleasant
dreams where she danced beneath the moon held
in Anthony's warm embrace, images of Dr. Smythe
and a recollection of his disturbing intimations intruded. There, on the threshold of slumber, she
found sightless eyes staring at her from heads that
floated in oversized jars filled with clear fluid.
Smythe's head. Anthony's head.

Delia's head.

With those terrible images filling her thoughts,
Emma finally fell into a troubled sleep.

Hours later, she woke slowly, disoriented. Some
noise, some sound had pulled her from a deep
slumber. She listened, her ears straining to detect
the source of her unease. There was no specific

cause of her disquiet, just a sensation that something was not as it had been. Pushing the coverlet aside, she sat up and swung her legs over the side of the bed. She ran her hand along her cheek, smoothing the strands of hair that had come loose from the braid that hung down her back. The motion of her hand, the stroke of her fingers against the skin of her face, brought to mind the glorious warmth of Anthony's caress.

Dropping her hand, Emma swallowed back the lump that clogged her throat, refusing to moon over him in his absence. She sniffed lightly, frowning at the elusive aroma that tantalized her. Anthony. The very air smelled like him, carried the delicious scent of sunshine and sandalwood that she had come to associate with his presence.

Disconcerted by the wayward turn of her thoughts, Emma lit the candle on the bedside table and gasped. Nestled on the far edge of her pillow was a single white rose, the perfect petals partially unfurled. Without thought, she closed her hand around the stem and then cried out in surprise as a sharp thorn pierced her skin. She stared at her finger where a bead of dark blood welled from the cut. Even a child recognized that the beauty of the rose hid the sharp edge of its thorns. She should have known better.

She took her handkerchief from her bedside table and pressed it to the scratch. The rose was a token from her lover. He had stood here watching her sleep. He had placed the rose on her pillow, perhaps rested his hand on her cheek. Touched her hair. She smiled at the realization that Anthony had returned a full day early. To her.

Rising, Emma hesitated, wondering where he was

now, and if she should seek him out in his chamber. What exactly was the etiquette of a clandestine affair?

She crossed the room to the washstand and poured fresh water in the basin. Setting aside her bloodied handkerchief, she splashed the tepid water on her face and then raised her head and looked in the glass. Her glance strayed to the reflection of the writing desk that stood behind her. Something odd caught her attention, and she peered into the mirror, frowning. Slowly, she turned, feeling as if she inhabited a dream.

The looking glass had not lied. Piled on the small desk were books. Fully a dozen leather-bound treasures.

Forgetting entirely about her damp face, Emma scrubbed her wet hands against her nightclothes as she crossed the room. She reached out and lifted a volume from the top of the pile, tilting it to catch the light of the candle. *Frankenstein* by Mary Wollstonecraft Shelley. Emma ran her hand across the leather cover and then opened the book with reverent care. Published 1818, she read. She stepped closer and peered at the spines of the other books, reading the titles. *Melmoth the Wanderer* by Charles Maturin. *The Romance of the Forest* by Mrs. Ann Radcliffe. Tracing the words with her index finger, Emma recalled her conversation with Anthony as they stood outside the icehouse on an afternoon that seemed an eon ago.

"Do you, by chance, enjoy the works of Mrs. Radcliffe, Miss Parrish?"

"Yes, I do, my lord."

"Pray tell me your favorite. The Mysteries of Udolpho *perhaps? Or* The Romance of the Forest?

He had listened to her words, and he had bought her books. Gothic novels. Her favorites. They were worth more than gems, or furs, or even . . . well, Emma could think of no gift that she would have preferred to these gold-stamped volumes. They were an offering from the depths of the heart, the secret chamber where Anthony guarded his emotions, holding them under lock and key. A gift from a lover who knew her heart's desire. Emma gently laid the book back atop the pile.

Snuffing the candle, she crossed to the door that separated her chamber from Nicky's. Allowing her eyes to adjust to the darkness, she peered into the room. The moon cast its light across Nicky's sleeping form. He lay on his back, one leg thrown over the covers, both arms flung wide.

He was the reason she had come here. Even before she had known him, before she had come to love him, she had been determined to make a difference in his life, to show this child the love and support that she herself had known from her mother before her tragic demise.

She had come here expecting that Lord Craven was a poor parent, half expecting even worse than that. But she had been wrong. Anthony Craven was a good father.

And he was so much more.

Pulling lightly on the door until only the smallest opening remained, Emma stood poised in the threshold, about to turn away. She paused for one last glance at the sleeping child. Suddenly, the insubstantial illumination of a single flame fell across Nicky's bed. Emma glanced up in surprise and found that Anthony had come to his son's room. She longed to fly across the space that separated

them and fling herself into his arms, but she was so
new to this role of lover that she was uncertain.
Moreover, she was loath to intrude on this private
moment between father and son.

Emma smiled, watching as Anthony set his
candle on the dresser across from his son's bed. He
stood, his face a contrast of light and shadow, and
he watched his son sleep. Emma thought he looked
sad and tired, haggard, as though a great weight
and consternation lay upon his shoulders.

Scraping his fingers through his long hair, Anthony stood at the foot of Nicky's bed. His clothes
were rumpled and his jaw darkly shadowed by a
day's growth of beard. He looked dangerous. Hard.
Emma shivered at the premonition that crawled
over her skin, the cold fingers of an ill portent
making the fine hairs on her arms stand on end.
There was something tragic in this scene, though
she could not name it. Anthony bore the look of a
man about to do something that did not rest easy
on his thoughts.

Suddenly, he glanced up, his green-gold eyes
fixed on the door that shielded Emma from view.
She pressed against the wall, holding her breath.
For a moment she wondered if he could see
through the gloom, like a nocturnal hunter fixing
its gaze on an unwitting prey. She knew she ought
to pull the door shut, to allow the scene the privacy
that was its due, or call out, tell him she was there,
but something, some sense of doom made her hold
to the shadows, unannounced.

Stuff and nonsense, she thought. 'Twas too much
imagination on her part, and too little common
sense. And why in heaven's name was she even
thinking such things? *Because you cannot trust*, a

voice whispered through her thoughts. *Because though he is your lover he has shared nothing of himself. Because he left you, and might well have gone straight to the arms of another. One who might make a suitable wife.*

"No." Her denial was the softest whisper. Oh, why did she allow such treacherous thoughts?

Sinking her teeth into her lower lip, Emma watched as Anthony moved softly across the thick carpet and then sat slowly on the edge of Nicky's bed. The child shifted in his sleep but did not waken when his father took his small hand between his much larger ones. He stroked Nicky's hair back from his brow and leaned forward to press his lips to the child's forehead.

Emma looked away, feeling as though she intruded. When she returned her gaze to the silent tableau she saw Anthony take something from his pocket. His shoulders rose and fell on a sigh, as though weighty thoughts encumbered him greatly.

The candlelight caught and reflected, shining off the metal object in Anthony's hand. Emma stood frozen in place, horror congealing in her veins.

Oh, dear heaven! He had a *knife*, a sharp, glittering knife held poised above his sleeping son.

Anthony straightened his shoulders, fingering the blade lightly as if testing the sharpness. What she could see of his expression was resolute. He had reached the point of action.

Her heart twisted, constricting to a painful knot. She could not fathom it, could not imagine that Anthony would do harm to his son. Yet, here he sat clutching the wretched blade. And Dr. Smythe's warning, so improbable, so impossible only hours past, rang through her thoughts.

And here was the most terrible, tragic tableau played out in wretched truth. Madness. This was madness.

Breath coming in short, sharp gasps, Emma moved on sheer instinct. She shoved the door open and it slammed into the wall with great force. Nicky stirred and rubbed his eyes, then cried out as Emma threw herself across the bed, using her body as a barrier between Anthony and his son.

She looked up into her lover's eyes, which widened, then narrowed, his surprise giving way to cold, flat wariness. Her gaze shifted to his hand, to the small sharp blade he held in readiness. Her heart pounded and wretched bile clawed its way into her throat. There was no mistake. Anthony stood over his son, his expression resolute, remote, and the blade in his hand could not be mistaken for other than it was.

"Get out," Emma said, her voice low and hard. She could feel the child quaking within her embrace, and she tightened her hold, pressing his face to her shoulder. Her gaze was trained on the knife. "You will not harm this boy."

Anthony looked at his hand. The blade glittered in the candlelight, sending rays reflecting off the walls. His eyes met Emma's and she was stunned by the hurt she saw there. Confusion coursed through her, and anger, and a terrible aching regret. Surely he was mad. *Mad. Mad. Mad.*

Dear heaven.

"Go." Her voice quavered, but she held Anthony's gaze, intent on protecting Nicky from whatever evil his father had devised. She felt as though she were caught in the midst of a most ghastly nightmare, a tableau too unreal to be believed. Never could she have imagined such a scene. And even as she lived the reality of it, she could not believe that Anthony would truly injure the child. Even faced with the glittering edge of the blade, a part of her was so very certain that Anthony would never do harm to his son.

So why, then, did he stand over the child knife in hand?

As he stood staring down at her, Anthony's expression turned bleak. Something tore away inside her, leaving Emma feeling as though she had somehow erred, as though *she* were the one who had done some vile, unforgivable thing. She looked away, thinking that there was some sorcery in his gaze that stole her common sense.

"You will not harm this boy," she repeated.

"I will not harm him. I could not harm him." Anthony's tone held a bitter edge. "You think—" He broke off and said nothing more.

Emma buried her face in Nicky's hair. Averse to frighten the child further, she bit back a sharp retort. Instead she made soft, soothing sounds, rocking Nicky in her arms. She could not look at Anthony, could not face her own urge to open her arms and include him in her embrace.

She was as lost as he, she thought, as she rocked Nicky and kissed his crown. *If he was mad, then she was his true consort, for she must be unbalanced to want to rationalize away that which her own eyes had witnessed.* She could barely breathe through the heartbreak that choked her.

She loved him. Dear heaven, that was the terrifying truth of it, even in the face of this, the clear evidence of his ghastly intent. She loved him, this wonderful, terrible man, and she questioned her own sanity, for despite the knife, the resolution in Anthony's expression, the appalling evidence that something was very wrong in this house, she longed for an explanation that would wash away even this.

Despair was heavy on her heart.

He had been about to harm his son. The one surety that had sustained her since her arrival at Manorbrier, the fact that Anthony Craven loved his son beyond all else, was now in question. She thought of the procession of governesses who had trooped through these walls, each one worse than the last, and she began to question all she had believed. Anthony had hired those women, allowed them into his home. He was indirectly responsible for the way they had treated Nicky. Could she have been so terribly wrong?

She felt as though a heavy band tightened around her ribs, pressing down on her. She had given herself to him, heart and soul, believing that despite his idiosyncrasies he was a noble man. And now? Now she knew not what to believe, for her heart argued against that which her eyes beheld.

And all the while, Dr. Smythe's innuendoes and whispered cautions circled through her thoughts like black-winged scavengers determined to gnaw at her soul.

She felt truly ill, for despite it all, she wanted to believe that her eyes, her ears, her senses had lied.

When at last she forced herself to look up, Anthony was gone. He had left with silent tread, without any explanation or expression of remorse.

Emma paced her chamber, so distressed that she could not order her thoughts or feelings, instead crying one moment and laughing darkly the next.

She pressed her palms to her cheeks and tried to reason out all she had seen, but there was no explanation, no revelation that could draw out the poison of what she had witnessed. Anthony had stood by his son's bed with knife in hand, his expression dark and grim. What possible justification could there be for that?

She was extremely grateful that Nicky had fallen asleep quite quickly, believing with a child's open and honest heart her reassurances that he had but had a frightful nightmare. Would that she could believe the same.

Searching for a distraction, she snatched up Delia's diary and sank onto the window seat. With forced concentration, she reread page after page of frivolous chat, soothed by the very monotony of the writing. After a time, she flipped ahead, skimming through a description of a visit to the aunts and a day spent with Dr. Smythe at the fair in Bosherton.

Suddenly, she gasped and reread—once, twice, thrice—a passage that jarred her.

The time has come to face the terrible truth. I am pregnant. Pregnant. The terrible, astonishing wonder of it. After the choices I made, I had not thought it possible.

Was Delia's pregnancy the terrible realization she had alluded to earlier? Heart racing, Emma read on.

He was so angry when I told him. Oh, God, nothing is as it seems. Nothing. How could I have been so wrong? Empty-headed girl to be so blinded, to make such decisions based on frivolities. A flower, pretty words. All meaningless in the face of this. I am in great danger, with no means of escape. And my baby, as well. He will kill us. I saw it in his eyes. Coward that I am, I cannot risk the truth. Instead, I shall seek the company of others and protect myself with the safety of numbers. And I shall pray it is enough.

Emma ran her fingers over the delicate script, her heart pounding with such force she feared it would leap from the confines of her ribs. *He will kill us. I saw it in his eyes.* Closing her own eyes tightly, she tried to block out the ugly words, but when she opened them once more the accusation was still there, flaunting itself, eroding her trust in herself. She could not love a murderer. She could *not*.

"No," she cried, the denial dragged from the depths of her soul. Slamming the book shut, she hurled it as far away as she could. It fell to the carpet with a dull thud. She pulled her knees up, drawing them close to her chest, and wrapped her arms around her legs. Tears seeped from the corners of her eyes. Ghastly. This was all too ghastly to be borne, and she had no idea how she could face the coming dawn.

Was it only a few nights past that she had lain in Anthony's arms, cocooned in his embrace, glowing with passion and the unspoken love that filled her? Emma's glance slid to the diary, to where it lay on the floor like a serpent, coiled and ready to strike, the words as poisonous as any venom. The implication was clear. Delia herself had named Anthony as a potential murderer, but did the suspicion that he might murder equate with the assurance that he did in fact take a life? Or was that diary merely the ramblings of a shallow, self-absorbed girl?

Emma swallowed. She swung her legs over the side of the bed, and reached for her robe. Rising, she reclaimed her candle and checked on Nicky. He slept, arms flung wide, one bare foot hanging over the edge of the bed.

She stood there for a time, her heart aching with love for him, love for Anthony, a dark torrent of confusion, and then she turned and quit the room. The house was still, reminiscent of the moment when a storm gathers overhead, ready to send forth its wrath. Invariably there was a period of quietude before the rage of the storm belched forth, a moment of calm. Emma felt exactly that way as she silently descended the stairs and walked softly across the tiled expanse of hallway to where it melded with wooden floor.

Something dark dwelled here. Something evil.

But why, oh why, did she have such difficulty believing that Anthony was the source?

She barely noticed the cold beneath her feet. The realization that she had forgotten her slippers was merely a flicker on the edge of her awareness. Determinedly she crept through the stillness until she reached her destination.

Holding the candle up, Emma watched as the flame cast meager illumination over the wall before her. There was Delia, her golden beauty displayed for posterity, her gilt-framed portrait gracing the wall with elegance. Emma fisted one hand by her side as she placed the candle on the small table that stood next to her cousin's likeness.

"What secrets did you carry to your grave, Delia?" she whispered, the soft sound echoing about the empty chamber. "You named yourself a fool, the accusation written in your own hand. But am I any less the fool if I too fall prey to whispered words and the lure of passion?"

Emma traced her finger along the painted edge of Delia's gown. She had thought to come here, to look upon her cousin's serene expression and know the truth, but the portrait gave no clue. The woman portrayed here was an artist's rendition of life. Whatever secrets had lain behind Delia's soft smile were not reflected here; they were buried beneath the rich, dark soil.

"Did you die in childbed, as so many women do? Or were you the victim of dire circumstance, murdered, and if so, by whom?" Emma could barely force the words past the lump that clogged her throat. Her happiness, perhaps even her immortal soul, hinged on the answer. Had she made love with a widower, or given herself to a murderer?

"Oh, Anthony." Covering her face with her hands, Emma fought to get her emotions under some semblance of control. She could not believe it of him.

Taking up the candle, she turned from the portrait and began to walk away. Suddenly, the floor seemed colder than the grave, the chill seeping through skin and muscle, to lodge deep in the small bones of her bare toes. A draft swirled about her ankles and rose up under the hem of her nightclothes. Emma began to shiver, her rapid, uncontrolled movements sending the flickering candlelight dancing eerily along the walls. Her pace quickened as she took a step and then another toward the darkened doorway that would lead her from the portrait gallery.

A sound came from behind her, and she spun back toward it. "Who is there?" she whispered, then louder, "Who is there?"

"*Ehhhmmmaaa . . . Ehhhmmmmaaa . . .*" Her name, a whisper in the darkness, and then the same terrible laughter that had haunted her that day in the icehouse. "*Do not search for answers. You may not like what you find.*"

"Show yourself!" she cried.

No answer came, and she spun away, running now along the corridor, her heart pounding, her fingers curled tight round the candleholder. Feeling suddenly foolish, she slowed, stopped, resting her back against the cool wall, dragging in deep, gasping breaths as she pressed one hand over her pounding heart. A slow perusal of the area revealed nothing, no one, only the deserted gallery painted in preternatural shades by the eerie moonlight that filtered through the many windows.

A loud bang came from the end of the chamber, the sound acute and sharp, hacking through the gaping silence, and again the laughter rose and swelled. Emma cried out, nearly dropping the candle as she spun toward the source of the noise. Her mouth was dry, her palms damp.

Slowly, she took a step and another, back toward the gallery, toward the source of the sound. She would not scurry away like a rodent to its hole. Better to confront her tormentor, to end this now. She froze, listening, eyes straining to see into the shadows that darkened the corners and dusted the walls. Again, she crept forward, drawn on despite herself. Perhaps a wise woman would flee. But that would leave the perpetrator free to persecute her another day.

She pressed onward, then stuttered to a stop, her gaze fixed on the oddest sight. There on the floor was Delia's portrait, ripped from its place on the wall. The gilt frame was cracked in half, one jagged sliver piercing the canvas and pointing outward directly through the place where Delia's heart would have been.

Too horrified to move, Emma stood frozen, staring at the foreboding image of her dead cousin, stabbed through the heart by a shard of gilt-edged wood. There was an awful and tragic menace to the sight. A message, or a warning. She stood so for a long while, not moving, not thinking, barely even breathing. And then some sense of self-preservation took hold, and she rushed back the way she had come, through the darkened house, her feet flying along the floor. She was almost at the stairs when she heard the thud of footsteps in pursuit, and the rasp of quickened breath. Almost upon her. Her pursuer was so close, so close.

"There now, lovey. What's this hurrying about?"

With a startled cry, Emma spun, tripping on the first stair and sprawling with a dull thud, her elbow smacking sharply against the wood. Her candle fell, the flame snuffing, leaving only dim shadows and a paltry light that seeped from a distant window.

"Cookie!" she gasped, squinting at shadows. The cook carried no light.

"I heard someone about and rushed from my bed to see what the commotion was," Cookie said. Emma wished she would step closer, a human comfort.

"There was someone in the portrait gallery. Someone in the house. He tore Delia's portrait. Speared her through the heart—"

"Someone in the house?" Cookie's voice rose. "Did you see who?"

Emma opened her mouth to reply when the flickering light of a candle heralded yet another nocturnal wanderer.

"Someone in the house? Are you certain?" Anthony stepped closer, the single flame sending dancing shadows over his features. He stared at Emma for an instant, his brow furrowing. "Are you hurt?"

She realized that she yet sprawled across the lowest stair, and with an embarrassed hiss, she scrambled to her feet. It seemed that she had become strangely clumsy, always falling or twisting her ankle. A wry and inappropriate humor seized her. At least she wasn't succumbing to a faint.

"I am unhurt, my lord." She felt awkward, uneasy in his presence, her emotions a roiling ocean of confusion and dismay. Glancing at Cookie, she found her clinging to the shadows, making no move to draw nearer.

"I will see to the portrait gallery and search for your intruder, Miss Parrish." There was the most peculiar inflection to his words. "Here. Take my candle and return to your chamber."

She shook her head, intent on refusing the candle, but more than glad to seek her privacy. He held the light out toward her, and after a moment, she took it, the brief brush of their fingers sending a prickle of awareness dancing through her. Even now, after all she had seen. Oh, treacherous, traitorous body.

"I—" Her gaze slid to Cookie, then away. Now was not the time for conversation, for questions, for answers. "Thank you," she whispered and turned away.

She heard the sound of his booted feet on the floor, and she turned back only to find that he had been swallowed by the darkness and the night. Slowly, she mounted the stairs, feeling that something was not right, that she had missed some important detail, but unable to place exactly what that might be. Quickening her pace, she collapsed through the door of her chamber and shoved it closed behind her. She was breathing heavily, struggling against the urge to push the massive wardrobe against the portal to block out the night.

She stumbled to the door that led to Nicky's chamber. He slept on, the innocent slumber of a child, arms flung wide, covers tossed aside. A sigh of relief escaped her.

Her feet were near to frozen as she climbed into her bed. She curled them underneath her, wrapping the coverlet around her body. The image of Delia's fallen portrait gnawed at the edge of her thoughts. Was it merely happenstance that her cousin's likeness had fallen at that very moment? Was it coincidence that the picture had been ruined, torn asunder by the sharp sliver, just as Delia's life and the life of her daughter had been ripped from this mortal coil?

Emma tried to reassure herself that there was nothing prophetic about it. The portrait had fallen from the wall, as portraits do. A poorly placed nail. A crack in the wall. Perhaps the shifting of the foundations. No ghostly undercurrent steered the course of her fate. But no matter how many times she silently admonished herself to be realistic, to be rational, to be strong, the image of Delia's painted likeness, punctured and torn, taunted her pitilessly, and the memory of the terrible laughter grated on her like gravel in an open scrape.

Emma wrapped her arms about herself and stared at the far wall, seeing nothing, lost in contemplation. She narrowed her eyes.

Surely no ghostly perpetrator, but perhaps one of *this* world.

Crawling to the foot of the bed, she hung over the side and dragged her fingertips along the floor searching for Delia's diary. When her touch did not discern its smooth rectangular shape, she shimmied closer to the edge and hung over the side, but though she twitched the bedskirts to and fro, and eventually bunched them in her hand and dragged them up to search beneath the bed, she found no sign of the journal. It was gone. Taken.

By whom?

An edgy anxiety gnawed at her and so many questions swirled through her mind. There seemed no possible explanation, no reasonable rationalization for all she had seen this night. Her heart was heavy in her chest, a dull ache burning behind her breastbone, and she wondered if Anthony had taken the diary, if there was some incriminating passage that he wanted kept secret.

And then she felt like a traitor for thinking it.

She sank her teeth into her lower lip and dashed at the unwelcome tears that stung her eyes, for the most terrifying questions were the ones she least wanted to confront.

What had he been doing in his son's room, blade held in terrifying ready? What manner of darkness gnawed at Anthony Craven's soul?

CHAPTER FOURTEEN

The following morning, Emma went in search of Anthony, intent on confronting him in his lair. A sleepless night had done little to sweeten her mood but much to sharpen her thoughts. And the one thought that burned brightest was that she must determine the root of his bizarre and frightening actions the previous night. She could not equate what she knew of Anthony Craven with the scene she had witnessed at Nicky's bedside, and her sensible nature demanded that she find some resolution. To that end, she bolstered her determination, girding herself for an inescapable confrontation.

She reached the open door of Anthony's study, resolute and sure in her course, her queries well ordered in her thoughts. Dragging in a deep breath, she closed her eyes, centering her thoughts, and then she stepped forward.

He was not there.

His absence dampened her confidence, leaving her as deflated as an empty bellows.

Turning to leave, she caught sight of a stack of printed booklets on the small table by the door.

The title of the top one caught her eye—*An Inquiry into the Causes and Effects of the Variola Vaccine.* The author was Edward Jenner, and the pamphlet was dated 1798. The year of her birth.

Frowning, Emma lifted the next pamphlet: *A Prospect of Exterminating the Small-Pox; Being the History of the Variola Vaccine, or Kine-Pox* by Benjamin Waterhouse, dated 1800. Smallpox. A shiver chased up her spine. Smallpox had killed her mother, and now there was smallpox in Derrymore. Mrs. Bolifer had said it was so. What could this mean, a prospect of exterminating such a dread plague?

'Twas likely a hoax.

Carefully placing the pamphlet back in place, Emma turned to leave. Her heart stuttered and stopped, for there, standing in the hallway, was Anthony, in his most disheveled glory. His dark hair was still damp from his morning ablutions, and the sleeves of his linen shirt were rolled back in defiance of decorum, revealing strong forearms etched with veins. He watched her warily, eyes narrowed, and she could not help but recall how only days past he had gazed at her with heat and need, how he had wrapped those strong arms about her body in a passionate embrace.

He had come upon her with silent tread, unannounced. With a frown, she glanced at his booted feet, wondering if he could have been the one in the portrait gallery last night, the one who had defaced Delia's portrait. But to what end? If he had wanted it gone, he had only to take it from the wall and store the thing in the attic. Or burn it, as he had instructed her to do with Delia's gown.

She opened her mouth to speak, but he looked away and with a start she realized that Meg stood on

the other side of the open door. The maid's eyes
were wide and anxious, and she wrung her hands
nervously over her distended belly before bobbing
an awkward curtsy.

"You have the look of a woman with something
important on her mind, Meg," Anthony said, his
tone kind.

"Yes, my lord." Again she bobbed a curtsy, her
expression revealing a mixture of adoration and
trepidation.

He sighed and said gently, "I could well become
dizzy if you persist in bobbing up and down like a
cork. What is it you wish to say, Meg?"

There she went again, down and up in another
curtsy. She wobbled unsteadily as she straightened
and Emma sucked in a breath in a nervous rush.
Anthony moved as if to steady the girl, but at the
last moment Meg righted herself, and Emma exhaled softly in relief. She had imagined Meg keel-
ing over forward, the great weight of her belly
dragging her to the ground.

"Would you like to sit for a moment?" Anthony
asked.

Meg grimaced, pressing one hand briefly to the
small of her back, and Emma felt a surge of sympathy. She looked positively worn out.

"I can't sit and I can't stand. In the morning I fair
need to be winched out of my bed," Meg said and
then fell silent, turning her gaze to Emma, then
away. She studied the carpet with inordinate interest.

"Out with it, Meg." At Anthony's firmly voiced
command, she jumped and began to speak in a
rush, as if his words had opened a spigot.

"I know you're a doctor. I know you don't physic
anyone, but I know you know how. I heard other

things, too, about how you're a mur—" Meg stopped abruptly and swallowed convulsively before continuing. She raised her head to look at him as he stood above her, and her huge blue eyes shimmered with a desperate plea. "I don't *care* what I heard. You've only ever been kind to me. I want you to be there when my time comes. My lying in. I want to know that you'll help me. I'm afraid and I don't want him—"

Meg shook her head, obviously unable to continue, and dropped her gaze back to the floor.

"I know you know how," she said softly. "Please."

"Meg," Anthony's voice was gentle, but Emma heard something else in his tone, a dark undercurrent that she could not name. "Meg," he said again, "you know not what you ask."

"I know I ask for help. A chance for life and the life of my babe. I've been having dreams, horrible dreams, of pain, and blood and darkness. Sally Firth died of childbed fever just last week. Despite that *he* was there. The doctor, I mean. Now her husband has three little ones and no wife. And the way she died . . . ." She paused. "I don't want to die, and especially not like that, fevered and ranting and taking so long to go. And though I didn't ask for this babe, didn't ask for what was done to me, I want the child to live. It's an innocent, with no crime on its head. You can help me."

Anthony laughed, a harsh sound laden with pain that made Emma's heart twist. He was suffering, and despite all her qualms and fears and distress, she could not stop herself from suffering with him. She wondered what it was about Meg's simple request that caused him such anguish.

"You think that I will save you?" he asked bitterly.

"You could not be more wrong, Meg. The last woman I attended died, and her babe with her. You know that."

Emma gasped, certain he spoke of Delia, so bleak was his tone, so laden with self-contempt. "But I thought she died in a fall—" Emma blurted.

Anthony shot her a sharp glance, then scrubbed one hand over his face, and when he spoke his voice sounded infinitely tired. "Go home, Meg. You are too far along to see to the heavy chores."

"Oh, my lord, never say it," Meg cried, her face twisting in distress. "No. Please. I am desperate for the coin. I can—"

"I shall pay you your regular wage regardless," he said gruffly, cutting her off. "Send your sister in your stead and I will pay her, as well." He paused for a long moment. "And when the time comes, have your sister come to fetch Mrs. Bolifer. Not the doctor. Do you understand, Meg? Mrs. Bolifer. She will ensure your safety and that of the child."

"Oh . . ." She hesitated, seemingly intent on saying something more, her hands twisting nervously in her apron.

Anthony gave her no encouragement, merely watched her through narrowed eyes, never looking at Emma, though she wished he would. His generosity to Meg, his offer to pay her wages though she could not work, was astonishing.

At last, the maid spoke. "Yes, my lord. I understand." And after yet another laborious and unsteady curtsy, she turned and lumbered away.

"You turned her down." Emma stood in the doorway, every sense focused on Anthony.

"'Tis for the best," he said brusquely, then stepped forward, his gaze roaming her face. "She asked for my help, asked me to deliver her babe, because she thought my presence would keep her safe." He threw back his head and laughed, a hard, ugly sound that bore no relationship to mirth. "Like as not my ministrations would kill her."

"Stop it," Emma whispered. "Stop this now. You wallow in your memories and you deny that girl your help."

"Do I disappoint you, Emma mine? I warned you that I would."

Her breath caught at his use of such tender endearment, and, too, at his implication that she had expected something unrealistic from him. Had she built a fantasy? Had she?

Steeling herself against the urge to step closer, to rest her cheek against the strong expanse of his chest, she forced herself to meet his gaze.

It was Anthony who looked away. "She should sooner ask the devil to guard heaven's gates than ask me to guard her life."

And then he strode from the study, leaving her feeling confused, bereft, alone. He had not trusted her with an explanation, and she had not trusted herself to ask.

The following morning, Emma dragged her feet as she descended to the breakfast room, knowing that she could not postpone facing Anthony and questioning him about what she had seen that night in Nicky's room. Each passing hour had lent her a calmer perspective, and she realized that she should have confronted him long before this, either that night, or the following day when she had spoken to him in his study. Meg's presence had precluded such a conversation, and later, Emma had found that she had lost her nerve. She was a coward, fearing whatever terrible explanation he might give, when in truth, her imagination was likely painting a grimmer picture than the reality would yield.

But there was more to her reticence. She was so confused, her heart yearning for him, her body aching for his touch, her mind distressed by the terrible image branded in her thoughts—Anthony standing over Nicky, knife in hand.

Do I disappoint you, Emma mine? I warned you that I would. Had she expected him to disappoint her, as her father had disappointed her mother?

Emma shook her head. She wanted him to come to her, to trust her, to share with her the truth of whatever he had been about.

"Here we are, Nicky," Emma said, looking up to find that Griggs barred the breakfast room, his massive bulk filling the doorway, preventing her from entering.

"Master wants to dine alone with the boy," he said gruffly. His scarred face was creased in a concerned frown. "You are to dine with the others in the kitchen, miss."

Emma glanced at Nicky, who sent her a jaunty grin and ducked around Griggs's massive legs, unaffected by this change in plan. And why should he be? He treasured the time he spent with his father.

"I found a mouse in the stable, Papa." Nicky's voice drifted into the hallway. "Mrs. Bolifer told me not to go near it, but I took a bit of cheese with me when I went riding last week, and I left it in the corner of the far stall. I'll have to check to see if the little fellow got my gift."

Despite herself, Emma felt a smile tug at the corner of her mouth. She wondered what the stable master thought of Nicky's munificence.

With a slow nod at Griggs, Emma turned away. Still, with the issue unresolved and the memory of Anthony standing in the darkness, knife in hand, she was loath to leave the child alone. Foolish, really. He had been alone with his father for six years before her arrival. And the naked truth was that despite what she had witnessed, she believed some rational reasoning lay at the root of all she had seen. She was not certain if that was willful blindness or calm rationality, or perhaps a contagion of lunacy that pervaded these walls, but she believed that Anthony could calm her fears should he so choose, could provide an explanation that would eradicate all her doubts and suspicions.

As she made her way along the hall, she heard the low murmur of Anthony's reply to Nicky. To her consternation just the sound of his voice made her heart kick against her ribs and her breath quicken. Dear heaven, she knew not what he was capable of, and her treacherous heart did not seem to care.

Oh, but you do know what he is not *capable of,* a voice whispered from the depths of her soul. *He is not capable of murder. And he is not capable of doing harm to his son.*

Emma shook her head and hurried along the hallway, glad for this reprieve. Her initial surprise at Griggs's edict quickly gave way to the realization that this plan was likely for the best. Anthony was protecting his son. Better for them to speak alone later in the day than to confront each other now with Nicky's big ears taking in every word of their exchange.

The kitchen was redolent with the scent of fresh-baked scones. As Emma took her seat at the wooden table where Cookie had put out the breakfast, she noticed that a place had already been set for her. So the others knew that she had been banished from the breakfast room. She wondered what else they had been told.

Though she had little appetite, Emma poured herself a cup of tea from the pot and helped herself to a scone.

"We were so glad when you came here, love," Cookie said softly.

The unexpected statement made Emma glance up in surprise as Mrs. Bolifer grunted noncommittally.

"All the ones before, the other governesses, I mean, they didn't *love* Nicky. Oh, some of them, the early ones, liked him well enough, but he wasn't *special* to them. Each child deserves to be special, don't you think?" Cookie asked, watching her earnestly.

Emma stared at Cookie, her heart constricting in her breast, for the cook put into words the deepest emotions of Emma's heart. Every child, no matter what his or her beginnings, had a right to be loved.

Even illegitimate children. Like her.

"Nicky *is* special," Emma replied.

"And every child should be loved, should be with their *rightful* and *true* and *loving* parent," Cookie pressed.

Emma frowned, wondering at the vehemence in the normally placid cook's tone.

"Yes, of course," she said, then hesitated. Cookie seemed odd this morning. Perhaps it was because she had opened the forbidden subject of Nicky's previous governesses. After a brief moment, Emma asked the question that had occupied her thoughts on more than one occasion. Now, more than ever, she needed an answer, needed to understand how Anthony could have allowed such terrible women to tend his son, so many women who had been anything but loving. "Why were there so many governesses, Cookie?"

Mrs. Bolifer rose abruptly and began to clear the remains of the meal. She gave Cookie a thunderous look but held her tongue.

The cook shrugged. "In the beginning, His Lordship hired one from the best agency. She was pleasant and professional. Mrs. Granger, her name was. She was more of a nurse. Nicky was just a wee thing. But she hated it here in Wales and left before the year was out. The next one, and the next, felt the same. They wanted a *London* placement, if you please, and the master's odd comings and goings made them uneasy. They had heard rumors, you see, and with each new governess, the stories seemed to grow larger and larger. The ones who came stayed for a shorter and shorter time, until we expected a fresh departure and a fresh arrival every few weeks."

"But what is so terrible about Wales?" Emma asked in confusion.

"I told you, love. They wanted a *London* placement. And if they couldn't be in London, then they wanted to work for a family who could give them excellent reference at the end of their employment." Cookie looked down at the table, rubbing her fingertips absently across the scarred wooden surface. "They didn't wish to remain in the employ of a man with a . . . disreputable reputation."

Emma did not hesitate as she fired the next question at Cookie, intent on understanding at last. "You refer to the gossip about Lord Craven? That he is a murderer?"

Mrs. Bolifer made an odd sound, but Emma did not look at her, keeping her attention focused on the cook's expressive face.

Cookie nodded miserably, her fingers now working the tabletop in agitated haste. "And Lord Craven's odd hours and even stranger ways helped not at all."

Reaching over, Emma placed her hand on the other woman's, stilling her nervous action.

"Go on," she said.

"Not much else to say, love. The time came that the best agencies wouldn't take his requests anymore. So he opted for the second best, then the third."

"But why hire a governess at all, then? Why did he not leave Nicky's care to the two of you?"

"I can't read a word. Or write," Cookie said. "Fine thing that, if Lord Craven's heir were to be raised by the likes of me." She closed her eyes and dragged in a breath, and when she opened them once more there were pain and loss and tragedy mirrored there. "Besides, I couldn't keep my own little one safe, couldn't stop death from claiming him. How was I to care for another's?"

Emma blinked. This was the first time Cookie had ever spoken of her dead child. "I am truly sorry for your loss, Cookie."

"Yes. Well. Little Nicky needed a proper governess."

Clearly the woman had no wish to discuss her

child, and Emma was loath to press. "I had not thought of the academic issue," she conceded, steering the conversation back to less painful ground. "But at least in your care he would be loved."

"True enough. And I do love him, but he needs to cipher and write and learn his Latin. He has a place in this world, a station. Besides, Lord Craven's stepmother was most insistent. Nicky was to have a proper governess, or she'd come and see to the matter herself."

A place in this world, a station. Emma swallowed the resentment that the words drew forth. How many times had she been reminded to know her station, her place? How many times had she been taunted and called bastard?

"The women who came got worse and worse," Cookie continued, warming to her topic. "Then the last two died, and *no* agency would fill the position. And after Lord Craven found out that the wee one had been hit, well, he was in a fine rage. He was away at the time, didn't know about it until it was over and done." Cookie smiled at Emma then. "So he sent for you."

"And aren't we lucky that you came." Mrs. Bolifer cut in abruptly.

Emma swung quickly to look at her, unsure if the housekeeper's statement had been heartfelt or sarcastic. Her customary sour expression lent no clue. Whatever the case, the moment was gone. Cookie rose from the table and began to tidy the kitchen.

"You think you know things," Mrs. Bolifer said. "But you understand nothing."

Putting down her teacup with great care, Emma raised her eyes to meet the housekeeper's.

"Then help me understand," she said simply.

"What manner of man do you think he is?" Mrs. Bolifer queried.

Emma looked at her, startled by the open challenge. What manner of man? A loving one . . . Or so she had thought. He was a man who stood in the dark with a knife poised and his expression set. She sucked in a breath. Who was Anthony Craven, really?

"I have no idea what manner of man he is. He is full of contradictions, with more twists and turns than the most intricate maze," she said at last.

"He has his reasons."

What reasons? she longed to cry out. What reasons for holding a knife to his son? What reasons for letting his wife's fear of him grow to such extreme that she left a written legacy implying he would do murder?

"He may have reasons aplenty, but my care is for Nicky. He is an innocent child and must be protected." Emma held her tone firm.

"Protected, yes. But not from the one you think." The housekeeper's lips turned down at the edges, etching deep lines that bracketed her mouth. "He would never harm the boy."

Chewing on her lower lip, Emma wondered how much the housekeeper knew, how much it was safe to reveal. Should she press the point, describing the tableau she had witnessed two nights past, Lord Craven standing by his son's bed with knife in hand? She felt it would be a betrayal. She must confront Anthony directly, not slink about behind his back prying morsels of information from the other servants. At length, she merely shrugged delicately and pretended an interest in her breakfast that she did not feel.

"Here now." Cookie brought her own tea back to the table and sat halfway along, using herself as a barrier between the other two women. "Here now," she said again, but seemed to be unable to think of any other words that could fill the leaden silence.

At that moment Anthony entered the kitchen with Nicky in tow. Emma's belly dropped as nerves twisted her insides into knots. Oh, she would never be used to the way the master of this house wandered about, right into the kitchen or the scullery. Right into every crack and crevice of her heart.

Though he had already breakfasted, Nicky snatched a scone from the plate and began to munch on it happily. The child seemed oblivious to the undercurrents and tensions that pervaded the room, but the adults were not. Both Mrs. Bolifer and Cookie busied themselves with pressing tasks.

Emma lowered her head, unwilling to meet Anthony's gaze. She could sense his eyes upon her, but he made no attempt to approach her. Hazarding a quick peek through her lashes, Emma watched him as he leaned negligently against the table by the far wall. His lean fingers plucked an apple from the bowl, and he began to quarter the fruit with a small paring knife.

Abruptly, he turned to face her and caught her in her clandestine observation of him. One brow lifted mockingly as he moved the knife up and down, the way one would move a wineglass when giving a toast. Yet, she sensed that mockery was a façade, for in his eyes she saw the same confusion and hurt that she had read when she confronted him in Nicky's bedchamber. And then his gaze became shuttered, the protective wall he maintained cutting off her momentary glimpse of his soul.

He lifted a slice of the fruit to his lips and bit into it with his straight white teeth. Emma looked away, hardening her heart. He was at fault here, at grave fault, and she could not allow herself to think otherwise. She could not allow herself to be beguiled by the dark lure of him.

"The cheese, Papa!" Nicky tugged on his father's arm.

"Ah, yes. The cheese." Anthony turned to Cookie. "It would seem that Nicky feels the need to feed the stable mice. We would like a slice of cheese to carry with us."

Cookie stared at him a moment, her face uncharacteristically solemn, and then went to fetch the requested item.

Emma felt like crying. The morning seemed so pleasant, so normal. A father and son sharing a moment in time. She felt like a thief, her suspicions stealing into those moments, carving the lines of tension that she saw on Anthony's face. He was waiting for her to come to him, to confront him. She could sense it. He would offer no explanation unless she asked, and some instinct whispered that he had his reasons. But she wanted *him* to come to *her*, to trust her, to share his secrets freely.

With a heavy heart she watched as Anthony and Nicky left the kitchen, laughing and carrying their cheese.

It seemed the longest day of Emma's life. Nicky was sullen and uncooperative. He balked at his lessons and went so far as to have a tantrum when Emma insisted he work on his sums. Her patience strained to the limit, she tried desperately to keep her mind on the task at hand. At last the day was done, and the child was washed and changed and more than ready for his bed. As she leaned over to place a good-night kiss on his cheek, she sensed a presence behind her. Her heart sped up, but she forced herself to rise slowly from her stooped position, hoping that her expression betrayed none of her thoughts.

Hope, confusion, sadness—all swirled in a maelstrom that threatened to overwhelm her.

Anthony stood on the other side of his son's bed, watching her, his expression shuttered. He had once regarded her with what she was certain had been some form of affection. Now, he looked at her, his eyes betraying nothing of his thoughts, his gaze distant and aloof. She could not read him, could get no inkling of what he contemplated behind that icy mask, and she thought that were she to reach out and touch him, she would feel the solidity of the protective walls he had erected about himself.

"Miss Parrish."

She thought perhaps he mocked her with the formal address, the lordly nod of his head. But no, there was no mockery in that smooth, rich voice. Rather, she detected a subtle undertone of grief. Emma ached to step back to nights past, to be able to look at him as she had, with a lover's admiring gaze. The compulsion to touch him, to find some reassurance in the human warmth of him was nearly overwhelming.

Something flickered in the depths of Anthony's eyes, an answering need. Emma recognized it and seemingly of its own volition her hand began to move toward him.

Nicky murmured drowsily, and Anthony turned his attention to tucking in the covers and plumping his son's pillows. He smiled down at the child, the hard curve of his lips softening as he looked at the sleepy boy.

Emma watched in puzzlement. Two nights past she had seen the knife in Anthony's hand. There was no doubt about his intent. He had meant to cut Nicky while he slept, for what nefarious purpose Emma could not guess.

Her confusion grew as she watched him standing there gazing at the boy with all the love that any parent could bestow. What possible answer could explain the absolute oddity of Anthony's behavior? Was he mad, with unseen demons gnawing on his soul urging him to perform horrible acts outside the normal bounds of society? She could not fathom it. He was eccentric, to be sure, a trait she found appealing, rather than sinister. Being unconventional was not necessarily an indicator of an unstable mind.

Suddenly, Emma realized that her hand hung suspended, poised in midair, the fingers stretched toward him as if pleading for his touch. Self-consciously, she tucked the wayward appendage behind her and was grateful that Anthony seemed not to have noticed her gesture.

Without warning he swung his attention back to her. Whatever warmth she had read in his expression was gone now, replaced by a cool façade that veiled his thoughts.

"I think Nicky may be feverish," she said softly. "He was out of sorts this afternoon."

"Yes, I expect he was. He'll have a fever and a sore head, but it shall only last a few days."

Emma frowned, for Anthony's words implied that he had anticipated Nicky's illness.

"Come. I would speak with you," he said.

Emma swallowed, his words bringing both hope and dread. "Yes, my lord."

He fairly grimaced at her answer, though she was unsure of whether it was her tone he disliked, or the formality of the address.

Following him from Nicky's room, Emma pressed her lips together as he strode confidently through the adjoining door into her chamber. Her gaze darted to her bed, then back to the broad expanse of Anthony's back.

"Perhaps we should speak in your study," she ventured, her tongue feeling thick and heavy as she spoke.

He glanced at her over his shoulder but said nothing. Instead, he crossed to the window and stared out at the oncoming night. The last light of the day barely lingered, illuminating Emma's bedroom with a soft glow.

"You thought me a monster. Then you thought me a man." His voice was heavy with emotion, and Emma longed to go to him, to press her cheek against the smooth expanse of his back and wrap her arms around him. Instead, she fisted her hands in the material of her skirt, her heart beating a hard and steady rhythm that pounded in her ears. "And again you think me a monster."

He turned, pinning her with the intensity of his stare. "You shared with me the beauty of your passion and now you shrink from my touch."

A soft sound of denial escaped her, and she sank her teeth into her lower lip, trying to hold back the words that sprang to the fore. Words of denial. Words of affection. Foolish words born of dangerous emotion.

His eyes narrowed as he watched her, and then his gaze shifted to the stack of books he had brought her. Emma followed his glance.

"I see you found my gift."

"Yes. Thank you. I . . . they . . . the gift means a great deal to me." *You mean a great deal to me*, she thought with anguish but held the sentiment trapped in her throat.

"So, it is done now," he said gruffly, then made a soft sound of disbelief. "Over before it even began?"

She had wounded him. Her heart broke at the thought. A single tear slipped from the corner of her eye, tracing a path along her cheek. If Anthony saw it, he gave no indication.

He hesitated, as though waiting for words she could not give, questions she was too afraid to ask.

"I shall leave you to your solitude," he said and walked toward the door.

The words sliced through Emma. Solitude, she thought, when she had so yearned for exactly the opposite. She had arrived at Manorbrier full of hope and optimism, and a wide-eyed idealism. More than that, she had arrived with dreams of finding a home, of hollowing out a place for herself. The last thing she had ever wanted was solitude.

Emma squeezed her eyes shut against the magnitude of her desperation. Would Anthony send her away for daring to oppose him, for questioning him?

"Wait!" she cried, the thought of leaving Nicky, of leaving Anthony, too terrible to consider. "You said you wished to speak with me, but you have said nothing." *Trust me. Come to me. Share yourself with me.*

He froze, and when he spoke his voice was rough. "Ask your questions and I will answer."

So many questions swirled in a dark eddy, fighting to spring forth. She took a slow breath and chose one, the one that demanded the least. "Will you send me away?"

"No." The denial burst from his lips; then he continued more softly, "I gave you my word."

"I remember," she whispered, her relief so acute as to be painful. Despite everything, he said he would honor his word, and she believed him. Dear heaven, was this trust, this feeling of warmth and clear, sweet relief? "I remember everything about that night."

In three strides he crossed the space that separated them. Looming above her, he held her gaze. Emma's head fell back as she watched his eyes. His beautiful eyes, full of promise and danger. She could smell the seductive scent of him, feel the heat of his body radiating toward her like the warmth of the sun. She longed to tangle her fingers in the hair at his nape, to pull his hard, firm lips toward her.

With a cry, she spun away, nearly running from him in her haste to place the solid bulk of the bed between them. His nearness mesmerized her, and she prayed that physical separation would lend rationality to her thoughts.

"Why?" he asked simply, and Emma could feel his hurt in that single word.

Why what? Why did she turn from him? Why did she stop him from whatever terrible thing he intended that night?

Why did she love him still?

"Why did you awaken in me this need to *feel*, to *care? To trust? Why*, Emma?" His words came in a rough whisper that rasped over her, leaving her flayed, her inner core laid bare.

She pressed her lips together, her control near to shattering. His question almost broke her heart. She had hurt him in a way she had never intended, had made him care. *He cared for her*. And she had turned on him. But with reason . . .

"Emma"—Catching her hand he drew her close—"I have some things to say to you."

"I—" She tried to pull away. Too close to him, and she was singed by his fire, her thoughts muddled and confused. She needed her wits for this discussion, her distance.

He held his fingers to her lips, halting her before she could speak.

"Listen." He whispered the word, and then replaced his fingers with his mouth, letting his firm lips rest on hers in a brief caress. She ached to wrap her arms around his waist, to pull him close and rub her body against the solid length of him.

Too quickly, he pulled away and then smiled ruefully as he continued, "Physician, heal thyself. Many times over the past years I admonished myself to do just that. But I could not. Instead, I allowed my wounds to fester and rot my soul, walling me off from life, from love. Leaving me alone in my crumbling tower. Until you came and began to knock down the wall, stone by stone, with your open nature and giving heart."

With a gentle touch he brushed a strand of hair from her cheek, tucking it behind her ear. She turned her cheek against his warm skin, reveling in the feel of his callused fingers against her face. He was so close that she could feel the heat of him radiating toward her, nurturing the hope that unfurled in her breast like a new leaf in spring.

"That night, when you stood over Nicky with the knife, what were you doing?" She asked the question that had been held back for too long, the words tumbling from her lips, opening the door to his trust, just a crack, but, oh, she prayed it was enough. Something tugged at her thoughts, some connection that hovered just beyond her grasp.

"Ah, I wondered when you would get to that." He looked at her sharply. "You thought I would *harm* him, harm my son? I sought to protect him. There is smallpox in Derrymore."

Emma stared at him, befuddled by this apparent non sequitur. Something teased her memory, and again she thought there was some correlation she knew, but could not define. "And the smallpox in Derrymore has a connection to your knife and to the fact that you near scared me to death?"

"You defended Nicky like a lioness defending her cub. I must admit that in retrospect I understand your concerns."

"You understand my concern at finding you standing over your son, knife in hand, your expression stark as a barren field . . . ?" she prompted. "Explain to me the connection between knives and smallpox." She studied him for a long moment, letting the certainty that there *was* a connection wash through her. For some reason, she thought of the pamphlets she had seen in his study, the ones that spoke of the eradication of smallpox. "You *do* have an explanation . . . ."

"I do. Twenty years ago, a man named Edward Jenner found that by and large milkmaids do not

develop smallpox. He concluded that their expo-
sure to cowpox rendered them safe from the disease. Hence, he began experiments in which he
purposely inoculated individuals with liquid from a
cowpox pustule. *Vacca* is the Latin for cow. Jenner's
process has come to be known as vaccination. That
is what I intended to do to Nicky that night.
Jenner's method uses quills to scrape the matter
from the cowpox pustule into the subject's skin,
thus conferring protection. The knife was merely to
pry open the box of quills. The lid was stuck." At
her soft exclamation, he shrugged. "I had hoped
Nicky would sleep through the worst of it, and wake
up safe from possible contagion."

"And you chose not to explain yourself at that
moment because . . . ?" Frustration lent a sharp
edge to the question. Such a simple explanation,
and had he but chosen to share it, much of her distress could so easily have been avoided.

"Nicky was awake, upset, already pulled in to an
argument that should never have occurred." He
raked his fingers through his dark hair, and the expression he turned to her was a tad sheepish. "And
then my ego demanded that you come to me."

"Ohhhh!"

He held up one hand, palm forward. "Ridiculous. I know."

Emma stared at him, her mind spinning, assimi-
lating all he had shared, and suddenly she shivered
with increased awareness. Cowpox. He spoke of
cowpox. She jerked upright, eyes wide with newfound insight.

"Farmer Hicks's cow! I was learning to milk the
cow," she cried, her anger and hurt forgotten in the
face of her dawning knowledge. Dear heaven, he

had gifted her with understanding, and he had not even been aware of her question. "I have wondered these many years why our entire household was struck down by that terrible plague. Three of the children, and their parents. The butler, the maid, even a sweep who came to do the chimneys. *My mother.*" She drew in a shuddering breath. "Yet, I remained untouched. The guilt of surviving while others died was terrible." She shook her head at the unbelievable strangeness of it. "And all because I was learning to milk the cow."

"I shall be forever grateful to that cow," he murmured, his voice husky. He eased closer to her, and she stared at him, her thoughts whirling.

"Oh, no! I stopped you from protecting Nicky! We must—"

"I took care of it later that night," he interjected. "He slept through the whole of it."

"So that is why you expected him to be feverish. He has cowpox," she said, with wonder.

"A benign form of disease that will cause him temporary discomfort but leave him none the worse for it. In fact, it will leave him better off, for smallpox will not touch him."

Emma fisted her hands in her skirt, suddenly unsure of herself and her place in Anthony's esteem. Was he angry with her? Disappointed? He had not been about any nefarious business. His sole intent had been the protection of his son. She should have known, should have trusted . . . And then the realization dawned. She *had* known. In her heart, she *had* trusted him.

With new perspective, she acknowledged the insecurities that had clouded her entire life. Her father had tossed her aside before she was even

born. Oh, she had had a mother's love but, at the
same time, had borne the scorn of others. The servants had gossiped, and with each new post that her
mother was forced to find, Emma had prayed that
this time would be different, *this* time none would
dig out the rumors and point an accusatory finger,
this time she would truly be home. But each new
place had turned out the same in the end, until her
mother died, leaving Emma alone and at the mercy
of her aunts, cast aside and offered to the highest
bidder, a horrible man who would take her as mistress whether she wished it or not.

'Twas no wonder she knew nothing of trust.

But she knew of heat and need and the pull of
Anthony Craven, the temptation of him so strong
that she would sell her soul for the taste of his lips,
the feel of his hard body under her palms, the
sound of his honey-smooth voice as he whispered
against her ear.

Her lips parted, and she jerked her gaze up to
meet his, trying to read the deepest secrets of his
heart.

Chapter Fifteen

"I am so sorry," Emma whispered, meaning the words with every fiber of her being. Sorry for her lack of trust. Sorry for breaking down his walls, making him care for her, and then disappointing him. Sorry because she knew the truth, that his caring was not enough. She wanted him to love her as he had loved Delia. No, *more* than he had loved Delia. Different. Deeper. Stronger.

A sorry state that, for he had clearly vowed that such were the emotions of the youth he had once been and not the man he was now.

But, oh, the emotion she felt for him, pure and clear as a mountain spring, welling from her heart to flood her veins. How to hold such a thing secret? How to guard it and keep it safe?

"The fault is mine," he replied. "I should have explained my actions right away."

"Yes. You should have."

Apparently caught off guard by her reply, he blinked. The silence spun its silken web. "I wanted you to trust me," he said at length.

Her heart twisted in her breast. Trust. There was

something in his eyes that made her think the word held a depth of meaning she could not begin to fathom.

"And yet, in the end, you did explain yourself."

He smiled ruefully. "I am unused to justifying my actions to anyone. I am afraid that I made a poor showing of it."

She stared at him, touched beyond measure that he had been willing to give her an explanation, and even more than that, willing to forgive her trespass.

"Emma." Her name. Only her name. But the sound of it on his lips, warm and rich with promise, made a twist of longing gather in her core. She could see the faint quickening of his breath, feel the heat rising off of him, telling signs that spoke of his own response.

He stepped closer, not quite touching her, but almost, the great shadow of the bed looming so close beside them.

Overwhelmed, she stared into his green-gold eyes, pulled into the depths, emotion churning hot and feral inside her, battering the limits of her control.

"I love you," she whispered and then froze, the enormity of her confession crashing over her.

His eyes widened, darkened, and a tiny furrow marked his brow. She stood poised, quivering, and then she did not want to wait even a second more. With a low moan, she threw herself against him, tumbling them both onto the bed in a tangle of arms and legs.

His lips slanted across hers, and she felt the rough texture of his tongue as he probed and stroked, demanding a passion that she readily yielded. She made a soft sound, a purr of pleasure. Oh, glorious relief to savor his kiss.

Bunching the cloth of her skirt in his hand, he drew it up over the skin of her thigh, his touch driving her half mad with wanting. Her tongue darted out searching for his, dragging a rough sound from deep inside him, something between a laugh and a groan.

He was Anthony, Lord of Manorbrier, a lonely castle set atop a hill, the thick crumbling walls and whispered stories holding all at bay, just as the walls around his heart let none draw near. But not her. Never her. Untouchable Anthony Craven touched *her*, and let her touch him, and together they were whole. She felt it deep inside.

With fingers made clumsy by passion, she tore his shirt open, and his trousers, and pressed her mouth to the smooth, warm skin of his chest, tasting salt and man. She licked him, nipped him, pressing wet kisses to his belly, and lower, until her mouth closed around the hard, velvet length of his erection. Drawing on him, she pulled a growl, and then a moan from his lips.

The feeling was indescribably lush. Delicious feminine pleasure. Power. He was there before her, sprawled in slavelike ecstasy, half clothed, his glorious body kissed by the dusk, by her lips, touched by her hands. She found that she liked this feeling, and she swirled her tongue around the proud thick rod that jutted forth, the smooth, round head of it, and then she sucked him deep inside her mouth.

"Christ, Emma." A growl rumbled from deep inside him as she drew hard on him, then ran her tongue from base to tip. "Where . . . ? How . . . ?"

She drew back, circling the hard thickness of him with her tongue, then letting him go as she met his gaze. "I liked it when you did it to me. I thought you would like it too." And he did like it. Of that, she had no doubt.

A raspy laugh rumbled in his chest. Rolling with her, he tumbled her back, pulled the clothes from her body, tossed them carelessly aside, kissed her, wet and openmouthed and deep. One hand tangled in her hair, and his mouth pressed to hers, rough with passion, his naked chest brushing her breasts. He bent his head, suckled one nipple, squeezed and stroked the other with his fingers, and she moaned, lost in the wet heat of his mouth and the pinch of his fingers, her nipples hard and aching.

"Now," she whispered, and then louder, "Now."

And, dear heaven, he was pushing himself up into her, stretching her, filling her as she moaned her pleasure, her body closing around him, her fingers grasping at the hard globes of his buttocks.

The feeling was unearthly perfection. Wicked torment and unutterable pleasure. She wanted him so desperately she was trembling with it, burning, half sobbing as he filled her, smooth and slick and hot, and she arched up, her knees bent, heels digging into the sheets as she struggled to draw ever closer, ever tighter, to make them one.

He went deeper still, each move a slow climb to madness, withdrawing then thrusting until she cried out, a high keening sound of wicked pleasure and aching need.

"Oh, please . . ." She panted, whimpered, every nerve so sensitized she thought surely she was half mad with longing.

Wrapping her legs tight around him, she angled to meet each thrust, gasping as he moved harder, faster, every muscle taut, and then he came into her and held still, his body rigid as a bow. With a cry, Emma shattered, and she felt the pulsing release of him, there, with her.

And in that moment, she thought she was finally, beautifully home.

As the hour drew close to midnight, Emma snuggled against Anthony's side, wrapped in the soft cloak of her contentment and the warmth of his embrace.

"Emma, we must talk. About . . ."

Ah. Her wayward tongue had betrayed her, and now he would speak of it. *I love you. I love you.* Oh, why had she let the words escape?

A frantic tapping came at her door, forestalling their conversation. Dragging the thick coverlet about her naked body, Emma tiptoed to the portal, relieved that her words of love, her frantic avowal, would not yet be opened to his denial.

She opened the door to find Mrs. Bolifer standing in the dark hallway, her hair falling wildly about her shoulders, her face white with strain.

"Meg's time has come," she said tightly. "And she's in a bad way. The babe's breach, and her being a wee thing, I have a fear for her life. Her sister's come for me. Alice. And she's dreadful afraid." She looked past Emma into the dim room, her expression indicating that she felt neither surprise nor censure at the discovery of her master in Emma's bed. "You must come."

Turning, Emma saw that Anthony was sitting on the edge of the bed, the sheet draped across his loins. He raked his fingers through his hair and shook his head. "I can offer her nothing."

Emma's heart twisted at his words.

"You must come," Mrs. Bolifer insisted.

"I will come, but I will not touch her. You know that I cannot. There is nothing I can do. We both know that now." He heaved a sigh. "You will be a far greater comfort and help to the girl, Mrs. Bolifer."

The housekeeper stared at him, her expression bleak, and then she nodded once before hurrying away.

"You *can* offer her something," Emma whispered, stricken by his refusal. "You are a doctor. A healer."

"No longer, Emma mine. I am a researcher, a scientist."

"You can save her," she insisted, her voice rising. "At least you can try!"

"Try? And fail?" He shook his head. "Never again."

Anthony tugged on his clothes and came to stand by her side. He ran the backs of his fingers gently across her cheek. "I cannot. Stay here in case Nicky wakes. There is nothing you can do for Meg."

Sinking down onto the soft cushions of the window seat, Emma stared at the empty doorway long after he had left the room, a feeling of indescribable sadness washing over her. She had won his affection, perhaps even a small corner of his heart, but she had not healed his wounded soul, had not chased away the demons that gnawed at him.

Only he could do that. And until he did, until he healed himself, what hope was there for her?

The clatter of hooves on the cobbled drive announced his departure. She thought he must have taken Mrs. Bolifer in the coach and left for Bosherton. She could only hope he would choose rightly once he saw Meg.

She frowned, rubbing her hands along her arms, feeling chilled. Reaching for her gown, she slipped it on first, and then her stockings, to warm her cold toes. Something felt wrong. The coldness came from inside her, clawing icy talons along her limbs. Shivering, she rose and crossed the room.

Silently she eased open the door that joined her chamber to Nicky's and moved to his bedside, then let out a soft gasp. The chill intensified, numbing her. Nicky was not there.

"Nicky" she called softly, hurrying to check the hallway. It was empty.

With mounting concern, she returned to her own chamber, wondering if he might have woken and crawled into her bed. But no, her chamber was empty as well. She realized she had expected that. Every instinct cried out at his absence. Something was terribly wrong.

Thoughts in turmoil, Emma crossed to the small table, intent on lighting the candle that rested there. She would need light to carry out a search of the house. Perhaps she should wake Griggs, and Cookie, and Glynnis, the downstairs maid. Her gaze skimmed the window, and a subtle movement outside caught her attention. She leaned closer, peering through the glass. Two shapes emerged from the shadows, a child and a man dressed in pale breeches. Together they hurried along the drive toward the gate.

Alarm made her stomach rise, then fall. Without pausing to think, she hurried from the room, down the stairs, and out into the night, her breath coming in harsh gasps as she gave chase.

"Nicky!" Emma cried, running now, stumbling at the sharp bite of stones into the soles of her stockinged feet.

The soft nicker of a horse carried on the breeze. An enclosed carriage waited just beyond Manorbrier's crumbling wall, its hulking shape somehow threatening in the darkness. She watched in horror as the man yanked open the carriage door and lifted the child inside.

"Stop!" she yelled, panic rising in a sickening surge. Oh, God! This was a nightmare. "Stop! Nicky!"

The man's head jerked up at her cries, and he melted into the shadows. Dr. Smythe, she thought. Dr. Smythe was stealing Nicky away in the dead of night.

Skidding to a halt directly before the carriage door, Emma curled her fingers around the handle. She tugged frantically on the door.

"Climb up beside me on the box," a voice whispered from directly beside her right ear. "We must be away. There is danger here."

"Cookie!" Emma spun toward the voice, her relief so acute that she slumped under the force of it, pressing one hand to the side of the carriage. "Oh, thank heaven. I thought"—she shook her head—"never mind what I thought. What are you doing out here at this time of night?"

"Hurry, now. Up onto the box," Cookie urged. "We must be away as quickly as possible."

"Why? What is amiss?" Suddenly, she thought of the night she had gone to the portrait gallery, and her certainty that someone had entered the house. "Is there someone in the house? Do you take Nicky to his father?"

"To his father. Yes. A child should be with his *true* parent." Cookie's voice was urgent, harsh. "Hurry!"

Frowning, Emma clambered up the side of the coach, felt the vehicle rock and sway as Cookie came up beside her onto the small bench meant to hold the coachman. Taking up the leads, the cook set the carriage in motion.

Fingers curled over the edge of the seat, pressing against the hard wood as the vehicle jolted wildly along the rutted road, Emma wondered at the sharp coil of unease that looped in her belly. Twisting, she sent a glance at the road behind her, watching as Manorbrier receded in the distance, a dark smudge against the night sky. *Wrong. Wrong. The night felt wrong.*

She turned forward once more, trying to calm her racing heart. A thin glow diffused from the face of the moon, lighting their way. She pressed her fingers harder against the wooden seat, welcoming the pain, focusing on it instead of on her growing distress. Turning her head, she glanced at Cookie. Her expression was intense, lips compressed in a thin line, eyes staring fixedly at the road ahead.

Emma glanced down. Cookie wore breeches. Buff breeches. And polished black boots.

And the smell of lemon mixed with horseradish and turpentine.

Oh, dear heaven.

Pulling away, Emma slid to the farthest edge of the hard little bench, but there was nowhere to go other than over the side and into the black void. Were she alone, she would fling herself from the seat and hope that she could land with little more than a bruising. But she was not alone. There was Nicky, her precious boy, locked in the carriage.

Emma struggled to stem the surge of mindless panic that swelled to monstrous proportions.

Clearing her throat against the knot that had lodged there, she raised her voice to overcome the pounding of the horses' hooves. "I . . . I should ride with Nicky. I do not wish for him to be afraid."

The cook did not answer. Instead, she stared impassively ahead, flicking the reins and encouraging the horses to greater speed. Emma thought they were traveling at a most dangerous pace already, but when she tried to bring the matter to Cookie's attention, the woman ignored her and flicked the reins anew.

As the carriage careened wildly to one side, Emma yelled, "Cookie, please slow down! This is dangerous! The carriage will overturn!"

Emma fought the urge to grab Cookie's arm, fearful that any sudden movement might cause her to lose control of the team. As if her thoughts became reality, the carriage wove precariously from side to side as it lurched around a curve in the road.

"Miss Emma! Miss Emma!" Nicky's panicked cries were muffled by the walls of the coach, the din of the horses, and the rising wind. But some maternal instinct allowed Emma to hear the terror in his voice. The sound of his fear mirrored her own.

"Please!" she cried frantically.

Perhaps it was her own desperation that reached the other woman, or the child's frantic cries, but at last Cookie eased their wild pace.

"Why are you doing this?" Emma asked. "Where do you take us?"

"A child should be with his true parent. Do you not see? His *true* parent. No child should be separated from his parent." A broken sob escaped the cook. "My child was taken from me, separated from me. It isn't right, isn't natural."

"Cookie, please. Take us back to Manorbrier. Take us home." Emma eyed the taut leather reins, wondering if she could safely snatch them away from Cookie's grasp. And then what? She had never driven a coach in her life. Dear heaven, she could kill them all.

"Not his home." Cookie sent her a dark glance. "You read the diary. You *know*. Manorbrier is not Nicky's home."

The diary, Delia's diary. So it was Cookie who had taken it. Suddenly, the puzzle solved itself. The boots and breeches she had glimpsed in the hedge outside the icehouse. The medicinal lemony scent that had haunted her. She recalled Mrs. Bolifer telling her that Cookie prepared her liniment. And Cookie had been nowhere to be found that day when Emma returned to the kitchen from the icehouse, and the night she had sensed an intruder in the portrait gallery, Cookie had been wandering about. It was Cookie. All of it. Cookie.

"Tell me about the diary. I never read to the end. Tell me," Emma urged, desperate to sway the cook's attention, hoping to make her slow the coach still more.

"Lord Craven is not Nicky's father."

Emma gasped and reared back in shock. "Not his father? What do you mean?"

But even as she asked, she knew the answer. Words from the diary, written in flowing feminine script, drifted through her thoughts. *The time has come to face the terrible truth. I am pregnant. Pregnant. The terrible, astonishing wonder of it. After the choices I*

*made, I had not thought it possible. He was so angry when
I told him. Oh, God, nothing is as it seems. Nothing.*

Delia became pregnant, not by Anthony, but by
some other man. The breath left Emma in a rush
and she wrapped her arms around her waist, trying
to hold in the wild emotions that tore through her.
Did Anthony know?

Yes. Oh, God, yes. He knew, and that had been
the cause of love turned to hate, the reason that he
had been so bitterly angry at Delia. And still, he
loved Nicky as his own. Loved him with all his heart.
A father's love, granted freely and unconditionally.

"Oh, Anthony," she whispered.

Cookie snapped the reins, driving the horses
back to their earlier frenzied pace, and then sur-
passing it until Emma thought the carriage must
surely overturn.

She pressed back against the seat, her throat closing with emotion. She thought she could hear
Nicky sobbing inside the coach, the sound harsh
and wretched to her ears.

"We could be killed. You and I, and the child as
well. 'Tis not safe here. Please, Cookie, please, let
us return to Manorbrier." She raised her voice to be
heard as they rushed on, striving to keep the panic
from her tone, though it welled inside her, dark
and sticky like the sucking mud of a bog, threatening to draw her in and suffocate her.

The carriage rocked and swayed, but the mad
pace did not slow.

"And if we are killed, then he will suffer all the
more as he stares at the boy's broken body."
Cookie's words resounded with a maniacal glee,
and spittle sprayed from her mouth. "He kept me
from my son. Bound my bloody wrists and kept me

from my son. All this time, I thought Nicky his, but he lied . . . oh, he lied . . ."

Mad. Truly mad. All the times Emma had thought Manorbrier a nest of Bedlamites, she had never truly thought to face such as this. Poor, poor Cookie, unhinged by the death of her son, pushed now beyond reason by . . . by what?

"Well, I'll fix it. Make it right." Cookie's laughter swelled, a wild crazed noise that rose and spread until it was nearly tangible, wrapping around Emma as she shrank from her. She gasped, smelling lemons and turpentine.

Pulling to the edge of the seat, Emma nearly gagged on the bile that burned her throat as her stomach heaved and shifted. Cookie's hand shot out and tangled in Emma's skirt as she grabbed a fistful of fabric. With unexpected strength she yanked her closer, barely guiding the horses with one hand while she held fast to the cloth with the other. Suddenly, she sawed on the reins, drawing the lathered beasts to a halt. The carriage rocked precariously, and Emma clutched at the seat, nearly sliding off the side.

Cookie turned to face her, and in her eyes Emma saw no reason, no soul, only cold, bitter hatred and terrifying madness.

"What do you think happened to Delia?" Cookie leaned close, her face a pale mask. Emma could feel her hot breath on her cheek as she spoke, smell the odor that rose from her. Rank sweat, lemon, and something sickly and fetid—a repulsive combination.

Emma pulled away, saying nothing, her eyes flicking back and forth between the other woman's twisted expression and the dark landscape as she tried to formulate some plan of escape. The sound of her own panicked breaths filled her ears.

Cookie snickered, her eyes rolling this way and that. She yanked Emma closer still.

"What happened to Delia?" she asked again, her voice high and shrill.

"I do not know."

"Don't you, lovey? Don't you?"

"Oh, please! Nicky! I must get to Nicky. I beg you, let me go to him."

Cookie laughed, the sound harsh, reminiscent of the protest of rusted hinges on an old gate.

"Delia. She told me what she'd done. Didn't want to spoil her pretty figure and so she ended her pregnancy—"

"What?" Emma cried.

"Not her second one. Her first. She got pregnant on her wedding night and she didn't want it. So she killed it. And I killed her. Pushed her to the bottom of a great long staircase. It was the only way. But she took a long time to die, a very long time, her belly writhing as she struggled to push forth the babe. One born living, the other dead." Cookie's tone rose and fell with an eerie singsong cadence, and then she slanted Emma a frighteningly cold glance. "Perfect justice. One babe to stay with the father, the other gone into death with the mother. A child must stay with its parent, don't you see?"

Oh, dear sweet God. No. This was too terrible to believe. Oh, Anthony, Anthony. Emma swallowed the bitter terror that rose inside her, rearing its ugly head, threatening to destroy her composure.

She raised her head, glanced about, wondering if help would come. No. No one knew they were gone. She would have to rely on her own ingenuity to save herself and Nicky both.

The thought was cold comfort.

Cookie's hand was still wound in the material of Emma's skirt. She tugged on it, as though sensing that Emma was contemplating clambering over the edge of the seat to get to Nicky.

"Please," Emma whispered, struggling to pull free. Nicky's piteous cries, growing weaker now, ate at her heart.

"Don't be afraid," Cookie crooned. "I won't make it hurt." She stroked one hand along Emma's cheek. Emma flinched, then curled her hands into fists and struck out, landing a blow to the other woman's cheek and another to her shoulder. Free. She had torn free!

With a cry, she made to leap from the seat, but Cookie caught her hair and yanked her back, then lashed the horses to resume their course. Again she whipped them, and again, until their speed surpassed all caution, all reason.

I won't make it hurt. Her attention divided between the danger of the runaway coach and her fear for Nicky, Emma barely registered the cook's meaning. She knew only that the other woman was mad as a hatter, dangerously so, and that she blamed Anthony for all the sorrows of her loss for he had saved her life, thereby separating her from her dead son. The carriage tilted precariously and Emma heard a sickening thud as the wheels on her right left the ground, then crashed back to the hard-packed road.

She could hear Nicky pounding on the carriage door and crying her name. His loud sobs crescendoed, tearing at Emma's heart like knife-edged talons. She dragged in a breath, wondering why she smelled smoke.

She glanced at Cookie, and with a renewed burst of strength, she dove at her, grabbing for the leads.

"Nicky!" Emma yelled, forcing the air from her lungs, through her larynx, desperate to project enough volume that the child would hear her. "Jump when the coach slows! Jump, Nicky! Jump! Jump and run! Run away, Nicky! Run!"

With all her might Emma pulled up, trying to stop the horses' mad dash. She felt the coach slow, and from the corner of her eye she thought she saw a small form hurtle out into the dark night.

Then Cookie was upon her, the back of her hand catching Emma across her cheek. Falling back, Emma strove to turn and search the ground, to see if Nicky had escaped. The carriage door was open, the jolting ride sending it crashing against the side, banging it back and forth.

"Run, Nicky!" she screamed, sobbing now. "Run!"

Emma struggled as Cookie snatched the reins from her hands. The carriage tilted crazily to one side and Emma slid, her head slamming hard against the edge of the seat. Pain lanced through her. The coach listed even further and Emma scrambled to right herself. *Too late,* she thought, as the world pitched and rolled, the smell of smoke stronger now, burning her nostrils.

She was flying, hurtling through the darkness. A great crashing sound rent the air, and an endless scream pierced the night. The ground rose up to meet her and she felt a sharp pain before the blackness closed in.

* * *

The light hurt her eyes. Emma opened them, then snapped her lids shut against the pain. Cautiously, she eased them open once more, frowning. It was night. Biting back a moan, she turned her head. Odd. It was night and the light was so brilliant.

"Nicky," she said softly, a whisper, a prayer.

"Miss Emma."

She felt his soft hand touch her brow and tears pooled in her eyes.

"Oh! Thank God!" She pushed herself to a sitting position, ignoring the terrible agony that streaked through her head and the vile nausea caused by her movement. Wrapping her arms around him, she pulled Nicky into her lap. She buried her face in his soft hair, inhaling the scent of him.

"Are you hurt?" she asked, in a strangled voice.

Nicky shifted in her arms, angling his leg so she could see the tear in his brown velvet breeches.

"I have a scrape." He sounded so forlorn.

Nearly sobbing with relief, Emma tightened her embrace. "Oh, what a brave boy you are."

Suddenly, the enormity of their situation hit her. A finely honed shaft of terror shot through her and Emma raised her eyes and scanned the vicinity searching for Cookie. A short distance away lay the remains of the coach, flames licking at its sides, but of the cook there was no sign.

Oh, she thought, blinking at the growing blaze, *so that is the source of the light.* Then she frowned, unable to force her sluggish mind to comprehend from where the flame had originated. She recalled no lantern, no candle. Nicky made a small sound of protest as she hugged him tightly.

"Miss Emma," he began tentatively, "I think I made that fire."

"You did?" she asked, angling her head to look into his face.

"Theodore, my soldier." He held up one hand and showed her the tin toy. "He didn't like the dark." He paused for a moment and then went on in a rush. "Papa doesn't like me to play with matches. He caught me once and was very angry. But I had a tin in the pocket of my coat. It's an old coat. Cookie put it on me to keep me warm. I forgot the tin was there, only when I put my hand in, I found it. Theodore was so afraid. I thought if I lit the match it would be light, it would help. But I dropped the first one, and the seat started to burn with a cheery flame, and I lit a second one and tossed it at the first, and when you yelled for me to jump—" Nicky began to sob in earnest. "I didn't mean to!"

Emma tightened her arms around him, even as she glanced about searching for some sign of Cookie. She did not trust that they were safe here.

"Oh, Nicky. None of this is your fault. None of it. Of course you were afraid—"

"Not me. Theodore," he interjected.

"Yes, of course. Theodore." She kissed the top of his head. "But you, Nicholas, are a brave boy indeed. You saved yourself, and you helped to save me."

He looked at her, his eyes wide. "Truly?" he whispered.

"Truly. But now we must be away from here. We must find our way home."

"But what of Cookie?" he asked.

Yes. What of Cookie?

Setting the child on his feet, Emma struggled to rise, pressing her hands against the rough ground. They must be away. They were not safe here. Suddenly, a terrible pounding slammed through her head, and the earth seemed to shake with its force. Emma clutched the child to her, the two of them adrift in a sea of noise. Nicky's head snapped up and he went still, like a small animal scenting the air. Then his face lit with a smile and he bounded to his feet.

"Papa!" Leaving Emma on the ground, he ran toward the source of the sound.

Again, she made to rise, to follow him, but the world swam dizzily before her eyes.

Pressing her fingers against her forehead, Emma felt a sticky wetness. *Blood,* she thought.

And then he was before her, Anthony, the bonfire that consumed what remained of the carriage illuminating the night, casting flickering shadows across the chiseled angles of his face.

His beautiful, beloved face.

He caught Nicky tightly against him and squatted at Emma's side, cradling his son.

"Anthony."

His name was a sigh on her lips.

He took her chin between thumb and forefinger, turning her head firmly toward him. His touch was warm and solid, and in his eyes she saw a blaze of emotion so deep, so stark it stole her breath. Tears of relief clogged her throat, and she could not force words past the blockage. They were not yet safe, she reminded herself. There was still the specter of Cookie, her madness, her bilious, irrational hatred.

"You are bleeding. Here, press this against the gash." Anthony's voice, so calm, so cool washed over her, and her gaze snapped to his. His walls were firmly back in place. He pressed a folded square of cloth against her temple, then lifted her hand and guided it to the spot. "Press."

She wanted to grab his hand, to press her lips to the knuckles, to babble her relief in a shining torrent of words. Taking over the chore of pressing on the cloth, she managed to croak only a single word. "Cookie."

Anthony rose, scanning the vicinity. The wind caught his coat, billowing the tail like great black wings.

"Where?"

A shrill scream pierced the night.

At the sound, Anthony's head jerked up and for a fraction of a second he stared at the flaming wreckage. Then he sprinted toward the source of the cry, his greatcoat fanning out behind him.

Emma struggled to her feet. The world tilted precariously. Holding both arms out from her sides she fought for balance, then stumbled after Anthony. She reached him as he pulled his coat from his shoulders and tossed it to the ground.

A second scream echoed from the growing flames, more shrill, more frantic than the last.

"I'm trapped! Oh, God! My foot!" Cookie's voice, laced with terror.

Anthony did not hesitate. Emma watched, her heart in her throat, as he strode toward the conflagration that threatened to destroy all it touched.

Cookie lay on the ground, a huge section of the carriage collapsed upon her, pinning her beneath its weight. The edges of her jagged prison were aflame, and she struggled to free herself, her eyes rolling back in her head as panic overwhelmed her.

Suddenly, a small hand clasped her own, and Emma looked down to see Nicky at her side.

"Will Papa save her?" he asked, his voice trembling.

Why should he? Cookie had murdered Anthony's wife, stolen Nicky away in the dark of night. She pulled Nicky against her, turning the child in to her skirts, hoping to spare him the worst of what would follow. And when she spoke, she knew without a hint of doubt that her words were true. "Yes. He will try to save her. Your father is a doctor, a healer."

Anthony would try to save even this woman, she who had cost him so much. His wife. His daughter. His good name, seeing him branded a monster, a murderer.

Looking back toward the flames, Emma watched as Anthony grabbed the woman's defenseless form, tugging and pulling in a desperate bid to free her. Cookie screamed and batted at his hands, hindering his every effort.

"Let me die," she cried. "This time, let me die."

With a snarl, Anthony seized the edge of the wreckage, struggling to pull it clear as the flames danced closer, higher.

Emma could see now that Cookie was covered in blood, a thick hunk of wood protruding from her belly. She sucked in a breath, her heart pounding as Anthony renewed his desperate bid to free the woman who had cost him so much.

Like a man possessed, Anthony jerked on the wreckage, using a broken piece of the wheel to hack frantically at the walls of the flaming cage. And then Emma realized that the dark shadow beneath Cookie's suddenly still form was a pool of blood, that even if Anthony succeeded in freeing her, she would die, her wounds too terrible to heal. Perhaps she was already dead. Emma thought she was.

"May God grant you peace at last," she whispered.

Anthony reached one last time into the fire, made one last attempt to pull Cookie free. Emma

watched, her belly clutched with fear, terrified now
that the licking flames would take him from her.

"Stay here, darling." She gave Nicky's shoulder a
firm squeeze, and then she wove unsteadily toward
Anthony.

The flames would soon reach his clothes, but he
remained frozen, seemingly unaware of the danger
to his own life and limb. With a cry, she threw herself against him, sending them both to the ground,
rolling away from the blaze.

He was warm and solid against her, his breath
coming in harsh gasps. She could smell ash and the
stink of burning hair and flesh.

"I'm sorry, Emma. Christ, I'm sorry." His arms
came around her, holding her so tight she could
barely breathe. His hand stroked her hair, his fingers tangling in the long strands, and then he
tipped her face, his mouth swooping down in a
hard kiss that tasted of smoke and desperation.

Together, they rose and staggered toward Nicky,
who flung himself into their outstretched arms.

Emma wrapped her arms around Nicky, holding
him close, both of them surrounded by Anthony's
loving embrace, cast in the flickering light of the
dancing flames.

Looking toward the indistinct shape of the
charred wreckage, Emma felt as though she had
walked through the fire herself, so raw and vulner-
able was her sensibility. Tightening her hold on
those she loved, she held them close and wished
that she could wake and find it all a terrible dream.

CHAPTER SIXTEEN

"Have you stopped bleeding?" Anthony asked, pulling back to examine Emma's head. The mere sound of his voice was a soothing balm after the frightful trauma of the past hour.

"Yes," she whispered, running the tips of her fingers along his soot-stained cheek. "How did you reach us so quickly?"

"Meg," he said sadly. "Smythe is the father of her babe. He told her of an encounter with Cookie. Called her a raving lunatic. From Meg's scattered account I managed to piece together something of the story."

"But how did you know which way to go? The road forked. If you had taken the wrong path . . ." She could not stop touching him, or Nicky, who nestled sleepily in his father's arms. She ran her hand along the child's soft cheek, and then traced the strong column of Anthony's throat, the hard line of his jaw.

"Oh, God." Tears clogged her throat. "And now? How is Meg now?"

"Now, she lies wracked by a labor that came too early."

"You must return." Emma gnawed on her lower lip, anxious to question him about all Cookie had revealed, to share her suspicions and certainties, yet she knew that her questions must wait.

"I—"

She pressed her fingers to his lips, stopping whatever protest he meant to make. "You must, Anthony. Free yourself of the past, of the ghosts who haunt you. The time is long overdue."

He was silent so long she thought he would balk, would refuse to do what must be done. And then he turned and strode toward the waiting coach, laying his sleeping son on the bench and handing Emma in along with him.

Then he closed the carriage door, leaving her alone with the child, and the dark. She could hear a soft huff of inhalation and exhalation, and she closed her eyes, tears pricking the backs of her lids. Full circle. She had come full circle, riding a coach in the blackness of night to a fate she could not be certain of.

The coach creaked and shifted as Anthony climbed up on the bench, and then it began to move, eating up the distance to Bosherton. She thought she might have dozed, for in the space of a heartbeat they drew up before a small cottage and Anthony came round to pull open the door.

She glanced at the sleeping child.

"Leave him," Anthony whispered. "Griggs is here to keep an eye."

She nodded and climbed out just as Mrs. Bolifer hurried from the cottage.

"You are back, my lord, and none too soon. My

store of knowledge is exhausted. Meg needs you now. Come," Mrs. Bolifer said brusquely.

If Anthony was offended by the housekeeper's inappropriate tone, he gave no sign.

"My lord, I think Meg is not long for this world," she urged. "The sheets are soaked with blood, and the girl's barely conscious. She is calling for you." Looking at the ground, the housekeeper hesitated, then whispered, "She says she does not want to die."

He blanched at her words, and Emma could sense a strange current pass between master and servant.

"I cannot, Tabby," he said, looking away to stare at the horizon. "You know I cannot."

Emma was startled to hear Mrs. Bolifer's given name pass his lips. She was even more amazed when the woman stepped forward and laid her hand on his arm, as though she were friend rather than servant.

"I brought your instruments. Even now they are in the kitchen, sitting for the past hour in a pot of boiling water, just as you used to instruct me." The housekeeper's voice was firm, bracing. "I know you can do what needs to be done. The girl will die without you. She doesn't deserve that. Doesn't deserve to be sacrificed to your demons."

"I am no longer a physician and surgeon," Anthony snarled. "I do not deal in life. Only death."

Emma rushed forward and drew abreast of the housekeeper, and standing side by side with the older woman, she faced him down.

"You deal in death to save life," she cried desperately, sensing that it was not only Meg's life that hung in the balance, but Anthony's battered soul. "I know nothing of your demons, nothing of the horror that haunts you, but I know that you risk your own life to try to understand disease. Terrible, horrible disease that you grow in a dank tower. You do that to prevent contagion. To save lives."

He said nothing, his silence a bitter constraint on her reckless hope.

"You risked your life to save Cookie, a woman who tried to steal your son, who by her own account murdered your pregnant wife, pushed her down the stairs." She heard Mrs. Bolifer's startled gasp, but it was Anthony's reaction she focused on. Time enough for explanations and tears later.

He grew still, so still that she thought he ceased to breathe.

"Delia told me that she had done the deed herself. All this time I thought—" His words broke on a strangled groan. "I blamed myself. I thought she would rather be dead than married to me. And in the end, she begged me—" He shook his head. "I could not do as she asked, and I could not save her."

He seemed hewn of stone, each muscle and sinew corded as he stood, stiff and unmoving, his expression glacial. She thought he would surely crack, so rigid was his composure. Staring at her with eyes dark and unreadable, he looked untouchable, unreachable by their pleas. Time hung suspended.

Emma held out one hand in supplication.

"Please," she whispered brokenly. "Anthony, please."

"And if she dies? As Delia died?" he rasped. "As I *let* her die?"

So this was his private hell. This blame he cast upon himself. Emma made a soft sound of denial, a gasp, a plea.

Raising his hands before him, Anthony turned

his palms upward, stared downward as he clenched them into fists. His fingers were blistered and raw, testament to his attempts to save Cookie. His hands, like his face, were blackened with the soot from the fire, and the smell of smoke yet clung to him. Emma saw these marks, badges of his walk through purgatory's fire, confirmation of his survival. If only he could see himself as she saw him, not as monster, but as hero, despite all his human flaws.

"If I kill her?" His tone was bleak. "Or worse, if I can save neither one? Neither Meg nor her babe?"

"Surely both will die without your intervention," Emma said simply, and she knew she spoke the truth. "You offer her hope."

Anthony's nostrils flared as he sucked in a breath.

"Such faith in me." There was no sarcasm in his tone. Only a sweet sense of wonder.

"Yes," she said simply. "Such faith. Unshakable trust."

He looked away from her, toward the house, and his expression hardened.

"Your faith is misplaced, Emma. I could not save Delia, and when she begged me to take the child from her belly, I refused. Coward that I was, I refused. I could not kill her in order to save her child, and to open her womb was a death sentence as surely as if I slit her throat. No woman has survived such surgery. And so I let them die. Delia, and her baby with her. My fault. My hands are stained with their blood."

Her heart felt as though it would shatter, like a delicate crystal cast against hard stone. So now she knew. He blamed himself for his wife's death, for the death of Nicky's sister, though she doubted any other surgeon would have done differently.

"No!" she cried, with such vehemence that the sound ricocheted through the silent night, echoing her denial. "You killed no one, and you let no one die. You are a man, Anthony. It is not your choice who lives and who dies." Emma dragged in a tremulous breath. "But think of Nicky. You *did* save *him*. Think of the love you bear him. Would you deny Meg that opportunity? Would you deny an innocent babe its chance for life? You can use your knowledge to heal. Or you can hoard it like a miser, hiding behind your own pain and misery."

Anger flared in him. She saw it in the way his pupils dilated, and the way his lips compressed thinly. His expression reflected such icy rage that she thought he might freeze her with a single glance. It was the cold, controlled fury she had seen before, and she stared him down, unafraid.

As suddenly as it blazed, his anger abated, and she watched, heart in her throat, as he reached a new resolve.

Holding Emma's gaze, Anthony spoke softly, and she thought he spoke only to her. A promise to her. Her heart swelled and blossomed, nurtured by hope.

"I will do what I can," he said, never taking his eyes from hers. And then in low tones meant only for her ears, "For you. I will do this for you. Face my demons and vanquish them, because you believe I can, and so I believe I can. And for myself, because I *am* the man I once was before circumstance and tragedy played havoc with my heart."

"I believe in you," she whispered, his words swelling inside her, bright as any star. *I love you.* That declaration she held back, whispering it only within her heart, saving it for later, for the time that would be right for the sharing.

He turned away and strode toward the house calling a rapid string of commands as he went.

"I'll need water to wash, and a fresh sheet to tie over my filthy clothing, lest I carry disease to the new mother. Mrs. Bolifer, fetch my instruments. Lay a clean cloth on a tray, and spread them on it for easy reach. I'll need fresh linens. Boiled water in basins so it may cool. And a bottle of carbolic acid. Hurry."

"Griggs," he called, turning back toward the coachman. "Take Nicky home. Send Glynnis to sit by his bed. Then fetch the magistrate. There is the matter of a dead woman on the road to Tenby." Anthony's voice caught on the last, and Emma knew the pain he felt at such tragic loss.

"Aye, my lord." Griggs gave a curt nod.

"And Griggs, see if you can find the horses. They escaped when the coach overturned, and I dislike the thought that they've been harmed by this night's dark deeds."

"Yes, my lord."

Emma watched Anthony's broad back as he strode into the cottage, and then she whirled to face Mrs. Bolifer.

"I want to help," she said resolutely. "Tell me how to help."

She wasn't certain what answer she had expected, but the housekeeper's nod of assent was a surprise.

"Come along then, girl." She led the way through the door. "There're clean linens there. Tear them into strips. Mind, wash your hands first so you don't carry His Lordship's 'wee animalcules' to Meg,"

Mrs. Bolifer ordered firmly. She rested her hand on Emma's forearm and gave a gentle squeeze.

Emma nodded, then frowned as a thought came to her.

"Has Meg been alone this whole time?"

The housekeeper shook her head. "No. Her sister, Alice, is with her. Come along, now." She marched toward the narrow door at the far end of the common room.

Less than twenty minutes later, Emma stood unmoving, bearing silent witness to the life-and-death struggle playing out before her, watching Anthony as he worked over Meg. The girl, whimpering piteously, writhed on the floor in a nest of stained sheets that had been set out close to the fire atop a bed of straw. The hours had worn away at her reserves, robbing her of her strength.

Alice moved away from her spot by her sister's side, weeping softly. Emma recognized her as the sullen-eyed maid who had given her the blanket her first day at Manorbrier. Her eyes were dull now, full of grief.

"Take my place," Alice whispered, gesturing toward Meg's limp hand that she had held fast these many hours. "I cannot—"

Emma gave her a reassuring smile, a heavy sadness tugging at her as she realized Alice was little more than a child herself.

"All will be well," she whispered, though it was a near futile hope, she knew.

"I stopped up the keyholes. Closed the windows. Drew the curtains. I've done all I can to protect her from evil spirits." Sobbing, Alice fled the room, and Emma heard the soft thud of the door closing behind her.

Moving to the low stool set beside the fireplace, Emma took Alice's place, weaving her fingers gently through Meg's. To her surprise, the girl squeezed her hand, and at that tiny show of strength, Emma's optimism was renewed.

"All will be well," she whispered again, this time with firm resolve. Her gaze collided with Anthony's, and he gave her a tired smile.

Emma stayed at Meg's side, wiping the sweat from the girl's brow and watching her suffering, her heart breaking bit by agonizing bit. The drapes were drawn across the windows, blocking out the light of the dawn. The fire in the hearth was fed, and though the room was stifling hot, Meg lay on her makeshift pallet, her body wracked by chills. Anthony said she shivered so because she had lost too much blood.

Dark shadows formed half-moons beneath Anthony's eyes, and his mouth was held in a grim line of fatigue and frustration. Emma longed to lay cool fingers on his brow and soothe his weariness. Watching him work, she had held out hope for Meg's life. At first, she had thought that if sheer determination could save the girl, then Anthony would succeed. But as time dragged on, Emma began to acknowledge that she may have asked for more than any mortal could give. Despite his efforts to turn the breached babe and see it safely born, Meg's fate was not Anthony's to decide. He had fought a valiant battle that Emma was only now beginning to suspect he would surely lose.

An involuntary sound escaped her lips as yet another spurt of blood soaked the fresh cloths that Mrs. Bolifer placed between Meg's thighs. Anthony's head snapped up, his eyes searching out

Emma's in the dim light. She pressed her lips together and shook her head, willing him to understand that she knew he had tried so desperately, had done all he could do. Willing him to see the love in her eyes.

"The craniotomy?" Mrs. Bolifer whispered, her face white and drawn. "It may well be the only chance to save her life."

Emma glanced at Anthony and saw all color leach from his cheeks.

"I cannot, Tabby. Christ, there has to be another way."

"What is a craniotomy?" Emma asked, more than half certain that she had no wish to hear the answer.

Anthony made a sound low in his throat, and it was Mrs. Bolifer who replied, her voice pitched low so Meg would not hear. "The craniotomy is a last resort. He'll take the crotchet, there"—she gestured at the array of instruments—"and he'll crack the babe's skull like an egg. Pull the child piecemeal from the mother. Likely it'll save her life. The mother's, not the child's."

Emma pressed the back of her hand against her lips, fighting the nausea that threatened to overcome her. Mrs. Bolifer's words painted a picture so horrific, so grisly, that she could scarce believe the possibility.

She looked again at Anthony, at the hard, set line of his jaw and the quiet sadness in his eyes, and she knew that the terrible thing Mrs. Bolifer described was no figment of a tortured mind.

Anthony held her gaze for a long moment and then he moved so quickly that she gave a soft cry of surprise. He bent over Meg's prostrate form, his back toward her face. His legs straddled her body, one knee to each side of her, and with a soft curse he pressed his hands, the right over top the left, against Meg's undulating belly. Emma thought he would crush her, so hard did he press, seeming to force his full weight upon that still and slight form.

Emma's teeth sank into her lip, drawing blood, and her heart pounded as she curled her fingers, sinking her nails into the palms of her hands.

"Let her live," she whispered. "Oh, let her live."

The muscles of Anthony's forearms bulged, corded with effort, as he pressed against Meg's abdomen as though he were kneading dough. His shoulders shifted forward, stretching the material of his shirt taut across his back. Emma thought that the force he used would break the poor girl in two. He altered his position and increased the pressure, his head flung down, his eyes closed in concentration.

Suddenly, Meg's eyes snapped open. Her head and shoulders reared up and her face contorted in grim effort.

"Push, Meg. Now. With all you have," Anthony urged, even as he pressed and manipulated her belly.

"Emma," Mrs. Bolifer said urgently, "here. I have not two strong hands."

Emma knelt at Meg's feet, steeling herself against the puddle of blood and tissue that pooled there.

"The head, yes. Like that," Mrs. Bolifer said, as she used her one hand to guide Emma's actions. "Now turn it, so. And once more . . . There!"

The baby slid from Meg's body, a slippery, red-faced miracle that resembled a gnome. Emma began to laugh as she wrapped the infant in a blanket, drying it gently.

"A girl, Meg. You have a daughter." Emma felt so happy she fairly sang the pronouncement.

Glancing up, intent on sharing her joy, she found Mrs. Bolifer and Anthony exchanging a look of grim acknowledgment. The feeling of euphoria evaporated and she glanced down to find a fresh spurt of blood draining from Meg's body.

"Oh, no," she whispered wretchedly, her eyes searching out Anthony's, silently begging him to deny the harsh reality her own mind refused to accept.

"Mrs. Bolifer," he ordered crisply, "press from there. Push with all you have."

As Mrs. Bolifer shouldered Emma aside, Anthony seemed to transfer his entire weight to his arms and hands, pressing against Meg's distended abdomen with unbelievable force. She made no sound but lay insensate upon the floor. Emma wished she would cry out, even whimper, give some evidence that life yet remained in her.

Then Alice was there, taking the infant from her arms, and Emma, unable to stop herself, moved forward, placing her hands on Anthony's, lending her weight to his.

"Push, Emma," he ordered.

And she did. She pushed with all her strength, drawing on reserves she had not thought she possessed.

"It's stopped." Mrs. Bolifer's words were barely a whisper. She repeated them, louder, and then she laughed, the sound bubbling from her lips. "It has stopped, my lord. She no longer bleeds."

"But does she live?" Emma asked, her voice hoarse and urgent.

"She does," Anthony said, wonder in his tone. "She lives, Emma. She lives!"

Tears blurred Emma's vision as she scrambled back, dropping her hands to her sides. Anthony swung down from his odd position straddling Meg's supine form and took a step toward Emma, opening his arms, and she fell into his welcoming embrace, unmindful of the blood that stained them both, caring only that in the end, there was life.

Glorious life.

CHAPTER SEVENTEEN

Slipping her wrapper about her shoulders, Emma moved to the window seat of her chamber. She sank wearily onto the cushioned bench. The sky was painted with an artist's brush in shades of pink and gold. Beautiful, she thought, gazing out as she ran her hairbrush through her freshly washed hair.

She started at a soft sound behind her. Anthony. She could sense his presence.

Turning her head, Emma saw him sitting on the edge of the bed watching her. His hair was still damp from his own bath, and he wore the collar of his shirt open, revealing the strong column of his throat.

"You were sleeping," he said softly. "And you were smiling."

"I must have dozed off." She had been dreaming of him. Kissing him. Touching him. "How is Nicky?"

"Sleeping. He has slept the day away."

"And how is Meg?"

"Fine. Weak, but amazingly optimistic after her ordeal." He smiled. "Come here, Emma mine."

She rose and crossed the room, her heart pounding a fierce rhythm. Sinking down on the mattress, she leaned into him as he twined his fingers through her unbound hair. She stared into Anthony's eyes, all the questions and conjectures that begged answers flying to the fore.

"Cookie said . . . about Nicky . . . she said . . ." she began uncertainly. How to ask a man if his son was truly his son? All her own insecurities about the circumstance of her birth writhed inside her and the words clogged her throat.

He did not respond immediately. Bringing her hand to his lips, he pressed a kiss to her palm. "What is it that makes a father, Emma?" he asked. "Is it enough for a man to spill his seed, then claim the title of parent as his right? Smythe was the father of Meg's babe. She was an unwilling participant in the deed. Does that make him a father in truth? Or merely a man who did something he had no right to do? And is Meg's babe to bear the burden of guilt for that man?" He paused. "Should Nicky have suffered for his parents' mistakes?"

She inhaled in shock at his pronouncement, his words clearly marking Cookie's ramblings as truth. "You knew. All this time you knew." He had known Nicky was not his son and had loved him nonetheless. Just as he had known she was of tainted birth and he had—

No, she would not think it. Could not bear to hope that he might love her and then have that hope shattered.

"I have known since before his birth. Since the day Delia told me of her pregnancy. Yes, I knew." He shook his head. "And that knowledge seeded my hatred. Delia became pregnant on our wedding night. I was happy. She was not. Without my knowledge she sought out a woman in Whitechapel, and when the deed was done and Delia was bleeding and distraught, she came to me to fix it." He shook his head. "She destroyed *my* child. I brought her here and left her, alone, my anger so great that there was no forgiveness in my heart. I returned to London. She hated me for that."

"And you hated her for her betrayal," Emma whispered. "But something changed. You love Nicky—"

"Nicky is my son in all ways that matter. I do love him. He is mine, borne to me by my legal wedded wife. Was I obligated to turn him out, toss him to the whims of fate for a choice that was not his, but that of his naive and lonely mother? Was I to call him bastard?"

"No," Emma said earnestly, understanding completely. "I love him, as well. I could not love him more if I had carried him under my heart for nine months and borne him from my body. He is my treasure."

"Yes." There was a wealth of meaning in that small word.

"But he looks like you," she blurted as her mind circled these new and confusing thoughts. "He has dark hair."

"As did Delia's father," Anthony pointed out reasonably. "And he has his mother's blue eyes."

Emma stared at him. "I once believed all men were like my father. He won my mother with pretty promises but lived up to none of them. He refused to claim his own child."

"As did Smythe."

She was almost shocked by the revelation that Smythe had been Delia's lover. Almost. But she recalled the diary, the reference to L.S.—Leonard Smythe—and she was not surprised. Only saddened. Anthony sent her a look of understanding. "Delia went to him, told him of her pregnancy. He demanded that she allow him to terminate it." He paused and then said so softly that she almost missed it, "She was afraid. Of him. Of me. Poor girl."

"That is why you hated her. That is what turned your love to ashes."

"Yes."

She sucked in a breath, remembering the words he had spoken that long-ago night in the portrait gallery when he had told her of his love for Delia, a love that had turned to hate. "Do you hate her still?"

He opened his mouth, paused, and then his eyes, his beautiful green-gold eyes, widened in surprise. "No. I don't."

Oh, how her heart swelled at his denial.

"How did she die?"

Anthony swallowed, and Emma read his torment. "For seven years I have believed that I killed her on a dark and storm-tossed night, and now you have claimed otherwise, that Cookie did the deed. My conscience will take time to adjust."

The night of her arrival, the storm, Anthony's comments in the coach—memories teased Emma's thoughts. "Is that why you dislike the rain?"

"The rain. The stink of tallow. They make me think of the night she died." Anthony rested his head in his hands. "I found her at the bottom of the stairs, broken, twisted. She was near death. And for the hours that followed, each minute that sapped her strength and her life, she swore she had thrown herself to the bottom of the staircase. Swore she had done it in a fit of repentance and guilt." He made a low sound of self-derision. "And I believed her. Perhaps she believed it herself."

Rising, he paced restlessly across the room and back. "We will never know for certain. But the truth remains that I failed her. Failed her child."

Emma lurched upward, catching his wrist. "That is not true! You love Nicky. You are a wonderful father."

"Ah, but he is not the child I failed." His tone was heavy with secrets and regret. "She begged me to cut the child from her, to give it a chance for life. I could not. To do so would have surely consigned her to death. I know of no woman who has survived such a procedure. Yet, I knew that she would surely die if I did not do the deed. A craniotomy would have saved the mother. Slicing open Delia's belly would have saved the child. Coward that I was, I could not wield the blade, and so I did nothing. *Nothing*. The first child, a girl, was stillborn. Delia was wild with grief. She pleaded that I take the second child. Still, I did nothing. Only after she breathed her last breath did I open her and take Nicky from her. My cowardice, my inactivity killed Nicky's sister as surely as if I had done the deed with purposeful intent. And the baby's death, coupled with my refusal to save the child yet inside her, surely contributed to Delia's loss of strength."

"All these years you have blamed yourself for this? Anthony, you are a doctor. You do not govern the fates. You do not decide who lives and who dies. You must let this go." She gazed at him earnestly, willing him to finally forgive himself.

He closed his fingers about hers, drawing her

hand to his lips, pressing a soft kiss to her palm. "So wise, Emma mine. I spent nights lost in despair wishing I had answered her differently. All these years I have dreamed of death, and in my nightmares, Nicky does not survive."

Emma snaked her arms around him, holding him close. "You saved him, brought him forth into the world. You are no coward," she said, thinking of the way he had thrown himself into the conflagration in an attempt to save Cookie's life, and later, how he had faced his own demons to save Meg.

He brought his lips to hers, a warm, sweet kiss of hope and promise, and together they sank back into the softness of the bed. "You complete me, bring light to my darkness."

"Anthony," she breathed. Her heart swelled with love, and she opened to him, shifting closer to lie full against him, to feel the hard length of him.

Arching back, he watched her for a moment. There was something in his eyes, some emotion, and it was so strong and bright that she thought it would surely singe her with its intensity. It was neither passion nor tenderness, though both were mirrored in his gaze. Something more. A reflection of her own heart.

"I love you, Anthony." She had told him this once before, and he had made no reply. Anxiety and trepidation iced her blood, but she forged on, her emotion so strong that she could do naught but share it with him. "I love you with all that I am, all that I will ever be."

He smiled, a glorious flash of white teeth, an expression of absolute joy.

"Then, Emma Parrish, I shall marry you."

She gasped, and the words hung between them. He would *marry* her?

"I am a bast—"

His fingers on her lips held back the words.

She pushed his hand aside. "Your stepmother—"

"Has no say in my life," he finished for her. "I *will* marry you, Emma mine." He paused and then added, "If you will have me." An afterthought.

Her blood thrummed through her veins and her heart pounded in her breast, thunderous, so hard and fast she thought it would surely burst from the strain.

"If I will have you," Emma echoed, a tiny squeak of sound. "That is all you will say to me? Nothing more?"

He smiled, that perfect curving of his lips that made her heart melt. "You asked me earlier how I knew which way to go, which fork to follow. . . ." And then the smile faded, his expression growing serious. "Emma mine, I but followed my heart and it led me straight to you."

Dear heaven. Had he said that? Truly said that . . . to *her*?

"Give me the words," she whispered. "All of them. I swear I will not betray them, betray you."

"I love you, Emma Parrish. Marry me. Be my wife. Make my house a home."

She smiled at his words. They were a beautiful gift that filled her with inestimable joy.

"Then, Anthony Craven, I shall marry you, and build a life with you, and share a home with you."

He grinned, leaned close to whisper against her lips, "Yes, you shall." And then he crushed her to him and kissed her deep and hungry, and she could feel her blood begin to sing.

A sound caught her attention and she shifted her concentration to the door that led from her chamber to Nicky's. The child stood in the open doorway, rubbing his fist against one eye, while regarding her sleepily with the other.

"Can I kiss Miss Emma, too?" he asked, stumbling drowsily toward the bed. Then he stopped and looked around. "We're home! That's grand!"

With a laugh, Nicky launched himself at the bed. Anthony tightened one arm around Emma, even as he opened the other to catch his laughing son against him. Emma felt the movement of his chest as he chuckled softly.

"Yes, Nicky, we are home," she said, her heart near bursting with the immeasurable joy of living as she met Anthony's adoring gaze. "We have all finally found our way home."

Please turn the page for an exciting sneak peek of
Eve Silver's newest historical romance
coming in August 2007 from Zebra Books!

Desperation made for a poor walking companion.

Jane Heatherington studied the horizon, dread gnawing at her with small, sharp bites. The sky was a leaden mass of churning gray cloud that hung low on the water, and the ocean pummeled the shore with a strength that heralded the furor of the coming storm. Breathing in the tangy salt scent of the sea, Jane clenched her fists. The edges of the delicate pink shell in her hand dug into the skin of her palm, grounding her, holding her misery at bay.

Life was burdened by tragedy. Naïve girl, to have believed that fate had dealt out all her cruel jests years ago. No, not fate. Jane shook her head. She could blame no one but the true perpetrator of this terrible thing that had come to pass. Her own father had consigned them both to uncertainty and despair.

How much money?

Five hundred pounds.

Yet fate was there too, lurking, laughing, and

playing her horrible game. Was not Jane's presence here this morning some act of chance?

Ill chance, to be sure.

Less than an hour past, as the cold, gray dawn had crawled into the heavens, Jane had left her father's hostelry, needing a few moments to understand and to accept the terrible choices he had made and the dreadful consequence he had brought down upon them. She had walked along the beach, mindless of any destination, seeking only to calm her concerns and fears.

She shuddered now, studying the two men who stood in the churning surf. They waited as the waves carried forth a grim offering, a single dark speck that dipped and swayed with each turbulent surge, growing ever larger, taking on defined shape and macabre form.

Indeed, desperation made a poor walking companion, but death even more so.

Wrapping her arms about herself, she watched the dark outline float closer, closer, discernable now as human: face down in the water with arms outstretched; long tendrils of tangled hair fanning like a copper halo.

A woman, bobbing and sodden.

And dead.

Heart pounding in her breast, Jane took a single step forward, as the men sought to drag their gruesome catch from the ocean's chill embrace. She was held in thrall by the terrible tableau unfolding before her, and she swallowed back the greasy sickness that welled inside her. 'Twas not morbid curiosity, but heart-wrenching empathy that froze her in place.

Most days, she could look at the ocean as a thing of great beauty.

Most days.

But not today.

Today there were disquieting clouds and churning surf; the icy kiss of the mist that blew from the water's surface to touch land; and the awful knowledge of her father's actions. And deep in her heart, the terrible feelings of foreboding and change, unwelcome and unwanted.

'Twas all too similar to a day long past, a day best buried in a dusty corner of her mind. The sea. The storm. And there, just beyond a great outcropping of rock, the brooding shadow of Trevisham House that loomed silent and frightful against the backdrop of gray water and grayer sky.

Separated from the sweeping curve of sandy beach by swirling waves, the massive house was a lonely, empty shell balanced atop a great granite crag that rose out of the sea like the horny back of a mythical beast. A fearsome pile of stone and mortar that offered no warmth, Trevisham was linked to the mainland by a narrow causeway that was passable at low tide or high. Unless there was a storm, and then it was not passable at all.

Chilly fingers of unease crawled along Jane's spine, and she tore her gaze away, glancing to her right, to her left, feeling inexplicably wary. She was given to neither fanciful notion nor wild imaginings, yet today it appeared she was subject to both. Her heart tripped double time, and her nerves felt raw as she scanned the beach, searching for the source of her unease. She could swear there was someone watching the beach. Watching her.

'Twas not the first time she had suspected such.

Twice yesterday she had spun quickly, peering into darkened corners and shadowed niches, finding nothing but her own unease. She sighed. Perhaps it had been a portent, not a human threat, but a warning of the news her father had been about to share.

"She's been in the water less than a week, I'm thinking," Jem Basset called grimly, drawing Jane's attention to where he stood, thigh deep in the water.

"Where's she from?" Robert Davey asked, wading a step further into the waves. "A ship, do you think?"

"There's been only fine weather for more than three weeks. No ship's gone down here. If she's from a ship, then it was wrecked on the rocks to the north, I'm thinking."

The two men exchanged a telling look.

Jem grunted and reached as far as he could, but the waves carried the body just beyond his grasp. He glanced up, saw Jane, and shook his head. "Go on, now, Janie. No need for you to see this."

He was right, of course. There was no need for her to watch them drag this poor unfortunate woman from her watery grave, but Jane could not will her feet to move, and his words of wrecks and rocks haunted her. There had been whispers of late that the coast to the north was safe for no ship, that in the dark of the night wreckers set their vile lights where no light should be, bent on luring the unsuspecting to their doom, tricking a ship into thinking it was guided by a lighthouse's warning beacon, only to see it torn asunder on jagged rocks.

Torn asunder like the fabric of Jane's life.

But at least she had *life*, she thought fiercely, watching the corpse bob down, then up, its copper hair swaying in the current like snaking tendrils of dark blood.

Pulling her shawl tight about her shoulders, Jane blew out a slow breath, steadying her nerves and battling both her fears for her future and the ugly memories of her past. Dark thoughts. Terrible recollections of storm and sea, and Trevisham House.

Jem lunged, and this time, he caught the dead woman's arm, and then Robert came alongside him; together they wrestled her from the frothing waves.

"You think there'll be others?" Robert asked, breathing heavily as they slogged toward the shore. The sand sucked at their booted feet and the woman's body dragged between them, her head hanging down and her legs trailing in the water.

Shaking his head, Jem cast a quick glance toward Jane. "Not likely. Bodies usually sink into the deep dark. Strange that this one didn't."

"They sink only until they fill with bloat, and then they float up again like a cork, don't they?" Not waiting for a reply, Robert waved his free hand and continued. "Her skirt. See the way it's tangled about her ankles? It must have caught the air when she went into the water and held her afloat. That is why she did not sink."

Drawn despite herself, Jane took a step along the beach, and another, gripped by the image of this poor woman, her limbs growing heavier and heavier as she was tossed about on a cruel sea. Struggling, gasping, praying.

And finally, dying.

Such an image.

Such a *memory*. The tightness in her chest. The great, gasping breath that brought only a cold burning rush of water to fill her nose and throat and chest. Her heart pounding a harsh rhythm in her breast, Jane struggled against the strangling recollection.

Jem laid the drowned woman in the back of a rough wooden cart, mindful of her modesty, though such was long past any value to her. With a twist of pity, Jane saw that the woman was both bloated and shriveled at once, her face white-green, in frightful contrast to her copper hair, and her eyes . . .

With a cry, Jane stumbled back a step, pressing her palm to her lips as she stared at the empty black sockets. Horror seeped slowly through her veins, a terrible dismay that chilled her to her core.

The woman's eyes were gone, gnawed from her skull.

Jane wrenched her gaze away, swallowing convulsively as she stared at the wet sand dusted with a smattering of white and pink shells.

Shells.

She had come to walk on the beach to soothe her soul, and to fetch a handful of shells to carry with her. Just a handful of shells for her mother. Those were her reasons for being on the beach. Now, instead of shells and ease of mind, she would carry the memory of the dead woman's bloated face, the empty sockets that had held her eyes, and the image of a razor-toothed fish nibbling away the soft tissues.

A new nightmare to haunt her rest, Jane thought. Imaginings of another woman's suffering, as though her own was not companion enough in the darkest hours of the night.

Suddenly, she froze, and her head snapped up. The hair at her nape prickled and rose. Jane rubbed her hands briskly along the outsides of her arms as apprehension chilled her from within, swelling in tandem with the rolling waves.

Someone *was* watching them.

Lips slightly parted, the tip of her tongue pressed between her top and bottom teeth, Jane turned to face the great wall of sea-carved cliffs that rose alongside the long, slow curve of sand. Tipping her head up and back, she studied the stark precipice with measured interest. The sound of the waves hitting the shore surrounded her and the cry of a lonely gull high overhead. From the corner of her eye she caught a hint of motion—a shadow, far, far to her left—up on the cliff.

There was a blur of movement, a dark ripple of cloth that might have been a man's cloak.

She spun so quickly, her balance was almost lost. Reaching down, she pressed the flat of her palm to her left thigh, adding sheer will and the strength of her arm to the paltry force of the muscles that would straighten her knee and hold her upright. If she was lucky. If not, her leg would crumple as it was often wont to do, and she would sink to the sand in a graceless heap. After a moment, she righted herself, and turned her attention to the place she had glimpsed the shadowy stranger.

But the cliff was barren. She could see nothing. There was no one outlined against the ominous backdrop of gray sky.

The man—if in truth she had seen one—was gone, but the sinister unease that clutched at her remained.

Leaving the beach, Jane inched along the narrow dirt path that hugged the sea carved cliffs, her thoughts awhirl with both her own personal turmoil and the horror of the drowned woman's tragic and pitiable fate. She climbed to the top, and paused, her attention snagged by her father's cousin, Dolly Gwyn. The frail woman stood by the edge of the sharp cliff, arms raised, her wild gray hair unbound, whipped by frantic eddies of air, and her form swathed in layer upon layer of faded black cloth. Before her lay the roiling turmoil of the angry sea; above her the leaden sky that pressed its ominous weight down upon her as she perched there atop her precarious roost, summoning the storm.

Jane sighed. "Cousin Dolly!" she called, cupping her hands about her lips to amplify the sound. "Come away from the crag!" The wind and the crashing sea swallowed her cry, or perhaps Dolly chose to ignore her. 'Twould not be the first time.

As Jane reached her side, Dolly stretched out a thin arm, waving her hand to encompass the storm-washed beach, and the sea cliffs that extended as far as the eye could see.

"I saw a light, oh, about a week past," Dolly said, diving into the topic without preamble. Her voice was strong, though her body was beginning to weaken as years and hardship took their toll. "High on the cliff it was, far to the north. An evil light. A false light." She cast a glance at Jane. "A wrecker's light."

"Never say it," Jane whispered, a sick feeling rising inside of her. A wrecker's light, so close to Pentreath . . . This morning, as they dragged the woman from the ocean, the men had said that she'd been in the water but a few days. They had hinted with brief words and subtle glances that they believed she had come from a wreck on the northern shore. And if Dolly spoke true . . . Dear heaven, let Dolly be wrong . . . let them all be wrong.

Enough. Jane wanted no more heartache, no more sadness this day.

"I say it because I saw it," Dolly insisted. "We'll be hearing the tale of a ship gone down within a short time, my girl. You heed me now. We'll hear of a ship gone down and all aboard her dead. What can that be but wreckers, I ask you? What?"

"I pray you are wrong."

"As do I, Janie. As do I. But I tell you . . . the woman that was pulled from the waves this morning . . . she came from that ship. She died for men's greed." Dolly wrapped her thin arms around herself and swayed to and fro in the wind as they stood, shoulder to shoulder, facing the crashing surf and listening to the building furor of the ocean.

"And it's *him*, his coming, what's brought the evil down upon us," she continued, stretching out one gnarled finger toward the sea, and toward Trevisham House, dragging Jane's unwilling gaze. This of all days, with the horrible news her father had shared, and the image of that poor drowned woman so fresh in her mind, Jane would have preferred not to think of Trevisham and not to remember.

"He is in league with the devil. I feel it in my bones." Dolly pulled back her lips in distaste, revealing the uneven outline of her three remaining teeth.

"The new owner?" Jane asked, loath to tar and feather a man without cause. "We know nothing about him."

With a careless shrug, Dolly shuffled a short way

along the path, clutching her tattered coat about her hunched shoulders.

"What do we know? What do we know about him?" She slanted a sly glance at Jane. "We can guess that he has a very, very *large* fortune, for Trevisham surely cost him more than most could ever imagine. But how he came by his money . . ." Dolly's voice trailed away, leaving her suspicions unspoken.

"I am sure that is none of my concern," Jane chided gently, for she knew from experience exactly where this conversation would lead. Dolly loved nothing better than to sniff out her neighbor's secrets, and if she smelled naught of interest, she was not averse to providing details from her own vivid imagination.

"His money's ill gotten, if you ask me. Smuggling. Wrecking. Mayhap murder." The old woman turned a jaundiced eye to the heavens.

Wrecking. Murder. Jane could not help but think of the terrible bloated face of the woman she had seen dragged from the sea, and of the hint of movement, the dark shadow she had sensed high atop the cliff that morn. Dear heaven, was there to be only darkness in the days to come, only sadness and loss?

"There's an ill wind blowing today," Dolly said, as though in answer to Jane's unspoken question. "You mind me well . . . it blows from Trevisham"— she stabbed a finger in the general direction of the house—"and from the man who will be master there."

"The man who will be master there," Jane repeated. She could not recall a time when Trevisham had been inhabited. The previous owner had left more than two decades past, before Jane had come to Pentreath, and the house had stood empty all the time since. Curiosity surged in her breast, an interest in who he was, this man who had purchased a forgotten pile of rock and mortar, a man of mystery and shadow.

He was a man of great fortune, if Dolly was to be believed. A pirate. A smuggler. A wrecker.

Turning, Jane stepped forward, moving closer to Dolly's side. Fierce breakers pummeled the jagged rocks that surrounded Trevisham House, and then crashed against the stretch of beach, churning the sand. She felt Dolly reach for her, the woman's age-twisted fingers curling about her wrist.

"Have you seen him, Dolly? The new owner of Trevisham House?" Jane asked, though for certes she already knew the answer. If Dolly had seen him, the entire village of Pentreath would have known within the quarter hour.

Speculation about the newcomer was rampant. Even without the man having actually put in an appearance, people had talked of nothing else for over a fortnight. Her father welcomed the gossip, for the villagers needed somewhere to meet and discuss their conjectures, and a pint of ale at her father's hostelry was usually the venue of choice.

"I've not seen him. Other than old William, no one has," Dolly replied, hooking her arm through Jane's. "He arrived under cover of night, never stopping at the pub for drink or conversation. I wonder what kind of man shuns the company of his neighbors."

"A man who prefers his privacy." Jane pulled her black wool gloves from the pocket of her coat and slid them onto her hands, keeping her arm linked with Dolly's throughout.

"Aye. But *why* does he prefer his privacy? There's a good question." Narrowing her eyes, Dolly tapped the tip of her forefinger against the sagging skin of her wrinkled cheek. "And why did he choose *this* place?" she mused. "There are less isolated houses about, and in better repair."

Jane thought she understood such a choice. She had long ago learned to appreciate the magnificence of the stark and lonely countryside that had been her home for over a decade. She knew the splendor of the moors, the harsh appeal of the wind-and-salt spray etched faces of the precipices that jutted into the sea and the tors with their caps of jagged granite. And she knew that Trevisham House called to those who would listen. "Perhaps he views isolation as privacy."

Dolly grunted. "Isolation is good for certain activities . . . activities that are carried out on a barren rocky coast with none to bear witness."

A heaviness settled in Jane's chest, stalling her every breath. She shook her head and said firmly, "Perhaps he chose Cornwall because this is a place of beauty."

Dolly hooted at some secret jest. "Aye. That it is. Barren. Lonely. Beautiful. But that is not why he came. Mark my words. This man is cloaked in death. I feel it in the depths of my old soul."

"Death is no stranger to Pentreath. No stranger to Trevisham," Jane replied, thinking of her mother's body as it had looked that long ago day, draped cruelly over the rocks, long dark hair hanging wet and limp like seaweed.

Thinking, too, of the pitiable, nameless woman that she had watched Jem and Robert drag from the ocean.

No, death was not a stranger.

At length Dolly gave Jane's arm a gentle squeeze. "I'll leave you now. I have mending to do and I need what there is of the light on this dreary day to do it. You'd best see to your visiting, Janie, and make your way to home before the storm."

Yes, she would do well to make her way home before the storm. The lesson was one well learned. Cold fingers reached forward from the past to touch her skin, making her shudder. She would have done well to hurry home another day, far in the past, to hurry home before that long ago storm. Memories nipped at her like a beast poked with a stick.

Gathering her thoughts, Jane spoke her farewells, and Dolly hobbled off in the direction of her small cottage nestled at the edge of the village. Watching her go, Jane tried to stifle her unease, to tamp down the restless urgency that gnawed at her and the sense that great misfortune was soon to come to Pentreath.

She sucked in a breath. Great misfortune had already come, if not to Pentreath, then to her, carried on her father's foibles and poor choices. Yet she sensed something bigger, stronger—something worse than even this wretched circumstance that had been thrust upon her.

Dolly had seen a light to the north, where no light should be.

A dead woman had washed ashore, her very presence testament to some terrible misfortune.

Wreckers.

Only once before had Jane felt such a strong forewarning building inside her until it seemed to take on a life of its own. On that day her world had tilted and all she knew as safe and good had shattered. Gone in an instant. She remembered the storm and her mother's voice calling out to her, the sharp crack, like a pistol shot, and the pain. She remembered the pain.

And she remembered Mama dead, calling out no more, broken like a porcelain doll on the merciless rocks.

"No." With a whispered denial, Jane tore her thoughts away from the cheerless remembrance; away, too, from the terrible guilt, for if she allowed it to surface it would easily overwhelm her. Her grief was old now and tinged with bittersweet recollection, misty memories of joy and warmth tempering the horror of her loss. She had learned over the years to control it, rather than letting wave after wave of crushing sorrow control her.

Turning, she shambled with her uneven gait toward the tall square bell tower that loomed in the distance, its crenellated cornice reaching to the menacing sky. The way was familiar to her. At least once each week she made this journey to the church and to the graveyard that lay in its shadow.

She paused beside the low stone wall that surrounded the building, and rested a wool-gloved hand against the chilly surface, silently acknowledging the ever-present dull ache in her left knee. The winter damp seeped right through the joint. She could barely remember a time when the muted pain had not been her constant companion.

A noise caught her attention. Frowning, she turned and looked over her shoulder, a chill chasing along her spine. But, no, there was no one behind her on the well-traveled dirt path.

She stood for a long moment, staring at the

empty trail. For an instant, she had been certain that she was no longer alone.

Turning to open the ancient iron gate, Jane set her teeth as the rusted hinges emitted a strident squeak. The gate was in need of oiling. She would mention it to the vicar's wife, who in turn would mention it to the vicar. Such was the way of village life.

Fallen autumn leaves, brown and parched, tumbled end over end, whipping between the headstones with a dry, rustling sound as Jane walked through the graveyard.

Suddenly the wind died and all was still. Uneasy in the eerie silence, she glanced about, her gaze coming to rest on the dead and blackened elm that stood in the far corner of the cemetery, its lifeless limbs arcing over the etched stones. High upon a narrow branch perched a solitary raven, watching her.

She let her gaze wander across the rows of gravestones. Something felt strange this morning. The silence in the face of the brewing storm. The portent of the raven. Dolly's doom-saying. And the faint whisper in the darkest corner of her mind that had haunted her since she had jerked from fitful slumber at the first rays of dawn. There was a wind of change swirling over Pentreath, carried by the storm. A wind of change, bearing menace and danger.

Resolutely Jane turned her thoughts to her task. She fastened the highest button on her coat and pulled her shawl tighter about her shoulders as she slipped between the graves, making her way to the carved granite headstone that marked her mother's final rest. Pausing, she reached into the pocket of her coat to pull out the small, perfectly coiled pink shell that she had taken from the beach. With a sigh, she trailed her fingers along the stone to the engraved words that were her mother's epitaph.

Sacred to the memory of Margaret Alice Heatherington, the wife of Gideon Heatherington of this Parish, who departed this life 18th day of July in the year of our Lord 1802, aged 29 years. In this life a loving wife and a tender mother dear.

Silently mouthing the phrases, Jane closed her eyes against the insidious tide of sadness that flooded her heart. There were still days that she awakened expecting to hear her mother's voice.

"Good morning, Mama dear," she whispered as she placed the shell on the top of the tombstone. A hazy memory flitted through her mind: her mother, running barefoot along the beach, laughing as she paused to gather shells. That night she had strung them on a length of yarn, making a necklace for her daughter. As a child, Jane had treasured the gift; as a woman grown, she treasured it still more.

Her touch strayed to the small painted miniature, fronted in glass, that her father had ordered embedded in the stone. An exorbitant expense, but one her father had insisted upon. Jane ran her finger over the glass, noting that the winter's harsh kiss had forced a jagged crack. Her heart twisted and a tear escaped to carve a path along her cheek. The glass would remain as it was, broken. Her father's folly had seen to that.

She traced the twining vines that the mason had carved about the picture to frame her mother's likeness. The artist had done a wonderful job; the minute painting resembled Margaret Heatherington in all details. Just as it resembled Jane, who to an uncanny degree took after the woman who had borne her.

Mother and daughter shared the same tall, slim build; the chestnut hair; and the ready smile. Jane well remembered her mother's flashing dark eyes, tipping up just a bit at the corners. She could see those eyes looking back at her in the mirror each morning. And she could see the subtle differences, too. Her nose was smaller, her lips fuller, her chin slightly squared where her mother's had been soft and round.

"Oh Mama. I miss you so."

Her only answer was the mournful howl of the wind, which had renewed itself and bit through Jane's coat and shawl with pitiless vigor.

With a single piercing cry, and a great flapping of feathers, the raven took flight from its lofty perch. Startled, Jane spun about. Her gaze sought the source of the sound and she watched as the bird spread its wings and soared above the secluded cemetery, flying free and unfettered.

Oh, to be that raven. To be free of the situation her father had thrust upon her.

She watched the bird until it was only a dark speck in the distance, and then she shivered. Again, she felt the sensation that she was not alone.

Slowly, she lowered her head, and her breath caught in her throat as her blood rushed hot and rich in her veins. Taking a stumbling step back, she felt the unyielding solidity of the granite stone at her back, and she leaned against it, touched by an equal measure of trepidation and fascination.

Her heart stuttered and then raced.

Because, no, she was most definitely *not* alone.

GREAT BOOKS, GREAT SAVINGS!

When You Visit Our Website:
www.kensingtonbooks.com
You Can Save Money Off The Retail Price
Of Any Book You Purchase!

- **All Your Favorite Kensington Authors**
- **New Releases & Timeless Classics**
- **Overnight Shipping Available**
- **eBooks Available For Many Titles**
- **All Major Credit Cards Accepted**

Visit Us Today To Start Saving!
www.kensingtonbooks.com

All Orders Are Subject To Availability.
Shipping and Handling Charges Apply.
Offers and Prices Subject To Change Without Notice.